A True-to-Life Western Story

~No Lookin' Back~

An Inside Look at One Man's Personal Struggle for Freedom

TED RIDDLE AND LINDA RIDDLE

Frontier Adventures in the 1800s

PAGE PUBLISHING, INC.
New York, NY

First originally published by Page Publishing, Inc. 2019

Story as given to Ted Riddle
Recaptured for print by Ted and his wife Linda Riddle

ISBN 978-1-64027-982-7 (Paperback)
ISBN 978-1-64214-719-3 (Hardcover)
ISBN 978-1-64027-983-4 (Digital)

Printed in the United States of America

Dedicated to All those who seek freedom

We would like to give thanks to the following people:

Jerry Charles
Janet and Mike Vines
Elaine Hazelwood
Pam Wells
Jan Bradford
Victor Jantz
Glennes Desbien

INTRODUCTION

Ted, my husband, asked me to introduce his story because I am the one who heard it first. We had been married for two years when his "gift" was given to us.

It was about 4:00 a.m. on a Sunday morning. We were both asleep in our home in Tonkawa, Oklahoma, when he sat up in bed and said, "I know how I died!" I awoke to those words, astonished as he began to tell the end of his life in a different-sounding voice and using words and a dialect I had not heard before.

After a few moments of an intense outpouring of emotional facts, places, names, and events, I knew I had to write "his story" down on paper. I climbed out of bed in the dark, found a legal-size yellow pad and pencil and began writing as fast as I could. He did not slow down to help me catch up; the tale just kept flowing from his mouth. The hairs on my arms stood on end and chills continued as he told in detail events that happened over one hundred years ago. My fingers began to cramp as I kept trying to keep up with him.

The descriptions were so vivid that I could visualize what he was saying like a movie playing before my eyes. Eventually we hurried to the living room after I found a small tape recorder in our dresser drawer. Ted continued to talk in this unusual voice, causing me to laugh and cry as this true-to-life saga of the 1870s began to unravel.

He told me how he died at about the age of sixty. Then he went to the beginning, when Tom Summers, who was sixteen years old, left home to join the Union Army. He lied about his age and was able to join the army and fight in the Civil War. The journey takes you into the war, on into Indian Territory and westward. Every day for Tom was an adventure, and Ted will share it with you.

Anyone who meets Ted is drawn to him instantly. His manner is one of confidence: of a very genuine, honest, loveable guy. He will win you over with his "Just one more story" or a big bear hug if you are not careful.

We met at a teen hop in the 1950s, when I was fifteen and he was seventeen. We dated in rural America for about a year. He was then leaving the farm to go to Oklahoma State University, and he asked me to marry him.

We both married other people and raised our children. Forty-one years later, we discovered each other again. This time, I said, "Yes."

Join us on our fascinating journey into the Old West as seen through Tom Summers's "beautiful blue eyes."

Linda Riddle

FOREWORD

I felt a surge of excitement as Ted, my husband and author of *No Lookin' Back*, turned into the gate at Fort Supply, located in northwestern Oklahoma, near the town of Fort Supply.

The day we arrived, September 16, 2009, the landscape and atmosphere was much different from September 16, 1893, the day of the opening of the Cherokee Outlet. I told Ted, "I need to see this place and get a feeling of it if I am going to help write this book."

We traveled from southern Colorado, where we live in the summer, to Fort Supply area after visiting with Frank Carriker and Bobby Rey on the phone. Bob is the head historian of the Fort. Frank had worked there many years. We also visited with Frank in his home and toured the excellent museum in Woodward, Oklahoma.

At this time, I took pictures that you will see in our book. We were privileged to be taken into the original blacksmith's shop that had been in Fort Supply in the 1800s. It had been relocated to the Woodward museum.

We parked in the visitor's parking lot, but I did not feel like a visitor. I had been here many times in my mind as I had helped to develop the characters in Ted's book. I am so thankful for the "gift" that was given to us and for the opportunity to help write this true-to-life story. I feel a responsibility to be as factual as possible while helping to paint a word picture for you, the reader.

As I headed out over the acres that take up Fort Supply, I could almost see and hear the hustle and bustle of everyday life of the Fort as it really was almost 150 years ago.

Homes and buildings were built with what they had, and what they had was not much. I was most interested in the teamster's log house. Trees, though they were scarce, were cut, and the limbs of saplings were fitted into an oblong trench, which had been dug into the earth. The poles were set vertically. I am sure the builder looked for the straightest poles so there would be few gaps. The gaps were filled with rags, mostly condemned canvas from covered wagons. Then a mixture of lime and water was used to whitewash the rags. It had two rooms with a wood-burning fireplace in each room. Windows were the only purchased items costing "five bits" each. Note: $1.25. Doors were made out of wood, and then strong timbers were added to form a roof. Grass sod was cut from the plains and laid on top of the timbers. A dirt floor completed the "decor." What more could you want?

Life was harsh. One story they like to tell is of a woman from the East, no doubt an officer's wife, who was brought in on the train and then by buggy to the door of her new home at the Fort. It is storied that she said, "Don't let me out at the stables. I want to go to my home." The orderly said, "This is your home."

Indians, extreme weather, lack of social contact, and proximity to civilization were just a few of the problems. As a woman, I could sense and understand the loneliness and the need for adjustment.

Alcohol was forbidden at the Fort, but I'm sure that was a rule broken many times. The guardhouse stands as a reminder of lives lived out of their comfort zone.

I was reminded that when a person left his family in the East to come West, many never saw their loved ones again. Letters were slow and often lost; travel was slow and treacherous. Disease and danger were an everyday situation. To bring a child into the world, as our heroine, Rachel, did at the Fort, had to be overwhelming.

Fort Supply was one of the central locations of our story. It was a melting pot of modern and European ways from the East colliding with the heathen, barren land of the West. This land was fierce but offered opportunity. It brought out the best in men and women and brought out the worst as well.

I just wanted to grab hold of the past, to hear the sound of marching soldiers, to taste the smell of the blacksmithing, and to watch wagons being unloaded. Where was the captain's wife in her big, bouncy dress and sun-shading bonnet?

Those things were gone like the sunset, only a glimmer remained—memories of the stockade, Indians attacking, and courage to tame the West. Fort Supply—you are still here!

Our deepest appreciation goes to Bob Rey and Frank Carriker of Fort Supply for their gracious help. The folks at the Woodward Museum were exceptionally helpful as well. Thank you for reading this book, and may "The West" always be a blessing to you.

Note: When Tom arrived at what is now Fort Supply, it was called "Camp Supply." It became a fort in 1888.

CHAPTER 1

Where's Home?

Nothin' but grass, buffalo grass all the way. My name is Thomas Jefferson Summers, and I am headin' West. The year is 1906 and I am getting a little older. I have seen sixty winters—some good, some not so good—raised my family and more cattle than I care to remember in the Cherokee Outlet on the Oklahoma Territory.

It is time now to join my daughter, Donna, and her husband, Justin Slader, and family on their ranch in the New Mexico Territory, near Cimarron. Donna wrote to me just about the time I lost my ranch to the government. She asked me to come live out my days with them and to be sure to bring my stud horse, Ranger.

We had a beautiful place leased on Comanche land, called The Big Pasture: good water, lots of grass, and the army nearby. What more could a man want? I would have liked to stay, but the government took over and started giving land to farmers and to the Indians. It wasn't the same after Rachel died anyway. She made every day special. Everyone loved her, especially me. I saddled up Ranger, a descendant of my first ranch horse. Guess I bought Ranger I in 1868; my, how times have changed. The war is over and the buffalo are almost gone.

I have my Colt .45, a Sharps .50-caliber rifle, some rations, a little cash, and my mother's locket that I had given to my wife, Rachel, when we married.

She gave me a beautiful daughter, a son, and years of devotion. Heck, we just had a lot of fun together.

I could have taken the passenger train to the New Mexico Territory, but I am an old cowboy. Why not do it right and ride the trail one more time?

I'm sittin' tall in the saddle; I finally learned to ride as well as any man. I'm now in the Texas Panhandle after leaving Fort Sill, Oklahoma Territory, a week ago. The sun feels good on my back after a fierce rain yesterday. Following the railroad track, I should make Amarillo by nightfall. It will sure feel good to sleep in a real bed and have a real bath.

"Come on, Dog," That's her name. I speak aloud, but the only ones to hear me are Dog and Ranger, my dun stud. In the stillness, it seems like I can hear Rachel whistling a soft, lonesome song, although she has been dead for eleven years. My son, Johnny, left with the Roughriders, and I have never seen nor heard from him since.

Ranger stumbled and brought me out of my daydream, then the earth began to move, kind of like when a herd of buffalo thundered across the prairie years ago, when the West was free and the Indians were one with the land. Then I heard the rumble of the engine tear through the open spaces. I can see it now, the Iron Horse, as some call it: big, black, and the end to a way of life.

I watch with fascination as it came closer. I am about fifteen feet from the track. I pull Ranger back, proudly thinking that I would let these Easterners see a real cowboy.

Just then, the engineer pulls the train whistle and lets a blast of white steam at my horse. It spooks Ranger and off we go, pitching across the prairie, giving the passengers a good show.

Ranger gallops toward the deep ravine and stops dead in his tracks. Thrown in the air, I land on a boulder, breaking my leg. I can see the bone sticking out and a good amount of blood.

"Now, what do I do?" I am in quite a jam. I pull my belt off and wrap it around my thigh, but it does not stop the bleeding. I've been in worse predicaments than this. Ranger will pull me out.

I have landed twenty feet almost straight down into a small canyon. Ranger bows his head and is looking down at me. Dog is whining, "Come on, let's go!" I am trying but I cannot climb up this slope. I can hear the train in the distance leaving me behind in distress. I rest a little, certain that I'll be able to get out of here. I look to the north and then to the south; it does not look good. It sure is cold for noonday; wish I had my coat. Minutes seem like years. I am too weak to move. Looks like the end is near.

"Look! There's Rachel, coming up the ditch to be with me! This can't be real, but it is!" I get up and we walk off together.

This is how my story ends and begins.

Thomas Summers

Steam Engine Train—This 1900 Steam Engine Passenger Train or "Iron Horse", as it was called, roars through the wide open spaces. Tom gambles and loses with this train. Drawing by Linda Riddle

CHAPTER 2

Tom's First Years

Tom was born in 1846 on a farm near Brownsville, Tennessee. He was named after the third president of the United States because his mother admired the leader from Virginia. His father, Frank Summers, was a big man and strong as an ox. Frank grew up in Illinois and headed west, got as far as Memphis, and ran out of money. He met his future bride, Anna Marie Rutherford, on the docks of the Mississippi, where he was working as a blacksmith and she had just arrived to visit her Aunt Mae.

The first ten years of their marriage were happy, although it was a hard life, living off the land, planting corn, and raising a few animals. Their first child was a son they named John Adams Summers. Then came Thomas. Thomas Jefferson Summers, full of vim and vigor, three years later. After Tom was born, Frank began to drink and would come to the house and fall on the floor, dead drunk, or beat John and Tom for no reason. The boys could do nothing right. Anna taught them to read, mostly from the McGuffey Reader and her Bible. They practiced their spelling and penmanship daily, but Frank did not think all that learnin' was necessary; it interfered with the fieldwork.

The older the boys got, the worse the beatings became. They never knew Frank to harm their mother, but they lived in fear of his drunken anger.

One day in early fall, the brothers had been picking corn all morning. The sun shone down on their bare backs with no mercy.

"Time for a break, little brother," John said. "Let's go over to the shade, and drink the lemonade mother made for us."

"Guess we better take this wagonload to the corncrib then haul in some water soon as we rest a minute," Tom suggested.

Just then, the crack of the whip cut through the moment. Their father came down on them hard, slashing their sunburned backs. "Git to work!" The harsh growl of their father was only slightly less painful than the salt from their sweat as it soaked into their whip-lashed wounds.

As they were about to finish unloading the wagon, Frank appeared again, this time enraged and wildly ranting about how lazy and stupid his two loafers were. "That's it!" John, now eighteen, shouted. "I've had enough of you, old man!" He turned on his father and almost beat him to death.

Although neither boy had yet to realize that it was the rotgut whiskey that made the old man crazy, their mother, Anna, long remembers the man she married and ran to his rescue. "Tom! Help me pull John off your father!" she frantically cried. When the struggle was over, Frank lay on the ground, weeping. "Forgive me! Please forgive me! I promise! I promise I will never hit you again!" After that episode, Frank did not lay a hand on John. But if John was gone, Frank would attack Tom when he got him alone, hiding behind the swig in the bottle.

When Tom turned sixteen, John now nineteen, they decided to join the army and help save the Union. "I will be back for spring planting," John told his mother.

"If you go, I want to go too," Tom, pleaded. "If you are gone, the old man will surely kill me."

"Mother?" Tom said, facing his aging mother, half-looking for her permission. With tears in her eyes and her voice breaking, she said, "I know what you boys want to do. I understand. May God protect you both. Always know I love you." She gathered some cured meat, corn fritters, and honey for their trip and put it in their knapsacks along with a few pieces of clothing.

Early the next morning before Frank awoke, the boys kissed their mother good-bye and started on a new adventure. Harvest was over, early autumn, October 5, 1862.

Two miles north of the house was the Allen farm. "Let's stop and tell Uncle Henry and Aunt Ethel good-bye," John said. "I'm hopin' she'll have some apple pie coolin' on the porch." Tom smiled with hungry anticipation. The couple was not related to the boys but loved the brothers and had asked them years ago to call them "aunt" and "uncle."

"Come in! Come on in!" Uncle Henry bellowed as he put down his tools. "Where you boys headed?" he asked.

"Well, sir, we're goin' to join the 34th Illinois Infantry," John proudly announced.

Aunt Ethel overheard them and interjected, "You boys are too young to fight in this awful war! Why, it will break your mother's heart for you to leave!"

"Yes, ma'am," John replied almost apologetically, "but she gave us her blessing and said she doesn't know how much longer she can stay. She would go back to Georgia, but the fightin' is pretty bad there, we hear."

"Please look after her for us," Tom asked his good friends.

"You know, I just happen to have some cornpone pudding and some potato soup on the stove. You must stay," Aunt Ethel begged. Tom was sure he could smell apple pie too.

As the four of them enjoyed the noon meal, they reminisced of days gone by. "You know the Lord never blessed us with any children—until you two came along. Please stay safe," Aunt Ethel remarked.

"Yes, ma'am, we will," Tom answered. "We will win this war in no time."

Uncle Henry cleared his throat and said, "We would have given you Molly and Lily, our last two mares, for your trip, but the army confiscated them about a month ago."

Just then, they heard a commotion. Outside, the chickens were squawking and scattered. "You boys git out here and git back home!" Frank yelled. He had showed up, hollering loud enough to be heard for miles and bullying with his pitchfork in hand. "You no-good, unthankful, no accounts! Git home before I kill both of you!" he shouted.

"I'll handle this," Uncle Henry declared as he took the long rifle from above the fireplace. Carrying his prized firearm outside, he demanded, "Frank Summers, git your drunken self off my property and go back where you come from!"

The drunken man, shaking his pitchfork, shouted, "Hell no! Not without my sons!"

"You've beaten them for the last time," Uncle Henry said. "They are leavin' to fight for our country. You leave them alone!" he shouted.

Still shaking his pitchfork like the devil, Frank cussed Henry and declared he would kill him.

Then Henry lowered his long gun at the old man's head and said, "Never take a pitchfork to a gunfight!"

Frank backed away down the length of the lane, still cussing somewhat. As he reached the end of the road, Henry shouted out, "Frank Summers, don't you ever come 'round here no more!"

Turning to John and Tom, he said, "Glad that's over." Henry said reassuringly, "Let's go back into the house."

With worry still wearing on his face, he reached into the pie safe and brought out two cap-and-ball pistols. "I want each of you to have a pistol to carry with you at all times," he told the boys.

"Oh no! We can't take your pistols!" the brothers said in unison.

"Nonsense!" Henry argued. "They sell these every day. But I want you to wait until nightfall before you leave; there are Johnny Rebs around that could be trouble."

CHAPTER 3

Going to War

Yesterday, John and Tom were farm boys harvesting corn. Now, after thanking their friends again, they walked into history as young men. In the still of the night, they headed north, up the old river road, up through Kentucky, into Illinois. On the way, they met up with other young men with the same idea. At Springfield, Illinois, the group mustered into the Union Army. They were issued blue uniforms, one of the colors of their beloved flag. The men joined ranks along with many others. Captain Robert Reynolds addressed his new recruits, which numbered over one hundred men that they were at the home of their president, Abraham Lincoln. "You will be made into the best fighting force in America," he announced. "You will make our president proud." Several hundred men, young and old—farmers, store clerks, and trappers turned soldiers—trained from dawn 'til dusk. Reynolds told them that this war would not last long because the Confederates would run as soon as one shot was fired.

John and Tom thought this was a glorious thing, much better than being farm boys. "We ought to be home by Christmas," said Tom's new friend, Jimmy Thompson.

Jimmy was a store clerk from the South, the only son of a Baptist preacher.

The Blue and The Grey—Private Summers, a Union soldier and a Confederate soldier battle it out at the Battle of Stones River. Half of the 34th Illinois Infantry were killed the 1st week of Jan. 1863. This was the bloodiest battle of the Civil War at this time.

Soon, Tom's unit started marching down to Tennessee, which was now part of the Confederacy. No war in Illinois, where the recruiting took place and the Union army had routed the Rebel army out of Kentucky, so this leg of the journey was peaceful. The eager soldiers arrived early one evening at Murfreesboro, some thirty miles southeast of Nashville, on the Stones River. General Rosecrans gathered some forty-two thousand troops in this area.

The troops bunkered down, making their beds out of what they carried on their backs. John was ordered to the south field, and Tom was ordered to stay on the ridge. The sergeant did not want brothers fighting side by side. John turned to go and then reached back for Tom, putting his hand on his brother's shoulder. "Stay low, little brother," John said as he walked down the hill. Tom watched his brother walk away, wondering if he would ever see him again.

Morning broke as a heavy mist rose over the land. The fog, over Stones River, lay like a bed of crystals dancing in the early morning light. Some of the men were eating breakfast. Tom awoke to a soft rumble in the distance: a sound he had never heard before. A lone hawk circled over the meadow, searching for food. In the distance, a shadowy form began advancing over the horizon. The noise increased as the form grew larger and larger. The sunlight caught the gleam of steel, and the new recruits were on their feet, scrambling for boots and guns. Some thirty-four thousand of Brogg's Rebels came as a surprise assault against the Union soldiers.

"To arms!" called the sergeant. Some of the men prayed, but most just looked for a place to fight.

It was December 31, 1862 when the battle of the Stones River began. The 34th Illinois Infantry fought hard. Tom and his friend Jimmy Thompson fought side by side with a silent understanding between them to protect each other at all cost. There was nothing glorious about battle and men killing each other. That was all there was, killing and more killing. Tom and Jimmy thought they'd go crazy with the thunder of cannons and the screams of death around them. The gray coats did not run, as was expected.

The weather too was a cold-blooded enemy. The icy rain showed no favorites and fell the same on both sides, making their lives even more miserable. Sleet and snow made it almost impossible for supplies to get through.

The fighting was so intense on both sides of the river that they began to run out of ammunition, and there was always the danger of snipers in the trees. There was a day's respite, during which the 34th finally received a shipment of ammunition.

During a lull in the fighting, Tom and Jimmy were assigned to unload the wagons and take the heavy boxes to the troops. On their last trip, Tom bent down to pick up his end of the box while Jimmy held the other end. All Tom heard was a whizzing sound, and Jimmy's head was gone. His body was still standing, but no head. Jimmy did not know what hit him.

Tom began to vomit all over himself, and his nose was bleeding profusely. He thought that he had been hit too. He wandered into the river, and that is what probably saved his life as the battle raged around him. Cold, wet, and afraid of the next moment, Tom lay on the riverbank.

"Here's a coat" was said by a welcomed voice from one of his own. "Stay here and I will get you some dry boots and another uniform." Tom never saw him again.

The next morning, the battle resumed. The fighting intensified as General Breckenridge's men again made a mighty charge. The noise of the gunfire and cannons was nonstop. Tom felt he would go mad from the screams of the dying, the smell of death, and the carnage surrounding him. Suddenly, Tom and about twenty of his company rolled into a ditch, trying to dodge the bullets that were ricocheting all around. The Rebs were charging and running over them.

Now, it was too close to shoot. Screaming war cries, the Rebs attacked. Tom looked up and saw a young man about his age jump into the ditch right by him. Tom's only chance to survive was to bayonet the Reb. Tom tightened his grip. The rifle was set with a bayonet; Tom lunged and ran him through. The startled look in the young man's eyes was one Tom could never erase from his mind. The Reb was so young; he thought he could not die.

Writhing in pain and his guts hanging out, the Reb cried out, "Help me!" Although no one was supposed to carry a revolver, Tom remembered the one his Uncle Henry had given him. Only officers were supposed to carry a sidearm. There, this dying lad lay cussing and screaming at Tom and God for putting him there. Tom pulled out his hidden pistol and shot him in the face. The screaming stopped. During the fracas, Tom felt a searing pain in his upper left thigh. He fell over on top of the man he had just shot. He lay there for hours with the battle raging all around him; bodies falling on him, he did not move. Lying there, looking at the sky, he was as a dead man, covered with blood, flesh, and excrement. Snow began to fall softly on Tom's face and the fallen all around him. Somehow, nature was trying to purify the carnage.

Finally, it was over. The gray coats were defeated. Half of the 34th were killed the first week in January 1863. This was the bloodiest battle of the war in terms of the number killed and those fighting at this time.

At some point, Tom had tied his belt around his leg to help stop the bleeding. He was weak and dizzy, and he had lost a lot of blood. The bullet had blown a gaping hole in part of his leg. The stench of death surrounding him burned his nostrils. Everywhere he turned, Tom could hear moaning and cries for help. The man on top of him was sobbing and begging for his mother. Soon, there was no sound at all—except for the wind.

Soldiers from Tom's unit set out to look for anyone yet alive. Someone heard Tom choke, found him, pulled him onto the top of the heap, and said to him, "You are the only one alive in this ditch." Two men put Tom on a stretcher and carried him about a hundred yards to the first aid tent.

There were so many wounded and dying that the unit's only doctor attended to the worst first. When he came to Tom, he said, "This one, take this one off," pointing to Tom's leg. He could not believe it. He tried to get up to leave, but the doctor pushed him down and said, "I know best."

The doctor's nurse, Jenny, a beautiful young woman, with long, black, flowing hair, argued with the doctor. "You've cut off so many legs today, and yet you have saved some that weren't any worse than this! Why don't you try to save this man's leg?"

The doctor said, "If you're so smart, you do it," and left Tom to die.

"Nothing but a bunch of butchers" was Tom's thoughts. Behind the hospital tent, they placed the dead along with discarded, amputated limbs. The burial party was hard at work burying the dead, but it was time-consuming. Even though the temperature was cold, the odor of decaying flesh saturated the air.

The young nurse, Jenny, came to Tom like an angel. She cleaned his wound and pulled the flesh together with bandages. She brought him food and made sure he drank water.

His wound began to heal and he gained back his strength. One day, Tom asked her if there were any books around he could read. She took a special interest in him. He thought it was because he had read all the old newspapers that she gave him. Reading to some of the other wounded helped him pass the time. He helped some of the soldiers write letters to their loved ones also.

Tom thought that he would be going home soon, as he was getting better. One day, the lieutenant in charge heard him reading to a young soldier and became angered. "You are ready to go back into battle!" he ordered. "If you can read, you can fight!"

Tom knew he wasn't going back; he had seen all of the war that he wanted to see. His unit commander, "Ol' Blue Hawk," was going to send him to the front come morning. Tom told Jenny that he didn't want to fight anymore. He thought to himself, "If I am in good enough health to fight again, then I am in good enough health to go over the hill." He told Jenny that he didn't know which way to go or where to hide. She told him, "If you travel three hundred or four hundred miles to the west, you will find neutral Indian Territory." Then she did a strange thing: she kissed him on the lips and told him that she would not tell anyone where he went.

That night, he slipped out of the camp and headed west on foot.

CHAPTER 4

You Can't Go Home Again

The battle of Stones River, often called the Battle of Murfreesboro, was a Union victory. It was there that Tom narrowly escaped butchering at the hand of the field doctor, cheating death. He felt older and a little wiser but feared being captured and sent back into the deadly war, so he headed west.

Stumbling and then running, he soon came to thick timber.

Which way was west? He remembered something his Uncle Henry had taught him, so he checked the moss growing on the trees in the old forest to find out which way was north; then he turned to his right and, hopefully, freedom.

Trudging through the virgin land, mostly at night to avoid being discovered, he continued on his way. In the two weeks since he had gone over the hill, the scant provisions carried in the knapsack given to him by the nurse named Jenny were almost gone. All that remained was deer jerky, an apple, and the memory of his first kiss.

February 1863 was an extremely cold period in the South. Clothed only in woolen underwear, uniform, boots, and a wool hat Jenny gave him, along with heavy mittens, Tom covered himself with leaves and branches to rest and hide. His wound was almost healed but pained him after the difficult hours of walking. "Thank God for my knife and my cap and ball revolver." Tom said to himself. He managed to kill a coon, skillfully skin it, cut it in pieces, and roast it over a quick fire. He had a few precious matches in a tin that he carried next to his heart. As soon as the meat was done, he stomped out the fire and covered the ashes with dirt for fear the Confederate or Union soldiers would see the smoke.

"This meat will last me a few days," he said as he tucked the pieces into his pockets. Every time Tom crossed a stream, he filled his canteen. He was always on the lookout for the enemy.

Hoping against hope, he headed in the direction of his old home place. He knew this part of the country like the palm of his hand. "I hope Mother is still alive," Tom prayed out loud. "I long to hear her voice," he said to himself; loneliness filled his every breath. He could almost smell the fresh, hot bread she'd bake coming out of her oven and remembered his favorite apple pie with fresh cream.

The trees were so close together that he couldn't see where his home should be until he climbed over a rise, breathless and anxiously expecting to see the whitewashed image of the house surrounded by outbuildings, the old well pump, and the apple orchard. His eyes ached for home, but as he searched into the valley, he looked in horror, as the landscape was black. The buildings, fence, almost everything on the farm he loved was leveled to the ground. Wind picked up a bit of soot and carried it until it lodged against a large rock.

As he slowly approached through the morning mist, Tom gazed into an unknown world. The only thing Tom recognized was the stone chimney that his father and neighbors built when Mr. Summers came to Tennessee from Illinois.

Home place—Wounded, Tom slips out of the army camp and heads west on foot. After many miles he eagerly climbs the hill overlooking his home. He longs for his mother, but all he sees is blackness before him. Confederate soldiers had burnt all he knows to the ground.

Carefully, Tom stepped through what had been the kitchen. The smell of burned memories sickened him to the point of dry heaves. "Where are you, Mother?" he cried out. "Who did this?" He stumbled and fell, tears blocking his vision and taking him off balance. Stretching prostrate in agonizing darkness, Tom felt he could no longer carry on. All that he ever knew and loved was gone.

Gathering himself up on his knees then to his feet, he looked around in hopes of finding some clue as to where his parents were. Maybe they left before the fire, he frantically wished. Maybe they were safe somewhere away from here. "No, no, it cannot be! Please, God! Do not let it be!" he cried as he faced straight ahead into the garden place, where a grave with a wooden cross set crooked in the dirt. The young man stumbled toward it, begging not to see what he feared most was written on it. "Anna and Franklin Summers, December 12, 1862" was carved into the wood. What Tom read spoke louder than a cannon blast. One common grave held the man from the North and a Southern lady, his mother.

"No, No, it cannot be, "Tom cried as he looked straight ahead into the garden, where a grave with a wooden cross set crooked in the dirt. Frank and Anna Summers, Dec. 12, 1862 was carved into the wood. His mother's golden locket lay close by.

Tom was not aware of how long he sat there, sobbing and hating the war even more. His heart kept telling him to get up and leave as fast as he could to erase the fear and pain of this terrible war. As he stood, he placed his hand on the cross to straighten it and said a silent "Good-bye." Just then, he noticed a glimmer in the now noon-day sun. The wind had picked up, and he thought he could hear his mother gently humming, "Hush, little baby, don't you cry." He looked down at the touch of light and saw what he thought it was—but it could not be. Yet, it was his mother's golden locket!

He bent over and picked it up; with his fingers, he rubbed the blackness away. Sure enough, it was the locket that her father had given her when she turned eighteen and left home in Savannah to go for nurse's training. Whenever she wore it, Anna told of warm summer days in Georgia and the fun times that she and her sisters had on their parent's cotton plantation.

Tom grasped the treasure and headed toward the nearest neighbors, the Allens, two miles up the road. Mr. Allen, or Uncle Henry, as Tom always called him, was working in his cornfield.

Henry saw the young man coming toward him as he raised up from picking up rocks; he ran to meet the boy that he loved. "Oh, Thomas, I am so glad to see you! Are you well? How did you get away from the war? I hear it is raging all over the country!" Mr. Allen grabbed Tom and hugged him. "Come, come into the house! Ethel will feed you and you can warm up," the old man said.

Slowly, Tom asked the couple who had always been so good to him and his brother John, "What happened?"

Reluctantly, Henry began. "Well, son, it was like this. A group of five men, Confederate soldiers, came to your folks' farm, probably looking for something to eat. They were up to no good. Your father was in a drunken state and tried to run them off with his pitchfork. The troopers taunted him until Frank hit one of the men. Without hesitation, the bully soldier filled him with one shot after the other, killing him. Your mother heard the shots, came running out of the house, and then the cowards shot her as well. They quickly looted the house and set the place on fire. Upon hearing the shots and seeing the smoke, I jumped on Mojo and raced that way," Mr. Allen continued. "I met up with one of the ragtag men who had just murdered your folks. He held me up at gunpoint and threatened to do the same to me if I protested. Then he began boasting as to what they had done."

The Confederate went on whining, "I told those bastards not to shoot the woman, 'cause we could have some fun with her." Mr. Allen did not relay this sickening message to Tom. He went on to tell Tom that he had hurried home to protect his wife. After the hoodlums were gone, he and Ethel went back and buried the couple.

Tom was truly dazed. They sat there and talked for a spell. The Allens wanted to know more about the war. Mrs. Allen sat a bowl of rabbit stew and dumplings in front of Tom and said, "You must eat something." His throat was so tight, he could hardly swallow.

"Thank you for your kindness. Now I will be on my way," said Tom.

Mr. Allen spoke up. "Thomas, we want to say something. We would be honored for you to be our own." Mrs. Allen shook her head in agreement.

"No, no. I love you two but I have to go." He grabbed his grungy knapsack and practically ran out the door then disappeared toward the Mississippi.

Tom ran for what seemed like forever. Finally, he fell to the ground, exhausted, and slept a fitful sleep. He awoke with a start, picked up his knapsack, which felt heavier than usual, and continued in what he thought was west. After a while, he realized that he was lost. "I've been going in circles," he said out loud. He waited until first light to see which direction the sun came up. He had slept off and on, still seeing the wooden cross whenever he shut his eyes. At last, he could see rays of soft light and he was on his way, westward once more. About noon, he saw a troop of Union soldiers in the distance. He quickly hunkered down and hid in the brush until they passed out of sight. While waiting, he checked his knapsack and, much to his surprise, found several sacks of dried fruit and a small smoked ham. No doubt, Mrs. Allen had placed them in his sack when he wasn't looking. "I'll eat a few bites and save the rest," he told himself.

He could hear the soldiers talking as they rode by him. "Just wait till we get you deserters to Memphis. There will be a firing squad that will take care of you."

Tom peeked out from behind a fallen log and saw the troop of Union soldiers leading four men on horseback with their hands tied to the saddle horns of their saddles. Tom tried to bury himself in the ground on which he lay. "My God, will I ever be free?" he prayed.

After days of travel and nearly walking right into a camp of bluecoats, he heard a strange noise. It became louder as he crept through the underbrush. It sounded like something splashing in water. He had never seen a steamboat, but there she was, the *Queen of the West*, making her way down the mightiest river that he had ever seen. "This must be it!" Tom exclaimed as he half-ran, half-jumped into the water and began to swim. The current was stronger than he was. Down the river he went, narrowly missing a logjam. He hit a small island in the middle of this "bad lady." "Now, how am I going to get from here to there?" he muttered, thinking he was foolish to try such a thing. It was daylight, and he was afraid that he would be seen from the shore. Besides being cold and wet, everything he owned was cold and wet, including his matches.

Dusk was creeping in all around him. It was almost dark when he saw a canoe coming his way on what he knew was the river that he had been looking for, the Mississippi. A bearded man, dressed in rugged skins and furs from head to toe, called out to him, "Monsieur, viens, garcon. Je ta'iderai!"

No doubt, this was a fur trapper taking his pelts to market. Once again, he called to Tom in French—"Viens, garcon. Je ta'ide-rai!" (Come, boy, I will help you!) as he paddled near to where Tom was standing, motioning for him to get into the canoe. Tom grabbed his knapsack and hoped for the best. The Frenchman took him to shore all the while rattling away in a language Tom knew nothing about. He understood nothing except one English word: "ignorant."

Tom was now on the west side of the river; the Frenchman paddled away, still muttering about, "River bigger than you—fleuve plus gran que toi!" Tom hurried to the underbrush. The countryside was flat, with a few trees and bushes. There were areas that had been cleared for farming. He skirted around these places with farmhouses for fear he would be caught. Nightfall came with big, bright stars overhead. There was a full moon, so he made his way while he could. He saw clothes hanging on a line. Some were hanging on a fence, so he crept ever so cautiously in the moonlight and pulled two shirts and a pair of pants from the line. He crawled a little closer and grabbed two pair of socks. He saw a coat on the porch, and he was tempted to steal it, but he was afraid of getting that close to the house, thinking the dogs might start barking.

Tom slipped away. Clouds had covered the moon, so he made good time. "I don't know where I'm goin', but I hope it's warm when I get there," Tom thought to himself. He buried the uniform that he had been wearing. He stripped off and put on the clean, warm clothes. The river water had washed off most of the black from his body, but he could still smell the nightmare. His new clothes were too big, but he didn't care. He needed to find a coat soon.

Arkansas Cabin—"Am I in Arkansas," Tom ask the man behind him with a gun. "What do they call ya?" the tattered looking man demanded. "John Johny Johnson," Tom quickly replied in hopes of covering his identity.

Tom could hear a rooster crowing in the distance. A small farm came into view, sitting on a hill covered with rocks. He could see steam rising from the livestock in the early morning light. Smoke circled in the sky over the one-room shack. The coon dogs spotted him and let out their signal cry. "What 'ja doin' here, boy?" a voice from behind demanded.

"Just passin' through. Do you have somethin' for me to do to earn some breakfast?" Tom asked.

"Let me take a lookin' at you'ens," one man said as another opened Tom's sack and dumped everything on the ground. The man looked harmless, just nosy, Tom thought of the tattered young man.

"I guess you'ens is all right," the first one said. "Come on in and feed yer face," he continued. "Maw, this here man needs some hog jowls and eggs!"

"Am I in Arkansas?" Tom asked.

"How come you'ens want to know?" the second man asked. "Interesting," Tom thought to himself, "the second man looks just like the first one."

The second man continued talking, "This here is my brother, Leroy, and my other brother, Roy Lee. Don't take no mind of him; he never talks. I am Jimmy Lee. What do they call you?" the two Cain brothers asked at the same time.

"My name is John Johnny Johnson," Tom replied.

"That's a funny name," Jimmy Lee said.

"Guess my maw liked the name 'John,'" Tom answered.

"How come you'ens a-wearin' army boots? Are you a Union or a Reb?" one man asked. But Tom couldn't remember if it was Leroy or Jimmy Lee.

"No! I just picked these up from a man that didn't need them anymore," Tom continued.

"You'ens sound like one of us'ens," Leroy said as he scratched his privates. "Yes, you is in Arkansas, and we don't want nothin' to do with no war. Now, come on, we got work to do. What can you'ens do?" Leroy asked Tom. "We want you'ens to clean out the chicken coop, but first, fetch yourself here in the barn and clean out these here stalls. Their downright knee-deep in horse crap!"

Tom realized that this was a test; these three backwoods boys were trying to provoke him. So he went along with their scheme.

When they entered the shed that they called a barn, Tom saw an assortment of old tools—harnesses, broken wheels, a large anvil setting off to one side, and a forge.

"Here's your pitchfork, John Johnny," Leroy said as he gave the old fork a toss. Put that crap in this here wagon and then pull it to the cornfield and scatter it."

"Yes, sir, I'll get right on it," Tom answered. The old milk cow heard the commotion and meandered in to see what was going on for herself. "Go on, get outta here," Tom said. "It's not time to milk yet."

As Tom was finishing with the stalls, he heard the call to supper.

"Come and get it before I throw it out!" a woman's shrill voice pierced the cold evening air. The meal was more pig jowls, eggs, and cornbread.

"Woman, we got ta' get us to town one of these days! I'm tired of not havin' no molasses!" Jimmy Lee announced.

The woman responded, "I've told ya and told ya, we got-a find a way to make some cash," she said as she gathered up the tin plates and spoons.

"Why, we is so poor, we can't even afford forks," the mother of the three boys told Tom. She looked at Jimmy Lee and said, "Fetch me some water so I can do the dishes." He simply replied, "I ain't goin' to do it."

Tom thanked her for the meal and ventured out with an idea. "I saw the anvil and forge today in the barn. With my skills as a black-smith and your tools, I can make us both some money."

Jimmy Lee questioned Tom, "What do you'ens know about blacksmithin'?" he said with a smirk. "That there anvil belongs to my Uncle Jeb Bob, who is off fightin' in that there war."

Tom replied, "I learned at an early age in Tennessee. Allow me to repair the broken wheels of your wagon. If you are satisfied with my work, we can take in jobs from your neighbors."

Leroy laughed and spit a wad of chaw on the old plank floor. He had aimed at the fireplace but missed.

The wiry woman slapped him and told him, "I told ya not to spit in the house!"

Leroy shoved her and said, "Old woman, I'll do what I durn near please!"

Tom stepped out of the cabin and went about gathering tools. He asked, "Do you have any blacksmith coal?"

Leroy bragged, "We got lots of that stuff from old Pennsylvania. How much do you need?"

Tom said, "A couple of buckets will do to get started." Tom built a fire in the forge, got it hot, and set about to do the job that no one there could do. Soon, the brothers had more work than they ever believed would come their way. Tom made enough money to buy a fine dapple-gray and some provisions to continue his trip westward. He thought he would aim for Indian Territory, maybe even Texas. "No one will find me. I'll keep lettin' my hair grow and let my beard cover my face," he said to himself.

"Run! Run! Come this way! Confederate soldiers are headin' this way!" Leroy said to Tom and the two younger men. "If you don't want to fight in that killin' war, go hide yourselves in the woods," Leroy cautioned. The scouts were out rounding up all the men they could find, forcing them to join the army. Leroy was safe from this recruitment as he only had one arm and could not see very well.

For two days, the men hid in the thicket about a half-mile from the cabin. Roy Lee had taken some moonshine that he shared, and Tom had some crackers in his shirt.

When they emerged from their hiding place; they were covered with "no-see-'em" ticks. The men helped each other get the ticks out from under their skin by using a lit match on each bug.

"I'm leaving in the morning," Tom announced.

"Oh no! You'ins can't leave yet. We will let you spend some time down in the cellar with our sister for a small price."

"What! You have a sister?" Tom said with surprise, as he had never seen the girl.

"You bet! She's a looker too. We keep her locked up so she can't run away. She has made us some pretty good money with the army passin' through. Why, we would even let you marry her if you stay and work," Jimmy Lee said, taking charge.

"No, thanks," Tom said and headed for the barn where he stayed, fearful for his life as the brothers were getting lathered up to have their way with him. He pretended to go to sleep. At first light, just when he heard a flock of geese flying overhead, he hurriedly packed his sack, being sure he had his money stash. Silently, he led his newly acquired mount, a beautiful dapple-gray to the edge of the clearing. He never looked back.

CHAPTER 5

Cherokee Nation

Knowing only that his destination was west, Tom soon settled into the old, worn-out saddle that he had found discarded in the barn, which he repaired right before he left the farm. The young gelding that he bought with money he earned as a blacksmith was named Star, for the marking on his forehead.

Quietly, they rode out of sight of the Ozark cabin near Pickle Gap, central Arkansas. Tom breathed a huge sigh of relief as the pre-dawn mist cushioned the sound of Star's hooves on the thick bed of moist leaves and vines. "Those brothers would have killed me if I quit making money for them, or they would have forced a shotgun wedding on me if I had stayed any longer," Tom said to himself. His main concern now was to keep away from any kind of soldier, Union or Confederate.

Any word from the war was tragic, brother against brother, father against son. Tom wept, not knowing where his brother, John, was or if he would ever see him again.

He avoided the small hamlets and campsites, and keeping to himself, he made good time. A couple hours each day before sundown, he would trot Star to gain more miles; then they both rested.

At first, the forest was thick, and Tom had no problem finding a tree to hobble Star at night while he did a little hunting or slept on the ground. A pile of leaves often made a good mattress with a blanket that he had bought from a traveling salesman. He had a good coat by now, long and made of wool, sheared and made right there on the Arkansas farm.

The land changed as he continued westward. There were not as many streams to catch fish or trees to hide in for cover. The cold April wind blew constantly, and frequent showers made traveling more difficult. The ground was hard and flat. Only the prairie dogs had shelter in their underground homes.

After several days of traveling, Tom saw hills covered with trees stretching as far as the eye could see. Tom found a suitable crossing and also found out that not only was Star a handsome horse, he was also sure-footed as a goat. "You got us across without a hitch," Tom told Star. "We must be in Indian Territory by now," he thought to himself. "I haven't seen an Indian yet. I just hope they are peaceful."

At the edge of the swift-running river, on the west side was a boat landing, a general store, and a few outbuildings. Tom rode up to the hitching post and dismounted. An old man stuck his bearded face out the door and shouted, "What can I do you for?"

Tom replied, "I would like to buy some supplies."

"Where you headed, boy?" The spry old man continued. "You sure are a tall drink of water!"

"Well, I would like to know where I'm at," Tom replied. "Is this river the Arkansas?"

"Your square dab in the darn middle of the Cherokee nation. You had better not do nothin' stupid," the gruffy man responded. "We don't need no trouble in these here parts. I do not suffer fools gladly."

As he spoke, a beautiful Indian squaw approached the headquarters. "Don't you pay her no mind. She belongs to me," he said with a thick Irish brogue. "What you doin' in these parts?" the Irishman quizzed Tom. Before Tom could answer, the man continued. "Me and the missus fled Ireland. Our crops failed again and again. No one had any potatoes or anythin' to eat. The missus and our three babies died on the voyage over here on the ship, and a mighty ship she was. Now, what's your business here?" he asked again.

"Just headin' west, and I need supplies. Been livin' off the land mostly. I have cash money too. I'd like a place for my horse and bed for the night," Tom answered. "I need some grub too."

"For four bits you can put your body down on a bed in my store," the burley, redheaded man answered. "Put your horse in the barn with mine. There's plenty of oats and hay in there for him. My name is Gruffy George. Why they call me that, I do not know. What do they call you, young'un?" he asked.

"You can call me Smith, Tom Smith," Tom replied.

"Oh! One of them, are ya? You runnin' from the army?" Gruffy asked.

Just then, the dark-haired beauty asked Gruffy a question in such a soft voice that Tom could not hear. The man answered, "Yes, he will be here for supper. Boil more corn."

Tom slept soundly in the feather bed, much as he had as a child; the smell of home surrounded him all night. He woke with a start. "Time's a-wastin', boy!" Gruffy said as he pulled the covers over the bedpost. "I want you to go to the river with these buckets and bring them back full of water. Breakfast will be ready soon."

Tom remained at the store, doing odd jobs for four days. He also washed his clothes and long handles and hung them on a fence. When they were dry, he put what he wasn't wearing in a burlap sack for traveling. The days were warm now, and the sounds of spring were everywhere. The river was alive with insects, frogs, and fish.

Having taken a liking to Tom, Gruffy asked him if he would consider staying on awhile. "I can pay you two bits a day with room and board for your wages."

"No, thanks, I must be on my way. People are asking too many questions," Tom replied.

Gruffy told him, "Tom, you best go back home."

Tom looked down and said, "I do not have a home. My folks were killed and their farm burned. No doubt my brother was killed in the war."

"Do what you must, but do not venture north. There is a battle raging on at Pea Ridge, northwest Arkansas. It's a killin' field, so the story goes. Here's a map for you to find your way west, young man.

It's Indian Territory, you know. Now the Cherokee are a smart, civilized tribe. Just watch out for the war parties and the renegades of the other tribes," Mr. George reminded his new, young friend.

Tom bought the first supplies he had purchased since he had left the brothers. He also bought some leather straps and repaired his saddle again. The storekeeper told him he had some canned goods that did not have labels, so nobody knows what is inside. "I'll sell 'em to you cheap, four cans for four bits. For anybody else, it's double," he said.

Tom bought four bits worth. He also bought a floppy leather hat and more bullets for his prized cap-and-ball revolver.

After bidding Mr. George good-bye, Tom and Star headed into the unknown. The roads, if you could call them roads, were few and far between. The only real guide he had was the heat of the sun on his back 'til noon. Then the sun hit his face 'til evening.

Each evening, after setting up camp, Tom would open a can of the unknown with his trusty knife. First night, there was sauerkraut. Second night, sauerkraut. He didn't like sauerkraut when his mother made it, and he sure didn't like it now, but the price was right.

One hot afternoon, Tom thought he saw a river but was afraid it was a mirage. As he came closer, sure enough, real water! What a welcomed sight. He decided to cross the river and make camp on the other side. He dismounted and tightened the straps holding the bag with all of his worldly possessions, except his coat and pistol. He put his treasured coat on because there was no room for it in the bag. His pistol was tight under his belt; his mother's locket hung safely around his neck.

Just as he was about to mount up, Tom turned around and saw a tall, dauber-looking gentleman approaching on a coal black stallion. "Where you headed?" the stranger inquired.

"Why do you ask?" was Tom's reply.

"Fine-lookin' horse. Just what I need!" the shady-looking character said as he pulled down on Tom with his Derringer. He ordered Tom, "Take that rotten-looking saddle off that horse, and get rid of that ugly ol' sack! I've got an important poker game to get to in Kansas City, and I'm takin' your horse."

Tom slowly unhitched the saddle and placed it on the ground. The sack fell with it. The bandit grabbed the reins of Tom's horse and took charge of him. "Bring him back!" Tom shouted.

The gambler just turned in his saddle, laughing, and said, "What are you going to do about it?" Tom pulled his gun out from under his coat and fired. Tom did not know if he hit the man or not, but the would-be thief dropped the reins and fled.

It took Tom the better part of the day for him to walk Star down. He finally caught up with him and rode him back to where his saddle was piled on the ground. "Guess the braves ride bareback all the time, but it sure puts a strain all over the body," Tom said as he quickly made camp and kept a lookout for the gambler. His plans were to cross what he figured was the Salt Fork of the Arkansas River in the morning. Just as the sun was slipping out of sight, Tom heard a rustle in the trees. He pulled out his pistol. "Who goes there!" he called.

"Put your gun up," the heavyset man said as he limped into the light of the campfire. Tom was taken aback by the large scar across the man's face and noticed he was missing an ear. "Yeah, I know I look scary, but I own this here crossing."

"I've already had trouble come my way once tonight. Who are you?" Tom asked.

"My name is Matt, but everyone calls me Scarface. Now if you want to cross this here river, you owe me twenty-five cents!" he ordered. The riverbank had a low place and looked like a good place to cross, so Tom paid the toll, and with that, the man who looked like he had fought the world and lost disappeared into the trees.

CHAPTER 6

Snakes and Cherokee Indians

Early the next morning, the sun woke Tom up with flies and mosquitoes doing what they do best. Tom saddled up Star, secured his bag onto the saddle, and started across what he later learned was Yellow Bull Crossing. Star carefully found his footing and, as the water became deeper, began to swim toward the shore. Star moved a little from the main crossing where the cattle and wagons crossed. For some reason, he got spooked and started to drift downstream. He began to falter and thrash around, throwing Tom from off his back. Star hit quicksand and was slowly sucked down into it, saddle, bag, and all. Tom started swimming to shore when he saw a huge black object floating toward him. He reached out and hoped it would keep him afloat. The current was swift so Tom held on tight. What he had hold of felt strange to him, but he had no choice.

The slick-feeling mass moved within itself, surrounding him at times. He felt a sharp pain on his forearm and another on his thigh. Tom let go and tried to swim, but the current was swift and he kept getting tangled in this mass of blackness. He felt something around his neck and then realized he was part of a ball of water moccasins. He took a deep breath and tried to escape toward the bottom of the river, all the while feeling paralyzed by the fear of what the quicksand could do to him. Yet was it the fear of quicksand or the poisonous venom from the snake bites? He looked up toward heaven and thought he heard his mother calling to him. "Thomas, look up!" the voice seemed to say. When he looked up the second time, he saw someone clinging to a large branch, holding a pole toward him. Tom grabbed his salvation and was pulled to safety. Two snakes were still hanging on him. He jerked them away as he felt their fangs tearing into his flesh. He felt like he was going to pass out, but a strong will to live came over him. When he was safely on shore, he looked into the face of a beautiful young woman. She looked like an angel. He did not know how to communicate with her, so he took his knife and showed her how to cut an "x" where the bites were, and then to suck out the venom like his mother taught him years ago. He was getting very weak and cold when he passed out in the young maiden's arms.

When he awoke, he was in an Indian camp. Lucky for him, Susan and her sisters had been picking sand plums along the riverbank when they saw a horrible commotion in the river. Susan Dushane and the other girls had carried him to safety.

Tom was in and out of consciousness for days. Susan, a young half-breed, cared for him. She made potions from herbs, tobacco, and mud and placed the mixture on his wounds. The morning that Tom's fever broke and he opened his eyes, he asked, "Where am I?" There were several children standing around him with surprised looks on their faces. One offered him a small fish; he took it, thanked the child, and quickly ate it.

Tom stayed with the Indians for more than a year and learned some of their language. He discovered that he could ply his trade as a blacksmith. The Indian town was located on a road called by some "The Texas Road," and it was a way for traders to travel from Kansas City to Texas to sell their wares. There were enough wagons breaking down on this market road that it kept Tom busy.

He earned enough money to buy another horse, which he named Ranger. This horse measured sixteen hands high and was the choice stud from the Cherokee Chief, Big Nose, himself.

Indian Village—The Cherokee Indians had title to the land where Tom ran into trouble in Oklahoma Territory, called the Cherokee Outlet. One of the authors, Linda Riddle's forefathers made "The Run" in 1893 and settled in Northern Oklahoma. Ted's forefathers came later and traded a horse for a 160 acre plot.

Having lost Star and all of his belongings in the quicksand, Tom had to start all over again. The only thing he did not miss were the unmarked cans of vegetables. Life was good with the Indians. They treated him fairly and made him feel welcome.

Tom saw Susan quite often, but she was always with her mother or her sisters. Her mother, Little Flower, was Cherokee, and her father was a French trapper. They spoke some English, but mostly French. Louis Dushane had been killed by a grizzly three years earlier on a trip up north.

The Cherokees had title to this land that the government had given them, called the Cherokee Outlet. It was a place to hunt buffalo and a passage to the Rocky Mountains. The Cherokee were leasing part of the land to the white man to run cattle.

Most evenings, some of the Indian braves would gather around their campfire and tell hunting stories. Tom joined them and began to listen and ask a few questions. Lone Boy, Tom's best friend, showed him a rough map one evening. Studying the map and pointing to the junction of Wolf Creek and Beaver River, Tom asked, "What is this here?"

Lone Boy said, "This is Camp Supply, the only white-man settlement on the Cherokee Outlet."

Tom made an agreement with Chief Big Nose to lease a certain plot of land even though he did not own even one cow. "I am not much of a cowboy," he told the Chief. "I am really more of a farm boy from Tennessee."

The Chief gave him his blessing, and Tom thanked him. "I will send a brave to you each year to collect the lease money. You take good care of the land, and we will get along," the old Chief spoke in broken English.

Tom's land was near Camp Supply, southwest, along Wolf Creek. He was eager to get started with his new life. He told Susan that he was leaving in the morning. That night, she came to his hut, slipped into bed with him, and their bodies met with sweet passion and surrender. She was the first woman Tom had ever known, she made him feel like he owned the world.

Tom asked Susan if she would go with him. "Oh yes, yes! I want to go! I will tell my mother," she whispered. She was gone as quickly as she appeared.

At first light, Susan once again came to Tom's hut. This time, she was dressed for travel. She had prepared food and had provisions in a flour sack. At her side were her pony, Thunder, and her dog, Happy.

Tom stepped outside to greet her. As he was gathering up her belongings, they both turned to a loud noise coming from the camp. Little Flower was followed by the Chief, and several braves were with them. "No, no, you cannot take her. She must stay," Little Flower cried.

The Chief addressed Tom. "Susan is to stay and take care of her mother since her provider is gone. Go, and never return." Susan obediently turned and walked back to her people, followed by her dog.

Happy whined, and the girl picked him up, hiding her tears in his coat.

Tom had packed the night before, so all he had to do was throw his new saddle blanket on Ranger then his prize possession, a new handmade leather saddle made in Kansas City. Camp Supply was his destination, but his heart remained in the thicket by the river.

Tom knew he had to navigate Yellow Bull Crossing again, this time with much trepidation. "If I fall this time, there will be no one to save me," he reminded himself.

Although the river was not as swollen as before, Tom remained cautious. He gingerly selected a place to cross. The year was 1867. The month was June. Tom would soon be twenty-one; in fact, his birthday was July 18.

In his mind, all Tom could see were Susan's beautiful brown eyes, full of tears as she turned and walked away. He could still feel her body next to his. He had never known such pleasure.

Tom kept the reigns tight on Ranger as they entered the river. Part of him just wanted to drift with the current and be swept away from the heartbreak he was feeling. Then, there was his strong sense of survival and the thought of a new beginning.

The sun was breaking out over the hot, windless, open prairie. Tom set his course west, after leaving the Salt Fork River and Yellow Bull Crossing once and for all. The tall bluestem grass reached the belly of his horse most of the time. There was no trail to follow, just grass and sky. Occasionally, a hawk would circle overhead. The wind picked up a bit, moving the grass like ocean waves across the vastness. There were very few trees in this part of the country, with just a few ditches and draws.

The country was nothing like home or anywhere Tom had been before. The farther he rode, the fewer trees he saw—just wide open space, no sound but the wind and the rhythm of his horse. The sun beat down without mercy.

Loneliness was his constant companion. He spoke and it listened, respecting him and his thoughts. He was forced out of his comfortable place and brought back to reality when his horse stumbled in a prairie dog hole. "Be careful, Ranger. We are almost there," Tom said.

The fifth day he came to the Cimarron River, or so the map showed. Many cottonwood trees lined the banks. His canteen was empty. Tired and thirsty, horse and rider drank to their hearts content. Upwind, Tom could smell something dead. Buzzards flew overhead about a quarter mile away.

Rider and horse walked the distance to where, from the limb of a large cottonwood, hung the frame of a man. An old leather hat was pulled down low on the dead man's skull, covering the eye sockets as a mass of black hair hung from beneath the hat. The rope holding his hands behind his back was attached to the rope around his neck. The shirt that once covered the chest was in ribbons around the body. A leather belt held what was left of dirt-covered trousers. Any sign of boots were gone. A pile of cottonwood branches was piled up under the remains. It appeared that the man once stood on a log upheld by other branches, and as the man moved, the wood began to break, causing the rope to tighten slowly around his neck.

Although it was a gruesome sight, there was nothing Tom could do. He had no shovel and there were no rocks to cover the body with, so he said a little prayer, mounted Ranger, and continued his journey.

He crossed what he believed to be the Cimarron River at a shallow crossing. Tom did not know where he was, and there was no one to ask. He figured if he just kept going that he would find someone or something pointing him to Camp Supply.

Here, game was plentiful, but it was difficult to get close enough to kill anything with his pistol. Tom wished he had a rifle. As he topped a ridge, he cautiously rode up to a large herd of buffalo. They did not seem to notice him and kept their heads down, eating the plentiful grass. Off to his left was a half-grown calf. Tom quietly dismounted and crept within twenty feet of the animal. He aimed his cap-and-ball pistol, shot the calf at the base of its skull, and the calf fell where it stood. The rest of the herd did not move and just kept eating. Tom jumped up with his knife in hand and cut the throat of the calf. The herd of about two hundred slowly moved away as Tom began to butcher the young buffalo. This was the darndest thing he had ever seen. Farm cows would have run to the four corners of the earth, but not these strange-looking animals.

With dry buffalo dung, he built a fire and cooked some meat. He ate his fill that night and slept soundly using his saddle for a pillow. Ranger was tethered on a bush by a stream. Sometime in the night, a wolf or coyote stole most of his fresh kill. He was just happy to be alive.

Tom gathered up a little bit of meat that remained and began his journey once more. As the sun peered through the thunderheads, traveling became much more difficult. The huge rocks reflected bright silver from the sun. Ranger picked his way through the large boulders and rocky ground. As the day went on, the sky became darker and darker. Cold wind surprised Tom as sharp lightning permeated the northern sky. Just to prove that nature was in control, loud claps of thunder followed the long lightning bolts that struck the earth, resulting in a wave of fire over the valley.

Hard rain, followed by hail, pelted down on Tom and Ranger. As the storm worsened, Tom sought shelter behind one of the large boulders. To his surprise, there was a small cave just large enough for man and horse. A dog from the Cherokee tribe had followed Tom when he left them, always keeping a distance. But he now joined the party of two and huddled with them in the cave for hours. The three partners were cold and wet to the bone, and there was nothing dry to burn although Tom managed to keep his new matches safe. The sun meekly came out just before sundown. "Beautiful sunset," Tom thought as he remembered his time with Susan.

It was a cold, wet camp that night. He cut off some of the raw buffalo meat he had salvaged, gave some to Cherokee the dog, and ate some himself, chasing it down with some sweet green grass. That was supper.

"Maybe I should not have left the Cherokees," Tom said out loud. The dog looked at him as if to agree. Ranger looked miserable. "I had it made," he said to his companions. "I had a job, shelter, food, and a good woman. I must be crazy to follow this wild notion of being a cowboy."

Tom had counted ten days of being on the trail to find his dream—Camp Supply and the land he leased.

"I must be getting close, but where is it? I have no clue as to where I am," Tom lamented. Four days later, he came to a road that seemed to run north and south. Discouraged and hungry, he dismounted and tied his horse to a marker stake alongside the road. Feeling completely lost, he sat down on the ground to wait for someone to come by. No one showed up all day. Tom slept beside the road with Cherokee beside him. When morning came, he watered his horse and dog by pouring water from his canteen into his hat so that the animals might drink.

"Someone must come by pretty soon, for that was the last of my water," he told Cherokee. From a distance, Tom could make out a team of mules and a wagon heading his way. The old trader stopped by Tom and asked, "What are you doin' way out here?"

Tom told the fat, bearded man, "We have come from the Indian nations from the east, and we're looking for Camp Supply."

The jolly man answered, "Well, now, it is about forty miles south, as the crow flies."

Tom asked, "Where am I now?"

"You are in Kansas" was the reply.

Tom could not believe it! He thought that he had always traveled west, but he had drifted north. "Where might I find water?" Tom asked the bearded man.

"Right here in my water barrel," he answered. "Drink your fill and water your animals, then fill your canteen. Here, young man, have some fresh sauerkraut I brought from Kansas City. You look hungry."

Tom took the plate and ate and was thankful, even for the sauerkraut.

"Tie your horse on the back of my wagon and you and your dog climb aboard, and we will mosey on down to Camp Supply," Tom's new friend said.

"May I put my saddle and gear in your wagon?" Tom asked.

"Sure" was the reply.

As they headed south, Tom asked, "What are you carrying? And what do they call you?"

"I haul anything that is not nailed down. But this time, I carry blacksmith supplies to Camp Supply. They call me Trader Tom from Tennessee. What's your name?" Trader Tom asked.

"I'm Tom Smith."

"Funny, you look like a man I knew in Tennessee. He had a farm but was killed, and his house burned early part of the war. War is bad, you know. I keep as far from it as I can."

They talked and shared stories, but Tom was afraid the truth would come out as soon as he reached Camp Supply and the old man had figured out that he was Frank Summers's son who had gone to war and was on the run.

The wagon lumbered along with its heavy load. Trader Tom would stop once in a while and adjust the harness on his mules and look over his load. "What do you do for a living, young man?"

Tom replied, "I have leased land from the Cherokees for a ranch to raise cattle."

"Do you know anything about blacksmithing?" the trader asked.

"Yes, I do," Tom answered before he thought.

"They need a blacksmith at Camp Supply. I will put in a good word for you to the Captain Charles Morgan. Are you any kin to the Summers family near Brownsville?"

The ride was rough and bumpy, each bump sharper than the last. Just then, the right front wheel came loose and fell off the wagon. "I can't believe this. Come help me, son. This is going to be quite a job. It's going to be like pluckin' chickens against the wind. You're goin' to get a mouth full of feathers."

The two had to unload the wagon of all the heavy equipment and supplies and then fix the wheel. When that was done, they reloaded everything into the wagon in the blistering heat of August. The weather was muggy, and because of that, they both found it difficult to breathe.

As the two men were boarding the wagon, Trader Tom gasped and grabbed his chest. Choking, eyes wide, and unable to speak, he fell backward in the wagon.

They were out in the middle of nowhere. Tom lifted his companion up by the shoulders and gently shook him. "Mr. Tom, wake up!" But he didn't. The man died right then and there.

There was nothing else to do but take the reins and drive the mules to Camp Supply and explain to someone there what had happened. When Tom pulled up to the first hitching post at Camp Supply, someone shouted, "Where's Trader Tom?" and "Who are you?" another asked.

The wagon was recognizable because it had sunflowers painted on both sides. "Do you have a doctor here?" Tom asked. "Mr. Tom is in the back of this wagon, and I'm afraid he is dead.

CHAPTER 7

Life at Camp Supply

A strange-looking man appeared. He looked like he had been badly burned, and part of his scalp was missing. "You stay right here. I will get Dr. Renfro," he said as he walked away with a strange, uneven gait—obviously a man with a wooden leg. The doctor rushed to the wagon that was carrying the old trader. "Looks like it's too late for me to help. What's your name, young man?" the man said, as he looked at Tom with the sternest, steel-blue eyes that Tom had ever seen. "Tell me what happened." Tom took a deep breath and told what had taken place. "Yes, I believe you," the doctor assured. "Our old friend had been having some heart flare-ups but would not slow down. Captain Morgan, who was in charge of Camp Supply, rode up and, upon learning the facts, asked Tom if he was Trader Tom's helper. "Well, yes, I was helping him."

"Well, then, you have just inherited this wagon," the captain ordered. "Pull it over to the cemetery; I will have my men take care of the body. Then you can take the wagon and supplies to the blacksmith's shop to unload."

Since Tom had left home to join the Union, he had grown into manhood—a full six feet, two inches tall with broad shoulders, a full beard, and long, dark hair. He hoped that no one recognized him. This was the place that Tom wanted to call home.

Tom had learned one thing about the West: it was best to not ask questions. When he pulled up to the blacksmith's shop, he observed a young army private slumped in a chair. Tom jumped down from the wagon and declared in rather a loud voice, "I'm gonna unload these boxes right here!" "I don't give a damn. Just give me a hand," the drunken blacksmith demanded.

There was such an influx of soldiers to Camp Supply that the work had become overwhelming for the young army blacksmith. "Them damn soldiers just keep a-comin'," Private Emmanuel Jones explained. "What's your name?" he asked.

Tom told him and went to work.

The next day, after sleeping on a cot in the shop, Tom proceeded to shoe several horses and heat up the forge to rebuild wagon wheels. By putting hot bands of steel on the wooden wheels and shrinking them with water to cool them, they became "iron tires." Over the next several days, Tom showed Private Jones, "Red" as they called him, tricks of the blacksmithing trade—things he did not know how to do. The Captain came by one afternoon and observed this. "You could learn a thing or two about blacksmithing from Tom. Private, I suggest you do."

The young Irishman became belligerent and attacked Captain Morgan for his disparaging remarks. Captain Morgan ended up with a black eye. Private Jones ended up in the stockade, and Camp Supply had a new blacksmith: Tom.

There was talk of a big Indian battle that was going to take place soon. The Cheyenne were wintering on the upper Washita River, fifty miles straight south of Camp Supply in Oklahoma Territory. The word was, the army would go right into the Indian camp and wipe them out. Tom did not believe that the army would do such a thing.

The West was changing; more and more settlers were moving across the Great Plains. Many treaties with the Indians were broken. A conference between the white leaders and the Indian chiefs in 1867 at Medicine Lodge, Kansas, was supposed to settle the problems, but there are always troublemakers.

Tom met one such man, George Custer, in late November 1868. This new soldier, a colonel, was one of the worst. He was very flamboyant, with long yellow hair, and he wore a fringed army uniform. His ego preceded him, and he thought he was the best show in town. He rode ahead of the soldiers as they entered Camp Supply like he owned the place. The Indians called him Long Hair. He and his hair dismounted in front of the blacksmith shop that day. Acknowledging Tom, the colonel ordered, "Feed my horse and brush him down. I have a party to go to." That same day, a lieutenant brought in his mount for Tom to shoe. "I'm in a bit of a hurry. We have a big assignment. Can you do it now?" he asked Tom.

"Yes, sir, I'll get right on it." As Tom spoke, their eyes met. Tom almost choked.

For a moment, the lieutenant stared back. "Do I know you?" he questioned. Tom silently prayed that his beard and long hair were enough of a disguise to keep the lieutenant from figuring out who he was.

"No, sir, I'm just the blacksmith here," Tom replied. He was glad that this man had never seen him do any blacksmithing work and probably did not remember his name.

"Damn, I ain't no good with names, but faces, I remember. I know I seen you somewhere, but I can't place you." Tom was glad he could not, because this was the very man who was going to send him back into battle at Murfreesboro. He spelled trouble to Tom with a capital "T."

Just then, Colonel Custer walked up and told the lieutenant to get the men ready to leave the camp the next morning. Tom felt relief until Lieutenant Lundberg said, "When we get back, I'm going to look you up. By hook or crook, I'll find out where I saw you."

The next day, the United States 7th Cavalry, about eight hundred in number, rode out in a snow storm, led by Custer. Lieutenant Lundberg went also. Tom was glad that he was not fighting in the army anymore. He had a small shack next to his workplace. It wasn't much, but it had a wood-burning stove in it to keep him warm, and since he was considered an "essential" part of Camp Supply, the soldiers were assigned to cut wood for him. He got to eat with the soldiers, and the food was not that bad. The soldiers cussed it, but Tom considered it decent compared to what he had to eat for the last two years.

When the 7ᵗʰ Cavalry returned, boasting about how they had surprised Black Kettle and his people at dawn, on the morning of November 27, charging this quiet camp from four different directions, Tom felt sick at this stomach. He tried not to listen, but everyone was talking about the victory and what a brave man Custer was. "Why, even Black Kettle's wife was killed alongside him after he was scalped by Custer's Osage scouts," one old-timer bragged. Even though some forty Indian women were killed, Custer, already a hero of the big war in the East, was commended by his leaders, Sheridan and Sherman.

The man with the wooden leg, Benjamin Booker, came to visit with Tom almost every day at the shop. Ben, as he was called, told horror stories of what the Indians had done to him years ago. "The next thing they were going to do to me after they killed my family in front of my eyes was skin me out alive, but the cavalry came just in time to save me. He paused a moment as he reflected then continued with tears in his eyes. "They say ol' Custer burned all the tepees and killed all of the Indian ponies. What do you think of that, Tom?"

"I think that their unprovoked attack will come back to haunt them," Tom replied.

"You know, Lieutenant Lundberg must have been killed during that killin'. I haven't seen him around," Ben said as Tom kept on working.

Soon, Custer and his troops left and went back to Fort Dodge for supplies. The officers were able to spend time with their wives. The troop left bragging about the glorious thing they had done— massacre the Indians. Tom was glad they were gone, and things got back to normal. Tom became acquainted with a young soldier boy named Robert. He was a private in the army and enjoyed talking about himself. "You know, all I really know about myself is that the wagon train I was on with my parents was attacked by Indians. We was comin' across Kansas, and everyone was killed and everything burned except for me and a Bible that was under me. The couple that took me in, the Youngs, said that there were two corpses on top of me, and that's what probably saved my life," Robert confided to Tom. "And in this Bible was the name Robert Thornton, so that's what the Youngs named me. I was only about two years old, so I don't remember anything. The Youngs, my parents, were good to me, but when the war came along, I joined the army and fought for the North."

Then Robert asked Tom, "How about you? Were you in the war? Did you fight for the South? You kind of have a southern accent."

"No, Robert, I am not much of a fighter," Tom answered.

"Well, when I returned from the war, I wanted to farm, but my folks had no land to give me and there was none nearby to work for, so I stayed in the army and was sent out here to Camp Supply. All I brought with me was the Bible that was found with me and my hunting knife. The army gave me everything else I needed. I carry my Bible with me wherever I go. I know you can read. Would you read my family history to me, please?"

Tom began to read the names of Robert Hugh Thornton and Jordan Isabelle Delano, married in the year of our Lord, 1840, Glenrose Township, Territory of Kansas, born to them Robert Wayne and Abigail Lorraine. Tears welled up in young Robert's eyes as he thought about the family he never knew.

On Christmas Eve, they all put on their best and gathered in the mess hall. They prayed and worshipped God. Since Tom could read, he read the Christmas Story from the Bible: reading a version from Matthew, Mark, and Luke. He was a good storyteller too, and he told the soldiers how his mother would decorate the tree. Because his mother was of German descent, she'd talk about the evergreen trees in Germany. The evergreen tree represented life in the dead of winter. The candle in the window represented Jesus Christ; the Light of the World. Tom would tell how they would decorate the tree with red berries and then sing Christmas songs. He and the soldiers sang whatever Christmas songs they could remember. Often, they did not know the words and someone would say, "Oh, it goes this way." And someone else would say, "Yes, but maybe it could be sung this way." They would sing the same song four or five different ways. It was one of the grandest Christmases Tom experienced in a long, long time.

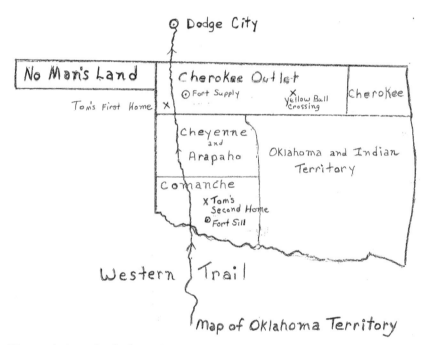

Map of Oklahoma Territory

Tom rode horseback through the Cherokee Nation and was rescued by an Indian maiden near Yellow Bull Crossing, as he was attempting to cross the Salt Fork of the Arkansas River. The authors made their home in near-by Tonkawa for several years. Tom made his first home near Ft. Supply. His second home was in Comanche County. The Western Trail shows where thousands of cattle were driven to Dodge City and beyond. Tom Summers drove his share to railroads in Dodge City, Queen of the West.

CHAPTER 8

Goin' to Texas
to Get Cattle

Spring was coming, Tom took time to ride out to the land that he had leased. He could see the breadth of his ranch—some forty thousand acres. He checked it out and found some water supply on it: a spring. He took a shovel and dug into the spring to see if he could open it up. There was a strong supply of water, and Tom thought, "Yes! This will be good enough to water cattle, if I can get some."

In the latter part of spring, while on his ranch, Tom saw a great dust cloud coming from the south. Thinking it was probably Indians riding through, he rode closer to see. It was a great herd of longhorn cattle, coming up from Texas. They were on their way past Camp Supply and then up to Dodge City, where the railhead was. Cattle were bought and sold there.

They called themselves "Texicans." They were grandly dressed with spurs, big hats, and bright-colored shirts. Yet they were a dirty breed. You could tell they were a proud bunch of boys and men. They said they had six thousand head of cattle. The herd could be seen for miles. The herders were driving the cattle slow so they could eat grass and gain as much weight as they could along the way. Cattle that were worth two dollars per head in Texas were bringing fifteen to twenty dollars per head in Dodge City. Tom asked about the price of cattle since he wanted to start a ranch.

"I can ranch cattle here at the Cherokee Outlet," Tom said, "but I need cows." The cowboys told him if you just follow the "Western Trail," as they called it, and travel south, you will come to Fort Worth, which is about a two-week ride. You'll find all the cattle you want. "We're just trailing out steers, but there are cows and heifers down there for sale."

"Will there be cowboys for me to hire down there?" Tom asked.

One old cowhand laughed and said, "There will always be cowboys in Texas."

Tom rode back to Camp Supply and told the soldiers, "I'm gonna be a cowman." They laughed and said, "But you've got this job." He said, "You can handle this for a while. I will lay aside this work, and we'll be back for the winter. My apprentice will be able to keep you goin', and I'll be back from time to time."

Tom bought a bunch of supplies. Robert, the young stock clerk, said, "I'll go over the hill and then head south with you."

Tom said, "How much longer do you have before you're mustered out?"

He answered, "I'll be mustered out in the fall."

The stock clerk didn't fully understand what Tom meant. Tom continued. "When you get mustered out, then we'll talk."

Tom bought a good pack mule, loaded up the supplies, and gathered up his money, making sure it was in gold. Tom knew the greenbacks had no value in Texas. They wanted the gold money. The Texans were already soured on Confederate money, and they didn't trust paper money. Tom built a special pouch in his saddle to keep his money hid so that no one would find it if he was robbed. This pouch would hold six hundred dollars. Tom had three hundred from blacksmithing. It took about a week to convert the paper money into gold, and then Tom headed south. He also had three hundred dollars from the sale of the wagon and mules.

At first, he was in a hurry, wanting to get to Fort Worth as quickly as possible. Then, Tom realized that he had only one horse and one pack mule, and it was going to take some time to get there. Tom had to take his time, or his horse would be out from under him.

On the journey, Tom had a lot of time to think. He remembered his folks and wondered where John was. He pleasured in bringing Dushane back into his arms and ached because she could not go with him. "Oh, I wish she would have come with me and that I could make her my wife," he spoke aloud as the miles slipped by.

After several days, Tom came to the Canadian River. Crossing this would take him into Indian Territory where there were many Indian reservations. He had heard about the Indians starving to death because some Indian agents were selling the food. Only an evil man would do such a thing, but that was not for him to change. Tom finally reached Texas. He ended up in Wichita Falls after crossing the Red River. River crossings would always be a problem for Tom after his experience with the snakes. When crossing a river, he would look upstream as far as he could, looking for snakes. He told people about this, and they would say they never heard of anything like this happening. One person said he had heard about the ball of snakes, but he had never personally seen one. Someone years later told Tom that the ball of snakes occurs only in the spring.

Longhorns—Tom was a greenie, who knew nothing about ranching or raising longhorns—but with the help of his ranch hands and quite a lot of jabbing—he learned the ropes!

Here stand two outlaws, the mossy horns, who was at least 12 years old—tough as a boot, with moss on his back and horns. The other is a steer, which had been neutered. They could run for three days when chased.

When Tom got to Wichita Falls, they said the cattle were farther south. He went on south and came to Forth Worth. Here you could get all the supplies you would ever want, and at a decent price. He was told to proceed where the longhorn cattle grazed on the open range. Not being a cowboy, he decided to buy heifers and cows, plus a bull or two, rather than trying to round them up as a real cowboy would. The good cowboys were rounding them up because they were free for the taking, and there were thousands of head of cattle.

While in this area of Texas, Tom heard about someone who wanted to sell out. Mrs. Bailey and her daughter had a ranch that they were trying to run even though Mr. Bailey had been killed try-ing to break a horse. She hired ranch hands to help her, but now the ladies wanted to quit. As Tom rode up to the old ranch house, he saw the aging woman was hanging clothes out to dry. At first glance, she looked more like a man than a woman; her skin looked tough from years in the sun, but when she spoke, there was softness in her voice. "Get down and tell me your business," she told Tom.

Tom found out that she just wanted to get back to St. Louis, where her family lived. Unfortunately, she lived a vicious cycle. She would range the cattle, hoping that the sale of them would pay her debt. But they never did. Each year, she had to go back to the bank and borrow money to get through the winter.

Tom visited with her and her fourteen-year-old daughter, Katy. He suggested that she sell the cowherd to him, and then when the boys came back from selling the calves in Dodge City, she would have enough money to leave for St. Louis. Mrs. Bailey pondered on it for a good while. Tom was beginning to think she was never going to make up her mind. Finally, she asked if he had "gold money." That cinched it! He offered her $500 for it all.

"The cows and heifers are worth more than that," she said.

Tom said, "Yes, ma'am, they are."

After more thinking, she said, "I need the $500. They are prob-ably worth more than 1,000, but I'll never get it. I can't sit here and wait for someone to come along with that kind of money."

Tom told her he would give her 500, and if she would give him the address where she could be reached, he would send her another

250 someday. Tom made no promises as to when, but he'd keep his word. She gave him the address of her sister and brother-in-law in St. Louis, saying, "They'll know where to find me."

Tom went back to Fort Worth and rounded up some men who looked like they might be worth something. Many of the men available for cow punching were drunks—unstable men. But Tom found four who were willing to come along and work.

The first man he found, Joe, was a black man who didn't know his last name, nor did he care. He turned out to be the best hand that Tom ever had. Then he hired Jacob Stevenson from Texas and Brent and Fred from Fort Worth. Tom gathered his men and told them, "I will pay you thirty dollars a month to start. From here at Fort Worth, we will drive the cattle that I purchase to my ranch in the Cherokee Outlet. This is a small operation. We will be lucky just to get where we're goin'. We don't even have a cook! But if you will stick with me, we'll have hardtack, bacon, and beans. If you will teach me how to drive cattle, I'll do the cookin' and bossin'."

Jake answered and said, "We have done a lot of strange things, so why not!" They all rode to Mrs. Bailey's and paid her for the herd. As she gave Tom the bill of sale, she gave him the biggest hug he'd ever had and said, "I want God to bless you real good." Tom said, "I sure hope He does, because I know I have bit off more than I can chew."

The five of them rounded up the herd and started north. This was more difficult than Tom thought it would be. Most of the animals did not want to leave home, but with some persuasion, the herd began to move. A few hours into the drive, Tom and his hands encountered a bunch of honest-to-goodness real cowboys coming home from the drive. The wranglers looked at us in a funny way as they thought we were headed for Dodge City. One of them said, "I've never seen such a bunch of fools like you guys."

Tom said, "That's correct." He never did tell them that they were not going to Dodge City. The leader shouted back at Tom, "They won't buy heifers and cows. They want steers." Tom answered back, "I imagine I'll talk 'em into something."

By the time they got to the Red River, the four men had taught Tom how to be a cowboy. He took to roping pretty well. Every once in a while, he would rope a heifer just for the heck of it and have trouble getting the rope off the hoof. One of the men would come help Tom and tell him, "You just leave that rope alone; we'll show you when to use it."

Tom also learned how to drive cattle; you couldn't get too close or they would turn the other way. He learned how to watch out for them and how to keep a count on them. Jake laughing, told Tom, "to count cattle, you must count their hoover, then divide by four!" It was a good thing that all the calves had been born, because Tom could not afford the extra wagon it would take to carry the newborns. He still had the pack mule, and it was loaded down with vittles and cooking supplies.

The men made camp near the river, knowing that in the morning they would cross. Tom made it clear that he would not be the lead or the drag. "I will be in the middle, and I want you to watch out for me," he said.

"Can't you swim, boss?" Brent teased. "Yeah, I can swim. I can swim with the best of 'em, but I don't like river crossings." It was years later when Tom told them about the snakes.

Tom had been gone from Camp Supply for three months. He and the boys finally arrived at his leased land in early summer with the herd. Tom showed the hands the spring that he had dug out. The water was still flowing and would for years to come. Jake spoke up. "You gotta brand your cattle soon."

"Yeah, you're right," Tom answered.

"Where are you gonna get a brandin' iron out here in the middle of nowhere? You look pretty silly, saying you're gonna brand your cattle and you don't even have a branding iron," Fred said. "That's really no problem for someone that knows what they're doin'," Tom replied. Brent and Fred laughed at him.

They were thirty miles out of Camp Supply. Tom left Joe and Jake with the herd, and he took Brent and Fred with him, "the doubters." They didn't figure that Tom could do anything right. They didn't even like the way he cooked bacon; said it was always too dry. So one morning, Tom barely warmed the bacon in the skillet and gave it to them raw. They did not like that either!

The three of them rode on up to Camp Supply and several soldiers came out to greet them. Tom's friend Ben said, "We heard you got shot." Tom replied, "Naaah, I'm too tough to die."

Tom and his two sidekicks rode on over to the blacksmith shop. He climbed down and shook his apprentice's hand. Bill Bradford was his name. Tom told him, "I need some of that brandin' rod in the back." Fred asked Tom, "Do you know what you're doin here?"

Tom said, "This is my shop, my blacksmith shop." The two cowboys were awestruck.

Brent and Fred gained quite a bit of respect for Tom real quick because there weren't too many around who could do that type of work. Tom made two branding irons—the Circle T. He asked Bill if anyone else had that branding name.

"Nope, nobody's got that," Bill said. "Captain Morgan said there's the Cherokee Cattlemen's Association way off up in Kiowa, Kansas, that meets in the spring," Bill remarked. "You can register your brand with them."

Tom replied, "I'll use it now and register it later."

The three men spent a few days at Camp Supply and gathered up some grub. They left to go back to the ranch and planned to start building on the bunkhouse. Hopefully, they would have time to build good shelter before branding season.

Nearing the ranch, Tom glanced off to the west of the spring. There was a huge grove of cottonwood trees. Tom had been there before and was amazed by it out there in the middle of the prairie—must have been a hundred of them. They went to cutting down the trees. Tom showed them how to build a log house like his father and his family in Tennessee had built. He showed them how to notch the corners and fit them together—how to lay one log one way and another log the other way. Of course, when it came to the roof, now that was a different story. They had wonderful walls and a door with buffalo robes hanging on it. Thank goodness, there were plenty of buffalo around to be killed.

They put chinking between the logs and fit them as tight as they could, but there was still some open space between the logs. Off to the west was a creek bed. On the bank of this bed was a real sticky clay soil. They took some buffalo robes and sewed them together to use for packing the clay soil. When the buffalo bags were full, the men put them across the back of the pack mule. This mule was probably the best animal Tom ever had. He was a worker. The men would dig up this sticky clay dirt and bring it back and mix some water and lime into it and then take the mud and stuff it into the cracks between each log. It would last for a year or two, then every fall or every other fall, they would have to redo the mud chinking and dobbin. This did make for a real tight cabin.

They took the rocks that were to the east of the cabin and built a large fireplace. Tom bought some cement at Camp Supply to strengthen the fireplace. They had difficulty in getting the roof on the cabin. They took the smaller limbs and made rafters out of them. Joe and Jake killed seven buffalo, skinned them out, and stretched them out over the roof. This was their first winter's roof. Not the best looking or most functional roof around, but it held until they could get shingles on it. There were wagon trains coming into Camp Supply from Fort Dodge. If you had the money, you could buy about anything you wanted, like shingles, but Tom could not afford them. Jake and Joe built a corral where they could hold the horses.

Tom found out quickly when branding season came that he was far more a farm boy than a rancher. They brought the cattle to the corral because it was easier to rope in the corral instead of out on the range. Jake and Joe were by far the best ropers.

The corral was quite large, about two hundred yards by one hundred yards. It had the bluff wall of a hill for one side so the cattle would be pinned in from that direction. The cowhands would run cattle in there, brand them, turn them out, and bring in some more. After two weeks of hard work, all of the cattle displayed the proud brand of the Circle T.

In early fall, Captain Morgan sent word to Tom that he was needed back at Camp Supply. The blacksmith apprentice Bill was being overrun with work and about all he knew was how to shoe horses. Tom left the boys in charge, making them promise they wouldn't leave and that they'd winter with him. They agreed.

Tom spent most of the winter at Camp Supply, taking a week off every once in a while to go back to check on the ranch and to take supplies to the boys. He was saving up as much money as he could because he knew a new roof was needed soon. In December, Tom told the boys to let the cattle go out on the open range, bring the mule, and to come to the camp and stay with him. They rode back to Camp Supply together.

Tom's old friend, Robert Thornton, whom he had met soon after he arrived at Camp Supply, found Tom at the blacksmith's shop one day and told him that he was supposed to get out of the army in two weeks. "But guess what?" he said, "I've been hoodwinked into staying until the first of the year. They're getting four months outta me for nothing. I guess that's how the army works! But I'm sure not signing up again. I would like to work for you, Mr. Tom, if you'd have me," the discouraged man said.

Tom replied, "I would be proud to have you on board."

"Thank you, Mr. Tom," Robert replied. "You can count on me."

Tom knew that the two men he called "the doubters" were ready to leave and go back to Texas. They had stayed longer than Tom had expected. Fred was always complaining, "It's nasty and too cold here. Besides that, the wind blows *all* the time." Brent wasn't much better. So Tom would be glad to have Robert there when they left.

This would be the second Christmas for Tom to spend with Robert. Tom remembered reading the Christmas story out of Robert's Bible, last year, and how, after, Joe had come to him and asked him about God who had sent His Son Jesus to earth for even a person like him, to save him from his sins. Joe ask God to forgive him. Joe was a different man after that night and would tell anyone who would listen, "I'm saved, and I know where I'm goin' when I die. I'm goin' where Jesus is, because I accept Him as my personal Savior. I believe He lived, died and rose again just for me, like the Bible says."

Tom and his wranglers joined the soldiers for Christmas. It was a time of remembering families and friends from the past. Robert Thornton was mustered out after Christmas and was eager to leave Camp Supply and lead the life of a cowboy on the Summers ranch.

The morning that Tom had chosen to leave for his ranch broke with a hard north wind and blowing snow. "It takes us a big, long day of travel to get home—even when the weather's decent," Tom told Robert. "Let's wait and see what happens."

That particular day, they heard tell of a gambler that came into the area. His reputation was known far and wide. Tom's two hired hands, Fred and Brent, who were once so eager to get back to Texas, decided to hang around a bit and cast their luck with the famous gambler.

"Please, Mr. Boss, give us an advance on our pay. We need some money to show that ol' gambler that we are 'cock of the walk.'" Tom felt a little sorry for them, knowing they wanted to do a little drinking and have some fun. He gave them each five dollars, allowing that was all the wages they had due them.

The boys made tracks into town. They immediately came up to this old barn-looking place they called "The Bar." It was on the outskirts of Camp Supply since there was to be no bar on the army post. They got to drinking old rotgut whiskey, one drink right after the other. As Fred and Brent guzzled the firewater, they got to talking meaner and bragged how tough they were.

"Why, I could kill a bear with one hand," proclaimed Fred.

"Why, I could kill two bears and a rattlesnake just by spittin' on 'em!" said Brent with a smirk.

Over in a dark corner, four weather-beaten cowboys sat, reeking of whiskey and foul language. One of the men, Brent and Fred had decided, was the one and only George Masterson. Handsome in a strange and mysterious way, Mr. Masterson had come down from Dodge City.

"We figured he was not any good," said Fred as he looked at him through blurred vision. He thought he might have even killed somebody or something, because this was not a nice place to be. Camp Supply, compared to Dodge City, was "hell on wheels."

Tom's two boys decided they wanted to get in on the action. Fred waited for a break in the cards and asked if he and his buddy could join the table. George looked up saw two greenhorns and said, "Sure, I can use some cowboy's money."

Fred and Brent were packing their sidearms, although they shouldn't have been because they didn't know what they were up against. George won every hand of poker. The losing and whiskey got the better of Fred, and he bellowed, "You're a damn cheater!" and he drew his gun. Fred had hardly cleared leather when the notorious gambler Masterson plugged him in the throat. Brent decided it was probably a good time to get out of there. He flew through the swinging doors of the bar as Masterson hollered at him, "Never let me see your ugly face here again!"

For some strange reason, after barely getting out the front doors and falling on his face, he stumbled back onto his feet and sneaked around to the back of the bar. Tom wasn't there, but later they told him Brent showed up at the back door of the bar, planning on shooting Masterson in the back.

As the drunken cowhand slipped through the old screen door, George Masterson, a man who lived with life and death all the time, heard a squeak from the screen door behind him. He spun around, his chair moving with him. While he was still spinning, he drew and threatened, "Don't do it."

He could feel a presence facing him in the shadows. Again, he said, "Don't do it." He was still and at the ready, with his gun pulled and pointed at the cowboy, telling him not to do it.

Young Brent, just short of nineteen summers, who had bragged about killing three men in Oklahoma Territory, reached for his gun and was shot dead before he knew what had happened to him. Masterson calmly turned around, put his smoking pistol in his holster, and said, "Whose deal is it?"

Tom was now short two cowboys. It looked like it was up to him to bury them. They were not the best guys in the world, but they had kind of gotten acquainted—almost close friends. Jake, Robert, and Joe took the dead men to the cemetery. It was not much of a cemetery. There were quite a few soldiers buried there, some who didn't have any place else. They buried them there, buried them with their boots on. Tom didn't know Fred's last name, but he chiseled Brent and Fred's first names on a wooden slab and said a few words over them. Hopefully, that made it better.

The men were all freezing when they left the cemetery. The earth had started to freeze, and they could hardly see their way back to the blacksmith shop, where they all holed up for the night.

All this time Robert kept saying, "I'm out of the army. I sure don't want to be here any longer." But the storm was so terrible, they could not be anywhere else. They could not even tend to the cattle if they were at the ranch. There was plenty of coal that Tom used in the forge, so they kept warm in the blacksmith shop.

CHAPTER 9

First Year at Ranch

The army had five or six wagons that needed worked over. Tom told them a good price that he would charge if he were to fix them. Robert, Jake, Joe, and Tom went through each one of the wagons. They bolted the beds down, put new lumber in them, and rebuilt the wheels. They did a lot of work on them, for they didn't have much else to do; you couldn't go outside in such a snowstorm.

After about thirty days, a schnook wind came a-blowing in. This is the warm wind that can cause the temperature to rise forty degrees in no time. By the end of the second day, a lot of the snow was gone. They probably should have waited a little longer to leave, but Robert wanted to get out of the camp in the worst way, so they decided to leave. He had clothes shipped down to him from Dodge City so he would have them and not have to wear his army uniform anymore. He didn't even want to wear his army boots. He had enough money to buy those things. He was not a drinker or a gambler, so he had managed to save a lot of his pay.

The four of them headed out, along with the mule with the pack on it and all they could carry on their horses. Tom wanted to carry home enough vittles to make it through the winter and not have to come back to the camp for more supplies. He could do it because he had managed to save some money. They headed down south toward the ranch, which was southwest of Camp Supply. They saw buffalo holed up, some dead antelope, and some deer in bad shape that probably wouldn't make spring. They wondered what kind of condition the longhorn cattle would be in. They feared they might be plum out of the cattle business if they had all frozen to death. But they had underestimated the stamina of these cattle. They were nothing but a wild breed—survival of the fittest. They knew how to get by in adverse circumstances. The strongest and best would survive over the long haul.

When they got close to the water spring, which was a few miles from what they called the ranch house, there were the cattle—mulling around the spring, their water source. Since the spring flowed all the time, there would always be grass. The cattle were digging in the snow with their hooves to get to the grass. Yes, Tom lost a few head, but by and large, they came through the winter very well, a lot better than he had imagined when they were holed up in Camp Supply for those long thirty days.

When they got to the ranch house, there was another herd of these smart longhorns making themselves at home. They had been branded in that very corral and no doubt hated it, probably didn't even want to be close to it, but there they were. The best part was they had been protected from the freezing wind by the high cliff on the north side.

They were licking themselves and sunning themselves as best they could. Tom and the boys felt good about it all, in fact congratulating themselves. "Boy, this is great! We sure were lucky!"

After checking on the cattle, they rode to the cabin, their ranch house. "Oh no, it can't be!" The roof was gone, all caved in from the heavy snow. Joe began asking, "Where we gonna sleep?"

"We'll sleep when the work gets done," Tom said, feeling upset at himself for not building a better roof.

Robert said with a grin, "You didn't know how to put a roof on. Lay hides on it like shingles, bottom ones first, then lap the next row over and sew them together with sinew. I'll show you how it's done, but first, we have to get some hides rounded up."

They all eagerly searched for three reasons: they were cold, they were hungry, and night was not far away. In a nearby gully, they found a herd of longhorns that had drifted away from the main herd—frozen to death. Actually, being frozen made them easier to skin. They each took out their knives and started to work. As they skinned the cowhides, they noticed the beautiful colors of each one. They loaded the skins on their horses and headed for their home on the prairie.

Robert took charge. "Lay each hide out on the ground so we can see the size of each one. Grab these two ladders so Joe and you can carry the hides up the ladder. Stretch them out over these newly constructed beams that we put together before we went searchin' for hides."

The hides were placed with the hair patterns going down so the rain or snow would move more easily to run off onto the ground. The angle of the roof was steeper than before, so it would shed water better.

The colors of the longhorn cattle hides created a beautiful roof. There are seven colors of longhorn cattle—brown, black, yellow, orange, red, gray, and white—and they had all the colors, like Jacob's coat of many colors in the Bible. They had never seen anything like it.

In later life, when Tom shingled a roof with the white man's shingles, he always remembered how beautiful the roof looked on his old ranch house cabin. The hides did not last but a few years. With the hot summer sun and the freezing temperatures turning them brittle and thin, they would eventually splinter away.

When summertime came, they moved the cattle up to some new grazing land. Tom had been told how destitute the Indians were, living on the reservation. When they were taking the cattle back to the ranch later that fall, they passed by the Comanche Reservation close to Fort Sill, where they had been camping. The Indians came out to look at the cattle. Tom was sure they had seen cattle drives before but still came out to see them pass by. Here we were with a lot of cows, calves, heifers, and about forty bulls. It shouldn't have taken all the bulls to service the cows, but we didn't know how well the bulls would perform, so we bought one bull for every ten head.

When passing through, we noticed their plight. Although Tom couldn't speak their tongue, he wanted to communicate with them and tell them he wanted to help them. He went into the office of Indian agent Willford Wilson. He was a very pitiful man: a Government appointee, probably somebody's brother-in-law that never amounted to anything so they sent him out West. Tom told him what he wanted him to do: it was to cut our a few cattle and leave them for the Indians. The agent said it wasn't necessary that they'd be all right. Tom's response: "You're wrong!" An argument followed. Tom said, "They're my cattle, and I'll leave them if I feel like it."

The Indian agent said he would see to it that the Indians would not get them. He said he would gather them up and sell them to someone at Camp Supply.

The argument continued. Tom drew his weapon, telling the dirty old man that he knew how to kill and that was about all he was good for. The agent backed down and said you can do as you wish. Tom holstered his Colt .45. He couldn't recall if he had ever been that angry before. He couldn't believe how cruel this agent was to those he was paid to protect.

Tom conversed with a young Comanche brave that could speak a little broken English. Tom told him what he was going to do. He left twenty bulls. He told this young brave that this was payment for them crossing their land. The young Indian expressed his appreciation by giving Tom a beautiful beaded breastplate with these words: "Take, wear in good health." Tom and the cowhands drove the cattle up on the hill. Of course, the twenty bulls still thought they were part of the herd and wanted to come along. A few braves came riding up on their paints. It was then that Tom noticed several of the Indians were but boys about ten to twelve years old. Even the young ones were excellent horsemen as they rode down the cattle, just like they would if the bulls were buffalo.

There was great excitement from it. The squaws came running out with their knives; they butchered several right there on the spot. Tom held the cattle on the top of the hill as they watched the Indians excitement. It was a grand sight. They thought they would probably never see anything like this again, and they didn't. This was as close as Tom had been to seeing the Indians hunt buffalo.

In the spring of '71, the cows were all with calves as near as Tom could tell. When the cows started calving in February, March, and April, they noticed the wolves were starting to hang around.

Tom told the boys, "We don't have enough bullets to kill all the wolves and coyotes. Plus, they are so crafty that we probably couldn't hit many of them anyway."

When the first cow calved, the men were out in the pasture with her as much as they could. They even thought of trying to be out there with her at night. This first experience showed them that wasn't really necessary at all.

Tom knew that a longhorn cow would protect her young, but when she's down in the calving process, who's going to save her then? And that's what they were concerned about. When the cow is calving, you don't want to be close to them anyhow. And thereafter, you might consider them almost a pet, but when she drops a calf, you'd better leave her alone for a couple of months. Then Joe and Jake, who had worked these cattle in Texas, told Tom, "You'd just better leave them alone."

Tom said, "Yes, but in Texas you didn't have the wolves that we have here. Maybe we'll lose 'em all." They didn't know.

Robert and Tom were working the area close to the spring when they saw a herd of cows, ten or twelve. They were in a circle, with their butts facing into the circle and their heads facing away from the circle. Tom couldn't believe it! He asked, "You know what they are surrounding?"

Robert took a spyglass he confiscated from the army and looked in and to his amazement he said, "Well, dad burnit, there's a cow in there giving birth, in the center of the circle!"

He handed the glass to Tom, and sure enough, those cows were protecting the little calf. When the cow had given birth, she licked the calf off and ate the afterbirth. Then the cows meandered off after they knew the cow could take care of her little one. The calf was up and sucking in a short time. They saw this happen on several occasions. Tom had never seen this in any other breed of cattle, where they would take care of their young like that.

As the calves grew, they would group together in herds of twenty or thirty. The men would see three or four cows protecting the young ones as they grazed. Later in the calving time, the wolves were getting more aggresive. They were after the downed baby calves.

The other boys were gone. Tom was tightening a shoe on a saddle horse. Joe came riding in and said, "Grab your rifle and come with me!" He rode out with his .50-caliber Henry rifle and his Colt .45. They came upon the same situation with the cattle in a circle, guarding a cow giving birth. The wolves decided they had been circling the cows long enough, and were plenty hungry for not having eaten for a few days. They were trying to attack the cow and calf in the center of the circle.

The guard cows had horns that were about three feet on each side and were plenty sharp. Plus, they had the inborn instinct on how to use the horns to ward off the enemy. It was almost as if they had eyes on the end of those weapons. They knew where the ends of their horns were and how to use them. You would think they would get their horns tangled in the bush, but they would just twist their heads just so and walk right through.

They were fighting those wolves. The cows had killed four wolves with no injury to themselves. The wolves were gored by the horns, and if they couldn't run away, they were stomped to death by the cow's hooves. The cows hated the wolves worse than anything.

It wasn't but a few minutes until the wolves left the cows. That was a sight to see. Tom never saw this event happen again; the prairie wolf was becoming extinct.

They had one cow that Mrs. Bailey must have treated as a pet. They found out that this particular momma cow loved sugar. She would actually eat it out of their hands. She was really too much of a pet. When this cow calved, she'd tend the calf but would soon head to the log house to get her sugar treat. She became quite a pest.

She was the amusement for the men but, again, just a little too much trouble. They were giving her sugar once in a while then decided to ration her only once on Sundays. It was their Sunday thing. She was around a lot, and her calf was becoming very tame as well. She was a beautiful cow, about four colors. She was orange and brown and black and white: just spotted all over. Several of the hands called her Speck. Tom just called her Ol' Momma. Tom did not know how old she was when they brought her up the trail, probably three or four years old. She was with them twenty years and never missed having a calf before succumbing to old age. One day Jake found Ol' Momma down and she couldn't get up. It made Tom weep when he had to shoot her. He cut off her horns and kept them.

Tom told the boys, "We're going to skin this one out and we're going to tan it." Joe knew how to tan hides with salt, much like the Indians did. Their beloved Speck became a rug on the floor or a blanket for the bed when someone was ill or needed the extra warmth it provided. It was as if that cowhide had healing power.

By mid-April, all calves were born—healthy and safe. The men still took turns watching over the herd. When Tom was out with the herd by himself, he thought of his family that he would never see again. His mom had such loving ways. When someone would ask her why she was so sweet, she would say, "I want to be like Jesus." She also made the best apple pie ever! His dad worked sunup to sundown. And John—"Oh, what I'd give just to hear his voice or hear him whistling while he did his chores," Tom cried.

The wind would catch his hair and blow it across his sunburned face. "I sure need a haircut and shave," he said aloud to no one.

As he drifted among the cows during a long watch, he could almost feel Susan's sweet lips on his, and it was like her hair blowing against his skin.

Tom yearned to have his own family, to be surrounded by love again. It still hurt that his Indian maiden couldn't come with him when he left the Cherokees.

The boys and Tom spent most of the summer working on the cabin. They made a door using scrap lumber from the camp. The hides would shed light rains, but holes were beginning to appear in the roof. You could even see some stars at night: that's good, but a leaky roof is not. One hot, muggy evening, the wind kicked up, then came a downpour complete with hail the size of marbles. Then it got real quiet—so still, one could hardly breathe. Tom heard a small rumble; it grew louder until it became a roar. It sounded like a train, but there were no tracks for miles.

Then Tom saw it, a long rope in the sky, dangling here and there, playing with the fear that was in his heart and kicking up dirt and dust the likes of which he'd never seen. "My God!" Tom said. "What is that?"

By then the cowhands had come into the ranch house—or cabin as they called it. Robert knew what was coming their way. He said, "That's a twister! You can't do nothin' to stop it!"

They stood frozen, watching this twisty, gray, twirling cloud dance on north of them, as if ignoring their presence. "Boy, that was close," all four of them said at once!

Next day, they rode out into the area where they had seen the monster in the sky. There was a swath fifty feet wide where all the tall grass was completely gone and all you could see was red dirt! "'Slicker'n a whistle,' like my grandpa used to say," Jake said. "I'd never seen anything like it. What if one of us had been caught up in that thing?"

The next week, when Tom was in Camp Supply, the captain came by. He said, "You know, we think quite a little bit of you. We think of you as an officer. You've got to realize that we officers don't usually patronize with the enlisted men. It just doesn't happen.

"We have over sixty troops here, plus a lot of officers. We're going to have a big St. Patrick's Day dance, and we want you to attend," he said with the tone of a commander.

Tom said, "I haven't anyone to bring or anyone to dance with. I'm a single man." Captain Morgan exclaimed, "There will be lots of fun, food and everything! All the officers' wives will be there. We want you to come and join up with us at this big dance. There won't be any intoxicating beverages at this here shindig. Lemonade is it."

Tom still didn't know with whom he was going to dance, but it sounded like a good time, so he said, "If I can get cleaned up, I'll sure go!" Fear came across him as he reasoned that someone at the dance could figure out who he really was and put him in the guardhouse or, even worse, back into the army to kill again.

Tom still had his beard. He figured he'd scratched that beard as long as he wanted to, so he shaved it all off, except for his mustache, and it was a dandy. He had always been proud of his mustache all through his life.

By now, Tom had lost some of his southern Tennessee accent. Hopefully, no one would recognize him. Tom didn't have any clothes that would justify going to this grand ball. He noticed more and more civilians coming into Camp Supply. They had a mercantile dry goods store setting up. Tom even heard of a tailor, Oliver Olson, from Boston, who was very busy fixing up uniforms for all the soldiers and officers.

Lo and behold, the dry goods man, Luke Smithie, walked up to Tom, shook his hand with a hearty grip, and spoke with broken English. "Howdy, sir! I understand you're quite the blacksmith. I must haul my goods from Fort Dodge to fix my new store. I love it here. My missus and my family will join me from St. Louis as soon as I turn a profit. But my main wagon has a broken wheel. I implore you to mend it. I will pay you. Please make my wheel new again."

Tom felt his urgency and knew his need was great. They walked over to his wagon. Tom looked at the broken wheel. He assessed that it wasn't that bad, but Mr. Smithie thought it was. It seemed to make Tom charge a little bit more when they didn't know what they had.

Tom slowly replied, "Yes, I can fix your wheel, with one stipulation: I need some new clothes." Smithie said, "I'll fix you up with what few I got."

Tom said, "No, you need to talk with Mr. Olson, the tailor, and acquire for me a good-lookin', citified suit plus all that goes with it. Even a good pair of boots—'cause I only have this one pair, and they are just run over 'til who threw a chunk under it."

They argued and fussed. Finally, Tom said, "I'll fix the wheel and put in three dollars to boot." Tom gave him three dollars for what he was doing. That way, maybe he was paying for his clothes.

Tom guessed that Mr. Smithies was at his mercy because there was no one else to fix the wheel.

Tom got his clothes a week later, just in time for the dance: a fine black silk suit, ruffled white shirt, black tie, even suspenders.

The tailor even fitted his new clothes to him. Tom was overwhelmed with Mr. Smithie's generosity. Tom sheepishly mentioned to Olson, "You know, a guy with this fine an outfit, I reckon, needs some new underclothes."

"Yes, sir, they're over yonder in that boot box with your new size 14, black-steer-hide boots."

"Oh!" Tom said. For once, he was speechless. All he could muster up was "Thank you, thank you! Tell Mr. Smithie I will be a lifetime customer." Tom said "Thank you!" again as he walked out of the tailor shop, loaded down with clothes befitting a duke from the old country.

Tom splurged. He got a real bath, shave, and haircut, all for two bits, plus some smelly good cologne from his friend Al the barber.

He had forgotten to get a good hat. It was Saturday night, the evening of the St. Patty dance, so he figured he didn't have to have a hat. He slicked his shiny black hair down, waxed his mustache, and hoped for the best. He began whistling as he leaped on his horse and headed for the dance.

Storm clouds were building, and a cold wind was coming out of the north as Tom arrived. He secured his stud, checked his tie, and made his way into the brightly decorated hall. He guessed that more than half of the officers were Irish, not only by their names, but also with the enthusiasm that this dance had brought to the men.

Everywhere, there were banners and flags, musicians warming up their instruments, and several women arranging the food and pitchers of lemonade. Tom was a stranger to these people because they had never seen him dressed and slicked up the way he was dressed. Although he was a little embarrassed at the attention he was getting at the party, he liked the way the women were smiling at him. "Boy, this is a pretty nice place to be." They had an orchestra, a fiddle player, and everything. "There's a guy playin' a horn! I've never been around somethin' like this before," Tom said to himself.

He didn't know if he was supposed to dance with the officers' wives or not. He knew there weren't any single women at Camp Supply. So he went to the captain and asked him, "What am I to do?" The captain replied, "Mr. Summers, you look right sharp. You may ask the husband of the lady you wish to dance with for permission. If he agrees, then, you may dance with her."

Well, this one officer, Lieutenant Sampson, had the nicest little black-haired wife you'd ever seen. Boy, she was something. So Tom asked the lieutenant if he might have a dance with his wife. "Sure, son," he replied. He looked at his wife and she smiled, so Tom danced with her.

Then, Tom went to ask the captain. Now, his wife was just a little heavyset, but she sure knew how to dance a jig. She must have had a lot of Irish in her, because she was sure teaching Tom a thing or two. He didn't know much about dancing, but like he would always say, "I never did know how to dance, but I sure like to hold them while they do."

Tom thought, "Well, it's time to go back and dance with Ruby, the dark-haired lady again, because she sure did dance nice and was a very beautiful woman." The lieutenant thought otherwise and thought Tom might be overstepping his bounds. He said, "No," when Tom asked him. He could justify his thinking, because he didn't know what Tom was thinking.

Of course, with her raven-black hair and sparking eyes, she reminded Tom of Susan Dushane, the Indian girl back in Cherokee country. Tom thought about Susan all night long, wishing she was at the dance with him so he could hold her. He enjoyed the whole night—even dancing a jig by himself once in a while. It was a fabulous thing.

Tom had a nagging feeling that someone was watching him and was going to find him out. He kept putting the feeling away and tried to concentrate on having a good time.

As he said his "good nights" and "thank yous" and began the short ride back to his quarters in the blacksmith shop, he began to feel Susan's presence around him. Tom could see her face; he could hear her laughter. The pain in his heart was still there from when she told him good-bye. He just could not get her out of his mind; he couldn't sleep for wanting to feel her body next to him.

"If I had a good excuse, I'd just go back and get her," Tom thought to himself. Then he realized that he didn't need an excuse—he would just saddle up and go.

Next morning, he got up early and got caught up on his black-smithing duties. Everything was pretty slow that day, so he rode back to the ranch after clearing it with Captain Morgan.

As he rode to the corral at his ranch, he saw the cowboys had stopped what they were doing. They were fixated on him, practically staring him down. His work clothes were in the saddlebag and he was wearing his new duds. He even stopped and got himself a new hat from a new shop at the Camp called Hal's Hattery. They glared at him as he drew closer. Jake put his hand on his gun. It was a wonder they didn't take a shot at him because Tom figured they thought he stole his own horse.

Jake did question him, "What can I do ya for, sir?"

"You can bring me a tall bottle of whiskey" was Tom's reply. They all had a big laugh over it when they recognized his voice and could see under the brim of the Stetson.

Tom's ranch hands were eager to know what he had been up to. Tom related to them about the evening at the dance. "I guess I must have told 'em three times," Tom said, "because they kept asking, 'What was this, and what was that?'" "Now just how big was the heavy-duty captain's wife?" Jake asked.

Tom replied, "She wasn't that fat. She was just a little heavy." They wanted to know what color of hair she had. What were those women wearing? Did they smell nice?

He told them that they could all go up there and look around, so everybody decided to go but Joe. He said, "The only place I'm at home is here at the ranch."

So Joe and Tom stayed at the ranch, and Robert and Jake went on up to Camp Supply. Tom told them to be back in three days. He gave them a little money. He didn't know what they did when they were there, but when they came back, they came a-whooping and a-hollering. He understood a wagonload of "ladies of the evening" had come into town. "Kinda wished I stayed!" Tom thought. They allowed that they had a good time.

The cattle were all looking good. They were staying where they were supposed to be, and they weren't having any trouble with the Indians or renegades.

Tom thought, "I think part of that might be because I am a blacksmith and thought of as a prized person." Every once in a while, a small patrol of troops would come by and ask how they were getting along and check things out and kind of protect them. It all worked out well for them.

CHAPTER 10

Back to Cherokee Nation

Tom said, "Boys, I've got to go back to the Cherokee country. There's a woman back there that I had shined up to. She had saved me from the snakes, and I am goin' to go back and get her." Tom saddled up. One of the boys had a leather bag that he always carried with him. Jake cleaned it up with saddle soap and put Tom's good clothes and his new boots in it. So when he did get to the Cherokees, he could clean up and look halfway nice. He packed his razor and took off, headed east toward the Cherokee country.

He kept thinking about Susan all the time while traveling there. For two weeks, she was ever on his mind. When he came to the Yellow Bull Crossing again, he took that bag with his good clothes in it and held it up high over his head, even though it was probably watertight; he did not want to take any chances that his clothes would get wet. Across the river he and Ranger went, hell-bent for election!

After crossing the river with much trepidation, Tom headed for the settlement of the Cherokees. These people were more civilized than most white people. There it was, the village nestled in the cottonwoods on the banks of the Arkansas River. They were planting spring corn. Tom rode to the cabin where he remembered Susan lived with her mother. Little Flower was so glad to see him, although she had to look twice to recognize him in the good clothes he had

84

changed into. Tom asked about Susan. Her mother said, "She's gone." Tom asked, "When will she be back?"

"She probably won't" was her reply.

He asked, "What happened?"

She gave him a long, hard look and turned back to the stove where she was cooking. He did not ask her again. It seemed like an hour, but he guessed it was maybe a minute or two.

She turned around and said, "You know the condition that she was in."

Bewildered, Tom said, "No, ma'am." Suddenly, he realized what she meant.

She said, "She had a baby—a baby boy." Tom was stunned. "There was this man, Jackson Martin, who said he'd marry her and take this child," the woman continued, "but they were gonna leave. They were going back to Georgia, which is where the Cherokees came from."

"I see," Tom told the woman. He was heartbroken. "If only I had known. If she'd only gotten word to me. But they didn't know where I was!" he thought to himself. Susan's mother said she would never come back. Martin had a farm and he would need her help to work it. Tom hoped he would care for the boy.

Tom fought back the burning tears and fumbled in his pocket for the silver bracelet that he had bought to give to Susan. "Thank you, Little Flower, for your kindness. I want you to have this." And he pressed the gift into her hand. With that, he turned away, mounted Ranger, gave him a hard kick, and rode off. He rode to the place where Susan had come to him in the night then headed north to a place he had heard of in Kansas, named Kiowa. By going this way, he avoided the treacherous Yellow Bull Crossing.

He didn't know how long he rode, but at last he saw a sign that said "Medicine Lodge Kansas." It was a grand town. It even had its own railroad!

Lots of cattlemen were there. These cattlemen were there for the Cherokee Cattlemen's Association meeting. The meeting focused on the ranchers registering the land that they had leased from the Cherokees.

Tom mostly listened until one man asked, "Where are you from?" Tom answered, and the tall drink of water said, "You're in the Cherokee Outlet!"

Tom answered, "Yes, sir."

He said, "You a rancher?"

Tom replied, "Compared to these cattle herds, I guess, just barely. I need to buy some cows, some more heifers, but I sure can't right now, because I don't have any money."

FT. Supply Blacksmith Shop—Photo of the original blacksmith shop in Fort Supply Oklahoma. The shop is now located on the Plains Indian and Pioneer Musuem in Woodward, Oklahoma. Ted Riddle stands where Tom made his circle T branding iron. Photo by Linda Riddle.

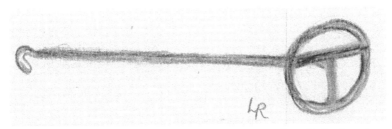

Circle T—Branding Day was a big day at the ranch. All the hands took part. Tom made the Circle T at the FT. Supply blacksmith shop. The men roped and bulldogged the steers one by one and put the iron to 'em.

Historic Fort Supply—Camp Supply was established Nov. 18, 1868. Five days later, Lt. Col. George Custer's 7th Cavaly departed for the Battle of Washita. In 1878 Camp Supply was officially named Fort Supply. This is one of the main sights of our story.

Courtesy: The Plains Indians and Pioneer Musuem in Woodward, Oklahoma

CHAPTER 11

White Gold

Later that day, an old-looking, weather-beaten man, whom Tom later learned had been a scout for the army, limped up to him and grunted, "You goin' back toward the Supply Camp, aren't you?"

"Yes, I am," Tom said.

His garments were worn leather, and he sported old army boots. One boot was larger than the other. Why? Tom didn't ask. His red wool long handles, which peeked out from under his laced shirt, were torn and frayed, and he was definitely ready for his once-a-year, whether-he-needed-it-or-not, bath!

He continued, "I guess you know, although you're too young to know much of anything, that down south of here in the Strip, there's a commodity that's almost as valuable as that there gold."

Tom couldn't figure out what he was mumbling about, thinking mostly that he had lost nearly all his teeth.

The old man explained, "You need some money, and I know how you can make some. It's hard work, but it'll be good for ya."

He began to meander down memory lane. "When I was a young whippersnapper like you, I came across this here ocean of white stuff. It goes for miles. You get out there alone, now, and you'll get lost. If the rattlesnakes don't get you, the red ants will. Summer is the worst time to go, 'cause you'll burn up and there's no good water for miles."

Tom's curiosity was getting the best of him. "Where is this place, and what's out there to make money?"

"Now just hold your horses. I'll tell you how to get there and what to do and what not to do, but first tell me, were you at an Indian settlement of the Cherokees about three, three and a half years ago?" he asked.

"Yes," Tom hesitated, wondering how he knew.

"I thought you were there. I recognized the horse. You don't see many dun studs that large in these parts. If you'd had any sense, you would have stayed there. Why, those Cherokees are good people, and there's good farmland in the area. You had a squaw there too. Why did you leave?"

Tom kept thinking, "How does this fella know all about me? I wonder myself sometimes why I left." Tom wondered what else he knew. Could he know that he was an army deserter?

He kept on. "You had a beard then too. What were you tryin' to hide?"

"Ole Scout," as he was known, spoke softly as he said, "I spec' you'ens was runnin' from something. But that's 'tween you and the Almighty. You know most out here are puttin' the past behind 'em as fast as they can."

Tom quickly changed the subject. "You must know these parts pretty well."

"You betcha I do," Scout declared. "I scouted for the army, mostly during the Indian wars in Kansas for about twenty years. I was the best they ever had. I'm not a bragger, just tellin' you the facts. I've even got a scar from a Comanche arrow on my back to prove it."

"So where exactly is this place?" Tom asked.

"It'll be about twenty miles south and a little east. You know, those buffalo hunters will pay good money for the desert brine. Make 'em pay with gold; that's the only thing that's worth totin' around. Then, find a place to bury it because you cannot trust the banks. There's a lot of robbin' goin' on. I've met some of those buffalo hunters," the old man continued. "They will kill the beasts all day and use salt to tan their hides with, if they can get it.

"I'm sure that Camp Supply is the jumping-off point for Fort Sill, Indian Territory, Fort Elliot, and Fort Wheeler, Texas. Any quartermaster would pay a pretty good price for the white gold," he said with authority.

That was a gamble Tom decided to take. He thanked his new friend for the tip. He bought a big wagon: a big wheel wagon. Oh, it cost! And he got six head of mules. He kept his saddle horse, of course; he was a beauty. He hired four hands, good workers. They lumbered along toward south, southeast until they came to this vast expanse of shimmering crystal-like sand, but it was salt. They had found the salt flats, stretching as far as the eye could see. And talk about hot! Tom had never felt heat like that, with the sun's rays striking up off the white ground.

As the five of them unloaded the shovels and white cloth bags to put the salt in, their skin began to burn. Every pore of Tom's body opened up with sweat and soaked up the salt vapors in the air. It was smothering; with the hot, humid air and the salt, they could hardly breathe. Tom kept telling himself, "This load will buy my way to being a real rancher." He was thankful that Ole Scout had directed him to bring rations and plenty of drinking water. Tom also brought several sacks of oats and a little hay and water for the stock. They began to load the wagon in earnest. One man held the fifty-pound sack open, and another would shovel it full. Tom instructed the men not to dig too deep or they'd come to sand. The pure salt was about eight inches deep, thinner in some places. They tried to keep from getting the dried manure in their sacks. They wanted to keep it clean.

It took them about two days to load the wagon with their precious cargo. They moved from one area to another to get the good, clean salt. There were rabbit droppings and other varmints to look out for also. At last, they were ready to leave for Camp Supply. Tom paid his hands, wished them well, and then remembered he'd better drive north to the spring and fill his barrels with water before he headed west. The good, sweet water, ten miles away from where they were digging, came from a natural spring. What a delight in a hot desert land. Who knew how long it would be before he found water again?

Will, the half-breed, didn't go with the other hands on their ponies. He lagged behind and said, "Mr. Summers, I wish to stay and work for you. I don't drink whiskey and I like you. I will work hard."

Man, Tom was glad to hear that, because he knew he'd need help unloading the wagon, plus he would need help buying and taking care of the new cattle.

"Come on, you've got a job! I'll pay you thirty dollars a month, plus room and board. What's your last name?" Tom asked. Will just shook his head and rode up ahead of Tom on his black-and-white pinto.

They headed off by dead reckoning. Tom didn't know any other way to get to Camp Supply, just kind of west and a little south. They were sunburned, but Tom had a good feeling that things were going to get better.

They ran across some renegade Indians. But they were not close enough to tell what tribe they were from. They could have been a mixed band of troublemakers. Tom told the half-breed, "I must look like such a fool that they don't want to bother with me." The Indians followed Tom, Will, and the wagon for several days. There wasn't much sleeping at night. Tom kept his rifle handy at his side. He was getting sick and tired of being followed. So the next morning, Tom planned to take some action.

Tom noticed that one of the five renegades was always holding up a shield. He told Will, "I'm gonna shoot a hole in that thing and see if that don't change their minds and leave us alone."

He adjusted his sights on his .50-caliber rifle, and as luck would have it, when he fired off the shot, it hit the shield right in the middle. The little band decided at once that there was somewhere else that they needed to be. They left in a hurry, whooping and hollering, leaving in a big cloud of dust.

Soon it was time to cross the Cimarron. "Why did God make so many rivers?" Tom told Will to tie the mules off, and he saddled his horse. Will rode with no saddle, only a blanket under his thin frame.

He and Tom scouted the river and the banks. Tom walked along the bank on the east side. As it was a hot summer day, the air was full of mosquitoes, flies, and gnats.

They were all being bitten even though they tied bandanas around their faces and tried to wave the insects off with their hands. The animals were in agony also as the relentless bugs persisted.

The river was almost dry, but Tom still didn't want any surprises. He didn't want the wagon to be bogged down, as it was fully loaded and quite heavy. It would leave a trail with deep ruts behind.

Tom came back and climbed up onto the wagon seat. He hollered at Will, "We'll cross over yonder, by that old cottonwood where there is no water, just mud."

He left his mount saddled and tied him up to the seat of the wagon. He wasn't leaving anything to chance. In case he had to, he could bail out on him for whatever reason.

Tom figured the salt could stay there in the river if the wagon got stuck in the mud. All of them got into the middle of the river. The mules were lying into it. It was a hard pull. Coming up a small grade on the other side, the mules just quit pulling! Now, what? The heavy wagon was above the water, but the wheels were mired down about four inches on each wheel. The wheels and the mules were bogged down in the mud.

Tom got down. Now, mules are just mules—no more, no less.

He talked to them and cussed them. He pulled them and pushed. They just kind of stood around. He cussed them some more, but to no avail.

Tom took the little wooden troughs down from the wagon. These were the troughs that he normally used to water his stock. Will and Tom carried the troughs to higher ground. Then, they came back to the wagon, where two water barrels were stored. Each one was about half-full. Will and Tom took the half-full barrels up the hill where the troughs were and went to pouring water into the troughs.

The mules started seeing that. Mules have a good memory. They're smarter than most humans. Tom had left Ranger, his horse, up on the ridge, tied to a sapling.

Tom hurried back down to the team and slapped them with the reigns, hollering, "Yaaah." It helped that they could smell the water, he figured. Will had a hold of the lead mule and was pulling on him with all his worth.

Finally, here they came, out of the mud. Tom guessed that these ornery mules would still be there if he had not tricked them.

They built a camp and spent the night there, along with the crickets, owls, and mosquitoes.

About forty miles from Camp Supply, they ran out of anything to feed the mules. The trip had taken longer than Tom thought it would. He had not put in enough sacks of oats. He told Will to hobble the mules—tie one of their front legs to one of the back legs with a short rope. Then, he turned 'em loose, knowing they wouldn't go far. After dealing with those darn mules all day, he slept the sleep of a very tired man.

Next morning came early. Tom awoke looking up at the biggest Kiowa Indian he had ever seen; he guessed that he was a renegade. He was standing over Tom, grunting at him and kicking his bedroll.

He had nothing to do but get out of the bedroll. He told Will, who sat there more like a stone than anything, "Will, let's don't make him mad. Let's see what he wants."

Tom told the brave, "We don't have anything to eat," motioning with his hands and mouth.

The big Kiowa had his hand on his knife, which was still in the sheath. Tom figured if he reached for his rifle that he slept with, the Indian would be right on him with knife in hand.

So Tom slowly got up and backed up to the wagon. Just as the hot August sun began creeping over the prairie landscape, he was aware of something strange. He could hear a loud beating and finally realized it was his own heartbeat. He felt like his heart was going to come out of his chest!

Slowly, Tom pulled the heavy tarp off the sacks of salt so the Kiowa could see what they were carrying. Tom kept speaking softly as if he could understand him. "We mean you no harm. We are just haulin' salt in our wagon. I wish we had food to share with you."

Tom opened one sack with trembling hands, hoping that the big guy didn't notice that he was shaking and hoping he couldn't hear his heart beating. Tom wanted to show him what was in the sacks, thinking that might save their hides.

The Indian reached into the sack with his big, long fingers and put the substance to his lips then tasted it. He let out a grunt of disgust. No salt in the world interested him, because he could ride over to the salt flat anytime he wanted to get some.

Now, here a white man and a half-breed had a whole wagonload of it. He acted as if Tom and Will were two of the biggest fools he'd ever seen. Tom didn't know how a Kiowa laughed until then. The Indian laughed and snorted, ran back into the willows, got hold of his pony by its mane, and leaped up on him, still laughing as he rode off over the ridge.

Tom was sure glad he did not have a load of gold or something that the Indian really wanted. Great relief came over them as they harnessed up the mules and saddled up their horses and headed on back to Camp Supply, arriving early in the afternoon. The mules were hungry, and so were the men. They stopped at the blacksmith's shop, where they watered their animals. Tom asked Bill, his apprentice, "Would you please take care of our horses and mules? They've had a long, hard trip."

"Sure will, but what you goin' to do with all those sacks of—well, what's in 'em?" he sputtered.

"You ask too many questions, young'un. Just feed my animals and rub 'em down too," Tom ordered.

Tom asked Will to go get them something to eat, then he walked over to where he knew the supply sergeant would be. Sergeant O'Riley was playing cards, his favorite pastime. He must have been holding a good hand, because he hardly noticed Tom. He ordered a sarsaparilla and mentioned that he had a wagonload of pure salt. "You interested?" Tom quizzed the sergeant.

"No, I ain't. Can't you see I'm busy? You'd best go see the colonel."

"Where can I find Colonel Whitley?" Tom asked.

"He's no doubt at the infirmary, lookin' after his sick wife. She got bit by a rattler, you know."

"No, I didn't know. Is she gonna live?" Tom asked.

"Next twenty-four hours will tell," the sergeant retorted, as if Tom was too stupid to know anything.

Tom found the colonel slumped over his wife's bed, pleading with her not to leave him. "Joella, don't leave me. I need you. Please don't die!" The poison was spreading up her leg.

Flashbacks of the snakes that bit him came flooding over Tom. The doctor had made the slash marks over the fang bites and had sucked out what poison he could. Then the doctor was getting sick, probably because he'd just had a tooth pulled and the poison had gotten into his bloodstream through his mouth.

Suddenly, Tom remembered what Susan Dushane had done for him and how she treated him with chewing tobacco. She'd made a poultice with it and applied it to his wounds. Tom did the same thing for the colonel's wife, Joella, and for the doctor too. "They'll be all right now," Tom promised, praying his words were true. He walked back to the blacksmith's shop, where Will was waiting for him.

"Did you sell the salt?" Will asked. "Here's some biscuits and ham. Thought you'd like ham for a change," he continued.

"No, Will, I didn't get the salt sold. We've had some problems. Let's just stay here tonight and maybe tomorrow will be better," Tom replied, his mind more on his memories than on what was happening then.

As he lay there in the heat of the night, his body ached for Susan, his dear little Indian maiden. She was no longer his. She belonged to someone else. She was so beautiful. He could still hear her giggling in the night.

He woke with a start; the pet rooster was crowing and acting his usual proud self. Tom pulled on his jeans, shirt, and boots and ran to the infirmary. The doctor looked much better and asked Tom to come in.

"You know, boy, I think you saved two lives yesterday, mine and Joella Whitley's. We will forever be indebted to you; thank you, bless you." Doc said. He hugged Tom like he was his son.

Tom almost cried but replied, "I was saved the same way once. I was just passing on what I know."

Tom decided to go to Captain Morgan and ask him if he was interested in some salt. It was a hot, muggy day, and he could tell the captain wasn't in a very good mood. As Tom approached, he was ranting about two of his men deserting the night before.

"I will find them, and when I do, they'll be sorry. They'll never see the light of day again, if I can just find them! Why, you knew both of them!" the captain said, looking at Tom, "Harold Glass and Ike Nelson. Where are they? How dare they desert my garrison?"

"Well, sir, I'm sorry about your men." Tom secretly hoped he would never find out about him. Morgan would send Tom back so fast, it'd make your head swim.

"Sir, I won't take up much of your time, but I've acquired a good amount of pure white salt. In fact, I've got a whole wagon full of it, all nicely stored in white cloth sacks. I'm sure you know the need for salt in the troops' diets and also quite a demand for it to tan the buffalo hides," Tom reasoned.

Captain Morgan showed no interest whatsoever and said, "No, I don't think so."

But Tom could tell by the way he answered and the tone of his voice that he wanted the salt. But more than that, he wanted the salt for a good price. Tom came up with, "Part of the money that the army pays me, I'll see that it goes to the orphan's fund."

"Captain Morgan grinned when he heard that.

"You take care of the orphan's fund, don't you, Captain?" Tom questioned, knowing full well that he did.

"Yes, I do," Morgan replied.

Tom said, "Okay, then it's a deal." The supply sergeant paid Tom the asking price. Then Tom paid the captain what amounted to nothing more than blackmail. But Tom paid him. Then to his surprise, Tom found out that the mules and wagon were in as much a demand as was the salt.

The road from Dodge City to Camp Supply was ninety miles one way. There was still a great need for a good solid wagon and strong mules.

This wagon had a little wider wheel on it than most. The wider iron tire made crossing the Cimarron easier. Tom was able to sell the wagon, mules, and harness, and make a real right, nice return. Tom sent word with one of the wagon haulers that shingles for his cabin were needed. They figured how big the roof was and how many squares it would take.

The wagon hauler, a big fella from Texas, said, "If I had the good cash money and you give it to me now, I'll see to it that you have the finest wood shingles on my next trip to town."

Tom knew that would be in about two weeks. He trusted him, so that's what he did.

After a good night's sleep in his quarters at the blacksmith's shop, which was a lot better than sleeping on the ground, Tom proceeded to pack his supplies. Poor Will had to sleep on the floor. Tom put everything he could carry on his trusted mount, Ranger. He left his suit and all of his new belongings carefully packed in a trunk by his cot. He didn't think anybody would bother it.

By now, Tom realized that Will was a valuable hired hand and would fit in well with his crew. Will rode well, without a saddle, but to work cattle, he needed one. So Tom bought a brand-new western saddle, and when he handed it to Will, the young brave knew he was accepted. Tom threw a new saddle blanket on Will's pinto and taught him how to cinch up the saddle to fit the horse. Tom showed Will how the stirrups adjusted to the length of his legs.

"That pony of yours will swell up his belly when you begin tightening the cinch, and if you leave it there, you and the saddle will fall off as soon as you ride off. So my advice is, cinch it tight! Ride a little, and then tighten it again. Your horse may not like it, but you're the boss," Tom said.

Will did exactly as Tom instructed, and then he mounted up. The Indian pony, who had never had a saddle before, pitched and tossed, bucked and caved. Will took it in his stride, showing him who was boss. Finally, the bronc gave in and accepted that this was the way it was going to be.

They proceeded on down to the ranch. All the while, Tom was telling Will about the ranch and how great it was. "It will be even better with all the cattle we get from the salt money," Tom explained.

On the way, he got to thinking about Susan and his baby boy. "By golly, he'd be three and a half years old." Tom remembered the evening they spent together. How she was so good to him. Tom thought, "You just got to do the right things when they happen, 'cause if you wait, there ain't no lookin' back."

They got on down to the ranch, and Tom felt a little better thinking about Susan. It helped to have Will with him. He knew that she had the baby with her. Hopefully, the man treated her right. He hoped she was happy. He figured the best thing to do was just put it out of his mind.

When they arrived, the boys were at the ranch house, arguing who was going to finish supper. There they were: Robert, Joe, and Jake.

They all wanted to know where this woman was that he went out after. Tom told them, "She made other plans. She's in Georgia."

Tom did not know much about Joe, but when he mentioned Georgia, Joe said, "She's damn close to hell, then." Tom guessed he must have been a slave in that part of the world at one time, because he certainly didn't have any use for the South. But Joe was always good to everyone.

"Boys, enough of that. I want you to meet Will, my new hand. I think he knows his salt." Robert looked at Jake and Joe. "They're real cowboys," Tom said. "If you'll pay attention to 'em, you'll learn a lot. Now, let's eat! What's for supper?"

Robert rescued the situation. He said, "I killed a young deer this morning, and the rump roast has been in the Dutch oven all day. I've been tryin' to get Jake to boil the last of the potatoes to go with it."

During supper, Tom told the hands that new shingles were on their way. You know the cow hides are all cracked and broken. Next rain storm we will be soaked to the gills. The shingles will arrive tomorrow, so we've get busy in the morning.

There was great anticipation as they took the old hides off and rebuilt the rafters so that there could be boards on them, then the shingles. They could hardly wait to make this old log house a lot better to live in.

CHAPTER 12

A-Courtin' Tom Goes

While Tom was at Camp Supply, getting ready to leave, his apprentice, Bill, who would come to be as good a blacksmith as anybody, said, "You know, they was a-cleanin' out the stagecoach that came down here from Dodge. It looked like some drummer left his newspaper. You might as well have it 'cause you like to read." Bill didn't read very well, although Tom tried to teach him a little.

Tom looked at it. It was a month old issue from the *Kansas City Star*. He thought, "Well, yeah, that's the outside world." Since Tom was in a hurry, he just wrapped the paper up in his work clothes, put it all in his saddlebag, and proceeded on down to his ranch.

The hands got caught up. They got the roof on the cabin and thought they were living like kings. Why, lo and behold, they were even thinking about putting in a wood floor! But that was something they just teased about. "Boy, we'll even have indoor plumbin' someday! Kind of like they do in Paris, France," Jake said.

When Tom unfolded his clothes, the newspaper fell out onto the floor. Robert picked it up and started to look at it. While he was looking at the newspaper, Tom said, "When we get us the indoor plumbin' and we get us a wood floor, I'll go lookin' for a woman. So I'll have me a wife someday."

Robert just grinned and said, "Here's one for ya."

In the newspaper was an article and picture of a family up in Iowa. Robert thought, "They sure must be well-to-do." The family had opened up a new hardware store. Someone had taken a photograph and put it in the paper. It was a man, Mr. W. E. Lentz, and his wife and their daughter, Rachel, and her brother, Walter. They were in front of their new hardware store, which looked like it had everything for the farmers in Iowa. It advertised the cultivators, plows, and harnesses. "Boy, it is such a good picture. A lot better than most pictures that are in the newspaper," Robert explained.

This young woman, she was a beauty! You couldn't tell what color her hair was. She wasn't a blonde; she wasn't a brunette. The boys decided they would just talk about her. They wondered if she was married or engaged. The article had the address of the hardware store in Leon, Iowa, which seemed like two worlds away to Tom.

If you wanted to order farm goods, you wrote to this address. They decided that if one could order merchandise, harnesses, and stuff, they thought they could get a letter off to Rachel.

After much kidding, prodding, and daring, "You need to do this, Tom! We're gettin' tired of your dang cookin!" they all teased.

Tom finally relented. He wrote Rachel a letter, thinking, "That's that!"

This is the letter Tom wrote:

Mr. W. E. Lentz of Leon, Iowa, General Delivery

Dear Mr. Lentz,

Saw your article and picture in a recent issue of the *Kansas City Star*. You should be very proud of your accomplishments.

I am interested in corresponding with your daughter, Rachel, with your permission and if she is free to do so. I have my own ranch in western Oklahoma Territory.

I'm a God-fearing man and a hard worker. Please reply to General Delivery, Camp Supply, Oklahoma Territory.

Sincerely,

Tom Summers

Even after Tom wrote this letter, with his heart racing and his hand shaking, he left it on the table for a week before he took it to Camp Supply, then it was carried on the stagecoach to Dodge, hoping it would soon arrive in Leon. Several weeks later, and much to his surprise, Tom got an answer!

Dear Mr. Summers,

In reply to your recent letter: I have never written to a cowboy. It sounds like you really have a frontier way of life. That's what all the men talk about up here, is going out west. You are already out there. How old are you? Where's your family?

"She seems so interested," thought Tom.

Tom pretty much let the boys run the ranch as he composed his second letter. That started a romance. As soon as he got a letter from her, he would sit down and pen one to her and mail it back. She was doing the same thing because he would get a letter from her almost twice a month. The relationship just blossomed and grew. They wrote about things he would not talk about with anyone else.

She told him that she was unmarried and twenty-one years old. Here he was, twenty-six; couldn't be, but he was. Ten years ago, he was fighting the war. Everybody said he was too old and too set in his ways to do anything except maybe meet the painted ladies' wagon up at Camp Supply.

They wrote to each other for the better part of a year. At Christmastime, he boxed up some iron works that he made at the blacksmith shop for her. The pieces could be bolted together to form a table, to put on the family's porch. She had told him earlier about the grand porch they had in front of their home. Apparently, it was one of the grandest homes in town.

She sent him a shawl. Whenever he was wanting to look his best, he would wrap it around his neck, and he would tell himself, "I really look grand." Anytime he had the occasion, he would put on his good clothes and wrap that soft blue shawl around his neck and go to the dances or the parties up at the camp.

In 1872, Tom finally had enough steers that he could take to market. A local rancher, Jack Lucas, who had about the same size outfit as Tom's, was out there in the Strip, probably illegally, but who cared? He had all he wanted of ranching, and Tom was able to buy him out pretty cheap. It was Christmastime, so the markets at Dodge weren't operating there during the winter months. Tom got his herd for almost nothing, just enough to get Mr. Lucas back to Missouri, where he came from.

Andrew "Andy" McMillian was the foreman for this outfit. Mr. Lucas made one stipulation when selling. He said, "You hire Andy or there's no deal."

Tom answered, "Okay by me. I need another hand, but I already have a foreman."

"That will work for me. I do not ever want to be in charge again!" Andy declared.

With that, Tom had five hundred more cows and five hundred steers, plus a new cowboy. With the Lucas's herd and his herd, Tom had well over a thousand head of two- and three-year old steers that they could take to Dodge in the spring.

Tom created some more money by working at the blacksmith shop, making trades and such. Will and Tom would even go to get salt. They'd buy a wagon then, when finished with the salt run, would sell it for twice what they gave for it. It was pretty certain in his mind that when he went to Iowa to see Rachel that he would bring her back.

They were doing a lot of building at Camp Supply, so they had a lot of carpenters there. Tom went up and made a deal with them to bring the lumber to his place and build a grand house out there on the prairie. There were not to be any permanent dwellings out there, but since Tom had always been faithful to rebuild equipment for them, the army overlooked it.

Tom helped them get the house started early in the spring. They had the plans, a very competent foreman, and men to build it. Robert assured Tom, "I'll make sure it is properly built."

They gathered up the steers in May and headed up the Western Trail around Camp Supply, across the Cimarron, and into Dodge City. This was not a very long cattle drive for them: about one hundred twenty miles.

When they were getting ready to cross the Cimarron, a storm came up. To the best of their ability, they could not keep the cattle still because of the lightning strikes. The herd was scattered all over that country. Here, Tom had great plans. As soon as the cattle were sold, he wanted to be on his way to meet Rachel.

It took them two weeks to gather the cattle. They even came up with a few strays which would make them a little extra money, but it was a long, hard two weeks getting the steers out of the Tamarack, there on the Cimarron.

They got them pushed on into Dodge; the cattle had lost some weight, but they still looked pretty good despite the stampede. The cattle buyer looked the herd over. Tom and his crew were some of the first ranchers to bring their cattle to town. The buyers started doing some figuring and said they would give Tom twenty dollars a head. Thinking Tom was illiterate, they intentionally made mistakes in their math. He made some good money showing where their mistakes were. He imagined they did that quite often to illiterate drovers.

Tom sold the cattle; then he went down to the bank, talked to the banker, and put all the money in his account, except for a thousand dollars to pay off the hands and to pay for his trip to Leon, Iowa.

Tom sure felt like a wealthy man. His suit of clothes didn't seem like it was good enough to meet Rachel in. They had gotten a little tight, as Tom had gotten more muscles. So Tom went over to Oliver Olson, the tailor there in Dodge, to see if he'd adjust them to fit him.

In his Swedish accent, Mr. Olson said, "Ya, it will be a couple of weeks."

Tom said, "I don't have that kind of time. I've got to be in Iowa." Tom told him to go ahead and do the alterations, and he'd pick them up whenever he came back through. Tom went on down to the mercantile and bought not one, but two suits of clothes, two sets of boots, and a hat—a new Stetson.

Tom went and got all cleaned up and put on some of his new clothes. When he stepped out onto Front Street, he was a sight to behold. Here came four painted ladies, headed for their place of work for the afternoon and evening. They sure did want to talk to him an awful lot. And they sure did look fine. Tom asked, "Well, where are you goin'?

Betty said, "We'll be down the street at the Variety Saloon."

Tom said, "I kind of know a man down there that tends the bar. Does George Masterson still work at the Variety?"

They looked at him kind of strange and asked, "Do you know him?"

Tom answered, "Yeah, he came down to Camp Supply one time. He killed a couple of my hands. I know him, but I don't hold a grudge against him."

They stared at him for a minute because they thought Tom was there to kill their friend George. Tom said, "No, they were grown men; they did what they did. I have nothin' to hold against that man."

That evening, Tom went on down to the Variety. There was Squirrel Tooth Alice. She had a pet squirrel, of all things, that she carried around with her. Tom often wondered if she took it to bed with her. Tom thought it must be quite a thrill to have a squirrel running across your naked body, digging its little claws into you.

There were these ladies of the evening: beautiful ladies. They enjoyed having fun. Maybe they drank too much; maybe they laughed too hard. But they were needed. Flirting and teasing Tom, they asked why he didn't go upstairs with one of them. They thought he had money, and that's all they really wanted. Tom didn't think he needed to participate in that type of thing. "Oh, I had a lot of fun," Tom said. "We did a lot of talking and a lot of 'I'll be up shortly,'" just to pass the time of day.

Next morning, Tom understood that there was a train leaving out of Dodge City with cattle. One passenger car to haul people was hooked on right after the coal car, so no one would smell the cattle as much.

Tom walked down to the depot and bought a ticket on this cattle train bound for Kansas City. It was a pretty good thing to be aboard this train, because they needed to get the cattle into the slaughterhouses as soon as they could. Cattle trains were a priority to the railroad company.

And away they went. This was his first time to be aboard a train.

He felt like he looked the part of a man who had been on a train several times, so Tom tried to act the part.

One of the girls from the saloon, Lil, was on the train. She decided she'd had all the life she wanted in Dodge. "I have a family back in Illinois. Maybe they'd take me back," she said with tears in her eyes. She and Tom sat together and talked for hours.

"I'd like to be treated like a regular woman," she continued.

Tom replied, "I can understand that." He held her hand most all the way to Kansas City.

Lil wasn't the type of girl he wanted to marry, but they passed the time together. She was a very intelligent person: well-read. They found they had a lot to talk about. As she told him about the books she had read, he decided he needed to be acquiring a library.

They arrived in Kansas City, Missouri. What a grand place. Big as big! This cowboy had never seen anything quite like it! Lil was able to catch a train on into the Chicago area quite quickly. Tom bid her adieu, giving her one of his biggest hugs. She kissed Tom right on the mouth, and she meant it. It made Tom wonder if he was making the right decision to let her leave. But away she went, her blond hair blowing back and forth across her shoulders as she ran to catch her train to Chicago.

Tom began making plans to travel on up to Leon, Iowa.

He had no idea which way Leon was, except north. It wasn't too far from Kansas City, so he caught a slow train that got him close; then a stagecoach with a team of fine horses that was part of the mail system. They all stopped at a station in St. Joe, Missouri, to rest and eat a bite. From there, he rode on another stagecoach. Tom thought he could have walked faster, but the price was right. Within two days, Tom was in Leon at last.

Rachel had told him about her home, a beautiful white frame with a white picket fence all the way around the house. Tom had the address in his pocket. She had also told him all about her family.

Tom headed for town. He thought about Rachel being a good Methodist woman, playing the pump organ in church and singing in the choir. He hoped she was as beautiful as her picture and that she could cook; but most important, he hoped she liked him enough to marry him.

He decided, first of all, that a man should go see her father because here he was, just courting her through the mail.

It wasn't difficult to find the hardware store in Leon. It made up a whole city block. Behind the building, there were wagons for sale and farm implements. Rachel's father, Mr. Lentz, had quite a sizeable business. Tom walked into his store dressed in his good clothes and new hat. Of course, he looked a little strange and a bit out of place in that part of the country.

Here came a rather large, redheaded, German-looking man out from behind the counter who asked Tom, "Can I help you?"

Tom said, "Yes, sir, you sure can." Then it got real quiet.

Mr. Lentz broke the silence with "You're Tom Summers, aren't you?"

"Yes, sir, that's who I am," Tom said.

They visited the better part of the day. Tom really didn't want to visit with him; he wanted to see the daughter! Mr. Lentz proceeded to tell Tom all about his life and how he'd wished he had gone out West and been a cowboy. His father had started this store with nothing but five dollars, a notepad, and a dream.

Mr. Lentz and his brothers had come to America from Germany in 1835. They were indentured servants before finding their way to Iowa. After his oldest brother, Albert died crossing the Missouri River, Mr. Lentz married Albert's fiancée.

"He picked a good one, that woman; but she talks a lot. Just nod and smile and she'll keep on talking," Mr. Lentz said of his wife, Ella.

Mr. Lentz continued. "Yes, sir, my father started this business, and at one time, I felt trapped to stay and work. Now, I'm glad I stayed. Bus, as his friends called him, willed the place to me. I inherited the business and built on to his original building. You saw the picture of our place in the newspaper, didn't you, Mr. Summers?"

Tom started to say, "You can call me Tom," but Mr. Lentz went on with his story.

"When I was twenty years old, I made plans to run away and head West, but that's when my mother died and father needed me more than ever. That's all behind me now, but sometimes I still think about when I was a young man and I could have made the gold rush into California or even Colorado. But I stayed put. Now, I'm glad I did." He banged his fist on the counter and said with a grin, "This is my gold mine."

He was a pillar in the community. Tom could tell by the way the customers spoke to him and their respect for him. Tom started to say, "I'd like to get on down to—" but he was interrupted by "We'll get on down to the house when we lock up the store."

Tom thought, "That is a hell of a deal."

Finally, Tom didn't think he locked the door any earlier than usual, because Tom could tell this man liked to make money. Some old farmer came in at quitting time, and Tom thought he would never leave. Tom said to the farmer, "I'll help you load your wagon."

"So here I am in my fine clothes loading harnesses, but I am happy to do it," Tom thought to himself.

"Good night, Mr. Smithiesler."

"Good night, Mr. Lentz, and who is this young fellow here with the fancy duds?"

"This gentleman is from the West, and he has a fine ranch with those longhorn cows on it."

Tom was afraid another two hours of conversation would follow, but to his surprise, Mr. Smithiesler cracked his reins and down the street he went.

"I'm goin' home to supper," the spry old man quipped.

Tom brushed off and cleaned up as best he could and waxed his moustache. Hopefully, he didn't look too straggly, as he hadn't shaved since morning. As they left, Tom grabbed his suitcase.

They walked to the home. Of course, Mr. Lentz just went on in, and Tom left the suitcase on the porch. Tom asked himself, "Should I knock on the door or something?" But no, he followed him in.

Rachel was in the parlor. She asked, "Is that you, Father?"

Since there was no answer, Rachel went on to say, "Mother has supper nearly on the table. I've already eaten because I'm going to choir practice. Janice will be here soon and we'll walk together to the church." Out the door she went. She just glanced at Tom as if he was one of her father's apprentices who was going to work in the store.

Suddenly, she reappeared and threw open the screen door and hollered, "Tom!"

He did not even have to answer her. She grabbed him and did not want to let him go. Rachel decided they could get along without her at choir practice.

As she led Tom into the parlor, Rachel called for her mother. When Mrs. Lentz appeared, Rachel introduced her to Tom. He was pleasantly surprised to see that both mother and daughter were blessed with beauty and grace. They looked more like sisters than mother and daughter, both with fiery-red hair and green eyes.

"It is very nice to meet you, Mr. Summers. Please join us for dinner."

The young couple sat down in the beautiful dining room, but Tom was not very hungry even though there was a lovely meal before him. After a polite period, Rachel asked if they could be excused and adjourn to the parlor.

They talked for several hours, but the time passed by so quickly that it seemed like no time before Mrs. Lentz came to the entrance of the room and said in a soft voice, "Rachel, it is time for your young man to say his good-byes. It was a pleasure to meet you, Mr. Summers."

Tom could hear the grandfather clock striking as he awkwardly arose and said, "May I call on you tomorrow?" he asked Rachel.

She smiled and asked her mother if he could join them for afternoon tea the next day. Mrs. Lentz agreed. Tom thanked her, shook her hand, and told Rachel good night.

Tom did not want to appear ignorant as to the ways of the world at this point. Even though he had not arranged for a place to spend the night, he jaunted down the sidewalk toward town.

Not knowing where to go with everything being closed up for the night, the only place he could think of to go was the police station. Tom found the station in town, and they wanted to know what he wanted.

Tom said, "Not really anything. Looks like the only place open. I didn't want you to find me sleepin' in some alley and throw me in jail. I didn't make arrangements for any place to stay tonight."

Samuel Means, the jailer, asked, "What's your name, and where are you from?"

Tom told him his story, and Samuel said, "If you intend to marry Miss Lentz, you'd better have a good pedigree!"

It was about midnight by the time Tom got settled. So his first night in Leon, Iowa, he spent it in the jailhouse. Of course, the door wasn't locked, but it was something he could tell his children—"The first day I went to court your mother, I spent the night in the jail-house. She'd always tell me to hush."

The next morning, after getting out of jail, Tom found a room at Mrs. Hagar's boarding house. The widow knew everyone in town, and was pleased to meet the man who was there to court Miss Lentz.

Tom rented a buggy, and made his way to the Lentz home for tea, where they got better acquainted. The next day, Rachel's mother packed them a lunch and they proceeded to go look at the flat farm-land. The land was plowed and corn was growing. Rachel would exclaim how wonderful the beauty of the corn was, and Tom would just say, "Yes, now that's corn!" Or "Yes, that's farmland!"

After he had courted her for about three weeks, he got up the courage to ask her to marry him. Rachel said, "Yes!"

Tom began going with her family to church on Sunday morn-ings and evenings, so he had already met the preacher, Reverend Ronald Bullock. The church was a grand style of German descent. The custom was that the gentlemen sat on one side of the sanctuary, and the women sat on the other side. On this particular Sunday, Tom and Rachel walked up the long flight of steps together and entered through massive hand-hewn wooden doors. As usual he turned to the left and sat with Mr. Lentz, Walter, and the other men of the congregation.

Rachel joined her mother and the other ladies on the right. Her best friend, Janice, was the organist. While they were singing the hymns, Tom's heart stirred with a special love for Rachel. He quietly slipped out of his place and joined Rachel and her mother. Rachel squeezed his hand, bashfully smiled and thought to herself, *I won-der what Reverend Ron is going to say about this.*" There was a small murmur, and a few heads turned, but Tom stood firm, continuing to sing "Rock of Ages."

Tom had not been to a church service since he lived with the Cherokees. It seemed like his whole life had come together for this moment—to be with Rachel and to share their lives together.

The preacher came to them when the service was over. He exclaimed, "Young man, I know you are new here, but our customs are different from those elsewhere." He looked at both of them as they were looking into each other's eyes.

"Yes, I can see you are in love. When is the wedding?" Reverend Bullock continued.

Nothing more was ever mentioned about Tom walking across the aisle that morning, except people referred to that Sunday morning as Crossover Day. The next Sunday, Mr. Lentz and more of the men crossed over and sat with their wives. Since then that day has been referred to as Crossover Sunday.

Tom and Rachel's wedding was the event of the year in that small German church. Rachel's father walked her down the aisle. He called her "Lizzie," as her given name was Rachel Elizabeth. She told Tom later that her father told her as they were approaching the altar, "Lizzie, you love this man with all your heart, and you both put God first in your lives."

Her younger brother, Walter, being sixteen years old and five years younger than Rachel, stood up with Tom. Boy, he was really proud because he was standing up with a cowboy!

After the wedding vows were exchanged and Reverend Bullock introduced the new Mr. and Mrs. Summers, the Reverend squeezed Tom's hand. With his parting words to the happy couple were the same ones he ended each of his sermons with; "Walk In The Sonshine."

Rachel's beautiful friend, Janice, her maid of honor, was dressed all in blue. She ran to catch the bride's bouquet of lilies, and caught it! The bells rang and the people cheered as they left the church. Before the wedding, Tom made reservations at the finest hotel in Leon. But before they could leave, the ladies of the church had a large reception on the church grounds for them. There were lots of toasts to good health and safe travel to where? Out West? Then there was a lot of talk about the Indians and if they would be safe and why they couldn't just stay in Leon and help with the nice hardware store.

The new Mrs. Summers put a stop to that, and with a hug, told them, "I'll always be safe in Tom Summers's arms." With that, he picked her up and whirled her around.

Walter and his friends had tied all sorts of things to the back end of the buggy to make noise and had hobbled the horse's legs. Someone had gone to the trouble of setting the buggy seat on backward. But Tom soon remedied all of that and picked Rachel up and sat her down in his rented buggy.

They spent their honeymoon night in the hotel. Rachel was such a grand lady. She was a lady wherever you put her and at whatever she was doing. Tom tried to show her how much he loved her.

The next day, they gathered her belongings and my, my! "The belongings this woman had!" Tom said. "She had shoes I didn't even know they made!"

She packed four trunks of her most prized possessions and kept telling her mother, "We'll be back for the rest of it someday."

Tom did not know that there could be any more. He thought they had the whole world in those four trunks. They were packed tight. He had to sit on each one to close it.

CHAPTER 13

Headin' Home with My New Bride

Money didn't seem to be too much of an object, but they had to buy an extra place on the stagecoach because of the trunks. So instead of a fare for two, it was a fare for three. They traveled to Kansas City, where they spent a whole week looking and sightseeing. How wonderful was this time together!

There was an empty cattle train headed west to Dodge City, so Tom bought three tickets on the only passenger car. The train wasn't in too big of a hurry. They were able to get off the train at Topeka and again at Wichita, Kansas. They spent the night in each town.

Of course, they had these four trunks that had to be moved each time they got off the train, went to a hotel, then back on the train. It was a great point to tease Rachel about. Tom never did get mad, just a little perturbed about those big trunks.

Rachel started asking him about the house they would live in. "Tom, what does your place look like?" she would ask and tug on his arm a little. He loved it when she'd touch him and call him by name.

Tom grinned and replied, "We have this wonderful log cabin. Me and the boys even put a roof on it!" He tried to describe how they put tree limbs on top of the logs and then covered them with buffalo hides. "Oh, this is going to be a great adventure living in a log cabin!

I've never seen a real buffalo. Will they hurt you?" She would ask question after question like that with excitement in her voice.

"I'll take care of you, don't you worry," Tom said as his heart just melted inside him like ice on a warm spring day.

"But, Rachel, guess what happened?"

"What happened?" she asked, her pretty, green eyes dancing in the light.

"The roof of buffalo hides was so flat and the snow so thick and heavy that—"

"Oh no!" she interrupted. "Were you hurt?"

"No, I wasn't inside the house when it caved in, but it sure was a mess. The boys and I cleaned up the debris; then we built a pitched roof and covered it with cowhides from the longhorns. It sure was a sight, all those colors of the longhorns, but last fall I had enough money, so we put a brand-new citified roof on, with real shingles."

"I was trying to fix it up for you," Tom said. He never did tell her about the new frame house the army crew was building for them.

That evening they arrived in Dodge City, a little tired but excited too. Rachel was almost jumping up and down as they strolled the boardwalk.

"Look there, Tom! Look," she questioned, "What are those?"

"Those are Texas Longhorn steers," Tom proudly pointed out to her. "That's the kind we raise."

Several cattle drivers were moving a herd of loud longhorns right through the middle of town on their way to the railroad corrals. There was a lot of yelling on that midsummer's evening. The cowboys were happy to finally get their half-wild longhorns to safety.

The couple walked over to the tailor's shop. Mr. Olsen, who had left Camp Supply for Dodge City, was just closing up, but he relented and let them in. Tom paid for his newly altered suit. He said, "I hope these fit after all those good meals your mother fed me."

Rachel exclaimed, "That is quite a hat!"

"You know, John Stetson, who made this hat, is a man who never gave up. He had several failures and, out of need, developed this style for you cowboys," Mr. Olson explained. "This one's called 'the Boss of the Plains.'"

Tom also retrieved his Colt .45 and strapped it on then took off his coat so everybody could see that he was packing iron. "I'd not want anyone to get out of hand and make a fool of themselves in front of Rachel," Tom said.

They put up in the Dodge House, waiting for the next day, so when the stagecoach left, they could be on their way home to the ranch.

Morning came bright and early. More cattle were being driven right under their upstairs window. Rachel was curled up in Tom's arms. He didn't want to wake her. He wanted that moment to last forever. Finally, his dream of having his own family was coming true. Rachel stirred and began kissing him and loving him while she was half-asleep. He never dreamed of such tenderness and complete joy.

"I don't want to get up, but, Rachel, we have to so we can get started," Tom whispered in her ear. Her hair was damp and smelled of sweet honeysuckle. "Come on, sweetheart, let me take you home," Tom urged.

They still had those four trunks of Rachel's clothing to contend with. Tom had carried them up two flights of stairs last night. She had every one of them opened by morning to decide what to wear on the last leg of their trip.

"Wear something that you don't mind getting dusty, "Tom said seriously.

"I want to look nice for you, Tom," she replied as she dug in the largest trunk.

They loaded up and headed to Camp Supply, a ninety-mile trip. Rachel thought it was a grand trip. She kept asking, "When are we going to get there?"

The Cimarron River was low as they forded it. They were coming up the far side when they heard a terrible noise! The stagecoach driver pulled his team to a full stop and jumped down. They all began piling out to see what had happened. One of Rachel's largest trunks had fallen off and had hit the back wheel of the coach and landed in the sand. The trunk broke as it hit a wheel, throwing shoes and garments everywhere. Rachel ran here and there, retrieving a couple of petticoats and fishing a high top boot out of the river. It took all four of the men to shove the now battered and broken trunk full of Mrs. Summers's wet belongings up the rocky bank and reposition it back on top of the stagecoach.

"Now, now, don't you cry, Mrs. Summers. Everything is going to be all right. Why, the last time we come across this here river, the road agents attacked and robbed everybody of their guns and money and jewelry too," the driver explained. Then he climbed back into his seat, let off the break, slapped the reins, and hollered, "Gitteeyup!"

The military road that led to Camp Supply was well kept. There were two stage stations along the way where the stage coaches could stop, trade horses, get out, and get a bite to eat. They stopped at the first one, run by two men whose names were Hank Arnall and Paul Casey. Beans and bacon were the fare, along with strong, black coffee.

Rachel whispered, "I'll wait 'til we arrive at Camp Supply; you go ahead and eat."

The beans were hard and the bacon, old, but the black stuff they called coffee washed it down. Two bits later, they were on the road. The summer sun was bearing down with no wind. "Thank goodness, we have fresh horses and we are moving right along," Tom said to encourage his new bride. "Civilization ahead! Camp Supply looks pretty good to me!" Tom thought out loud.

"Oh! We're here at last! Look at all the little houses! Who lives in them?" Rachel asked.

"Those are officers' housing. This is a military camp," Tom replied. Soon, they would start their life together on their little ranch on the plains.

Captain Morgan had arranged for the newlyweds to spend the night in one of the empty officers' quarters. Tom was proud to introduce his bride to Captain and Mrs. Morgan and to several of the officers. "We must turn in early," Tom told the Morgans, "We have had a long trip."

They didn't sleep much. Rachel thought she heard a dog howl. "No, that's a coyote, my dear," Tom told her. She just snuggled a little closer. Then she started to worry about the Indians. Tom assured her not to worry. "They will probably be afraid of you," he said with a chuckle.

Dawn came too soon. Tom got up first and pulled all the covers off the bed. Rachel went into a spin. "Now, Tom, give me those quilts!" Tom replied, "Not now, we have to get dressed and get to the mess hall."

The morning was spent meeting friends, and Tom had to repair the tongue on the buckboard.

"We can spend the night here," Tom said to Rachel.

"Oh no!" she said. "I want to see your ranch. I want to go! Please, let's go!"

He said, "It will be dark by the time we get there. Let's wait." She looked at him with those pleading eyes, and he gave in.

"Okay," Tom relented, "I'll load the trunks in the buckboard."

Tom met Robert at the blacksmith's shop, where he came for supplies. Tom introduced him to his new bride.

Robert said hello to the new Mrs. Summers. "Rachel, this is my foreman, my right-hand man," Tom told her.

"I'm so pleased to meet you, Mister . . ." She paused, and he said, "Thornton is my last name, ma'am. I'm pleased to meet you too."

She told Tom later, "He's a pretty good-looking man. Is he married?" Rachel teased him.

"Now, now, you're a married woman, Mrs. Summers."

She replied, "Now, don't be talking like that. I'll just be a friend to him. We need to find him a wife," Rachel said with a giggle.

Tom took Robert off to the side while he was helping him load the buckboard. "You go down and get the boys out of the cabin. We are going to come in tonight. For heaven's sake, tell them to pick up their dirty underwear and straighten up the place. They can stay outside tonight; they can bunk out."

Robert replied, "There's a room already finished in the new house. You and the missus could move on in."

"Now, let's don't do that. I'm afraid we'd stumble around and fall through the floor or something. I know my way around that cabin" was Tom's reply.

"Please leave a lantern burning for us," Tom said as Robert leaped on his horse and bade Mrs. Summers a good day.

Tom helped Rachel onto the wagon seat. He adjusted the trunks, his suitcase, and some supplies. "I'm glad I rented a freight wagon," Tom teased. "We got everything all tied on. I'd planned on going home with a single horse, but now we have a new team." Tom told Rocky Read at the livery that he would get the team and wagon back shortly.

The captain and Mrs. Morgan wished them well and waved as the newlyweds headed south. There was a strong west wind blowing across the empty land. Rachel had never seen tumbleweeds. They blew across the trail one after the other. The team didn't like them but kept plodding along.

They began their journey to their new home and a new life together. Rachel had no idea that a new house awaited her or, for that matter, what surprises the prairie would reveal to her.

Dark clouds suddenly appeared and big heavy drops of rain began to pelt the horses.

"Here's my hat to keep the rain off," Tom hurriedly said. "There might be flash flooding near the creek, but I think we'll be all right."

Soon the late afternoon sun turned a sultry, dark red. As the clouds rolled away, the gnats and mosquitoes come out in droves.

"Cover your face, Rachel," Tom told her. He stopped and found some peppermint leaves in his satchel. He told her, "Rub these on your hands and arms and a little on your face, and the bugs will stay away. It's an old Indian remedy."

As they traveled, a beautiful full moon climbed over the horizon and lit up the lonesome land. Crickets were the orchestra for the last few miles. A coyote cried in the distance, and Rachel was asleep on his arm. Tom was picking his way down the trail, trying not to awaken her, although they jostled around a lot.

Tom could see the cabin in the distance; a flicker of light could be seen from the only window as they approached. The harvest moon hid behind a cloud bank. It was dark when he pulled up to the hitching post.

Tom woke up Rachel. "Honey, we're home." Tom tied the horses to the hitching post in front of the cabin and helped his sleepy girl out of the wagon.

Robert appeared and said, "Welcome home. I'll take care of the team."

When Rachel and Tom came to the door, Tom said, "Let me carry you in." He kicked the door open. They found the bed. Tom gently laid her down and began to remove her clothes. They made sweet love, the first time on their ranch. "Such a lady," Tom thought, "such a lady wherever you put her, playing the organ at church or in bed with her husband."

Next morning, Tom slipped out of bed to check on the house, leaving Rachel asleep. Her beautiful red hair flowed across her pillow. She stirred in the homemade log bed, which was about big enough for one person, but they seemed to get by pretty well.

Tom went outside to check on their new house. The carpenters had just showed up, getting ready to work that Monday. They'd done a grand job so far. The house looked great.

In the meantime, Rachel woke up. She wondered where her new husband was and sleepily looked around at her surroundings. It was dark and dingy. No lights—the lantern had gone out during the night. The logs in the fireplace were wrapped in ashes, and there were no pictures on the walls.

She observed a small table, some mismatched wooden chairs, a cookstove, and a fireplace. The only window was dingy, like a film was covering it. A pile of wood was stacked near the fireplace. She was starting to remember where she was. All of a sudden, out of the corner of her eye, she caught a lightning-fast movement along the floor. There it was again, two mice chasing each other! As she started to scream, a large black scorpion crawled across the bed. Panic filled her as she grabbed her nightgown and headed for the door. Her bare feet hit the dirt floor and she got sick at her stomach.

Tom was on his way back to the cabin to wake her up when he saw her flying out the door, with only a nightgown in her hand. He was about four feet from the door when she ran into him and knocked them both to the ground. Tom guessed she would have run all the way back to Iowa if she hadn't run into him!

"You've got to put a floor in this place!" she exclaimed.

It wasn't "Good morning," "I love you," "How are you?" or nothing.

She repeated, "You've got to put a floor in that house! There's mice in there and this big, crawly, crab thing! What was that? It had a big claw up front and lots of legs! I can't live in there! You've got to put a floor in there!" she squealed.

Without so much as a flinch, Tom said, "Oh, that's not a priority now."

"It's not!" she cried. "What are you going to do? I am not staying in there! You have to take me back to Camp Supply!" Her red hair was on fire, it seemed. Tom realized right then that she had a temper.

"No, no, that's not my plan. My wife stays with me," Tom said with a grin.

"I am not going back in there!" she said, pushing away from him and standing to her feet. Tom reached for her, putting his arms around her in an embrace. Then he said, "I will take you wherever you would like to go, Mrs. Summers, but you might want to get dressed first."

"I guess," she said as she looked down at her body and suddenly realized she was totally bare naked.

"Oh!" she exclaimed, rushing back into the cabin even though it was the last place she wanted to be. She pulled on the clothes she'd worn the day before and put on her boots without taking time to put stockings on her feet.

Finally calmed down, she came out of the door. This time, she looked to the right, and there was her new home.

Tom said, "It may not be as grand as your home in Iowa, but it is all for you. I love you."

"Oh, Tom! I love it! Look at the porch! We can sit out there in the shade all summer!" Rachel twirled around and squealed, "Oh, Tom, oh, Tom! Why didn't I trust you?"

Tom said, "Well, maybe you will now. He could hardly keep up with her as she ran toward the new house. They looked the house over together. He showed her where the kitchen would be, the bedrooms, and hopefully, where there would be children to fill up the house someday.

There was a large pantry and a back porch for doing laundry. The carpenters installed a pitcher pump in the kitchen, which was of great interest to her.

Robert and Andy had brought the trunks and Tom's suitcase to the new house.

"Sweetheart, we can stay in this room while the carpenters finish the house. We can cook in the cabin and bring meals over here. I'm sorry you had such a frightful experience this morning," Tom sweetly offered.

Rachel replied, "I'm sorry too that I acted in such a manner. I'm sorry I let you down."

"Let's just forget it," Tom said, "I love you very much." Tom held her close and kissed her tenderly.

"Let's go for a ride. I want to show you your new ranch!" Tom exclaimed. "I'll go saddle up the horses. You might put on your riding clothes," he suggested.

They rode the range most of the day. He showed her the spring, some of the longhorn cattle, and some of the closer boundaries of the ranch. In the late afternoon, on their way back to the ranch house, they stopped by the spring. Tom showed her the grove of cottonwood trees. The wind was making a soft whistling sound, whipping the branches of the trees.

They stopped in the shade, where it was cooler. Tom decided to let the horses rest. He tied them off. On a mound of leaves, the newlyweds came together again, underneath the old sheltering trees.

Through the years to come, they remembered that time as a special day. Later in their private moments, they would talk and reminisce about this time in their young married lives.

The now invigorated couple mounted up and rode back to the ranch. Tom was impressed that Rachel was quite the horseman. She handled Whisper with ease and was in control at all times. Rachel was happy with her new horse—a beautiful dapple gray.

Tom loved watching her ride. She loved to gallop ahead of him so he would have to catch up. It became a game for them. Rachel called out, "Race you to the house!" with her long hair flipping in the wind.

Tom realized that he had not had a woman since he was seventeen; not that he hadn't had a few opportunities, but it never seemed like the right thing to do. He wanted to be sure he always treated Rachel with love and respect.

Tom began to ponder how he could be the kind of husband Rachel would want. He realized she would want a flower garden. They would need a fence to keep the cattle away from the house. Another thing was a privy, one thing he hadn't thought about before!

When they got back from their ride, they stopped at the new house. Rachel dismounted and started to take the saddle off Whisper.

Tom said, "Let Robert do that. I'll go see what I can find for supper."

The hands moved the small makeshift bed from the cabin into the house. They piled the quilts on the floor.

Rachel asked, "Joe, would you please shake each one of the quilts to be sure there's no varmints in them?"

"Yes, ma'am. We want you to be happy here," Joe said. "Ma'am do you mind me askin', do you cook? We's a-sure hopin' that you do!"

"My mother taught me how to make bread and pies. Guess I can learn the rest," Rachel said with pride.

While getting things set up, Tom asked one of the craftsmen carpenters, "Can you build us a real bed?"

The foreman, a middle-aged German named Adolf Kunzie, said, "I know exactly what you want," in broken English.

Then Tom told the foreman that there was something that they had completely forgotten. He became indignant because he was in a hurry to finish before the winter came.

Tom persisted, "We don't have an outhouse."

Mr. Kunzie laughed and slapped his knee. "Yes, sir!" he exclaimed. That's a pretty important item right now, isn't it?"

Tom replied, "Yes, it sure is."

He continued, "We'll just stop everything and we can have a dandy one built real quick. You want a two-holer, Mr. Summers?"

Tom went to Rachel, where she was unpacking, and had her come out into the yard. He hemmed and hawed around and finally told her what needed to be built.

"Yes, yes, that's true," she said, holding back a grin. "I will show you just where I want it—downwind from here."

While she was looking, Tom got his shovel and said, "If you just point to the spot, me and the boys will start diggin'."

Rachel pointed and said, "Oh, here will be fine."

Tom put the shovel in the ground as hard as he could. "'Cause you know if you tell me where you want somethin', that's where it's goin' to be."

"Oh no! Wait a minute. That isn't quite right," Rachel exclaimed.

Tom thought, "What difference does it make—a hole's a hole. We are in the right direction from the house with prevailing winds. Please make up your mind!" he said out loud.

She said, "Well, I think for sure I want it over here," which was about six feet away from the original location.

Right then, Tom realized he had learned a valuable lesson about Rachel and most women: they don't make snap decisions. You make sure that they are sure before you start. You just don't start digging the hole the minute they say, "Here."

The carpenter finished the outhouse and made the bed frame while Tom made a mattress tick out of dry grass. "We can use this until we can buy a proper featherbed," he said to the foreman. "Two more days and we will be done and leave you alone."

Adolf told him, "It's been good workin' for you."

CHAPTER 14

Buildin' the Ranch House

After Tom and Rachel had been on their place on the Cherokee Outlet for about two weeks, Tom found out he did not have quite enough cash to cover all of the expenses—the story of his life. He had money set aside for the winter and so much allocated for the house. He thought one thousand dollars would do it for building the ranch house, but the carpenters wanted more money.

The carpenters were stationed at Camp Supply, working for the government, mostly building officer's quarters and expanding their facilities. Adolf figured Tom owed them two hundred dollars more. Tom promised them that when they needed blacksmith work done, he'd sure do it. Each would keep track and Tom would pay it out that way. They agreed that would be the thing to do.

Rachel had been in the kitchen all morning. The fragrance of fresh bread filled the air, and sure enough, here she came out on the porch, flour all over her pretty face.

She said, "Let's have a party to celebrate our new home. Tom, you call the men together. I've made bread and meat pie." She grinned and said, "I also made a special dessert."

"Sweetheart, you don't have to tell me twice. I'll go get those boys right now," Tom said as he jumped off the porch.

Those cowboys came a-running to see what Rachel had cooked up. She said, "Are you hungry?"

As the group arrived, "We're always hungry," the youngest one, being Andy, responded. They all gathered around the wooden table built just for such occasions.

Rachel brought out big bowls with all kinds of food. She placed them on the table that stood on the porch. It was such a wonderful time! She had even picked some wildflowers for the table and spread the tablecloth from her hope chest.

"Wait a minute before you start," Tom demanded. He pulled out a chair for Rachel to be seated, took her hand, and said, "Let's give thanks to God, who brought us all here safely."

After a short prayer, Tom said, "Dig in fellas." They did just that. No one spoke for several minutes as they were too busy eating.

"Boy, this is sure good. Mrs. Summers," Robert exclaimed. "What did you put in this meat pie, Mrs. Summers?" Andy asked.

Andy, with his mouth still full, muttered, "Sure glad Mr. Summers married you, Miss Rachel. We needed a cook real bad."

Tom looked around to see who had said that, but no one confessed. Everyone started laughing and telling stories about each other, mostly about bad meals on the trail.

"None of you starved," Tom quipped. Then he remembered Rachel's promise of a special dessert and asked, "What's for dessert?" Rachel giggled and ran back into the kitchen. She came back with the biggest pie ever made and proudly said, "This is bumble-berry pie. I picked blackberries and boysenberries and sand plums and put them all together. I hope you like it." They did. In fact, they could hardly wiggle when the meal was over.

Rachel said, "I have one request, please." She added with a smile, "I love cooking for you boys, but I ask that when the meal is over, everyone carries their plate to the kitchen sink."

"We can do that, happy to oblige you. And thank you for a wonderful meal," Joe exclaimed.

With that, everyone except Tom started carrying plates and bowls back into the house. Tom looked at Rachel with a grin and started chasing her around the table. Finally, she let him catch her.

He picked her up and carried her into the house. The screen door slammed behind them.

Tom ordered the boys outside and said, "We will be out to join you after a bit."

Joe found his banjo and Robert had a harmonica. Together they began to play some old Negro spirituals. By sundown, everyone was singing and telling more stories.

"I love my new porch swing," Rachel cooed as she and Tom enjoyed the cool of the evening on their porch. Crickets were joining in with the singing, and the fireflies lit up the summer sky.

"Good night, my friends. We are going to call it a day. Tomorrow being Sunday, you can sleep in and we'll have a late dinner. Someone can check the cattle on the east side," Tom said.

Next morning, Tom fixed breakfast for Rachel and himself. He fried up some sausage, adding sliced potatoes. When that was done, he added four eggs and some wild onions. She loved being waited on but didn't eat much. Tom said, "How am I going to fatten you up if you don't eat?"

She replied, "Oh! Tom." As she began clearing the table, she said, "I'll clean the table since you fixed the meal." Tom thought to himself, "This lady will probably run for office someday and I'll vote for her!"

Soon the happy couple joined their hands on the porch, this time on the west side, as the hot sun was burning holes in the sky. Robert and Tom read scriptures from the Bible. Tom asked if anyone had a need for special prayer. Andy raised his hand and said he did but declined to explain. Some prayed and some just listened. They longed for a church to attend.

Will spotted some prairie chickens scampering across the yard. He jumped up, threw a washtub over them, and exclaimed, "I'm the mighty hunter, here's dinner!"

The men put together a campfire, much like they did on the trail drives. Joe rung the chickens' necks. Robert scalded them then plucked feathers. He speared each one with a stick. They took turns turning the meat over the fire. It wasn't long and before you knew it, they had roasted chicken!

A bit of a breeze cooled the muggy desert as they finished their surprise dinner.

They thought they heard thunder, but not a cloud in the sky could be seen. The noise came from the north along with a show of dust. They could see in the distance a band of wagons and riders on horseback. Apparently, the commotion was from Camp Supply, as they could make out uniforms, but why would so many be headed their way and in such a hurry?

Several wagons and buggies pulled up in front of the house, and officers and their wives began piling out with arms full of baskets, blankets, and they didn't know what all!

They began to hug Rachel, shake Tom's hand, and slapped them on the back with a hearty, "Congratulations! It's time we welcomed you and got acquainted," Mrs. Whittaker announced. She was a sturdy woman who could give orders as well as her lieutenant husband.

"You men here," she said, "and women over there." She continued to bark orders. "Now, girls, time to put Mrs. Summers on the pole." She was referring to a long cottonwood pole they had brought with them. Rachel hung on for dear life as the women carried her clear around the house.

The men did the same to Tom, except he fell off. One of the men picked him up and dusted him off and said, "Now it's time for the real fun." The men surrounded Rachel and Tom and tied them up with their backs facing each other as they sat in a wheelbarrow. Two men began to run down the road with the young couple. They were scared to death as to what was going to happen next.

The two flunkies ran with Tom and Rachel in the wheelbarrow for about a mile, then took them out of the wheelbarrow and left them beside the road.

"Rachel, don't be afraid. This is no doubt a shivaree. It's a time of partying and a time to embarrass the new bride and groom. It's their way of saying, 'Welcome.'" Tom tried to sound cheerful as he spoke to Rachel. "First thing we must do is get untied." Rachel was small enough; she slipped down from the ropes and freed herself. Then it was easy to untie Tom.

Just as they started walking back on the trail toward home and toward those loud people, they saw a buggy approaching. It was the itinerant preacher from Dodge. He stopped and asked, "May I give you a ride?"

"We are sure glad to see you, Reverend," Tom explained. "Our friends are just having a little fun with us. Come join us."

When the three of them arrived, the folks were still whooping and hollering and shooting in the air. Things calmed down some as the sun slipped behind some thunderheads.

The ladies brought out the lemonade and cake. They had never seen so much cake! "What kind of cake is that?" Tom asked Mrs. Witherspoon.

"Why, it's my secret molasses-rum-cake recipe!" she replied with great enthusiasm. "President Lincoln's favorite."

They all had a grand time visiting and sharing stories, allowing that all of them would soon be well acquainted and that many would always be friends.

Joe sought out the graying preacher man, Reverend McReynolds. He encouraged him to visit and to let them know when he was to hold services at Camp Supply.

"Where are you from?" Tom asked as he sipped the sweet lemonade.

"I am from Tennessee, near Brownsville," Reverend McReynolds said. Tom almost choked when he heard the word Brownsville. "Should I tell him that is where I'm from?" Tom thought to himself. Just then, Mrs. Johnson pulled him aside to speak privately with him. "I don't mean to be rude," Tom said as he left Mrs. Johnson, but he had to get away from the preacher.

"Rachel, I am going to go into the house and fetch a shawl for you so you don't catch a chill" Tom remarked hurriedly. Rachel thought it was anything but cold but just thought he was being thoughtful.

The lieutenant's wife, Ruby, with whom Tom had danced with a couple of years before, had been eyeing him. Every time she caught his glance, she smiled. Tom thought there was something wrong with her eyes because she fluttered her eyelashes whenever she looked at him.

As he walked to the house, some thirty feet away, she followed him. He opened the door around back, as he knew Rachel's shawl was hanging near the wash stand.

Ruby came inside, exclaiming, "It sure is hot out there. May I have a drink of water?" Tom walked to the kitchen and dipped a cup of water from the pail they kept on the counter. When he turned around, she was right up against him, standing on her tiptoes. Tom was startled, and he dropped the tin cup and splashed water all over her face.

She looked surprised then disappointed and said, "I just wanted a little kiss. You sure are a handsome man. How about just one little kiss?"

She was sure shining up to Tom. He was trapped between her and the sink. He knew he was blushing as he stuttered, "No, no, thank you, Mrs. Sampson. We had better get back to the party. My wife will be wanting her shawl."

As it approached sundown, they all hooked up their buggies and wagons and headed back home. Some were still whooping and hollering and carrying on. It was a great change for them to get away for awhile and come see the newlyweds. Tom wondered, "Who is minding the camp?"

Tom and Rachel felt safe, knowing the military was nearby and that they knew they were welcome on their ranch. Quite often, a troop of soldiers would come by to check on them.

Within a couple of months, Rachel came to Tom and told him she was with child. Tom was so astonished on how grand this would be. He couldn't seem to care for her enough. She would tell him that he was being foolish, that she could take care of herself. Tom told her that he would make arrangements for the army doctor to care for her when that time came. He was a happy man.

The carpenters who had built their home had work for Tom to do at the blacksmith shop. They needed all of their horses shod then needed some repairs on their wagons.

Tom asked Robert to be especially watchful of Rachel as he was going to be gone for a few days. "She is to do no heavy lifting," Tom warned him. "Have Will hang the laundry on the line for her, and you guys bring in the wood for the cookstove. If she even looks pale, you bring her to Camp Supply immediately".

With an anxious heart, Tom left her. They had not been apart since the blissful days in Iowa. "She will make a good mother to our son," Tom thought as he headed for Camp Supply. What made him think he was going to have a son? He didn't know, but what a joy just to think about it. The two of them could go rabbit hunting together and punch cattle and sing songs on the porch with Rachel.

When Tom arrived at Camp Supply, he leaped from Ranger, tied him to the hitching post, and headed for the infirmary to speak to the head surgeon. His feet barely touched the ground as he skipped along the wooden sidewalk.

"Dr. Renfro is busy," the hospital steward informed him as he entered. The post hospital was the first frame structure to be built at the Camp. Dr. Renfro had been there since it was built in 1870. He had seen a lot of changes.

The first hospital facilities were located in tents and dugouts. Then the soddies were built out of grass sod and cut by plow from the plains. Some cabins, like the teamsters, had been built by digging a trench the size you needed, standing wooden poles from fallen trees or from logs that had been carried in on wagons. They were then stood on end, held together tightly, hoping that the trees were straight. They were nailed together with a pole on top.

A sod roof was added over rough beams. Rags and condemned canvas from wagons were stuffed into the cracks. Whitewash made from lime calamine was used to put on the walls. The only purchased item was a window costing about $1.25. The floors were dirt and were packed down hard.

When Dr. Renfro appeared, he was splattered with blood. "We lost a good man today; his appendix ruptured. I tried to save him, but he had a long way to come over rough terrain and was too late. May I help you?"

Dr. Renfro looked older than his forty-five years. He had come from St. Louis from an affluent family, but the call of the West stirred in his soul. After attending medical school for one year, he told his parents, "I'll go and stay a year. If it's not for me, I will head home." He said with a weary smile, "Now this is home."

"Doctor, I'm sorry to bother you, but I have a huge favor to ask of you. My wife is with child, due in the spring. You know where we live. Why, you were there the day of the shivaree!"

The doctor replied, "Yes, lad, I was. I was one of the first people you met when you brought the wagon to the camp years ago."

Tom continued. "Would you deliver our child when he is born?"

He replied, "Normally, I just work for the army, but in this case, I'll sure do what is needed for you and your wife. It will be good to bring life into this world. I've seen enough death. I'll make sure there's a room available here at the hospital quarters when her time is near. You assure her that everything is going to be fine. By the way, how do you know it's going to be a boy?"

Tom just grinned and shook his hand. "Thank you, thank you very much."

For four days, Tom was kept busy in the blacksmith shop. It seemed like everyone had something that needed fixed. The morning that Tom was getting ready to leave, Ruby, the lieutenant's wife, showed up. She was all gussied up with ribbons in her hair and smelling pretty strong of some kind of flowers. It seemed like she made sure Tom was alone and began talking and moving around in a strange way. She came out with, "We didn't get to finish what we started back at your ranch in the kitchen. I know you want me, and now we are alone at last."

This time it made Tom mad. He told her that his wife was his only desire and that he did not want her. She became very indignant and spit out, "You will live to regret this," and left in a huff.

Tom ran after her and asked, "How's that?"

"I'll see to it that your precious wife finds out a thing or two about you!" she sputtered.

He hollered, "You should not lie about somebody." She just laughed and went on her way, tearing her billowing skirt on the iron fence gate.

Tom didn't know how he was going to handle this when he got home. He gathered up his belongings, saddled Ranger, and left the Camp. He was glad to be going home to peace and quiet and to his pregnant wife.

When he rode up to the front yard, Rachel ran out to meet him. "I've missed you so much. Tell me all about your trip and everything that you did."

Tom told her about the trip and the work that he had done and that Dr. Renfro had assured him that she would be well taken care of once her time was near. But he made no mention of the crazy lieutenant's wife. He also wondered how he would handle it if Rachel ever accused him of the lie.

Robert went up to Camp Supply later in the month to get supplies. He came back with the story that Lieutenant Sampson's wife had been caught in bed with Sergeant McHoney. He explained, "The woman's husband had been out on patrol for several days, and when he came back, he caught them red-handed in bed."

Tom said, "What did the lieutenant do to the sergeant, kill him?"

"No, Lieutenant Sampson gave him a fate worse than that," Robert replied. "He sent him up to be with General Custer. He will be under Custer's command." All the officers and enlisted men hated Custer with a passion, one reason being that he unfairly pushed his men beyond endurance. Robert finished with "I understand Custer is on his way with his men to fight in the northern campaign against the Cheyenne in Montana territory."

The betrayed lieutenant sent his wife packing back to her mother. She caught the stage back to Missouri. She was gone, and now Tom didn't have to be concerned.

Fall was a busy time for all on the ranch. They were branding the spring calves, castrating the bull calves and getting ready for winter. Rachel spent time making clothes and blankets for the baby. She loved the night; many times after a busy day, she could be found on her porch swing.

One night Tom reached for her and she was gone. He went outside on the porch, and there she was, just looking at the stars. He asked her, "Is anything wrong?"

"Oh no, this is my special time to think and ponder," she replied.

"Do you want to go back to Iowa? Is this life too harsh?" he asked her, half-afraid of the answer.

"Oh no, I love it here with you. This is where I want to be," Rachel replied.

"This is where I want to raise our family. Besides, I've made some good friends here too," she added.

Tom warned her, "There's hardship out here, more than you know. This has been my whole life since I was sixteen. I left my home and family to come here," Tom continued.

She wanted to know about his past. Rachel said, "You know, you have never told me about your early life. He confided in her about when he left his parents' home at the age of sixteen to fight for the Union in the Civil War.

"After I was shot in the leg, I deserted. I made my way west on foot and horseback."

She commented that he was too young to even be in the war. Tom agreed with her somewhat.

She said, "Being out here, you have helped the army more than if you had stayed and died." What she said helped some, because he'd always had a problem because he was a deserter. He felt like he had let his country down. He still wanted to bring peace to himself and others.

CHAPTER 15

Them Thievin' Renegades

Another evening in late fall, Rachel had slipped out of bed and went to her favorite place on the porch. It was a beautiful moonlit night. She heard noises in the direction of the horse corral. Listening intently, she thought she heard voices and saw shadows of movement. She quietly went back into the house, where Tom was sleeping. She woke him up and told him what was happening.

Tom pulled on his clothes, grabbed his pistol, got a rifle from off the fireplace, and went outside ever so easily. In the cover of night, he could barely see the outlaws taking the horses and herding them over the ridge behind the corrals.

Tom thought, "Oh boy, here I am on foot. These hoodlums are stealing our horses!" Then Tom whistled. His mount, Ranger, a big dun stud horse, broke loose and came running back. Two of his mares followed him.

The horse thieves took the ones that were left and hightailed it out of there. "Thank goodness, I trained Ranger to come to me when I whistled," Tom said, very much relieved.

Tom roused the boys out of the bunkhouse and told them what was going on. He said, "We've only got three mounts and there's six

133

of us." Robert, who had been a soldier in the military, was first to mount and lead the chase. Jacob was close behind.

Andy, Will, and Joe were instructed to stay and protect the ranch. "You watch over Rachel," Tom called as he followed Robert and Jake. "Thank goodness, they didn't get the saddles," Tom breathed under his breath.

Rachel pleaded, "Tom, please be careful!" Clouds had covered the moon and stars, but there was an eerie glow that covered the flat land. The rocks even reflected what light there was as they sped toward the sound of horse's hooves.

Tom was livid with anger. He was so angry with these fools, these outlaws, for stealing their horses. "It's a wonder they didn't get them all, and we would be out here on foot." Tom could see why horse thieves were hung in this part of the country. They proceeded to ride after them. Tom guessed they thought they weren't being followed because they were not riding very fast. Yet they still lost the thieves. They simply disappeared. They stopped and listened—nothing. Nothing but the sound of their beating hearts.

The men searched for about two hours until first light. They had been riding hard. The horses were lathered up, pretty well spent, and needed a rest.

All of a sudden, they came upon a canyon. At first, they didn't see anything. Then Jake spotted movement. Horses were being herded single file along the bottom of a deep gorge. They didn't know how they got down there, and they sure didn't know how to reach them.

Tom gave Ranger his head, and he found the opening to the trail to the bottom. Robert and Jake followed. They suspected these outlaws were renegade Indians no doubt, but Tom didn't know what tribe. They were dirty red men; they had stolen the horses—Tom's livelihood!

As they were riding along, Jake sidled up close to Tom and said, "I know this area. I've ridden it before. We can get up on top and look down into what looks to be a natural holding pen."

So unbeknownst to the thieves, they cut across and hightailed it over the ridge to get ahead of the herd. Tom and Jake were hoping and guessing where they might be. They reached the top and tied their spent horses to an old dead tree.

Tom said, "Boys, this has got to be it. These horses need rest or someone's goin' down. They can't go any further. We have got to get these outlaws now!"

Robert asked, "What are we goin' to do, boss?"

Tom said, "Far as I'm concerned, we're goin' to kill every last one of them!"

They could see them more clearly as they approached the top of the canyon on foot. There were five of them. The thieves were focused on their newly acquired mounts and did not suspect they were being watched. Slowly, Tom, Jake, and Robert took out their lever-action rifles and cut down on them all at once. It was like shooting fish in a barrel, but the hombres deserved to die because it was a terrible thing they had done.

It also was a terrible action that Tom took by killing them without giving them a chance.

As they were approaching, there was no doubt that the thieves were all dead, all five of them. These men were no more than horse thieves who had been ransacking and terrorizing the area for quite some time.

The men walked back to their horses and rode to the bottom of the canyon as it was now broad daylight. As they prepared to bury the dead, Tom and his men could not tell what tribes they were from. Some were wearing white men's clothes with moccasins on their feet and feathers in their headbands, some just buckskins.

The outlaws had built a brush corral at the head of the canyon, they had about forty head of horses enclosed in it. The horses all had different brands, including some that were unbranded. It looked like this was living quarters for them, and it would be hard for even the soldiers to find.

Each man checked a few horses. They found some branded with the Circle T, culled three of those ponies out from the herd, and saddled them up to give the other horses a chance to rest.

The dead were buried and the horses retrieved. They were about ready to leave when Robert noticed Jake lagging behind. He watched

Jake get down from his horse and walk over to the brushy area. He got down on his knees and disappeared into the unknown. Moments later, he came out with a small white child! The boy whimpered a little and looked scared, his eyes as big as the fear within him. Jake gently untied the naked child, wrapped him in a dirty blanket he found nearby, and held him close.

"Does anybody have something to feed this baby?" No one did. They didn't even have any water because they had left the ranch in such a hurry.

Robert looked inside the hut and found some cornmeal. Jake licked his finger, covered it with cornmeal, and offered it to the boy. The little fellow, about three years old, was too scared to talk but finally allowed Jake to put his cornmeal covered finger to his mouth. He sucked it eagerly, then he wanted more. Jake kept reassuring him, saying, "We won't hurt you, boy. We won't hurt you."

Finally, Jake was able to set the boy on his horse and climb up behind him, and they started back home, one more ranch hand in tow.

Rachel was frantic by the time they got back to the ranch. She had sent Will to run on foot to Camp Supply for help. She was more than a little surprised to discover their new little ranch hand. They called him "Buddy" as they had no idea what his name was or where he came from.

Rachel took Buddy into the house and fed him some pudding and green beans. He loved Rachel and wouldn't let her put him down. She washed him up and wrapped him in a clean shirt, put socks on his feet, and rocked him all day and into the night.

Next morning, soldiers from Camp Supply arrived with Will. They told of a wagon train that had been ambushed and everyone was killed, and all the horses were stolen. They could only gather that this child was the only survivor.

"We will take the boy to Camp Supply and try to notify next of kin as to his whereabouts," said the sergeant who led the soldiers.

"Sergeant Stone, we now have forty head of horses that don't belong to us," Tom said. "What are we going to do with them?"

He said, "Anything that's not marked is yours."

Tom continued, "I don't know if that's right."

The sergeant said, "That's the way it should be." He had a map that showed the different ranches in the area and their brands. It also showed the Texas panhandle and "No-Man's Land" off to the northwest.

Tom and Robert took the map with the brands on it down to the corral where the horses were and looked them over. Near as they could tell, the outlaws had raided four different ranches.

The sergeant said, "I'll send riders to those ranches so the owners can come collect their horses."

"That will be just fine," Tom replied. There were a couple of ranches that were as far as forty miles west and sixty miles to the northwest. The horse thieves, as Tom would rather call them, had established a pretty broad range. It was a wonder that they had not been detected. It seemed that they were good at keeping to themselves.

The sergeant again asked, "How many men were there, and what happened to them?"

Robert answered him and explained where they were buried.

Sergeant Stone said, "It's a done deal; we will just forget about it. You did justice. It would have been better if you had gotten the army, but then you would have lost them or been killed yourselves. I can understand why you hightailed it after them and that you handled it as you did."

In the weeks following, different cowboys showed up to identify their property. All but four were claimed, and Robert figured they were Indian ponies. Andy and Jake snubbed those four up and branded them with the Circle T brand. Tom had made up a small branding iron just for these horses, it had the Circle T followed by "75" to indicate the pony raid of 1875.

Winter was closing in; the creeks were frozen, which meant the men took turns going out each morning and evening to chop holes in the ice for the stock so they could drink. The wind howled around the corners of the buildings and threatened to suck the life out of them.

"Will it ever stop blowing?" Rachel whispered to Tom one night as they snuggled, warm beneath the thick comforters that she made at her sewing group.

Tom whispered back, "It will hush. Now, come here, and I will make you forget about the wind."

CHAPTER 16

New Life on the Ranch

"Tom, the baby just moved! Here, put your hand on my tummy! Feel," Rachel said with great excitement.

"Yes, he's going to be a fine, healthy boy. Don't you think we should take a trip into Camp Supply to see the doctor and make sure everything is fine?" Tom ask.

"Yes," she replied, "And I want to see if Mrs. Morgan has the material I ordered to make some baby clothes and blankets."

Tom did not sleep the rest of the night, just thinking what it will be like to have a son. He really wanted a son.

Indian summer was almost magical on the plains; it was nature's way of giving you a second chance to get chores done on the ranch before the hard winter hit. The sun was not as hot, and there was a glow through the cottonwood trees that made the yellow leaves almost hurt your eyes.

There was a peaceful, relaxed feeling in the air as Tom and Rachel stepped outside early the next morning. Tom harnessed up the horse and buggy and told Robert that they would be back tomorrow or the next day and that they would start branding steers then.

As Tom helped Rachel into the buggy, he realized that this was his second chance to do the right thing in this world. "I will raise this lad to be better than I am. He will be strong and never do anything that will make him always be lookin' over his shoulder," Tom thought.

"Why, Mrs. Summers, it's good that you came to see me," Dr. Renfro said after examining her. "Everything looks good. You are perfectly fine. I expect no complications when you deliver this spring. Even though this is your first child, everything will be fine. Now, I want you to come see me two weeks before the baby is due and plan to stay with us until the blessed event. My wife, Dorothy, and I would count it a privilege to share our home with you. Plan to stay here also for at least two weeks after the birth." Dr. Renfro was beaming as he spoke.

"How kind of you and Mrs. Renfro to extend such hospitality! My mother wanted to be here with me, but she won't be able to make the trip until Easter. Thank you, and thank Mrs. Renfro also!" Rachel exclaimed.

Tom and Rachel were giddy with excitement. They left the hospital like a couple of kids, laughing and talking at the same time.

The captain's wife, Sally Ann, approached them. She had her shawl tied up over her hat to keep the wind from blowing it away.

"Does the wind ever stop blowing?" she questioned.

Before Tom could answer, she continued. "I certainly hope you are well, Mrs. Summers. I saw your buggy in front of the infirmary, and I trust you have not taken ill."

Sally Ann Morgan was a bit of a busybody, but the couple was so happy with their news that both Rachel and Tom looked at each other and said, "We're having a baby!"

"Oh my, I didn't know that! When are you due?" she asked. Tom thought she was looking for someone she could be the first to tell.

Rachel exclaimed, "March! About two weeks before Easter."

Mrs. Morgan just stood there, smiling. Her face was an open book. One could tell she was counting the months in her head to make sure that nine months had passed from the wedding date until the baby's due date. A huge relief came over her as she grabbed Rachel and gave her a hug.

"Now, if there is anything I can do to help, let me know. Why don't you two join me for a cup of tea? We're right here in front of the officer's quarters," Mrs. Morgan said, probably hoping for more news.

After the young couple was ushered into her living quarters, Mrs. Morgan proceeded to tell her story. She was delighted to have someone new to pass along the latest gossip. As she poured the tea, she began with her favorite bit of news.

"You remember Lieutenant Sampson? He is so well regarded by my husband and all of the officers here. Well, he was gone on patrol and came back early. You would think that his wife would be glad to see him back alive, but instead she was in bed with another man, Sergeant McHoney. I am here to tell you they got what they deserved. Sergeant McHoney was sent away to fight with General Custer, and Ruby was sent packin' back to her mother or somewhere. Why, we ladies, of course, snubbed her royally. She was so pitiful, crying and begging to stay. She even had to load her own luggage! No one was there to see her off when she took the next stage to Dodge. I just happened to glance out my window as she was leaving. I say good riddance! She was a brazen thing—always making eyes at all the men." Mrs. Morgan finally took a deep breath and then changed the subject. Tom was relieved to know that Ruby Sampson was gone.

Tom was still counting his blessings when he heard Mrs. Morgan say, "The captain and I would be honored if you and the missus would stay for supper and rest yourselves overnight. It's too late to start back to your ranch at this hour. We have to take care of our little mother, don't we?"

Rachel looked at Tom and smiled. "Thank you very much. Your invitation is very much appreciated," he said. They spent a pleasant evening with the captain and his wife. She served roast beef, cabbage, and rice pudding for dessert. Sally Ann retold the story about the sergeant and Ruby again, except that this time, the sergeant was whipped at the whipping post and Ruby surely was tarred and feathered. The next morning, Mrs. Morgan sent word to the other ladies to come spend some time with Rachel. They had a splendid time asking Rachel about her baby plans.

"What are you going to name your baby? Mrs. Morgan asked. Will it be Thomas Jr. if it's a boy?" someone asked.

"I love the name Penelope, if it's a girl," another lady commented. Rachel was enjoying every minute.

Tom realized Rachel needed more time with womenfolk. He would try to make arrangements for that later. They gathered up the fabric that Rachel had ordered, and they headed back to the ranch in their buggy. They were both in such good spirits with everything in life to look forward to.

Rachel snuggled a little closer as the wind kicked up. "You know, I think this baby was conceived that day in the shade of the cottonwoods."

"I think so too," Tom said as he held her close.

He then tied the reins of the horse to the buggy to free his hands. The horse knew the way home. Tom gave his full attention to Rachel as they rejoiced in a day well spent and slipped slowly into the land beyond.

Tom prayed as dusk turned to nightfall. "Lord, please bring this child safely into the world, with no harm to his mother. Let me be the kind of father you would have me to be. I promise I will never abuse him like my father did to me. I pray he will always know that his home is a safe place."

The next day started while it was still dark; the cowhands and the cattle were ready. They branded the newly purchased cattle and cut the bulls.

Rachel fixed rabbit stew with spoon bread and lots of coffee for supper. "I'm going to make hardtack tomorrow so you will have it to eat when I'm gone," she assured her husband.

The men told stories as Rachel washed the dishes. "Andy, would you please empty the dishwater on the turnips I planted by my window?" Rachel requested.

"Yes, ma'am, I'd be glad to. Anything else?"

Next day, Rachel began to prepare the hardtack. She began with three or four cups of white flour, which she put in a pan. She added water until the dough was stiff. Then she added salt and began to roll the dough about one-half inch thick. She loved using the rolling pin her German father had made for her hope chest. One handle was a little shorter than the other. The imperfection made it even more precious to her. Rachel whistled as she worked, cutting the dough into three square pieces then piercing each piece with a fork. She had banked the fire to cook for a long time at a low temperature. These handy squares could be kept for years, if needed.

It had been a beautiful fall. Rachel made preserves from the sand plums and currants that she gathered down by the river. She also made apple butter from the apples that Andy brought to her.

The buffalo grass was turning amber brown, with a hint of purple; the short grass was still green. One morning, the hands woke to a hard freeze—a killing frost. The carefree days were over. The cowboys began to bring the cattle closer to home so they could eat the grass that had not been pastured all summer. Many days, the ice in the creek had to be broken so the cattle could get water.

Rachel began to prepare for Christmas. She asked all the cowboys to save any paper, especially colored or shining, and give it to her so she could make decorations for the tree. The four cowhands rode out on the prairie, looking for a perfect evergreen tree.

Christmas morning broke with ice crystals sparking in the air. Robert had killed and dressed an eight-point buck and put it on to cook in two Dutch ovens over an open-fire pit. Will shot a turkey, plucked the feathers, and roasted it with dressing made with wild onions. Jake picked a sack of crab apples, which were added to the dressing. Rachel cooked a kettle full of her prized turnips. Joe brought a jug of molasses into the house and told Rachel how his mother made molasses raisin pie. Andy presented a bottle of southern whiskey and went about finding glasses for everyone.

The huge evergreen stood in the middle of the room. The men had brought home the largest tree they could find, and when they tried to bring it through the door, it over powered all of them. Andy was too busy to help, but the rest took turns cutting the base off to make the tree fit the room. They made chains out of the colored paper, and Joe made a star for the top of the tree out of a metal can lid.

After singing songs and sharing memories of Christmases past, Tom presented Rachel with the cradle that he made for the baby.

An unusually warm January and February followed. There was evidence of green grass out on the prairie.

In March, the Sunday before St. Patrick's Day, Rachel packed her smallest trunk for her stay at Camp Supply. The clouds had moved in and brought a gentle snow. Tom asked his mother-to-be to dress warmly. "And don't forget the lunch you packed for us; it will be an all-day trip."

Although he tried to hide it, Tom was nervous. He took even greater care at helping Rachel into the buggy. Even Babe, the horse, was nervous. Will held Babe's head as Tom boarded. The hands surrounded them and all wished them well.

"Safe trip!" "Hope it's a boy!" "Hurry back!" they called to the excited couple, waving.

"Is Babe all right? She's barely moving," Rachel commented.

"Don't want to jostle you around," Tom explained.

"At the rate you're going, this baby will be born on the trail before we get there," Rachel pointed out.

They finally arrived at Camp Supply. The temperature had dropped. It was getting colder and ice, snow, and sleet were beginning to fall. The wind was no longer a friend and was showing off the best it had to offer.

The doctor was in the infirmary, standing in the door as if he knew the anxious couple would soon arrive. Some of the officers' wives were huddled together on the porch.

"Come in! Come in and get warm," Dr. Renfro beckoned. "I want to see how you are doing, and then we will get you settled in."

The time for Rachel to give birth finally came. The doctor was there, along with two women, Vera and Naomi, acting as midwives. The room was clean and sparsely furnished. Rachel was placed on a padded table. There were several lamps and a table with instruments lined up in a row. The smell of strong coffee filled the air. The wind whistled through every place it could find. A door banging outside kept rhythm with a dog barking in the background. Such love and attention was given to Rachel that she probably had better care than if she had been in Kansas City.

Rachel gave birth to a son: a beautiful baby with strong lungs. They had already decided on the name of John, after Tom's brother, whom he had not seen since he was sixteen years old. Baby John did not have much hair, but what he had looked like it would be sandy in color, after Rachel's side of the family.

Tom was at Camp Supply the day little Johnny was born; no prouder man ever walked the face of the earth. Over and over again, he thanked Dr. Renfro. He thanked the midwives, and he thanked Rachel. Most of all, he thanked the Creator.

One of the midwives, Naomi Hudson, took Tom aside after the birth and said, "You know, Dr. Renfro really isn't a doctor! He served in the Civil War as a medic. He lost his two brothers. Their home was ransacked and burned. His parents also lost their lives. He headed West and vowed to help where he could. This is the first child that he has delivered! Just thought you should know."

Tom was stunned. "What if something had happened?" he thought to himself. He lowered his eyes and thanked God again then went in to see his son.

After Johnny was three days old, Rachel said to Tom, "We need to give him a second name."

The proud father said, "That's entirely up to you. I wanted John, so I will leave the second name up to you."

She said, "I want to add the name Gail for his middle name."

Tom said, "Okay, that is a good name, but why? Is this a family name?"

"No," she said, "It's because here, the wind always blows a gale."

They always laughed about that. Sometimes, especially if he was in trouble, his mother would call in a stern voice, "Johnny Gail Summers!"

CHAPTER 17

To Market, To Market, Get Along, Little Doggies

The following spring, 1876, they began rounding up the herd and prepared to make a drive to Dodge.

Since it would take all of the cowboys to get them to market, Tom wanted his family, Rachel and Johnny, to spend this time in Camp Supply while they were on the trail.

"You won't be alone, and both of you will be safe. Who knows what could happen here!" Tom told her.

She replied, "What about our home and our outbuildings?"

Tom said, "Not much we can do about it. If someone wants to come and sack them, or worse, burn them, well, there's not much we can do."

Tom wrote a note and stuck it on the door. It read, "Whoever comes on these premises and needs food or shelter, go ahead and help yourselves." As neighbors, they were more than happy to help strangers in need.

The hands headed up the cattle and started up the trail toward Camp Supply. In the lead were Rachel and Johnny. They were in the new buggy Tom bought just for them. She had Johnny all bundled

146

up beside her. Tom could not help but admire her. Here was a young woman from the city and from a wealthy family, and she was out here, leading their herd to market!

Suddenly, the buggy lurched and threw Rachel and Johnny to the ground. The wheel on the new buggy had hit a rock and fell off. Rachel had curled herself around Johnny Gail, screaming for help. Even through the commotion, the oncoming steers weren't even fazed; they just walked around them. Tom had never moved so fast in his life!

He found the wheel nut not far from where the wheel fell off. Will had a piece of wire in his saddlebag and wired the nut on. It would hold until they reached Camp Supply.

They arrived at Camp Supply later than expected, leaving the cattle on the west side, beyond the twelve-mile limit outside Camp Supply. They knew they could not bring the cattle any closer for fear of being arrested. Rachel and Johnny were fine, just a little shook up. Tom took them on into Camp Supply. The hands camped on Beaver Creek.

Rachel had made several friends at the Camp, especially Sally Morgan, the captain's wife. They were more than happy for Tom, Rachel, and Johnny to stay in their quarters when they came to the Camp. The next morning, Tom kissed Johnny and Rachel good-bye and said, "We'll be back within four weeks after we sell the cattle in Dodge." Shaking his finger at his infant son, Tom said, "Johnny, you mind your mother."

As Tom was leaving, a grizzly-looking old man flagged him down. He allowed that he had heard there was a cattle drive going to Dodge City, and he wanted to go, too.

The man put a big chaw of tobacco in his mouth as he approached. " I've been on lots of [spit] cattle drives [spit], I can hold my own."

Tom asked, "Do you have a good horse?"

"No, I lost him [spit] to a gambler in Dodge. I [spit] am not much of a rider [spit], but I'm one hell of a [spit] good cook!" he exclaimed.

Tom said, "Buddy, if you want a job for a short time, you got it!"

He responded, "I need to get back to Dodge. You know there's lots of women there, and maybe I can win my horse back. What do you pay?"

Tom replied, "Name your price."

He allowed that Tom would give him twenty-five dollars and plenty of chewing tobacco; he would do the cooking.

Robert found an old wagon built by the Studebaker Company and began to fit it the way the new man wanted. First, he built a support for the small cast-iron cookstove.

"We need some gunny [spit] sacks so the cowboys can collect the buffalo and cow [spit] chips, so we'll have plenty of fuel," the old man reminded Tom.

Next, they built some shelves to hold supplies. Hardtack, as they began to call the new cook, suggested, "Let's throw in some boards [spit] and plenty of nails and a saw and axe [spit], and I can work on this wagon later."

"Okay," Tom said. He could tell he had better buy up a large supply of chewing tobacco. Hardtack, the mule team, and the partly fitted chuck wagon full of supplies rode ahead of them, heading north. The land was hard and rocky. They could see for miles and hoped they could see trouble before it saw them.

Tom told Hardtack to travel about twenty miles, where to look for water, and then to make camp. They would bring the herd up and find him.

The first day on the drive, they had almost completed their twenty miles when they heard a noise like sawing and hammering. Sure enough, as they approached the noise, they could see Hardtack working on his chuck wagon.

"Over here! Come and get it before I throw it out!" was Hardtack's greeting to them. Yes, they were hungry, and Tom was relieved that he didn't have to cook.

The fresh pork with pinto beans, complete with corn fritters, was delicious. The men guessed that Hardtack had already eaten and then got busy building a drop board on the back of the chuck wagon.

He was a good cook with what he had to work with and a fairly decent carpenter to boot. They had their doubts that he could cook with good stuff, but he did a fine job with ham and beans. The boys were always on the lookout for a small animal they could kill and skin out for the cook to turn into a meal.

"Now, you guys remember, no gunfire around the herd," Tom reminded them. "Make yourselves a slingshot or something; no gunfire or we'll have a stampede!"

Rio de Los Cameras, or the Cimarron River, was before them. It was a long, winding, open river, shallow in some places, deep and dangerous in other places. It was named for the wild sheep at its headwater in New Mexico, winding through the panhandle into Kansas and Oklahoma Territories, and ending in Arkansas. Many Indian tribes hunted along the banks and fished its waters.

Tom held his breath as they approached the sandy banks. They were about sixty miles out of Dodge City. Sixty miles and they would be safe—safe at least from the tricky river that was always changing its channels. It kind of reminded Tom of some women that he knew about—beautiful to look at, but treacherous.

Tom decided at the last minute to cross on the military road. No one was supposed to use this road for cattle, but it was firmer, hard-packed dirt and made for a better crossing. Even at best, it was not an easy crossing.

Tom's lead cowhand, Robert, and Pete, the new man he picked up at Camp Supply, were about halfway into the river. All seemed calm until one calf apparently lurched up too close to the others, got scared, and began floating down the river. Pete took off, scrambling up the bank. He was a good cowboy, with lariat in hand; he went after the one steer. He followed the shoreline and was waiting for the perfect moment to lasso him. His horse stumbled, throwing Pete into the crook of a cottonwood tree. It caught him in the throat. He just happened to be in the wrong place. When he didn't return, Robert went looking for him. He found him hanging in the fork of the tree by his head.

As they prepared to bury him, Robert found a letter in his pocket from his mother in Fort Worth. Why Pete was at Camp

Supply, they did not know. He had just said he wanted to hire on. Tom took the letter, and when he got to Dodge, he wrote to Pete's mother, extended his sympathy, and sent her his pay.

After they gathered up the cattle and crossed the foreboding river, they could feel a change in the weather. There were dark clouds in the northwest. It looked like a bad storm was headed their way.

On the prairie, there is always the danger of a storm starting a stampede. When the lightning strikes, it is terrifying to the animals. Then the loud production of thunder, as if the sky was breaking in two, causes even the best-natured animals to panic.

The horses were already restless. The men all saddled up on fresh mounts. Tom told his men to keep the horses and cattle moving. They circled the herd as best they could, nudging the occasional stray back into the fold, calling each a name.

Lightning struck the ground, leaving a black mark; fire flamed for a moment, but it was soon raining so hard, the fire was extinguished.

The lead steers acted surprised by the show of nature. They turned around and headed for a bluff nearby for protection. This place was a natural corral on three sides. The five cowboys secured the open end until the storm passed.

They were more than soaking wet when they finally met up with the chuck wagon. "I was worried about you, you know!" Hardtack angrily said, "I've got more to do than worry about you."

Tom thought he was mostly mad because his chewing tobacco had gotten wet. Tom started to say, "You're going to get it wet anyway," but thought better of it.

They called him Hardtack because he could make good biscuits, but there were times the biscuits would be more like rocks. They would give him a bad time, telling him if they needed bullets for their guns, they would just use his biscuits. They always said it in his presence just to rile him up.

Much to their surprise, even in that thunder and lightning storm, Hardtack had supper ready for them. They each had a piece of cheese, molasses on some hardtack, and milk that came from a can.

They sat around the fire and tried to dry out and changed their clothes. The men took turns trying to sleep and ride herd throughout the night. "Next trip," Tom vowed, "we'll have a tent!"

Next morning, after a breakfast of fried bacon, good biscuits, gravy and lots of black coffee they proceeded toward Dodge with very little trouble. After three more weeks on the trail, Hardtack came to Tom and said, "I'm ready to get paid. I can almost smell Dodge, and I'm wanting to go." Tom replied, "Okay, when we get there, we really won't need you. It looks like we'll be driving into Dodge today!" Tom paid him up and gave him an extra five dollars.

Hardtack said, "I'll leave your team and wagon at the livery stable on the south end of town."

Tom said, "That will be fine. I'll see you when we get there!"

He answered, "You may see me, but I plan to be so drunk, I won't see you!"

Tom and the boys wanted to hurry up because they would soon be in Dodge City, "Queen of the West." Tom wanted to obtain the best possible price for these cattle right off, but he knew he may have to wait to get what he wanted. The cowboys had been through a lot to bring the cattle here. They had lost one good man and several steers. Tom now had a family that depended on him. He would sure be glad to get on back to his wife and son.

The herd was moving along and looking good. A man in a big western hat rode up from the direction of Dodge City. He was a buyer from Kansas City who spoke with some kind of an accent.

"Good afternoon, sir," he said. "I saw you headed toward the railroad corrals. Would you be interested in selling your steers to me?"

"I would consider it for the right price" was Tom's answer.

He looked the steers over. Shrugging his shoulders, he said, "They look a little drawn. I'll offer you twelve a head. Tom allowed that twelve dollars per head was not enough; in fact, Tom was offended. He realized that buying and selling anything was a war: one must remain calm and confident to win.

Tom replied, "I was shootin' for fifteen."

The eastern-talking guy trying to look like a cowboy cussed and said, "You'll be lucky to get that!"

Tom said, "Is your twelve still strong?"

He replied, "Yes, I will keep my word."

Not believing him to keep his word, Tom replied, "If you don't mind, I will go ahead and try for more. These are strong, healthy steers."

The stranger gave his steed a slap and said, "You'll never get it!"

Just as he left, here came a fine-looking buggy. In it, was a man accompanied by a lady in stylish western wear. They approached Tom and said, "Good day. I am Mr. Nathan Hoffman and this is my wife, Mina. We are buyers from Iowa. If we can agree on a price, we will take these steers right away and feed them out. I will offer you fifteen a head."

Tom replied, "You can have them for twenty."

Mr. Hoffman come back with eighteen. "That's my final offer." He stated. Tom answered, eighteen it is. Where's your pens?" Then he realized that they all used the same pens, only at different times. This was his second cattle drive to Dodge, and he had a lot to learn.

They shook hands on the deal, and the boys and Tom began pushing and driving the herd into the empty pens. These were strong, tall corrals. The cattle in no way could jump over, but they wanted to. It's a wonder they did not die of fright, being the wild animals that they were. Longhorns did not like being confined or being so close together.

There was one long alley built from the main holding pen to the railroad cattle car that was waiting. They used long poles to jab and prod each steer into the open door.

Sometimes their long horns were caught on the sides of the pens or the edge of the door. Occasionally, a sharp-pointed horn would be in the way of another steer as he tried to move along. It was a slow process.

Mr. Hoffman and his wife joined them and were full of questions. The favorite question was "When are you going to start cutting off those horns?"

Tom answered with a grin, "Never!"

Mr. Hoffman wrote Tom a big check. Once every last steer was loaded, about twenty-five steers to a car, Tom thanked the Hoffman couple, mounted up on Ranger, and rode to the bank. He deposited most of the money, keeping enough to pay his hands and some to keep them through the winter. After his account and his holdings, he even had some extra that they called "interest." He felt better as he had been concerned if his money would still be there. He really had not trusted that bank man, but maybe he was wrong.

Tom rode back to the cattle pens to find his hands. In a way, it was somewhat sad. His herd was gone; they had given it their all to get them to Dodge.

"Mr. Summers, would you join us down at the saloon?" Jake asked.

He answered, "Yeah, I wouldn't mind going down to the Variety." He had a gnawing feeling that something was not right.

He promised the boys that he would buy for them. "Now, not all day and not all night, but a few drinks," Tom explained. "We're going to leave out in the morning," he said with a note of excitement in his voice.

First thing they did was find a barbershop right there on Front Street on the north side. They wanted to clean up and get rid of the cockleburs. A shave and a haircut were two bits, and a bath cost extra, but it was worth it!

They marched into the mercantile store next door and bought all-new work clothes. The guys put them on right there in the store.

"Excuse us, but we've been on the trail for a while," Tom said, a little embarrassed. He told the owner, "I'll be back tomorrow to pick up that suit that I left for you to alter a year ago. I might even buy some more work clothes! My wife is starting to call me Mr. Ragtag."

They left looking a whole lot better than they did when they came to town. Smelled better too. Will, Robert, Joe, Jake, Andy, and Tom walked a wide swath down to the Variety, the finest saloon west of the Mississippi, with a little swagger in their step.

Tom knew that the north side of the Santa Fe railroad tracks was the least dangerous and more respectable place to be. No telling what could happen in the Lone Star Saloon, which was on the south side. It was next to the jail, so it was handy when trouble arose.

Walking through two huge swinging doors of the Variety Saloon, a favorite of many, they looked the place over and made their way to the bar. Tom had never seen so many glasses or so many bottles of booze. Whiskey was the drink of choice for a real cowboy. A huge mirror that reached to the ceiling behind the solid mahogany bar made the place look like it went on forever.

A piano was playing loudly. Although it looked like it was playing by itself, there was a skinny old man sitting in front of it on a round stool, trying to keep up. Several ladies were on the job, laughing and trying to act as if they were having a good time.

Tom ordered a few rounds; the ladies clustered around as they were "the new men in town." The talk was that in May of that year, 1876, an assistant to Marshal Larry Deger was hired. This man was from Ellsworth, Kansas, where they say this Earp fellow had worn a badge for only an hour. This fascinating story captured their curiosity. "What kind of man is he?" Jake asked one of the ladies.

"I don't know, Mister, but they are paying him two hundred and forty dollars a month! Hope he comes my way."

Hortense chimed in, "He got to pick his own deputies too. Wayne Murrow is one, and Sandy somebody is the other one. They are getting seventy-five dollars a month. I could be nice to those boys anytime."

There were no taxes in Dodge, just fines and bonuses for each live arrest and a ten-dollar bonus for arresting a dangerous person. Tom hoped that he would get to meet, or at least see, this mysterious new lawman.

Tom, Jake, and Andy ambled over to a large round table where the fellows were playing cards. The three cowboys asked if they could join them, sat their drinks down, and looked around. To Tom's right was a rancher that he knew, Ned Legg, who had a ranch east of his on the Cherokee Outlet.

Ned told him that it wasn't going to be very long before all the ranchers on the Cherokee Outlet were going to have to form an organization to deal with the Cherokee Nation.

Tom said, "Yes, I suppose. Who do you think we could get to be the president and get it going?"

Ned said, "Why don't you?"

"No, there are much larger ranches than yours and mine out there, and they are closer to the Cherokee Nation. Why, it would take us four to five days to get there if we hurried." They visited about their cattle and their families.

The music was loud, but the laughter was louder the longer the evening rolled on. As the patrons drank, more ladies appeared. Some were dancing on stage, and some were singing, but mostly they were trying to get the boys to buy more drinks. Tom wasn't paying much attention, but his boys were. They thought this was pretty much a good idea—a good place to be.

Andy said, "This place is a lot better than those other places."

Tom replied, "Hey, but it's going to cost you more."

"Well, since you're buying the drinks, we'll have more money to spend," Jake said as he put his arm around a cute little blonde.

Out of nowhere, Tom felt someone grab his arm and say, "Tom Summers, it's sure good to see you again."

"I'll be darned, if it isn't Ruby Sampson," Tom thought, the lieutenant's wife whom he thought had been sent packing back to her family. Ruby was highly painted, her eyes baggy and her voice rough from the whiskey.

"Buy me a drink, handsome, or do you want to dance?"

"No thanks, Ruby" was Tom's reply.

"Oh, come on. I'll take care of you real cheap!"

He said, "No!" And he meant it. "I don't need you, Ruby, and I never did!"

Andy looked at Tom right in the eye and said, "Mr. Summers, what kind of a past do you have?"

Tom replied, "Andy, you will never know all there is to know about me."

Every year after that for several years, Tom would see Ruby hanging around the cowboys. She never approached him again; she shunned him and that was just fine with him. Tom would look at her and determine how much uglier she had gotten over the years. Her way of life was telling on her.

Tom never did say anything to the lieutenant through the years. Then, one day, Lieutenant Sampson was mustered out of the army and went back East, where Tom hoped he found a good woman and a good life.

Next morning, Tom's head felt as big as a number 3 washtub. He didn't think he could even get his hat on. He walked down a huge flight of stairs of the Dodge House and paid Lucky Smith for his night's lodging. Next door was Del-Monaco's Restaurant. They served a hearty breakfast, but Tom was more interested to learn more about the man who had come to what was once called Buffalo City. He wondered if the man could tame this most lawless city of the West. It was now renamed Dodge City, after nearby Fort Dodge. Tom learned that young Earp, named Wyatt, had moved out West in his early twenties. He was a student of "Buffalo Bill" Cody. Soon he was known to kill up to twenty-eight buffalo in a day by himself, shooting from his saddle. So that told Tom that he was quite a marksman. After a couple more cups of coffee, he tipped the server, who had shared what she knew about the man who would become Dodge City's most famous marshal.

Tom found his boys healing up from their hangovers and told them he would appreciate it if they would get back to the ranch in a week or two.

"Yessir, we sure will! One night was enough for me," reported Robert.

In addition, Joe did not like Dodge at all, but he said, "I'll watch out for these three young-uns till we's go home."

Robert said, "Joe and I are staying at the blacksmith shop close to the cattle pens. The marshal said we could stay there for free if we would watch for cattle rustlers, who sometimes help themselves to a steer or two."

"Fine," Tom replied, "See you soon; stay healthy. Dodge is a rough place."

Tom rode back to the mercantile, bought more work clothes, and paid for his altered suit. He was hoping that Hardtack had taken his wagon to the livery stable just as they had agreed, and sure enough, there it was. Tom threw his saddle in the wagon and tied Ranger, his stud, on behind, and away they went, Tom driving a team of mules and a chuck wagon—his favorite thing, looking like a cook! Tom hoped he could reach Camp Supply in a couple of days because he was sure missing Rachel and little Johnny. He realized more and more that city life was not for him.

Tom stayed with Paul Casey and Hank Arnall at the stage stop and followed the Cimarron for quite a while, looking for a good place to cross. That military road was the safest way to go, and it was patrolled. The soldiers just waved and rode on by.

That river, like most rivers in the west, was treacherous. If it rained heavy upstream, say fifty miles, you could have a wall of water coming at you without warning. That day, the river was down, so Tom felt fairly safe as he hurriedly cross the fickle, winding woman of the West. Cowboys love water but hate rivers.

Rachel and Johnny Gail were on Tom's mind as he rode into Camp Supply. He had lost all track of time. He knew it was midsummer. Looking around, there was a lot going on.

There were American flags flying everywhere, streamers and banners of red, white, and blue decorating every building and house. He could hear a band practicing in the distance. Everywhere there was activity and excitement.

Wagons were being painted, horses groomed, and soldiers in the courtyard were marching in their dress uniforms. Even though it was blazing hot, no one seemed to mind.

The officers at Camp Supply always looked forward to a chance to celebrate and take advantage of a good time. As he approached the officer's quarters, Tom realized that this was now a full-fledged stockade with a fence completely surrounding it. It looked like the entire encampment of six hundred men were preparing for something special.

Tom wondered what was going on and then it came to him. The next day was Independence Day, July 4, 1876! His struggling republic was one hundred years old! A big lump suddenly came in his throat. He could not hold back the tears. Memories of the Civil War flooded his soul. He had lost his parents and his home, and where was his brother, John? How he longed just to hear his voice and to tell him all about his new adventures. So many men died to save the union. In the last battle where Tom fought in, over seventy thousand were killed. Even though it had been eleven years since he had fled the war, Tom knew he was a coward that could not face death one more time.

Tom was glad Camp Supply was ramping up to celebrate. He would help where he could, but he must be guarded as to not be found out and lose all that he had worked for.

There she was, more beautiful than ever, her long red hair done up in curls, tied in ribbons. She was sitting on the front porch of the captain's quarters, holding their baby. She sat there beaming at him. He could hear her say to Johnny Gale, "Look! There's your daddy!" There was his world. He jumped down from the wagon seat, threw the reins at a soldier walking by, ran up to Rachel, and kissed her in front of God and everybody.

"Why, it looks like Johnny's grown a foot! I have only been gone six weeks, and look at you, big guy!" Tom said as he led them back into the shade.

"We have missed you so much," Rachel said, hoping Tom didn't notice her sunburned face and arms.

"Did you have a safe trip? Tell me all about Dodge City. I keep hearing how dangerous it is." Rachel was full of questions and began telling him about the big party coming up the next day. Rachel was hoping and praying that he would show up in time for the festivities.

"You know, this is America's one hundredth birthday, and we are going to celebrate!"

"I'm sure glad to be here!" Tom replied, "And to be with my little family." He squeezed Rachel's hand and winked at her, noticing that her face was a little red, maybe she was just blushing.

Tom was concerned that Johnny would be a little scared of him since he hadn't seen him for a while. But there he was, squealing and reaching for his daddy; so Tom picked him up and said, "Here's my boy." Tom was so proud of him.

The captain and Mrs. Morgan soon joined them. Sally had a large pitcher of cold lemonade and a basketful of her famous sugar cookies.

Sally said, "Now, Tom, you sit down here. You've been on the trail a long while, and look at you, just melting down with the heat. Sure glad you are back for the celebration. You and your little family just plan to stay here. No need to get back to the ranch just yet."

Sally was all aglow with excitement. The four of them visited a bit. The captain pulled Tom aside and told him of an Indian uprising down at the Fort Reno area, southeast of there.

Soon, Rachel excused Tom and herself and asked Sally if she would watch little Johnny for a while. Tom was glad to get Rachel all to himself. She drew him a nice bath and washed his back. As things progressed, he pulled her into the tub on top of him. She laughed and squealed and kept saying, "Oh, Tom!" Soon, she lay in his arms on the huge four-poster bed. There were no words as he kissed her and loved her again and again.

They could hear voices below and reluctantly bathed their warm bodies with cool water and dressed for the evening. Several officers and their wives stopped by to welcome Tom home and to talk about tomorrow's festivities.

Before dawn the next day, the hustle and bustle began. The household was welcoming a new time in history. What would the next century bring? Tom's prayer was that there would be no more war.

Rachel and Johnny were dressed in fine, crisp, white cotton. Her dress swished as she walked; the skirt was red gingham with lots of petticoats. Tom donned his fine duds and polished his boots.

Black powder rounds started the day off with a bang. A parade was assembling behind the teamster's building.

Cowboy Chuckwagon of the 1800's—The Circle T brand boosted a well-equipped wagon, which set-up for lunch break after traveling about 6 hours. After another 6 hours, the herd would be rounded up for the evening and the guys would have supper. "Come and get it, before I throw it out," rang out loud and clear. 20 miles a day was average to travel with the herd. Some tobacco juice in the eyes kept a man awake if the day got too long. "Hardtack" was in charge of food and supplies such as, lanterns, water barrel, kettle, coffee pots, tarpaulin, washboard, extra wheel, pot, wash tubs, brake and boot, first-aid items, canteens, extra horseshoes, bed rolls, coffee grinder, tool box, food and necessities, such as whisky, tobacco and a Bible. To clean their clothes, many times they would spread shirts and pants over an ant den and let the ants kill the lice.

CHAPTER 18

Independence Day and Back to the Bank

A s soon as the parade was over, Captain Morgan gave a speech from the steps of the church. The chaplain gave the blessing and the largest picnic Tom had ever seen began. There were hogs roasting over an open fire pit; the smell of pork alone was enough to get a man hungry. The fragrance of roast beef, fried chicken, and fresh roasted corn on the cob filled the hot July noon. One whole table was laden with pies, cakes, and cobbler. Rachel made her famous apple pie with caramel glaze and her sourdough bread. The band continued to play as they all ate to their heart's content.

After the meal, the soldier boys lined up their favorite mounts for a lively horse race. The race ended in a tie between brothers Scott Love and his brother Steven.

Another showstopper was bronc busting. The soldiers put a bucking cinch around a young horse's flank and tried like crazy to stay on the wild, thrashing beast the best they could. They were pretty good, but Tom wished his cowboys were there to show them how it was done.

The games and rowdiness continued into the night. Someone had rigged up a dunk tank out of a horse trough. Above it was a board to sit on that would collapse when the target was hit by a ball.

They lined up for that one, mostly to be cooled off at a moment's notice. Johnny laughed whenever someone hit the water.

Tom and Rachel decided to go back to their room so Johnny could have a nap and they could get ready for the dance. Rachel put Johnny down on the cool sheets of the bed. They got rid of their dusty clothes and came together as man and wife. A somewhat cool breeze wafted over their bodies.

They fell asleep and awakened to "You newlyweds better get ready!" They figured that although they had been married nearly a year and a half, they were still the newest newlyweds at the camp. "You better git your dancin' duds on because the dance is about to start," the captain's voice filled the upstairs.

Rachel was especially beautiful that night. Her hair hung in long curls down her back, and she wore a dress that she had made out of red, white, and blue silk. She looked like a picture out of a magazine. When they danced, Tom twirled her around and around so everyone could see her. She was the belle of the ball.

Rachel said, "I want to show you a dance we danced to in Iowa."

Tom teased her about dancing with all the boys. She replied, "Sure didn't dance with any girls!" They danced up into the night. It was so much fun, and Johnny was nearby in a little cradle, just taking it all in.

Next morning, they went to chapel. It was a time of thanksgiving for their young country and their many blessings. The young chaplain challenged them, "Freedom is not free. Preserve what you have, or you will lose it."

That afternoon, upstairs, while packing for the return trip to their ranch home, Tom said, "I'm really concerned about the money that I left in the bank at Dodge City. I don't trust the banks."

Rachel commented, "I've been wondering about that myself. Do you think we should go get it?"

Tom answered, "If we're going to do it, let's go in the morning. We can go in the buggy."

Sally met Tom, Rachel, and the baby just as they reached the bottom of the stairs. "Oh, are you leaving now for the ranch?" she said as she looked like she might cry.

"No," Tom assured her. "If we could, we would like to stay a little longer."

"Oh! Good. Then Rachel can go with me to the quilting bee in the morning."

"I'm afraid I won't be able to go with you as we want to leave early for Dodge City," Rachel said as she handed Johnny to her husband.

"Why are you going to Dodge? Tom, you just got back from there," Sally remarked in a flutter. Before Tom could say anything, Rachel explained, "Tom is going to buy me a sewing machine and something special for Johnny." Tom just stood there with a dumb look on his face.

Tom spent the day in the blacksmith's shop. Rachel helped with laundry and enjoyed the day with her lady friends. The next morning after breakfast, the little family began their first trip to Dodge together.

First thing Tom said to Rachel was, "I'm glad you thought fast enough to say that I'm going to buy you a sewing machine when Sally was drilling you as to why we're going to Dodge. You know if we told her that we were going to take our money out of the bank, everyone in the country would know it before we even got there!"

Tom talked to Johnny on the trip like he was a grown man. He pointed to the place called "The Big Basin." He said, "You know, it is almost a mile across and surrounded on all sides by hills. There are still a few buffalo in the area. Not too long ago, when you looked out over the horizon, all you could see were thousands of the mighty beasts. The noise they made as they ran across the hills was deafening. They made the earth shake. They are mostly gone now. Damn shame. The buffalo was a gift from God, and it was abused.

It is a two-day, ninety-mile trip from Camp Supply to Dodge City. They had good weather, although it was hot. The dust began to blow, so they covered Johnny and his basket with a damp blanket.

About halfway to Dodge, near sundown, they arrived at the stage stop. It was manned by two men whose job it was to both hook up and unhitch the teams of horses or mules on the stagecoaches. They also provided shelter and a bite to eat for passengers. The shack was devoid of any real amenities; it contained a few pieces of hand-made furniture, two oil lamps, and a small cookstove. In dry weather, the floor was swept; in rainy times, it was just plain muddy. Hank Arnall and Paul Casey were glad to see them; the job at the stage stop was a lonely one.

"I see you've brought your missus," Hank remarked to Tom. "I remember when you brought her here from Iowa as a bride."

Tom replied, "Yes, sir. Say, we need to stay overnight. Is that possible?"

Sneaking a peek at Johnny, Paul Casey joined in, "Yes, sir. See you have a new one. Bet he's a dandy! You folks stay inside and we will bunk outside. As you can see, we have a coach here that needs repair, and we can just bunk up on top of it and maybe catch a breeze."

Rachel was still nursing Johnny. After everyone ate, they settled in for the night in a small bed that sounded like crunching leaves every time they moved. It was a good time for memories. They were tired and just happy to be together.

Next morning, they were awakened by a loud noise of horses, harnesses, and wheels coming to a stop. The stage from Dodge had arrived early, traveling all night to avoid the heat.

When Rachel climbed out of bed with Johnny in her arms, she noticed something big, dark, and heavy hanging on the wall. She asked, "What is that, and what is it made of?"

Tom replied, "That is a buffalo robe. The men wear it in the winter to keep warm."

"Oh, and look, Tom! What kind of gun is that?"

"I think that is a Colt Lightning slide-action rifle. We should feel very safe with such weapons close at hand," Tom assured her.

He watered and fed his horse before he hitched her to the buggy. Paul Casey had been busy with the new arrivals. He came over to say good-bye, and Tom handed him a generous bill to cover their night's lodging.

"Anytime, sir, anytime!" he said as he shook Tom's hand.

They headed north, northeast; the sky was clear. The crickets and June bugs were everywhere, singing to the reluctant dawn. They knew which way was east—the hot sun made itself known. Rachel sang to Johnny and Tom. Tom felt like the wealthiest man in the world. With that thought, he encouraged Babe, their flea-bitten gray, to go a little faster. Tom began to be very anxious about their money in Dodge. There were bank robbers, but it was the banker that he did not trust.

They stopped to rest in the shade of an old cottonwood near Bluff Creek. Rachel tore a piece of her petticoat, got it wet in the creek, and bathed Johnny as best she could. He had developed quite a skin rash from the heat. She would be glad to get to Dodge City and rent a real room.

Johnny was quiet, and it was good to cool off if only for a moment. It was difficult to leave the shade and the tranquility of the moment, but they had a purpose waiting for them in Dodge—that was their goal.

The hot prairie wind kicked up about noon, sending tumbleweeds across their path. Most horses would be spooked as the weird-looking spheres bounced here and there, as if they held life, but not their faithful mare, Babe.

Off to the west, Rachel spied wind and dust tangled in the air going clear up to the sky. She pointed, "What is that, Tom?"

"It's a whirlwind, but we've always called them 'dust devils,'" Tom replied. "Makes me thirsty," he said.

As Rachel handed the canteen to Tom, she asked "How much farther to Dodge City?"

"We are about two hours out," Tom replied.

It was hot. Rachel poured water on a clean rag and tried to cool her baby, hoping that the rest of the trip would go quickly.

When they pulled up in front of the Cattleman's Bank in Dodge, the three of them were tired, dusty, and thirsty.

"Let's go in and get our money," Tom said to Rachel. Tom opened the massive door for Rachel and followed her to the teller window.

"We are here to see Mr. Nickolson," Tom said with a voice so dry, it could crack.

"He is gone for the day, sir. May I help you?" replied the teller.

"Sure." Tom handed him a receipt and said, "I want my money." The teller looked at the receipt with surprise.

"Oh, Mr. Nickolson will have to handle your request, sir. He will be here tomorrow at nine o'clock sharp," he said with assurance.

Tom replied, "We will be back tomorrow at nine o'clock sharp, then. Do me a favor, and don't tell Mr. Nickolson that we were here."

"Yes, sir. I won't say a word. I'm a God-fearin' man, and I wouldn't dare go to the establishment where I know my boss holds court!" the fearful teller responded.

Tom gathered up his family, and out the door they went. "Now, let's find a room," he said as they walked to the buggy and drove the short distance to Beebe's Iowa House.

"We need a nice, quiet room for my wife, child, and myself, one away from the street noise," Tom told the clerk on duty. Tom took the key and got their luggage, and up the stairs they went. They came to a landing with a divan, a few overstuffed chairs, and a couple of tables and lamps. On that floor, there were six doors with numbers on them, another room that had kitchen facilities, and a bath making a circle around the parlor.

"Here's our room, number 2," he said, opening the door. "You two rest and freshen up. I'll be back and we will go shopping."

Tom headed for the livery stable. "Jim, it's good to see you," Tom told the liveryman. "Want to leave my horse and buggy here a night or two. Babe needs a good rubdown; feed and water her, of course. I want to leave the buggy here. We are going to buy a sewing machine, and I will have it delivered here. Please cover it with a tarp and secure it to the buggy. I'll be back after I attend to some business.

"We'll get you all fixed up, Mr. Summers," Jim replied.

Tom joined his family back at the hotel. "I'm going to show you off tonight. I've even got a young lady to watch Johnny Gail. But first, let's buy you a new dress with all the trimmings."

Next door to the Beebe's Iowa House was a ladies' dress shop called The Finery. Rachel tried on dresses, and Tom sat and held Johnny Gail and complimented her as she modeled each frock. She chose what was called "the latest fashion from New York." The silhouette was slimmer than usual and had a low neckline. As the emerald green taffeta surrounded her body and highlighted her bosom, she was a vision of loveliness. Tom suggested that she buy the matching shawl. He secretly wanted her to cover up some of that loveliness. She bought black lace boots and a velvet bag for her gloves.

Next on the list was to find Rachel a sewing machine that she would be proud of. The one she decided on was beautiful. "Look, Tom, at this wooden cabinet, and the treadle moves with one foot!"

Tom turned to the clerk and asked, "Is this a good one?"

"Yes, sir. This is the best! Mr. Singer has been improving his machine for twenty-five years."

The mercantile also had a variety of baby buggies.

"I like this one, Tom," Rachel said. "The white wicker will be cooler than the leather, and it has nice big wheels. I think this will be good for Johnny and maybe a little sister someday."

Tom asked the clerk if the sewing machine could be taken to the livery stable. "Jim knows all about what to do," he stated.

"Yes, sir. We will be glad to do that for you; anything else for you and the missus?"

"Yes," Tom replied. "My wife wants to pick out material and some sewing supplies. I will be back soon. Rachel, after I find the boys and give them my orders, we will go back to our room and get ready for a night on the town."

Rachel placed Johnny in the buggy with his blanket; he loved it. She then went about selecting denim for shirts and calico for aprons, buttons, and a lot of thread. She was so excited, she said, "I can hardly wait to return home and start sewing. I want to make gifts for everyone for Christmas!"

"You are a very lucky woman to have a husband who loves you so much." the clerk said.

"One more item, please," Rachel mentioned. "I need a leather sachet and I'll take it with me."

Tom returned, a bit impatient. "How much to do I owe you? Please deliver all this to the livery stable. Come on, Rachel, let's get you prettied up for tonight. I have a surprise for you."

"What's the surprise, Tom? All day has been like Christmas! What now?"

"You'll have to wait until after dinner. We had better hurry, though," Tom replied.

On their way to the room, Tom told Rachel about his experience at the bar.

"I found my boys and asked them to return to the ranch. Robert will be heading out after he picks up supplies. The rest will retrieve the horses from the pasture south of town and head towards home with them," he said.

As they crossed the street, Tom continued his story. "While I was sitting at the bar, I overheard two ladies chatting with each other. One said, 'Which one of us is going to service ol' moneybags tonight?'

"'You mean Mr. Nickolson?' the second lady replied. 'Yes, I hope it's me because he always pays more than anyone else.'

"'Yeah, he even smells like money,' said the second lady."

"That's interesting," Rachel replied to Tom. "I'm glad we came to Dodge for our money when we did."

"Me too," Tom said. "Now, let's try to forget him and have some fun this evening. I love you!" Tom exclaimed even though his heart was heavy with worry.

After a fine meal of lobster and steak with all the trimmings, Tom reached for Rachel's hand. "Do you want to go have some more fun?"

"Yes!" Rachel giggled. Tom reached over and kissed her and said, "We are going to the opera house and laugh all night with Eddie Foy!" All eyes were upon the handsome couple when they stood to leave as Tom helped Rachel with her shawl.

Later that night in the hotel, Rachel lay in his arms with the moonlight softly sifting through the window. Johnny Gail was sleeping soundly in the buggy. Next thing Tom knew, it was morning and time to go to the bank!

They dressed early and killed time; neither of them wanted breakfast. Finally, at fifteen minutes until nine, they walked to the bank. Tom walked up to the teller and asked to see the bank's owner, Mr. Jim Nickolson.

He replied, "He is not here yet. Please have a seat."

Thirty minutes later, the banker appeared, walked over to the teller, and whispered in his ear.

The only response Tom heard was "All of it?" as his face turned chalky white. As Mr. Nickolson approached them, his demeanor quickly changed.

"Good morning, folks. Why, you must be the beautiful Mrs. Summers." He knew who Tom was from previous dealings.

"And what a handsome child," he said as he grinned from ear to ear.

"Tom, you ought to be glad you sold your cattle when you did. You know the price has dropped $1.50 a head; it's even worse in Abilene."

With that, Tom said, "Let's go into your office. We have business to conduct."

"Yes, yes. Please step right in. Have a seat. Would you like a cool drink of water, Mrs. Summers?" Mr. Nickolson inquired.

"No, thank you" was her reply.

Tom began, "I don't trust you or your bank. I want my money now. Here is my receipt."

Mr. Nickolson looked at the receipt and responded, "Now, Mr. Summers, surely we can work something out. You've been one of our best customers for a long time."

"I know," said Tom. "Please get my money together."

The banker looked to Rachel as if to ask for help. "Are you and your family leaving the country? I hope nothing is wrong."

"The only thing wrong is that you don't seem to understand that we want all of our money and we want it now," Tom jumped in sarcastically.

"Now, young man, don't get upset. We don't have that kind of money in the bank right now. We are probably a few thousand dollars short, but we can get it for you in a week or so."

Tom, who had his Colt .45 on his side, tapped the handle and said, "I don't care if the bank doesn't have the money. It's up to you to get it."

"Well," the man behind the desk stammered, "it's going to take me a while to get your money." With that, he put on his hat and coat and was gone for over an hour. When he returned, he said, "It's here. It's all here."

Tom watched closely as Jim Nickolson and the frightened teller began to count the paper money. When they finished counting, the banker reported, "Yes, yes, that's it! Every bit of it!"

The teller's face fell even further south. Tom jumped in as he had been counting also. "You are three thousand short! You have been shorting some stacks by a hundred or more. We are going to have a recount. This time, only the teller and I count," Tom demanded.

The old man, whose living was counting, could hardly speak, as he was so nervous. Tom kept his coat open so all could see his .45 shining in the noonday sun.

The teller spoke, "Yes, sir. We need three more thousand dollars. That's . . . that's right, isn't it, Mr. Nickolson, sir?"

"Okay, okay, you miscounted the first time. That's reason to lose your job. Gather up your coat, hat and that stinkin' lunch box and get out of here!" the pompous banker bellowed.

The banker, thinking he was in control, remarked, "Now, Tom, you and the missus just come back tomorrow and we will have all of your money," as he began to gather up the piles of money.

"Stop everything," Tom warned as he caressed the holster of his gun and continued. "You don't understand. We are not leaving this bank until we have all of our money in cash or gold!"

The scared banker covered with, "Oh, you will accept gold? No problem! You wait here, and I will return with your three thousand in gold."

"In the meantime, that money stays on the desk until you get back," Tom demanded. "You'd better hurry!"

With the one teller gone, the bank was left with only one man to wait on everyone. Some of the customers became unruly, impatient for service.

"I'll just take my money to the bank down the street," one cowboy muttered as he stomped out of the bank.

After what seemed like an eternity, the banker returned about closing time with whiskey on his breath. "Here we go, young-uns', just what you need," the old thieving banker extorted. "I've got some fine gold watches, a watch fob, chains, rings, and some old gold coins. I promise you, this is worth more than three thousand dollars."

Neither Tom nor Rachel fell for the "promise" part, but they realized that they were becoming part of a dangerous situation.

"Okay," Tom demanded. "I want you to write me a receipt stating that you have paid me in cash and gold totaling the full amount of my balance. Date it and sign it. I don't want you coming after me saying I robbed your bank!"

Jim poured out the withdrawal on bank stationery with the letterhead at the top: "Your Cattleman's Bank—We are here to help you. Dodge's Finest, James Nickolson, President."

Tom picked up his sachet and filled it with cash and gold and then adjusted his revolver.

Nickolson could not leave well enough alone and boasted, "You'll have a hard time holdin' on to that."

Tom reached for his pistol and responded by placing the barrel against the banker's forehead, "Nobody better try to take it from me."

Rachel covered her baby's head with his blanket, and out the door they went, almost running.

"I couldn't wait to get out of there, Tom. I am so proud of you. Thank God, all went well!" she exclaimed.

When the couple reached the hotel, Tom asked the clerk to send up some fruit and lemonade. They climbed the stairs, so relieved and thankful.

"You know, Rachel, this is our life's savings."

"Yes, Tom. You have worked hard and saved, but we are not out of danger yet. I am going to divide the money, put some in pockets in my petticoat, some in my shoes, and I am going to make a mattress to put in the buggy under Johnny for the rest of it. I will sew the jewelry onto a belt under my dress."

"What are we going to do with the sachet that the money is in now?" Tom asked.

"That will be our decoy, just in case," Rachel said as she got busy sewing. Suddenly, there was a knock at the door. Rachel hurriedly covered what she was doing.

"Oh! It's the food," Tom said as he paid the errand boy and brought the tray into the room.

"You go ahead and eat. I want to finish this," Rachel replied. She quickly ripped up part of her petticoat and fashioned the pieces into pockets that were sewn back onto her petticoat. She stuffed the hundred-dollar bills tightly into each one and sewed them shut.

"Tom, I need your belt," she called.

Tom asked, "How am I going to keep my pants up?" as he handed over his worn leather belt. Rachel ignored his questions and used lace from her corset to bind the jewelry to Tom's belt and put the belt around her waist. She took a pillowcase from a pillow and stuffed it with cash and then sewed it shut. By covering it with a blanket and her baby, no one would be the wiser.

"Now I'm ready for dinner. Where are you going to take us tonight?" Rachel was feeling giddy after all of the excitement.

"We'll go to the Dodge house. I hear they have good food" was Tom's answer.

They carefully carried John Gail, his buggy, and its hidden contents down the long flight of stairs. "I look kind of fat around my middle, don't I, Tom—with the extra padding?" Rachel questioned her husband.

"Come on, you look cute" was his answer.

They enjoyed a dinner of pasta, cheese, and the best cheesecake ever, but it took them longer than they anticipated. Over a glass of red wine, Rachel reminded Tom that they had to get up early in the morning.

"This afternoon was quite stressful. I'm glad to be here with you and just relax, but yes, we must go and get ready for our return trip," Tom said as he paid the bill.

They stopped at the hotel's registry and paid up telling the clerk they will leave tomorrow, careful not to give any details. Again, they carried the buggy up the stairs, being careful not to awaken their baby boy.

"It's good to be back in our room. I'm really tired," Rachel said. When she entered the room, however, she let out a scream. Everything in their room was in disarray: the dresser drawers were

172

all open, the mattress was ripped apart, chairs were turned upside down, and feathers from the pillows were floating around the room as they moved toward their luggage. Their clothes were tossed like dead animals on the floor.

"The sachet is gone, Tom, the sachet is gone!"

"No, honey, I put it under the buckboard seat as a decoy, like you said," Tom told her.

"What shall we do? We can't sleep here. What if they came back?" Rachel pleaded with Tom.

"I don't think they will come back. They pretty much ripped this place apart and didn't find anything. I'm sure they were looking for the money, and I'm sure ol' Jim is behind it. You wait here, and I'll find us another room," Tom told Rachel.

"Oh no, you're not leaving my side. We are going with you!" Rachel demanded.

They gathered up what belongings they could find, put them in their suitcases, and quietly headed downstairs. Tom had his .45 drawn as his feet gingerly found each creaking step.

Rachel remembered the handgun that she bought the day before. It was strapped to her thigh, just above her knee. She reached for it, just in case.

Tom was in the lead; the only light came from the coal oil lamps on the wall. A moth flew by and startled Rachel. She dropped her end of the buggy and Johnny Gail woke up. He cooed a little and went back to sleep.

"In here," Tom said, "in here."

The frightened family stepped inside a storage room.

"Wait here while I get a lantern from the hall. Okay. That's better. We will stay here for the rest of the night," Tom said after lifting the light from its holder.

Rachel quickly placed blankets from the storage shelves on the wall and made a pallet for them both to lie down on. Rachel lay behind Tom, clutching his body. Baby Johnny slept the sleep of an innocent child as he lay in the buggy. The scared parents heard every sound of the city, it seemed. Laughing couples began to arrive in their rooms. Riders on horseback were leaving town, and the cattle were bawling from the cattle pens.

Neither Tom nor Rachel slept much. Tom decided to get up and pulled away from Rachel and whispered in her ear, "I'm going to go get the horse hitched to our buggy. I will tap on the door when I get back." He looked at his newly acquired gold watch, and to his surprise, it read three o'clock.

"Tom, be sure and fill the canteens with water. I've got beef jerky to hold us over until we reach the stage stop," Rachel whispered back. "I'll be ready." She kissed him and then said, "Please be careful."

Tom quietly opened the storage door and proceeded down the hallway in the dark. Some of the coal oil lamps had burned out, leaving a sickening smell mingled with too many cigars. Someone had cranked the Victrola and it was playing "Auld Lang Syne" one more time.

All was well until Tom stepped on a cat's tail and nearly fell through the screen door that he was about to open. "The cat probably alerted everyone within three blocks of the hotel," Tom thought to himself. He walked in the shadows of the building with his hand on his holster until he came upon the livery stable. He saw Babe, but she was not hitched up to the buggy yet.

Jim, the liveryman, heard Tom and called out, "I'll be right there. You're a bit early."

"Yes," Tom replied. "But we need an early start." They harnessed Babe in the moonlight. Jim warned Tom that the toll bridge would not be open for two more hours.

"We'll just go around it," Tom replied as he reached in his pocket. "This will cover what I owe you, and keep quiet about where I'm heading."

Jim shook his head and said to Tom, "How can I tell anybody where you went when I don't know?"

Through side streets, Tom carefully led Babe back to the Iowa House. He fastened the reins to a tree, entered through the screen door, feeling for the cat this time, and tapped lightly on the storage door. Slowly, he opened the door. In the dim light, he saw that Rachel had a gun pointed at him.

"Honey, it's me, Tom," he quickly stammered. "Are you ready? And where did you get that gun!"

"You bought it for me yesterday. I just didn't tell you," she answered.

Rachel handed Tom the suitcases and pushed the baby buggy with Johnny in it down the hall and outside as Tom opened the door for her. "Let me help you."

Tom gave her a hand as she climbed into the buggy, petticoat and all. Tom placed the suitcase under the buckboard seat, where he'd placed the sachet the night before. After giving the baby to Rachel, he placed the baby buggy between them.

"Now we're ready to travel," Tom said.

Rachel cradled her baby, offered him her breast, and fed him. Her main thought was to keep him quiet as they left town.

The moon slipped behind a cloud as Tom turned to the left on Front Street. Rachel pointed out softly, "Is this the wrong way to the toll bridge?"

"Yes, it is," he replied. "It is closed for the night, so we will cross the river where we forded it with the cattle two weeks ago. We will cross right after we reach the stockyard."

A large campfire burning on the other side of the Arkansas River helped to guide the fleeing family. Tom skillfully drove Babe in the direction they needed to go. Even though the water was lower, a running river is a great deceiver.

They reached the other shore after a safe but bumpy ride.

Rachel, very much relieved, said, "I hope we don't do this again. I was scared."

"So was I," Tom replied.

They made about ten miles before sunup. "If anyone is after us, this will give us a good head start. By the way, do you know how to use that gun?" Tom asked.

"Yes, sir! I sure do!" Rachel said with a grin.

By now the morning sun was burning holes in the sky. Tom pulled his mare to a stop under a large cottonwood tree.

"I'm going to feed Babe some of the oats I bought from Jim. Maybe we can find some water down that gully," Tom said, helping Rachel down from the buggy.

"Sure feels good to stretch my legs," she replied, checking her sewing machine to make sure it was still intact.

"We need a good rain to cool things off. I can't find any water, so I'll give Babe some of ours," Tom said.

After resting themselves and Babe, Tom stood up. "It's going to take us a little longer to get back to Camp Supply because this buggy is heavy, so let's load up," Tom said.

As far as the eye could see, there was only flat, dry, unforgiving land. One mistake could be your last. There were only a few trees scattered to break the landscape. Sagebrush dotted the hills. The heat shimmered on the parched, cracked earth. Buzzards hovered in the distance—not a good sign.

"The best part is that we're together and my city girl can shoot a gun!" Tom said with a chuckle.

"Just how much money did you sew into that pillowcase that has become Johnny's mattress?" Tom asked Rachel.

"Exactly ten thousand dollars," was Rachel's response.

Tom replied, "I want to remember that so when Johnny is old enough, I can tell him that he was not born with a silver spoon in his mouth but that he slept on a ten-thousand-dollar mattress!"

In the distance, they saw the halfway stage stop, or was it a mirage? They were tired and thirsty as the midafternoon sun showed no mercy.

Hank and Paul could see them coming and ran out to meet them.

"We are sure glad to see you. Here, have a drink of water. You look wornout from your trip," Paul said to Rachel.

"Thank you," she said and passed the canteen on to Tom after she took a long drink.

"You and your family are getting to be regular customers," Hank chimed in.

Tom replied, "I sure hope you two can put us up again."

To which Paul said, "We'd be proud to have you! Here you go, Mrs. Summers. We'll help you and the little one out of the buggy."

"Yes, thank you," she replied. "Please bring the baby's carriage also."

As the men unharnessed Babe, Tom asked if they could put the buggy in the barn behind the stage-stop building.

"Yes," the two men replied.

"Do we need to hide it?" Paul asked.

"Yes." Tom explained that there could be trouble. Both men assured Tom that if there were trouble, they would help in every way.

"We don't want any harm to come to you or your family," Hank assured them again.

The night before in Dodge City, Jim Nickolson was at the Variety. And as was his custom, he was drinking and flirting with the ladies. But he acted differently, pushing the women back and asking, "Where is Sam, my man, and his sidekick, Issy?" He grabbed the bartender's arm and demanded, "You tell me where Sam is, and tell me now!"

"There they are. They just walked in," Cliff said and pulled his arm away.

"Well," the irate banker barked, "well, did you get the money?" As the two men leaned on the bar, Jim said, "Did you find that rancher and get the money like I told you?"

"No!" Sam finally answered. "We found out what room he was in, busted in through the door, and opened fire. Then we realized we were only shooting pillows under a blanket."

"Yes, I heard the shots, but what did you find in the room?"

Sam replied, "Nothing. We tore the place apart. The moneybag you talked about was not there."

"Where is it?" Jim shouted.

"Do not know," muttered Issy. "I need a drink." He continued. "We need another bottle."

"No!" Jim replied. "You two are drunk enough!"

Jim looked Sam square in the eyes, "I told you that if you did what I said and you got my money back and took care of that fancy rancher that I would see to it that the marshal would not find out about the preacher and his wife that you murdered last week. I'm sure Earp would love to hear all the gory details! So you sober up and, at first light, check and see if their buggy is still at the livery. If it's gone, you head for the stage stop south of town. And take your no-good friend with you."

Jim stood up, trying to look important. "I've got some personal business upstairs with Alice," he said. "You come back with that money, or the next hangin' in town will be yours."

As the banker disappeared upstairs, Issy told Sam, "You may have to do Jim's bidding for him, but I don't. This rancher fellow is tougher than you think, so you are goin' this alone. Besides, the gold fields of Colorado are calling my name." And with that, Issy got up and walked out the door.

Sam called out, "Issy, you're a sissy. I don't need your help anyway."

Sam proceeded to drink until he passed out. The bartender woke him up at sunup when he and his helper were cleaning up the saloon.

Sam woke with a start, cussed, and left in a hurry to where he figured the buggy would be. Not finding it, he saddled up and hurried to the toll bridge just as it was opening for business. "Has there been a man and woman came through here in a buggy this morning?" Sam asked the owner of the bridge.

"Hell no! Can't you see I'm just opening up now?"

Sam paid the dime toll and spurred his mount across the river bridge, thinking, "I've got to get that money back or I'm dead meat."

The seasoned thief nursed the bottle of whiskey he'd grabbed as he left the Variety Saloon. He was so full of artificial courage that he could barely sit in his saddle. After several near-miss accidents, he found the stage stop as dusk settled over the land. A quick but violent rainstorm had passed through, making the air muggy.

With the boldness of the booze speaking, he rode up to the soddy that housed the stage stop. He shouted out to the elusive rancher, "Come out and bring your moneybag with you, or I will come in and get it."

Tom whispered to his friends, "Let's shoot under his horse and see if that will get him bucked off."

Just as Sam took another sip of courage, the three men opened fire from their hiding places.

Sam hit the ground with a thud, holding his precious whiskey bottle high in the air. All three of his enemies were on him like fleas, and Tom took his still holstered .45 before he could move.

"What should we do now, kill this son of a bitch? I hate drunken thieves!" Hank exclaimed.

"No," Tom said, "let's tie him to his horse and send him back to Dodge. I'll put his feet and stirrups together and tie them under his horse."

Tom took the precious bottle with the last few drops of hooch in it. As Tom started to throw the bottle into the rocks, Sam cried, "No, please don't break my bottle. All I wanted was your moneybag and the money you stole from the bank." As the bottle hit the rocks, Tom said, "Tie his hands to the saddle horn."

Tom went into the soddy, brought out the bag, and showed it to him. "Look, you fool. It's full of baby toys."

Tom was angry now. "You go back and tell your lyin' banker friend that I'm filing charges with Earp against you and Nickolson for attempted robbery. If I ever have any more trouble of any kind out of you, I'll get my drovers and burn his bank down with you in it!"

With that, Tom pointed Sam and his horse toward Dodge, slapped him on the rump, and did a little shouting for good measure. What a strange sight as horse and man became one, riding over the horizon.

"Boy, I'm glad that's over. I hope things will quiet down now, and maybe we can have some supper," Tom said as he ran over to where Rachel and Johnny were hiding. He opened the door of the root cellar and said, "You can come out now. Trouble is gone."

"Are you all right?" Tom's anxious wife asked.

"Yes, we're all fine."

"We're fine but hungry," Tom continued. Paul came to the rescue. "I will rustle up some supper for us."

Rachel followed him and said, "I will help."

"I killed a rabbit right before this ruckus. It is soaking here in saltwater," Paul said. "Good!" replied Rachel. "I will fry that rabbit and make gravy. Why don't you peel some potatoes?"

"Best meal I ever ate," Hank remarked.

"Yes, we wish Rachel could be here all the time and brighten up the place. We might even let her cook too!" Paul joked with Tom.

As they finished their supper, the southbound stage arrived. The driver, Ron Love, and the shotgun rider, James Langdon, jumped down, and the two passengers climbed out of the coach.

Ron said, "I see you have a full house, so James and I will sleep on the ground. We have our bedrolls."

Tom did not recognize the first man to climb out of the stage-coach, a big, burly Mexican. As the second man appeared, Tom reacted, "Why, that's you, Ned Legg. Why in the world are you riding the stage?"

Ned looked up in surprise and replied, "I lost it all."

Tom took him aside and asked, "What do you mean?"

"Remember when you left me at the Variety, I decided I would try my luck at poker? We played awhile and I got a really good hand, but this gambler kept raising every bet I made. He sure was smooth. I lost all of the money I had on me, my horse, and worst of all, my saddle. I'd rather take a beating than give up my saddle."

"What kind of hand did you have?" Tom asked Ned, "if I may ask."

"I had a full house: three kings and two queens," answered Ned, "but the gambler had four aces."

"What are you going to do now?" Tom asked the embarrassed man.

"I know my wife will skin me alive, but I still have my ranch lease and my cowherd. The horses should still be there. I am glad my two sons did not stay to see it happen. It will be bad enough to have to tell them. I know my gambling days are over."

Tom inquired, "Are you going to try to stick it out on the ranch?"

"Yes," Ned said. "I think I can make it through the winter. I did it the first year we were here, and we can do it again!"

The driver interrupted the conversation. "You men grab a bite to eat. We are going to load up and travel the night to Camp Supply. We will beat the heat that way."

"Okay," Tom instructed Ned. "When you get to Camp Supply, go see Bill the blacksmith. Give him this note and ask him if you can sleep in the shop, and maybe he will feed you breakfast."

"Stay there until we arrive, and I will help you get home," Tom told his friend.

"Thank you, Tom, thank you. I really appreciate this," Ned replied.

The travelers climbed aboard, and away they went into the night.

As Tom and Rachel settled in for the evening, Tom explained to her about what happened to their neighbor, Ned.

"What can we do to help?" she asked.

"I have been thinking about that. Why don't we let Ned drive our cook wagon from the blacksmith shop back to our ranch, then I could loan him a horse to continue on to his place," Tom said.

Rachel thought a little more before replying. "You know, Tom, we could have lost our savings there in Dodge City, but we were looked down on from Above. Why don't we loan Ned the money he needs? He can pay us back next year when he sells his cattle."

Rachel continued, "Do you think we should go with him as he faces his wife and family? They may not understand."

"We will see," Tom answered. "We had a big day. I love you."

"I love you too," Rachel whispered as her husband began to snore.

Tom woke up to the smell of bacon and the sounds of the morning. "We have had this rooster here for weeks. We don't know where he came from, but he makes a good alarm clock. Hank wondered whether to keep him as a pet or turn him into chicken and dumplings."

Paul chimed in, "I go with the latter," grinning as he enjoyed the fine breakfast Rachel had prepared.

"Bet you are proud of your windmill," Tom said to the two men as they watered the horses.

"Yes, the stage company put the well and windmill in a year ago. Now we don't have to carry water from Jacob's well, which is nearly a mile east over yonder at the top of the basin."

While the men harnessed Babe to the buggy, Rachel bathed Johnny and packed a lunch out of the leftover bacon and biscuits. She carefully packed the sand-plum jelly that her new friends gave her.

"Now if anyone noses around looking for me, just tell 'em that I kept talking about the road that leaves the military road westerly to Meade, Kansas," Tom said.

"Sounds good to me," Paul replied.

"Thank you again for helping us in a time of need and for putting us up for the night again."

Tom tipped his hat, and they began their way to Camp Supply.

"The Cimarron River is up ahead of us. I'm going to stop and make sure everything is tied down good and tight," Tom said. Just as he was walking back to the back of his buggy, he noticed a rider coming, hell-bent for election from the north.

Tom called to Rachel, "Get down and stay down." Rachel reached for her small gun, holding Johnny close to her breast. Tom paused and placed his hand on his .45, waiting for the rider to identify himself. "It's Robert! Thank God, it's Robert," Tom called out in a loud voice. "Don't worry. No trouble this time."

Robert pulled up close to the buggy and stopped short. He dismounted, hugged Rachel, and kissed Johnny.

Tom said, "It looks like you miss them more than you do me."

Robert laughed and said, "That's for sure."

"It's sure good to see you," Tom told his foreman. "We have a lot to tell you, but let's keep it 'til we get to Camp Supply."

Tom and Robert were busy checking the ropes when Rachel heard a strange and scary sound. She leaned around and saw a coiled rattlesnake threatening to strike. It was between Tom and Robert, about three feet behind them.

"Don't move!" Rachel cried out. In one swift movement, Rachel grabbed her gun, aimed, and pulled the trigger, blowing the head off the deadly serpent.

Tom fainted; he dropped like a rock. Rachel and Robert rushed to his side. As he was coming to, he saw the blood on the rocks from the snake and thought it was his own.

"I can't . . . I can't believe you shot me," Tom sputtered.

"I didn't," Rachel answered, holding back a giggle, "I killed the snake. Now, come on. Let's go home," Rachel said as she helped him get up.

Johnny began to cry, and even Babe was unnerved.

"How did you learn to shoot like that?" was all that Tom could think of to say.

"I will tell you someday. Besides, someone has to take care of my men!" was his wife's reply.

Now on the trail, Robert began a conversation. "Have I ever got something to tell you, and it can't wait!" Robert exclaimed.

"Go ahead! What is it?" Rachel and Tom said together.

"I saw the strangest sight on the north side of the stage stop. I met a man whose feet were tied together under his horse. His hands were tied to the saddle horn. He was screaming and cussing as his horse sped by me."

"Did you try to stop him and untie him?" Tom warily inquired.

"No, he was too busy cussin' for anyone to help him."

"Hmmm," he said, "you never know what you're going to see out here on the plains," Tom remarked.

They approached the river. Tom asked Robert to stay with them until they made a safe crossing. Always in the back of his mind was the memory of the ball of black snakes when he was a young man, nearly killing him.

Now in a different place and a different time, another woman saved his life. Tom asked himself, "What is my destiny? What is the reason for my being here?"

Then Tom remembered his friend, Ned, who was waiting for him at Camp Supply.

"Robert, you will find a man named Ned Legg at the black-smith's shop. See what you can do to help him; we will arrive as soon as possible. We will be at the captain's house for the night."

When they pulled up in front of the two-story residence, Sally Ann came running out, full of questions.

"How are you? How's my baby? Did you get your sewing machine?"

"Yes, we are all good but tired," Rachel began. "But how did you know we would be here this evening?"

"Oh, Mr. Robert came by. He told us. You know, he's a good-looking man. Are you hungry? We have a lovely roast beef ready and waiting on you. I cannot wait to see your sewing machine! What kind is it? Did you buy a Singer? Oh, I talk too much, but I want to hear all about your trip. Did you see any shows? Any dance-hall girls? Oh, I want to go to Dodge City so badly, but my husband says it is no place for a lady. I told him Rachel went, and here she is, all safe, and sound. No problems."

"Thank you, both, for a wonderful meal," Tom said as he excused himself from the table. "I need to find Ned Legg and my foreman, Robert," he continued. "I will be back in a little while," he said.

He found the two men at the blacksmith's shop with his friend Bill the blacksmith. "Sure glad to see you, Tom," Robert said. "Ned here has been telling me his troubles. I told him not to worry, that we would all work together on this problem."

"Yes," agreed Tom. "Rachel and I want to help Ned get back on his feet."

"In the morning, Robert, I want you and Ned to take the chuck wagon and my horse back to our ranch. Rachel and I will follow in our buggy." Tom began to give more instructions when an odd-shaped metal box caught his eye.

"Bill, what kind of box is that over there?"

The blacksmith replied, "That box was once used to hold forging tools. Now I use it for trash."

"Could I talk you out of it?" Tom asked. "I'll trade it for one of Mrs. Summers's blackberry pies next time you're here." Bill replied.

"That's a deal!" Tom said.

He carried his newly acquired treasure to the chuck wagon, told everyone good night, and headed back to the officer's row. Rachel had just finished nursing Johnny and was putting him to bed.

"How is Ned doing?" asked Rachel.

"I think he will be all right. He and Robert are going to leave out in the morning for the ranch, and we will follow them." Tom replied.

"I will pack a lunch. Sally Ann will probably let us have some leftover roast and fresh bread," Rachel said.

They all got an early start to avoid the heat of the day. Later that day, they stopped to let the horse, Babe, drink and rest a bit. They enjoyed their "little picnic," as Rachel called it.

"Boy, this is sure better than when I was cook on the cattle drive," Tom stated.

"You bet," Robert chimed in.

"Now, it wasn't that bad!" said Tom, defending himself.

"No, it was worse!" Robert laughed. "We have had some good times on our drives and some not so good," he went on to tell Rachel a couple of stories that he figured she had never heard from Tom. Ned chimed in with "You all are a funny bunch!"

The note was still on the door when they arrived at home. There was another note from a family that had taken their welcome and thanked them for their hospitality.

"We humbly thank you for the comfort of your home. Our little girl, Eve, fell off our wagon. She cried all night, and by morning, she was gone. We buried her on top of the bluff behind the corrals. May God bless you and yours."

The sad note revealed the heartbreak of a traveling family.

"Oh, Tom, look! They left this beautiful rocking chair!" Rachel said sadly. There in the living room it sat, empty of mother and the child that had once loved it.

Robert and Ned helped unload the buggy. "Where do you want the sewing machine, Mrs. Summers?" Ned asked.

Robert asked, "What is this old iron box for?" as he lugged the beat-up, old box onto the porch.

"I will tell you later," Tom answered. "Let's hit the hay early tonight," he replied wearily.

Over breakfast the next day, Ned asked Tom what needed to be done. Tom frowned. "What do you mean?"

Ned replied, "I want to help with the work around here to repay you for your hospitality."

"We appreciate that very much, but we think you need to get on back to your place," Tom explained.

"Robert, I would like for you to saddle up and check cattle; we have been gone a long time," Tom added.

"Ned," Tom continued, "Rachel and I have talked this over and we want to help."

Ned responded, "I need all the help I can get after the foolish stunt I pulled."

Tom suggested, "Take my horse, Ranger, and my saddle, and start for home—"

Ned, interrupting, said, "But that's your horse and saddle!"

"The boys will be back with my herd of horses in a week or two. I will have a horse then, so take him," Tom stated.

"Okay, but I'm not taking your saddle. I will ride bareback," Ned replied. "And I promise to return Ranger as soon as I can."

Rachel spoke up and told Ned that they were willing to go with him. "Also, Tom and I want to loan you enough money to make it through the winter."

To this, Ned replied, "No need for you two to go. I will work this out with my family, but much obliged. As for the money, I do not know how much it will take. My wife handles things like that. Hopefully, she and I can work this out. Thank you again. I will take good care of Ranger and bring him back soon."

Ned shook Tom's hand, hugged Rachel, picked up Johnny, and said, "You have the best parents in the whole Outlet." Ned bridled Ranger, jumped on his back, and took off north by northeast.

Turning to Rachel, Tom said, "Sweetheart, I finally have you alone, but we have work to do."

"We need to find a place to hide the money," Rachel told her husband.

"Yes, yes," Tom replied as he ran out onto the porch. "Look what I found!"

When he brought it into the house, Tom said, "It even has a lid, and I think it will be the right size to hold all of the money and the gold." Tom walked over to the fireplace and pried a large rock away, leaving a hole. He placed the box in the hole. "It just fits!"

"Oh, Tom, you are so smart." Rachel praised him. "We need to leave some money out for expenses. I could hide some in the bedroom in one of the small sewing drawers in my machine. That would be handy."

Tom gathered up the money that they had put under the mattress overnight for safety, put it in the box, and closed the lid. "You know," Tom said, "this box is so strong, fire would not even bother it."

"Okay, that's good, but you forgot to give me some of the smaller bills," Rachel reminded Tom.

He filled the box with as much money as he could, wedged the box into the hole, and covered it with a large stone. "No one will ever know it's there," he said as he handed her some cash.

Robert returned about sundown. He said he did not cover all of the ranch, but he was able to find seven hundred of the thousand head of cows in the herd. Tom said, "That's good; we will get a more complete count when the boys return."

Late in the morning, Jim Nickolson was in his office at the bank, checking the books. He was sweating so profusely that beads of sweat dropped onto the ledger. He found out that if he did not retrieve the money that Tom Summers withdrew, he would be broke and would have to shut the bank down. In his mind, he reconciled that as soon as Sam got back with the money and gold, everything would be all right. Jim planned to give Sam a hundred dollars, forget about squealing on him, and send him out of Dodge. Then the bank and his life would get back to normal, or as best as it could be.

On his way to the café to get a bite to eat, he heard laughing and cussing at the livery stable. There was Sam, tied to his horse, cussing everyone around him, begging to be cut loose. Several hecklers were laughing at him. Jim ran over and cut Sam loose. "What happened to you?" the anxious banker inquired.

Sam answered, "That no-good rancher got the drop on me and tied me up this way! He must have had twenty men holed up, waiting for me. I didn't have a chance!"

"I suppose you didn't get the money, then, you wimpy, no-good loser!" Jim took him by the arm and led him away as the crowd dispersed.

"I didn't get the money. I didn't even see it," Sam repeated himself. "I bet he put that money in another bank in town, Jim." Sam desperately begged his boss, "Don't hurt me, please, don't hurt me."

Banker Jim realized the fix he was in and told Sam to calm down. "You will be all right here behind the stable. I'm going to get a jug and we will figure this out."

Sam responded with, "Good, I'm sure dry," as he drank his fill from the horse trough. Jim returned quickly with a jug of whiskey he bought on credit, for he was broke.

He proceeded to get Sam drunk in no time. When he passed out, the thieving banker helped himself to the money in Sam's pocket. Jim then hurried to the Variety Saloon. He asked for Alice, his regular lady of the evening. When she got him alone in her room and started to undress, she put her arms around him in a provocative way, kissed him, and said, "You know I love you, but when will you pay me back the ten thousand dollars and the gold you borrowed from me, Jim, sweetheart?"

Kissing her neck, Jim quickly replied, "Tomorrow, as soon as the bank opens."

"Oh, Jim! Thank you. That is the money I've saved to open my own business. I keep a stash hidden under a loose board, right here under my bed."

"Good idea," the banker acknowledged. "Now come here and give me some lovin'."

"Do you love me?" Alice asked her lover.

"Of course I do, just trust me," Jim mumbled, taking control. After a few minutes, as she slipped into sweet surrender, Jim brutally clasped his hands around her neck and strangled the life from her. He quickly arranged the bedcovers to make it look as if she was sleeping. He got dressed and slid the bed to the side. There it was, Alice's secret hiding place. "Hmm, not much money here, but it will buy me a train ticket," Jim said, relieved that he had some cash.

"Thanks, darlin'," he smirked as he checked one more time to make sure Alice was dead. He closed the door behind him, not realizing he left his prized fedora on the dresser in the room, and rushed down the stairs. Marshall Wyatt Earp just happened to be standing at the bottom of the stairs, their eyes met, Earp laughed and quipped "Did you get all you wanted?"

He replied, "Yes, I did, and Alice did too. By the way, Sam is passed out behind the livery stable. You should question him about the death of Reverend Reams and his wife. You will find the preacher's saddle in Sam's shack, down by the river. The marshal thanked Jim and headed out the swinging doors toward the stable.

Banker Jim headed for his room and packed a duffel bag to make his escape.

He wanted to go back to the bank and get some checks out of the drawer, but fear took over and instead, he headed for the train station. "I hope no one sees me buying a ticket; if they do, I will just tell them I am on important banking business," he said to himself. Seeing the westbound train at the station, he hurried to buy a ticket. The Iron Horse, as some called it, was loaded up with coal and water for the long trip to Pueblo, Colorado. Jim boarded the train, trying to blend in with the crowd, until a young lad who was skipping along the aisle dropped his lollipop onto the lap of the now-much-disgusted banker.

The conductor said, "Here, sir, let me help you. Aren't you Mr. Nickolson, the banker? My mother banks with you here in Dodge City. I bet you know her. Her name is Mrs. Coyle."

"Yes, very nice lady" he said as he reached for his hat. Suddenly, he realized that he had left his hat in the dead girl's room. He knew if he got off the train to retrieve his hat, he might be found out, and even if he was not arrested, he had no more money for another ticket.

Long Branch Saloon—Photo of The Longbranch Saloon in Dodge City Kansas, in the Boot Hill Musuem. This is where many cow hands celebrated after a long cattle drive. Recently this is where Ted Riddle, the author, celebrated with Adam Mc Elwain, the bartender and Ash-Leigh Drake, Miss Kitty. Photo by Linda Riddle

CHAPTER 19

Life at the Ranch: Gets Back to Normal?

The clouds were gathering in the north: dark and rolling in fast. It looked like a hailstorm was headed their way. Tom saw four riders coming in from the northeast. Tom grabbed Robert's spyglass and made out Ned and his crew following close behind.

Tom called to Rachel and told her that company was coming. Ned was riding Ranger, a woman riding sidesaddle, and two young men leading another horse.

When they arrived, he said, "This is my wife, Helen, and sons, Dan and David. We made it just ahead of the storm," Ned said breathlessly.

"Come on up to the porch, and we can watch the lightning. I think the worst of it is going around us," Tom beckoned to his guests. "Sure been a scorcher today!"

Rachel brought a large pitcher of lemonade out and met the Legg family. The young men were polite and quiet. Helen, their mother, said, "These two boys know better than to ever do what their father did. When they go to Dodge. I don't allow them to even go into a saloon. Dan here is seventeen, and David is fifteen, although he looks much older."

Mrs. Legg was a beautiful brunette, about thirty-five years old. "I am still trying to get over the shock of Ned losing all that money," she said.

She did all the talking, and Ned just sat there with his head down.

"We want to thank you for your help," Helen continued. "Is it true that you would loan us money for the winter?"

Tom answered, "Yes."

Helen responded, "I just want to get the straight of it. Sometimes, I just can't trust him."

"Now," Tom said, "do not be too harsh. All men make mistakes; I know I have made my share."

Rachel, wanting to smooth things over, said, "Would you like to come in? The storm has cooled things off quite a bit. I have supper on the stove. Why don't you all spend the night?"

A cool rain awakened Tom and Rachel. Tom played with Johnny Gail as Dan and David helped Rachel in the kitchen fix breakfast.

"Yes, ma'am, we know our way around the kitchen. We do most of the cooking and cleaning up. We have two pet calves that we take care of too. We left our dog at home to watch over the herd."

The young men were quite talkative until their mother appeared. Ned was behind her as she headed for the table. She looked like she had been crying all night, and Ned had nothing to say. They mostly ate in silence. Johnny Gail was full of giggles and kept everyone entertained, much to Tom and Rachel's relief.

"I hate to eat and run, but we need to get back to the ranch," Ned reported.

Tom asked, "How much money will get you by?"

Mrs. Legg snapped, "Five hundred dollars."

Tom looked at Ned and asked him if that would be enough.

Ned just nodded his head and said, "Yes, thank you."

As Rachel went to the bedroom to get the money, Helen told the boys to get the horses saddled. When Rachel handed the money to Ned, Helen grabbed it and stomped out the door, shouting to Dan and David to hurry up with the horses.

Ned told Tom and Rachel, "I do not know what I am going to do with her."

He thanked them both again and quietly walked outside. He was so upset, he started to get on his horse on the wrong side. "For heaven's sake! Can't you do anything right?" Helen hollered at her husband as they rode away.

Tom stood at the window for a long time, watching his friend Ned and his family as they rode away. Shaking his head, he said, "Well, it is good to get Ranger back. I hope things work out for them."

Tom's trusted cowboys, Joe, Jake, Will, and Andy, arrived the next day with the remuda. Even after tailing the cattle drive to Dodge City and returning, the horses were still in tip-top shape.

"Welcome home. Put all of the horses in the corral, because in the morning, you will have to saddle up and go looking for the rest of the herd," Tom shouted. "Be careful! Don't break the gate down!"

Next day, at first light, Robert and the boys got ready to ride. "See you tonight, Mr. Boss Man," Robert shouted as they cleared the yard.

When Rachel finished washing clothes in her round galvanized tub using a washboard, she carried the wet clothes from the kitchen in her basket outside to the clothesline. She had made a clothespin bag to keep her wooden clothespins in, just like her mother's.

Rachel was busy hanging laundry on the line that Tom stretched out for her. "I like this job. I can feel a cool breeze whenever the wind blows across me," she said to herself.

Tom was nearly finished repacking grease in the wheels of the family buggy. Johnny was on a blanket, watching his father work. Now being midmorning, Rachel saw the dust of a lone rider. "I wonder who that is?" she said to Tom, who was hunkered down next to one of the back wheels. As the rider approached, Rachel called out to Tom. "There's a man on horseback wearing a Confederate cavalry hat, headed our way!" The words "Confederate" sent chills down Tom's spine. The stranger pulled up. He said, "I sure hope I am welcome here. I have a herd of longhorns on the Western Trail about twenty miles east of here, headed for Dodge City."

Tom replied, "You are welcome. Step down, and tie your mount to the hitching post. What can I do for you?" Tom asked.

Rachel finished hanging the clothes and moved Johnny into the shade.

The cattleman began, "My name is Charlie Reams, and I am from near San Antonio, Texas." He shook Tom's hand, which was still greasy from the wheel he was working on.

"I'm Tom Summers. This is my wife, Rachel, and my son, Johnny."

"Pleasure to meet you all," Charlie said. "I have a strange request."

"Well, you just tell me what it is," Tom said.

Charlie, a bit older than Tom, was once a soldier for the South. "I have been on the trail for three months and have had more trouble than two men put together could ever have. We've had three stampedes, been attacked twice by Indians, and a crossing over the Red River that almost did us in. My horse herd is plum wore out. What I am asking is, can I rent some of your horses?"

"Gosh," replied Tom, "how do you want to do this?"

Charlie said, "If you will loan me twenty head of fresh horses, I will leave you twenty head of mine. Then, on the return trip back to Texas, we will trade back, and I will pay you for the use of your horses."

"I see, Mr. Reams. I want to talk to my wife about this. You may go down to the bunkhouse to clean up if you like and look the horses over," Tom instructed.

The man mounted his weary horse and rode to the place where the horses were gathered. Tom looked at his beautiful wife and asked her, "What do you think?"

"Looks like he needs fresh horses," Rachel replied, "but we need paid first."

"I agree," Tom responded.

When Charlie returned, Tom told him, "We run about forty head. How many do you need?"

"Twenty will work, and I will pay you up front. I am short of cash, but I have gold. Will that be okay?"

"Gold is always good," Tom responded in agreement.

After settling on a price of five dollars per head, Charlie rode off to fetch some of his hired hands.

Like soldiers on patrol, here came ten riders, each leading a horse. They all looked like death warmed over. You could see it in their eyes. Tom met them at the corral and said, "I will help you pick out what you want, as there are a few horses I don't want to part with—even for a little while."

Each man saddled a fresh mount and led another one back to the trail drive.

The two ranchers returned to the ranch house, where they signed an agreement of rent. Charlie said, "I will take this with me, proving you have rented your horses to me, just in case someone questions me. You are well-known in these parts. I am sure both you and your brand speak for themselves."

"Thank you, Mr. Reams. You also may want to hire a couple of my men to finish the drive. They are good hands and well experienced."

"Thank you kindly, but I think I can make it with the hands I have," Charlie responded.

"Well, why don't you stay for supper? We would be happy to have you join us."

"Much obliged, but I must get back to my herd. While we are in Dodge, I am going to look up my brother, Chase Reams, who is the preacher there. I will be gone quite some time."

"Yes, I have heard of him. Isn't he the preacher at First Union Church?" Tom remarked.

"Yes. Well, thank you again, and good day to you!" the cowman said as he rode away.

CHAPTER 20

Mother Comes to Visit

As they settled in for supper, Rachel thought it was time to bring something to Tom's attention—growing oats to feed their herd of horses. As she talked, Tom could just picture himself with a plow. He allowed that the day he started planting oats would be the day he quit ranching.

Then Rachel started talking about sewing for Sally Ann. "I want to make her the finest ball gown in all of the army, and now I can with my new Singer that you bought for me," she said.

"Before we get busy with the fall roundup, why don't I send Joe with you and Johnny to Camp Supply with your sewing machine?" Tom answered.

Rachel loved the idea. Immediately, she began packing. She thought the world of Joe. They had talked for hours on the porch about his experiences during the slave days in Georgia. The slave issue was one that she had a hard time relating to, being a northern Yankee; but he was always good to explain what it was really like in those days.

After a few days, she was ready to travel. Joe hitched Babe up to the buggy and loaded Rachel's Singer and sewing supplies, baby supplies, and finally, Johnny Gale, and his baby buggy. It looked like she was leaving for good. Tom sheepishly commented, "You are coming back, aren't you?"

"Yes, Tom, we will be back, and I will bring molasses and fruit with me, enough to last the winter. Please water my new apple trees while I am away," Rachel said.

They had planned to leave early that morning, but with all the extras to pack, the sun was already heavy on the land when they finally departed.

Joe drove the buggy, and Rachel tended to Johnny Gail. As they rode along, Rachel was a good listener to Joe's many stories. "You know, Miss Rachel, I would love to have a family someday like you and Mr. Tom."

Rachel asked, "Do you ever want to go back to Georgia?"

"Sometimes I think I do," Joe said. "It's a beautiful place, lots of trees and lots of water. I liked to go fishin' when I could."

"We would hate to lose you, Joe, but I am sure my husband would help you return if you wanted to," Rachel continued.

"No, ma'am, there is too much pain back there. I can still hear my mother cryin' when the boss man would take her into the shed."

Rachel said, "You never talk about your father, Joe."

"My father was a huge black man, straight off the ship from Africa. He brought more money than the other slaves, I was told. The boss man was rich and had a huge plantation where he worked many slaves in the cotton fields. My father was called 'the stud.' Boss man did not allow my father to work in the fields; he kept him chained to a tree day and night, where he was given young girls to father their children. I have many brothers and sisters, but I don't know where they is."

"Were you able to be with your mother?"

"Only sometimes," he said. "She taught me to be kind and to hold my temper. She said, 'It don't do no good to be angry. It only hurts you.' She died in childbirth. She was such a small woman."

"I am so sorry, Joe," Rachel consoled her friend. "You are a good man. Your mother would be proud of you."

"We should be at Camp Supply soon, Miss Rachel." Joe put the past behind him and looked to the future and said, "I am thinkin' about lookin' for a bride in the mail order way. Do you think that would work?"

197

Rachel encouraged him, "Yes, I would give it a try."

The cowhands and Tom began moving the cattle around the land to find the good, sweet grass away from the ranch house. Then, in the winter months, they would move the cattle close in to take better care of them.

When Rachel arrived at Camp Supply, she surprised Sally Ann and the captain. "We're back! I hope it is all right to spend a few days with you. I brought my new sewing machine to make you a ball gown for the fall dance in October."

"Well," said Sally Ann, "do I have a surprise for you! Here is a letter from your mother! Remember, you had written her, asking her to come visit you? I'd wager that she's writing to say she is coming. Hurry and open the letter and tell me what she said!"

Rachel tore the letter open and read aloud: "I will arrive by stagecoach at Camp Supply, August 18th." Rachel looked at Sally Ann and said, "Oh my! That's tomorrow! I can't believe it! I haven't seen her since my wedding! Johnny, your grandmother is on her way to see you!"

Sally Ann responded, "That's wonderful news. We have lots of room right here. She can stay here. We'll all have a good time!"

It was late afternoon the following day when Rachel's mother, Mrs. Lentz, arrived.

"I sure am glad to be here!" she said, giving her daughter a quick hug and kiss. "You look wonderful, Rachel! Where's my grandson?"

"Oh, Mother, it's wonderful to see you! Johnny Gail is with Sally Ann, my good friend over in the officers' row." Joe loaded all of Mrs. Lentz's belongings and drove them all to the captain's home. "Now you all have a pleasant evening. I'm goin' to go visit the new soldiers in camp."

Rachel explained to her mother that Joe was going to see the Buffalo Soldiers in the camp. She explained that the soldiers got that name from the Indians. When they first saw the black man, they named them after the buffalo because their hair was curly like the buffalo's.

As Joe, Rachel, and Mrs. Lentz pulled up to the captain's house, Sally Ann came out the front door with Johnny Gail in her arms.

Mrs. Lentz didn't wait for help getting down from the buggy. She rushed to Sally Ann, swooped up her first and only grandson in her arms, and began to cry. "Oh, Rachel, he is precious! He's beautiful! So handsome, and just look at his red hair!"

Sally Ann had prepared a comfortable place for her guests. They had the sewing machine set up in a separate room, and Rachel got busy fashioning a special gown for her beloved friend. The ladies had a grand week together, spoiling the little one. Captain Morgan knew that it would serve him well to stay busy or at least leave the three talkative women alone since he would not have gotten a word in edgewise.

A week later, much to Tom's surprise, Joe showed up at the ranch—bringing not only one woman and a baby, but two women and a baby and trunks tied on the back of the buggy.

Tom was trying to make some sense of the situation when he realized that it was his mother-in-law, Ella. Ella Lentz had never been west of the Missouri River. She had lived most of her life in the civilized world of Iowa. One of her favorite outings was to travel to Kansas City, to go to the theater, and to shop. She acted like she was happy to see Tom, but the ranch, this place he had taken her only daughter to, didn't quite live up to her expectations. She was surprised, however, to see the fine home Tom had built for Rachel and her grandson.

"Are the people down there in that log house your only neighbors?" she asked.

"No, the closest neighbors are where you came from, Camp Supply and Dodge City. As far as I know, the closest ranch is sixty miles west into Texas," Tom answered.

"This is the most desolate, forlorn country I've ever seen or heard about!" she exclaimed.

Tom replied, "This is our home. This is where your daughter and grandson live."

Rachel told her mother, "Mother, I've always looked at being here with Tom a great adventure, and I love it."

Tom left the women to unpack. He thought that no matter how hard the wind and rain blew or the coyotes howled, Rachel would just snuggle a little bit closer. He would tease her now and then, saying, "The only reason we have coyotes and wolves is so that you will reach for me in the night." She would giggle and say, "Oh, Tom!"

Although Rachel loved her life on the ranch, it was a different story for her mother. "There is no corn growing here. This land needs plowed up and the cattle fenced out. Besides, you are too far from town!"

She went on to say, "You know, the farmers now make fences out of barbed wire to hold the cattle in."

That was when Tom got irritated and snapped, "Boy, that would be great to ride your horse up against and rip his hide open."

"Now, Tom. That barbed wire is the coming thing," she said.

He got so mad, he left the house.

Rachel and her mother had a good visit, although she detested the West. The wind blew more than it did in Iowa, and the heat! There were no trees around the house, and she did not much like the cottonwood trees down by the creek.

"They don't even look like trees," she said. "Why, back home we have hardwoods, you know, oak, maple, and hickory."

She wanted to know when they were planning a trip up north so Johnny Gail could be baptized in a real church. "Your father and everyone wants to see you and the baby," she persisted.

Tom and Rachel allowed that was the thing to do and that they would make sure that it would happen. Unbeknownst to Tom, Rachel told her mother they were hoping to have another child, and when that happened, she would come to see her then, if not sooner.

After only two weeks, Mrs. Lentz decided she'd had enough of the prairie and announced it was time for her to go home. She hugged and kissed Rachel and the baby then hugged Tom too. The hug told him she felt there was no hope for him. He got the buggy ready and took her all the way to Dodge City.

"I know you're doing the best you can, Tom," she said tolerantly.

He bought her a ticket and said his good-byes. She hugged Tom again and said, "Take good care of Rachel and my grandson!"

He said, "I will!"

As he stood there waiting for the train to pull out, he overheard two women sharing the latest gossip. "Well, you know the bank is closed," one lady said. "The banker stole all the money and then left town."

"No!" replied the second woman.

"Oh yes! And that's not all! His girlfriend was found strangled in her bed, right up there in the hotel. They say he went out West on the train and no one knows where he is."

A third woman joined the conversation. "A lot of people lost everything they had because their money was in that bank. You know the preacher got killed too. I'll bet he stole that money and killed that whore too!"

"Excuse me," Tom interrupted, "what preacher are you talkin' about?"

"Reverend Reams and his wife, Catherine, were shot to death. No one knows why," one of the ladies answered regretfully.

The train was loaded down and slowly pulled out of the station, as Tom watched it heading East. Tom had no desire to spend any more time in Dodge City, but before he headed out, he thought he would stop by the livery stable to say hello to his old friend. Jim welcomed Tom but had more to tell him about Jim Nickolson's thieving rampage. "I'm glad you and the missus left when you did. Right after you left is when all this trouble when down," he explained. "How are things goin' for you at the ranch?"

"Oh, everything is fine. Our son is growing fast, and we are getting ready for winter. You take care of yourself. See you next year." Tom stepped up in the buggy, slapped the reins, and gave a "Yup, now!" to Babe and headed out. He was glad to be going home.

Tom drove until nightfall and staked out Babe by a creek with lush grass and slept in the buggy under the stars.

Next morning, he fed Babe some oats he bought in Dodge, harnessed her up, and headed south in a steady trot. Just south of the Cimarron, he met up with three men who stopped him. Tom could tell they were up to no good—road agents, he was sure. Tom guessed he looked more like a dude than a cowboy. He had his suit coat on as there was a little nip in the air that morning. He had his sidearm underneath his jacket. They pulled him up and were "who-rawing" him. Tom told them, "Go on about your business—you don't need to bother me."

They continued their taunting and asked, "What kind of peddler are you exactly? What kind of money do you have? We'd sure like to help you count it," one said as they all laughed with a wicked laugh.

Tom told them, "Now, just get on down the road. You are likely biting off more than you can chew."

One said, "A man that doesn't ride horseback can't be much of a man." The tall one reached over and tried to take Tom's hat. Tom reached up and grabbed him by the handkerchief around his neck and pulled him down on top of him then, just as quickly, pushed him away and threw him across the other side of the buggy. The other two had a bewildered look on their ugly faces as Tom pulled his Colt .45. He told them, "I've had all the foolishness out of you that I need. Get the hell out of my way!"

The one on the ground, the one they called Homer, was more than perturbed. Tom had two of them on one side of him and Homer on the other. Homer decided that although Tom had his gun pulled, he would make a play. He reached for his weapon, and before he could fire, Tom blasted his gun hand. Tom turned back to the other two hombres and said, "Load up this son of a bitch, and get out of here before I kill all of you!"

They loaded up Homer on his horse and hightailed it to parts unknown.

Tom took a deep breath and gave Babe her head. Tom was so ready to get home that he sped past Camp Supply and onward across the plains faster than you could go when driving cattle. Babe was quite a trotter. Tom was thankful that God had given her to him. It was late when he reached the ranch. Rachel was rocking Johnny, who had the croup.

Rachel asked, "Did you get Mother aboard the train?"

"Yes," Tom said, "I did, and she hugged me and thanked me."

Rachel asked, "Did you have any trouble on the way?"

He told her about the road agents and said, "I talked them out of doing me any harm." But he didn't tell her how.

"Tom, I wish you would be more careful. You are all I have, you and little Johnny," she cried.

Tom was asleep before his head hit the pillow. Next morning, Rachel said, "I don't know how you could talk someone out of robbing you."

"Guess I'm a good talker," he said as he picked her up and squeezed her. "I had a little help," Tom replied. Rachel did not know what he meant. He was so busy kissing her that she did not realize he was talking about his Colt .45. With a sly grin, he paused long enough to say, "I'm a pretty good talker. I talked you into marrying me, didn't I?"

She answered and said, "Yes. You know you told mother that you were going to put a fence around this house so that the cattle wouldn't be up here so close. I want to keep them off the porch and away from the baby."

"Boy, did I ever open my mouth and say the wrong thing, trying to impress grandma!" he said. "All I had in mind was to make love with my wife, and I got instructions about a fence!" Tom said to himself. Guess she's tired with the baby being sick and me being gone.

Tom fixed his own breakfast then rounded up the hands. "Okay, boys, we are going to quit being cowboys and start being fence builders for a while."

They took some axes and wedges with them to split the cottonwood branches into rails. "Bring the wagon, Will. We will load it down by the creek," Tom told him. Tom remembered how his brother, John, and he had helped their father build a split rail fence to keep the cattle out of the corn back in Tennessee.

Tom and the boys were proud of their job when they finished. The fence surrounded the ranch house, and Tom decided it was a good idea after all.

CHAPTER 21

Donna Is Born

By now, life on the plains was changing dramatically. The buffalo, once the answer to all of the Indian's needs, were all but gone from the area. The ruler of the plains had moved mostly to the Texas panhandle. With their demise, the red man soon lost his freedom and became completely dependent on the United States government to feed, clothe, and rule their lives.

The army contracted Tom to drive one hundred of his Texas Longhorns to the Cheyenne Reservation, south of the Summers place just beyond the Cherokee Outlet. The soldiers at Camp Supply were stationed there to keep the drovers and the Indians separated and to keep the peace when the cowman drove their cattle up to the railhead.

It was early fall. The colors of the cottonwoods and the wild plains grass were changing. One day, Charlie Reams showed up at Tom's door. His hair had turned completely white. He was thin and drawn. "Come in, we are glad to see you. Are you all right?" Tom asked as he opened the door and showed the old rancher inside.

"My brother is dead along with his wife. Someone shot them both." Shaking his head with regret and disbelief, he said, "They never hurt anyone, and now this."

"We are so sorry, Mr. Reams. Is there anything we can do for you?"

A TRUE-TO-LIFE WESTERN STORY

"I don't know. I am going back to Texas. We brought your horses back. They are in very good condition. Thank you. We would not have made it without you and your horses," Charlie reiterated.

"You are welcome to spend the night," Rachel said.

"No, I must get back to the men. They are anxious to get home."

"Well, next year when you're through these parts, we hope you'll stop by," Tom told his friend.

Charlie shook Tom's hand and said, "Thank you. I don't know if there will be a next year. Good-bye and thank you again!"

The north wind told Tom it was time to bring the last of the cattle in and cut more wood. Gathering the herd and chopping wood kept the boys busy for several days. Tom decided to stay home with Rachel. He had noticed some changes in his bride; she just seemed different in some way. "Maybe she's tired," Tom thought to himself. He felt that he needed to help her more.

Word came that there was going to be a grand party. Everyone at Camp Supply was going to celebrate Captain Morgan's birthday. Tom, Rachel, and all of the hands were invited. The news of the event seemed to revitalize Rachel. Tom could hear her whistling in the mornings as she went about her household chores. "Oh, I am so excited about the party! I am looking forward to seeing all of our friends at Camp," Rachel told Tom. "I remember what a grand time we had on the Fourth of July," she continued.

Tom thought to himself, Military Service at Camp Supply was difficult. Most of the men were far from home and in a hot, danger-ous, desolate land. These men look for an excuse to have a party, and Captain Morgan's birthday is a good excuse.

There was no alcohol allowed at the Camp, but Tom thought there was a jug or two on the outskirts of most festivities.

"What dress are you going to wear?" Tom asked his wife.

"It will be a surprise, Tom," she replied.

Rachel was lovely as always, as he took her on his arm for the grand march. An orchestra from Dodge City was brought in, in honor of the Captain's party. The pavilion was decorated in style and was full of soldiers all telling stories. Each tale was bigger than the last. Gold was discovered in Colorado, which caused much excite-

205

ment. Tom's cowboys asked many questions concerning how to strike it rich, and they dreamed about what they would do with the money.

The women all gathered around Sally Ann and made over her new ball gown. Even her husband told her she looked pretty, something the captain was not known to do. The gown was the color of her blue eyes. She seemed to glow with all the attention.

They toasted the captain, wishing him long life and good health; in between, there was much merrymaking and dancing, which lasted until dawn.

They all stayed at Camp Supply for three days. It did Rachel good to be with other women and have some time in "town." Johnny enjoyed the excitement too.

On their way home, Rachel sat close to Tom, holding Johnny. "I don't want these good times to ever end," she told her husband.

As anyone with children knows, time flies by. Johnny was three years old now. It was a warm day, and Rachel and Tom sat on the porch, watching him pretend to shoot a gun and ride the range. Tom said, "Looks like he wants to be a soldier the way he rides that stick horse and salutes every chance he gets."

"Yes, he is growing up so fast," Rachel replied. "He will soon have a baby brother or sister to play with too."

"What?" Tom almost fell off of the porch. "When? Oh, Rachel, I love you! How are you feeling?" he questioned.

"I am fine. I want to make the same arrangements with the doctor at Camp Supply as we did with Johnny," Rachel said as she calmed Tom down.

Being an old cowboy and dealing with cows, Tom thought the second birth would be easier. But it wasn't. They went to Camp Supply in early July and stayed with the Morgans at Sally Ann's insistence. Rachel was in labor for two days, with no relief. Tom worried he would lose her and the baby. Finally, Dr. Renfro was able to turn the baby, and in a short time, they had a little redheaded girl. They named her Donna. The baby was fine, but Rachel was weak and developed a fever. Tom prayed to God that he, Johnny Gail, and Donna would not lose her.

When Rachel's milk came in, it was thin, and the baby was not satisfied. Sally Ann made little Donna a sugar teat for her to suck on out of twisted cloth tied with a string and dipped in sugar water.

Tom's prayers were answered as Rachel's fever broke and she began to regain her strength. Her milk came back rich, and Tom's baby girl was content. If it had not been for the surgeon and the midwife, the outcome would have been different. Rachel and Donna remained at what was now Fort Supply under the watchful eye of the doctor. Donna was the first child born in the same year that Camp Supply was changed to Fort Supply. Johnny was his father's charge to take care of. Johnny loved to imitate the soldiers, marching on the parade grounds. The two Summers men remained for a while to be sure mother and child were doing well, but there was work to be done; it was time for Tom and Johnny to head back to the ranch.

As they were leaving, they met up with a family that was being relocated from Fort Reno, Oklahoma Territory. They introduced themselves as Sergeant and Mrs. Miller and their teenage daughter, Janell.

Tom got to thinking, "Maybe that young lady would be able to come to our place and help Rachel when I bring her home."

When Tom and Johnny pulled up, the ranch hands all met them before they even got out of the buggy. "How is Mrs. Summers? Do you have a boy or a girl?" Each was eager to hear the news.

"Rachel is doing well, and we now have another little lady to run the ranch," Tom announced proudly. "We named her Donna. How are things here?" he asked.

Robert reported, "We've had some rustlers. We lost ten head last night, so I have set up a night patrol schedule. Sure glad you are back, Boss."

"Robert, you're in charge. I don't want to put Johnny in harm's way," Tom told him.

The night passed uneventfully. Tom hoped the rustlers moved on off and this was the last of the cattle thieves.

Although Rachel had prepared food ahead for them, Tom could not seem to the get the pancakes right according to Johnny Gail. He missed his mother. Tom knew Johnny was lonesome for Rachel, so he decided to teach him a thing or two. Tom looked at Will and said, "Bring the new colt to me." Moments later, Will had a yearling colt with him, one Ranger had sired.

"Johnny," Tom said, "this will be your horse if you take care of him. What do you want to name him?"

"Soldier Boy," Johnny said.

Will, being part Indian, had a natural way with horses. Tom chose him to train Soldier Boy. He did a fine job of breaking the colt. He placed sacks of oats on his back and let him get the feel of weight. In the corral, with a halter he made out of rope, Will led Soldier Boy around in a circle then got on his back for a ride. This took several days, and much to everyone's delight, he got bucked off a few times. Then, one day after Will had ridden Soldier Boy for several hours, he rode up to the house and picked up Johnny, and the two of them rode together. After that, the horse and little boy were inseparable.

It was early fall 1878. Rachel and Donna had been at the Fort a few weeks. Johnny and his father loaded up the buggy and headed for the Fort. Tom looked up the Miller family and asked if Janell could come to their place to help Rachel with the new baby as Rachel was still recovering from childbirth. The Millers agreed and asked what kind of payment Tom would give them for their daughter's services. "Whatever you think is right," Tom responded. "We will see to it that she comes back to see you as often as possible," he continued. Janell joined the Summers family.

Johnny was full of chatter as they headed back home, telling his captive audience all about his new pony. "I can ride all by myself!" he told his mother.

For a young girl, Janell was very good with Johnny, and he loved her stories about the military and the Indians. She was good with Donna too, and she was able to help Rachel a great deal. "How did you learn to cook and care for children?" Rachel asked her.

"I helped raise my little brother and sister; but when my father rejoined the army, he gave them to my aunt in Illinois. I am the only one they kept. I guess because I could work."

"Well, we are sure happy to have you here with us. We want you to be part of the family," Rachel told her.

Anytime Tom was in the house or walking nearby, he could hear the women talking and laughing. Rachel began to teach Janell ciphering and grammar. They spent time reading the Bible together. Janell even wrote poetry.

After Donna was born, Rachel did not renew like she was before. She was still a loving wife, but without Janell, it would have been too much of a hardship to care for her family.

One Sunday afternoon, Tom asked Janell if she had ever ridden a horse. "No, I never have," she said, "but I would love to." Tom saddled up one of his favorite geldings, named Wisdom, and let her ride. Janell was a natural.

Several days later, Rachel and the children were napping, and Janell asked if she could ride Wisdom out on the range. "Sure enough, and if you should get lost, just give him his head. Wisdom knows the way home," Tom told her as he saddled the beautiful roan.

"Be careful, and don't go too far," Tom called as Janell rode away. If you were unfamiliar with the prairie, you could easily get lost; every direction looked the same.

Janell enjoyed the wind in her face and the fragrances of wet grass after a rain. After a while, she pulled the reins for the big gelding to slow down to a walk. Ahead was a small gully with a clear running spring. She guided Wisdom to stop for a cooling drink for both of them. Her dismount was quick and effortless. After splashing her childlike face and her womanly body with refreshing water, she watched Wisdom tickle the surface with his nose first and then nibble the water for a long drink. Then, she lay down near the fountain of water on a patch of soft, green moss. She used a piece of driftwood for a pillow to cradle her head and gazed for a long time at the endless heavens.

From the north, a large formation of geese made their way south, right over her head. "Mr. Summers says it is going to be an early winter," Janell said aloud to Wisdom. She counted the silver-winged birds just as Tom had taught her. Two, four, six—there were sixty-four in the flock. They kept changing leaders. Now, number three was at the front like an infantry captain, leading his winged soldiers to battle.

She was already to her feet when a stranger came riding up beside her. "What's a girl doin' out here all by herself?" he smirked, not really caring. There was a sound in his voice that sent chills up her spine. "What's your name, pretty darlin'? You look like you need a man." With that, he leaped from his horse and grabbed Janell with both hands. He was whiskered and weathered and smelled of urine and sweat, a sickening odor of unclean deeds. "Moe's my name," he said as he threw the frightened young girl to the ground.

She fell headfirst into the mud and struggled to get to her feet. The monster tore at her shirt and groped along her body. The ruffian's horse eagerly drank from the small stream and bit off the lush vegetation as fast as he could, ignoring the desperate fight that had begun.

Wisdom threw up his head and whinnied as if to command the assailant to leave his master's rider alone. The crazed man had twisted Janell over on her back, her head half buried in the mud. "If I can get this damn belt off, I will teach you a thing or two!" As Moe straddled the struggling, helpless girl, Wisdom, sensing Janell's fear and anxiety, somehow knew she was in trouble. In a stance like a stallion protecting his mares, ears back and nose to the ground like a battering ram, he rushed to her side, swung his head, and stuck Moe hard. It was just enough to catch him off guard and gave Janell a split second to break away from Moe's hold and jump to her feet. The bastard caught her by the foot and pulled her boot off. "I'll have all your clothes off before I'm through with you!" he swore.

With the boot still in his hand, Janell scampered up the bank and ran a few feet before she felt crushing arms around her. While he was struggling to hold her down, she took the flap of her belt and turned it under along her waist, making it almost impossible for the would-be rapist to tear the belt from her riding pants.

As he reached for his knife, Janell rolled away from him. Wisdom was enraged and reared up and caught Moe's head with a hoof. Dazed, he slumped to the ground. Janell grabbed a handful of Wisdom's mane and jumped on the back of her rescuer. She kicked him hard and let him have his head. He knew the way home.

Tom was beginning to worry as to Janell's whereabouts. "She is a smart girl and a good rider, and Wisdom is steady; he knows what to do," Tom told Rachel. But maybe I ought to go look for her just in case she stumbled into a beehive or a gopher hole."

He was cinching up Ranger when he first heard the screams. A childlike form with trails of rags alongside the horse that he knew was his, was heading toward him. "Oh no, God in heaven, what has happened?" Tom cried.

Robert and Jake grabbed their horses and raced out to meet the terrified young girl. "He's out there! He tried to—he's got a knife!" She cried and then fainted in Robert's arms as he came alongside her. He held her and tried to calm her. He assured her that she was safe and that he would never let anyone hurt her again.

The mud on Janell was a dead giveaway as to where she had been assaulted. Robert brought her to the house and briefly explained to Rachel what had happened. Rachel gently soothed her as she cleaned her face and body and wrapped her in a warm, clean blanket. She rocked her and listened as Janell recalled the chilling events of the day.

Tom, Robert, Jake, and Joe raced to the spring, about five miles away, leaving Andy to guard the ranch. Sure enough, there were signs of the struggle, pieces of Janell's clothing in the mud, and her boot. This precious young girl had become family to all of them, and now they were furious by what had happened to her. They were determined to find the perpetrator. They divided up into two groups and began looking for him. Jake and Tom had been looking for what seemed like hours and were about ready to give up when a man came riding up to them. He fit the description Janell gave. Jake asked what he was doing in these parts and then let him do the talking. "Oh, I've been on a big cattle drive, and I'm on my way back to Texas. I've been havin' a little fun too! You never know what you're goin' find out here on the prairie!" The stranger laughed.

Jake said, "Oh, really, what did you find?"

"Now, don't tell no one, but I found this sweet, pretty young thing out here, all alone. She was a feisty little white girl. I got me a real good feel. I'll bet she ain't never been with a real man before!"

Tom said, "Are those scratches proof of your story?" Tom asked, pointing to Moe's face.

"Oh yes, she was a wildcat!"

That's all Jake needed to hear. He drew his gun on Moe and said, "Throw down your gun and knife, you worthless piece of . . . crap"

"What's the problem?" Moe interrupted. "What's she to you?"

Jake was so angry, he could not speak. He stared at him coldly and held his Colt .45 on him. And Tom tied his hands together and then to the saddle horn. Jake fired two shots into the air, signaling Robert and Joe, who were quick on the scene.

"Here he is. This is the guy who hurt our little sister," Jake said.

"What are we going to do?" Robert asked. "Are we going to take him to the marshall?"

"No," Tom said. "They would just let him go. We are the law out here. It is our property. Head to the cottonwoods and let's see if he has any final words."

"What do you mean? Let me go!" Moe cried out.

Tom turned and looked at him hard. "We are not going to have your kind out here. You are going to hang!"

They did not use a hangman's knot; they used the regular knot on the lariat. They threw the rope over a limb of a large cottonwood, put the loop around his neck, and busted his mount across the butt, and the horse jumped out from under him.

Awhile later, they cut him down and he was dead. They dug a grave for him nearby. Robert said, "I'm going to bury this son of a bitch facedown. He don't deserve no respect."

Tom had some composure. He asked the Lord to forgive his men and Moe. Tom vowed that this was the last time he would ever be the law again; but he felt that the range was his, and he did not need people like Moe.

A feeling of sadness entered their home. Janell cried often; she did not want any one close to her except the children. Her comfort was holding and rocking Donna. Sometimes, she would read to Johnny Gail but was withdrawn the rest of the time. She stopped wearing her fitted dresses and began wearing oversized, loose men's shirts. Her long hair covered her face almost every day now.

Rachel asked Janell if she would like to see her parents.

"No," she replied, "They would not understand."

One morning, weeks later, Janell asked Tom, "Will that terrible man ever come back here and hurt me?"

"No, Janell, he will not. He will never hurt you or anyone else again. You are safe, I promise," Tom assured.

Robert brought a yellow calico kitten home one day when returning from the Fort. He knocked on Janell's door and told her that the little cat needed a home and asked if she would take care of it. She took the kitten in her arms and did not let it go for hours. Rachel warmed some milk for the kitten. Janell could not bear to risk losing her furry friend, so she held on to both the kitten and the bowl of milk and watched as it ate its fill.

"What are you going to call her?" Rachel asked.

"I think 'Goldie' fits," she replied.

As fall turned to winter, Rachel asked Janell if she should like to learn how to sew.

"Yes, could we make something nice for my friends, please? They helped me, and they've been so good to me," Janell responded.

They began a sewing session every day while the children napped. Rachel showed Janell how to measure and cut fabric and how to use the sewing machine. Before long, they had made denim shirts for each cowhand and Tom.

"You have done a beautiful job making these shirts, Janell. Would you like for me to show you how to embroider each man's initials on his shirt?" Rachel asked.

"Oh yes, that would be grand" was Janell's answer. "Can we surprise them and give the shirts for Christmas?"

"Good idea. Now, let's make you a pretty dress for the Christmas party at the Fort," Rachel told her young student.

Suddenly, Janell's excitement about the shirts turned to shame and embarrassment. She said, "I don't want to go to the party. I would like a new dress, but I don't want to go to the party. Could it be blue?"

TED RIDDLE AND LINDA RIDDLE

Rachel looked in Janell's eyes, hoping for a glimmer of a change of heart. She knew that Janell needed to be with people to help get over the attack on the prairie. When Janell's expression didn't change, Rachel said, "Yes, if you want a new blue dress, we will make you one. We will buy some blue velvet from the drummer the next time he comes by."

As the days passed and winter set in, joy, sharing stories, and playing games returned to the Summers ranch. You could hear Janell laughing as she played with Goldie. She was riding on the range again whenever one of the hands had some free time and could ride with her. Janell loved her blue velvet dress and decided, after all, that she would attend the Christmas party at the Fort. The dark days of her attack were mostly behind her.

Christmas was a happy day of eating and singing at the ranch. The boys brought in a small cedar tree, and everyone helped decorate it. Janell made a large yellow star for the top from yellow calico and wire. The girls fashioned garlands out of red sumac berries to go around the evergreen. Johnny's favorite gift was a pistol that Andy made for him out of wood. They ended the day reading scriptures and singing "Silent Night," accompanied by Joe on his banjo.

CHAPTER 22

Janell Goes to School

It was 1881. Two years had passed since Janell's attack. Tom's family was growing up. Johnny was six; Donna, four; and Janell was a beautiful seventeen-year-old. She had been with them so long that she was indeed family. Tom had even put her in his will.

Sergeant Miller, Janell's father, had put in enough time in the army that he could now muster out; the gold fields of Colorado were calling to him. Meanwhile, Tom and Rachel realized it was time for Janell to receive further education. They asked her if she would like to attend finishing school for young ladies. Rachel told her that there was a famous one in St. Louis, Missouri. Janell liked the idea. "But what will my parents say?" she inquired.

Tom answered, "I will ride to the Fort tomorrow and ask them. Do you want to go with me?"

"No, thank you," she replied. "Please just ask for their permission. I don't have any money for school, and they don't either, I'm sure," she continued.

"Don't worry about the money," Tom said. "We will take care of all the expenses."

Tom rode to Fort Supply. It was a clear, cold day in January. He found Sergeant Miller in the teamster's cabin. All he could talk about was getting out of the army and going to the gold fields. "You know," Miller said, "you could strike it rich in one day!"

"Yes, that's probably true," Tom replied. "If you leave here, what are your plans for Janell?"

"Damn!" Miller barked, "she's a full-grown woman now. She'd just be a burden to her ma and me. She ought to get married and let someone else worry about her, not me and her momma!"

Miller's harsh reaction surprised Tom. "If it is all right with you, Rachel and I want to send her to a fine finishing school in St. Louis," Tom said.

The two men walked toward the quarters where Sergeant Miller and his wife lived. "You ask her ma," the sergeant said. "I've got to finish inventory."

Mrs. Miller came to the door and did not mince words. "What do you want? We ain't got no money for Janell if that's what you're here for."

"No, Mrs. Miller," Tom said. "My wife and I would like your permission to send your daughter to finishing school in St. Louis. We will pay her expenses."

"That girl don't need any more schoolin'. Your wife's taught her all she needs to know. She needs to get married. Why, I was carrying my second child when I was her age," the bitter woman replied.

It was all Tom could do to not show his anger, but he continued patiently. "Janell is a fine young woman, and we want the best for her."

"Fine. Do what you want, but you're not gettin' no money out of us." And she shut the door in Tom's face.

Tom was taken aback by Mrs. Miller's reaction, but he was glad that Janell would have the education she deserved. He headed for the blacksmith's shop because his horse, Ranger, needed shoes. Even more, he wanted to talk to his good friend Bill.

"How in the world are you, Tom Summers? Haven't seen you since the dance."

Tom told him about Rachel, Johnny Gail, Donna, and Janell.

"That will be great," Bill answered. "You've done a real good thing, getting her away from the Millers. They are just plain mean. You can hear them most every night—fightin' and carryin' on. I say get them out of here and let them try to get rich in the gold fields. Good riddance."

Bill grabbed two glasses and a bottle. "How about a drink?"

"I think I need one," Tom said.

Tom spent the night on a cot in the blacksmith's shop, his old quarters when he first came to that part of the world.

The next day, with a headache, Tom returned home with the good news. "Your folks said it would be fine if you want to go to school, and they send their blessings," Tom told Janell.

"Oh, thank you! Could I go see them and tell them good-bye?" she asked.

"Yes, that will be fine. The weather is getting bad, though. Looks like a blue northern is headed our way. As soon as the storm is over, we will go see your folks. We'll telegraph the school and ask if they will register you when we get to the Fort," Tom explained.

The storm raged for days. Janell asked, "What are we going to do?" She had never heard the wind blow so hard.

"We will just hole up for a while, and everything will be fine," Tom answered.

One night, the girls cooked up some caramel, and they put it on fresh, hot bread.

"Tell me, Janell, how do you make this? Just in case I ever get married, I can show my wife how to make it," Andy said through bites of bread and dripping caramel.

"Rachel showed me how to take evaporated canned milk, get it hot in the skillet, and then add sugar until it turns brown and cook it until it's thick," Janell explained.

"You will make some lucky man a good wife," Andy replied, shoving another piece of caramel bread in his mouth.

Some nights, the men played cards, and Rachel and Janell worked on a quilt that Janell would take with her when she left for school. "It's sure going to be different being in a big city and a big school," she said. "You have meant so much to me. I will never forget you. Will you write to me?" Janell asked Rachel.

"Yes, honey, and we will come to see you," Rachel responded.

Every day they were busy planning for their trip to Fort Supply. Janell said, "I am looking forward to seeing my folks. They will be proud of me if I'm accepted at such a prestigious school. What will I wear at school?" she asked Rachel.

"From what I know, the girls all wear uniforms, so that makes it easier," Rachel said.

"I won't have to be around any boys, will I?" Janell inquired.

"No," Rachel responded, "but you will be invited to the dances, I'm sure."

Tom interrupted. "I do believe the storm has passed. Let's go see about the livestock."

During supper, Tom announced, "You, me, and the children will go to Fort Supply tomorrow, see Janell's parents, and telegraph the school. We will leave early, so bundle up and take provisions to stay a few days."

That was good news. They had been cooped up for days because of the storm. "Boys, if everything is all right here, I want you to ride over to Ned's place and see if he needs any help," Tom told his hands.

Tom and his family arrived at the Fort the next afternoon. Everyone was happy to see them, especially Sally Ann. The first thing Janell told Sally Ann was that she wanted to see her folks before she left for school. With a bewildered look, the captain's wife said, "Honey, your folks left yesterday for Colorado."

"Well, did they leave me a note or anything?" Janell asked hopefully.

"No, honey, I'm afraid not," Sally Ann said regretfully. The words cut like a knife. She tried to act as though she wasn't bothered by Sally Ann's information, but she was. The young girl looked lost, like she did not know what to say or do.

Sally Ann, ever the hostess, rushed over to Janell, put her arm around her, and said, "Now, don't you fret yourself none, Janell. You have your whole life ahead of you. You come on over here and warm up. I have apple cider brewing on the stove and a fine brisket roast in the oven. Janell, you can have the room on the left, and, Rachel, you know where your room is.

The next morning, Tom and Janell walked to the telegraph office and sent a message, asking for admittance to the finishing school in St. Louis. The reply came back that they would mail an application for Miss Janell Miller. Janell's mood lifted a little, but then she asked if they could go by her parents' quarters.

She opened the door. The room smelled of tobacco and whiskey. Nothing but emptiness filled the space. Tears came to the young woman's eyes. She couldn't understand why everything was happening as it was.

Tom watched in silence as Janell's eyes looked around the room for what seemed like hours. Finally, in a whisper, Janell spoke. "I must never look back. I will succeed and remember that you and Rachel have been more like a mother and father than my own parents. I will work hard and make you proud of me."

Janell spent the evening reading. "I want to learn all I can," she said as she pored over *The Life of William Penn* by M. L. Weems, a popular historian of the day.

At breakfast the next morning, Janell asked, "Captain Morgan, may I borrow these books?"

"Yes, you take every one you want. I want you to become governor when we become a state."

Captain told the little family, as they left the next morning, that when the letter from the school arrived, he would send it with a rider to the ranch.

A week later, a lone rider and a cloud of dust descended upon the ranch. Lieutenant Perkins delivered the important-looking letter to Mr. Summers. "Let's look and see if it's that application!" Tom said as he opened the envelope. "Yes sir, it is! Janell, Rachel, come here! Look!"

"Upon return of this application and a review of the board, you may be eligible to attend the private summer session as preparation for school, commencing Fall, 1881. Signed, Therron Reneau, President."

"Oh! This is grand! Come in, Lieutenant. Have a bite to eat and rest your horse," Tom exclaimed.

There is a chemistry that seems to happen every spring. It may happen in the city as two people pass on the street or in a factory, working side by side. Whatever it is, it was happening in the Cherokee Outlet that day in March. After reading the words of her acceptance letter, Janell seemed to walk taller and smile more. She hurriedly brushed her hair back and pinched her cheeks to make them blush. She served the young man in a winsome manner, and he became proper and charming. When he excused himself from the table and thanked Mrs. Summers, Janell spoke up and asked if she had permission to show the lieutenant the horses in the corral.

They strolled toward the excuse she dreamed up. "How long have you been in the army, Lieutenant?" Janell inquired.

"Two years, ma'am," Lieutenant Perkins shyly replied.

"I will be going away soon to the East," Janell told the young man. She began to talk, barely catching her breath, letting her nerves get the better of her.

"We will miss you, Miss Miller," he answered.

Caught between worlds of past memories and future hopes, she heard his words but could not respond. "Here's my favorite horse, Wisdom," she said, stroking the horse's soft nose. "He saved my life once. I will never forget him. His name fits him, I think. He is very wise."

"What do you want to do after school?" the young lieutenant asked.

"I want to be a nurse. I want to help children with problems."

They lingered and engaged in polite conversation. Finally, the young soldier asked, "I must get back to the Fort. Miss Janell, may I write to you?"

She smiled and said, "Yes, please do!"

The family continued making plans to take Janell to St. Louis to start school in July. The cattle drive would be over, and the cowhands could handle the ranch.

As was the habit of the army, a squad of soldiers would ride by to check on the Summers ranch, but with one difference. Lieutenant Perkins was always in charge. One time, Janell was hanging clothes on the line. As the army rode by, a wave and a smile would suffice.

Another time, during a toad strangler, the wind and rain came down so hard, you could not see your horse's head in front of you. The squad stopped and found shelter in the bunkhouse. Tom commented one night at supper, "I've sure noticed the army is patrolling our place more and more these days. Have you noticed that too, Janell?" She just blushed.

It was a busy summer. Johnny Gail was everywhere pretending to be a soldier on his pony, Soldier Boy. Little Donna was walking and playing with Goldie, the cat. Rachel and Janell cooked a lot of meals and worked from sunup 'til sundown. They counted sewing as a recreation and made clothes for Janell's new life.

Tom's family stayed at the Fort during the cattle drive, which gave the new romance time to blossom. Lieutenant Perkins was off on patrol quite often.

June at the Fort was an especially difficult time because of a renegade band of Cheyenne Indians that harassed the farmers and ranchers for miles around. Fort Reno sent for help. Lieutenant Perkins and several other soldiers responded. It was a hot, muggy night. All but one man in the platoon was asleep. The renegades were stealthy. The guard's throat was slit, and Lieutenant Perkins was carried off. News soon reached the Summerses.

Janell was distraught. "He was a good man. He did not deserve that!" Through tears she said, "He asked me to marry him! He gave me his mother's brooch! I want to get out of here. It's time for me to leave this country."

As soon as the trail drive was over, Tom and the crew returned to the Fort. Upon paying his men and securing the horses and buggy, Tom made his way to find Rachel. Sally Ann heard they had arrived and ran to tell Rachel and the little ones. "Mr. Summers is back! He's back! You go give him a proper greeting," she said. "I'll look after Donna and Johnny."

Although Tom and Rachel had been married several years, their reunions were always true and passionate, like young lovers. "I've missed you so much," Rachel spoke between Tom's kisses. "But, Tom, we've had a terrible tragedy. "Lieutenant Perkins was horribly killed while on patrol. You must go to Janell and console her. Nothing I say seems to help."

Tom knew Janell well enough to know where he would find her. He headed for the horse corral. As he approached, he heard someone crying and knew it must be Janell. Like a father, he put his comforting arms around his daughter.

"Why did this have to happen?" she cried. "Everyone I love leaves me."

"We don't know all the answers right now. When we get to heaven, we will know all these things. I know you loved him. Do you know if Adam knew the Savior?"

"Yes," she sobbed, "we even prayed together and talked about what heaven would be like."

As the sun was setting, they headed for Captain Morgan's quarters. "I know it's hard now, Janell, but you are going to be all right," Tom said, his arm around her shoulder. "You are my daughter."

After supper, Tom took his family into the parlor and suggested they leave early for St. Louis and Janell's school. Rachel pointed out to Tom that they needed to go back to the ranch: not just to get their clothes and provisions for the trip, but for the quilt the two women had made for Janell's new life.

Tom agreed to this and later told Rachel, "The sooner we get Janell away from here, the better for her."

He thought to himself, "We could buy new clothes in Dodge City . . . and why is it that where you need to be is always the farthest from where you are going?"

"Hang on," Tom told the women. "It's going to be a fast trip," he said as he slapped the horse with the reins. Sally Ann had offered to keep the children while they made the trip to the ranch.

Everything seemed to be in good order at the ranch. Before dawn, everyone was in the packing mode. Tom brought in the trunks after breakfast. "I remember the day I hauled all of these trunks to the ranch for the first time," he said, giving Rachel a wink. "I'm goin' to grease the buggy wheels."

When he approached the buggy, he laid his holster and gun down on the leather seat. The sun was just starting to rise over the desolate land. It was already so hot and humid, you could barely breathe the air. As he began to squat by the wheel, he heard a very familiar sound. He sprang to his feet, grabbed his .45, and shot instinctively. He walked back into the house, holding a three-foot rattler by the tail; its head was blown off.

"See here, I'm as good a shot as you are, my sweet Rachel." Rachel and Janell screamed, and Tom laughed. "We could have rattlesnake stew for lunch!"

"I don't think so!" Rachel replied. "Now, let's get packed and get out of here!" she stated.

Janell began to weep as they approached the Fort. "Why are people so cruel to each other?" She was thinking two things: how the Indians attacked and killed her friend and how her parents treated her.

Tom reassured her, "I'm glad we have each other."

Captain Morgan met them on the porch as they pulled up. "That was a mighty fast trip to the ranch! You had better leave Babe here, and I will loan you a trotter, number 76. You can take him and be on your way in the morning," he said.

"That will be fine," Tom answered, "but he has the US brand on him."

"I will make out loan papers on him so you will not get hung. I'll make an army man out of you yet." The big man laughed as he handed the loan note to Tom. "When you get to Dodge City, telegraph Fort Dodge to come and get 76 and the buggy, and they will bring them back when you get ready to return," Captain Morgan said.

"We are off on a new adventure," Tom told his family as they began their trip in the early morning. Sally Ann rushed in to give everyone a hug. As they pulled away, she called, "God bless you all! Janell, don't you worry now. We'll be praying for you!"

"You know, this country has a beauty all its own, but you have to look hard to find it," Tom mused as they headed away from Fort Supply. "This trotter has a much smoother gait than Babe, so we'll make good time."

"Are there Indians around here?" Johnny asked.

"We're safe, Johnny," his father replied.

"I know, but where are the Indians?" Johnny asked again.

"Watch for big white smoke signals in the sky, and that is where the Indians are," Tom instructed. Johnny fervently watched the sky until he fell asleep.

The family arrived at the stage stop without incident. Hank and a new man greeted them.

"Where is Paul?" Tom asked.

Hank introduced Edwin Rodriguez. "This is our new hand. Paul was ambushed by some Cheyenne. He had gone to pick up two teams of horses for the stage line. This group of renegades had left Fort Reno and headed for Montana country. They came across Paul, killed him, and stole the horses. Those Indians were headed back to their land. The cavalry chased them but could not catch them."

"Paul was a good man. I'm sorry," Tom said. "Do you think it is safe to go on to Dodge?"

"Yes," Mr. Arnall replied. "Those Cheyenne are moving about seventy miles a day. The army cannot keep up with them. They are riding their horses into the ground and then stealing more horses as they go. The last I heard, they were up in Nebraska somewhere."

Tom and Edwin unharnessed 76 and put him in the corral after they gave him a good rubdown. During supper, an army sergeant interrupted them with his gun drawn as he bolted through the door.

"Where is the horse thief?" he demanded. Tom threw up his hands the moment he recognized the man. "Sergeant Burns, I could be the man, but I'm not! Put up your gun. Captain Morgan at Fort Supply loaned me 76, and I have a letter to prove it!"

"Oh, is that you, Mr. Summers? I will take your word. I do not need to see the letter. I believe you!" the young man exclaimed.

Tom laughed and said, "You could not read it if I gave it to you. The captain's writing is getting worse every day. Listen, I will read it to you."

Burns looked sheepish and said, "Okay, I'm sorry to bother you ladies. Please accept my apology."

The next morning, as they were preparing to leave early for Dodge City, Rachel said, "I am glad you had the captain's letter."

"Yes," said Tom, "I will keep it handy."

As soon as they reached Dodge City, Tom bought five tickets on the Santa Fe train to St. Louis. Then he telegraphed the army at Fort Dodge to come and get the horse and buggy. Then he began loading the trunks into the baggage car. "Dealing with all these trunks have become part of my life," Tom mused to himself under his breath.

What an exciting time for the Summers family! They all climbed aboard with the help of the conductor. Their destination was Kansas City and then on to St. Louis: the Gateway of the West.

Seated two rows in front of him, Tom thought he recognized a cowboy, someone he had met in the past. As the train picked up speed, black smoke billowing onto the clear frontier sky, Tom excused himself and walked forward.

"You cannot get to Texas goin' this way," Tom said as he patted the young twenty-year-old on the shoulder.

The cowboy dressed in a suit and tie jumped up and shook Tom's hand. "Mr. Summers! How have you been? Please have a seat!"

Tom grinned at the handsome young man and said, "Where are you goin', and why the suit?"

"My cowboy days are over. I am going home to Missouri. My mother and father wrote to me, and they need me back on the farm. I sure hope they're in a forgiving mood for leavin' the way I did four years ago."

"Where is it you're going to in Missouri, Larry?" Tom questioned.

"Poplar Bluff," Larry replied. "Do you know where that is?"

"Yes," Tom replied, "that is close to the boot heel, some of the best farmland around."

"Yes, sir," Larry said, "I will be glad to get back. I've been gone too long."

"Did your father treat you well?" Tom asked.

"Oh yes!" Larry responded. "He's a hard man at times, but he's also fair-minded. My mom is the best cook anywhere. I can't wait to sit at her table."

The two men talked as the miles rolled by. After a while, Tom asked Larry to come back to where his family was seated. "This is my wife, Rachel, my daughters, Janell and Donna, and my son, Johnny."

"Larry, I'm sorry, but I don't know your last name."

"Rupp. I am sure glad to meet you," he said as he looked at each member of the Summers family. Janell, looking young and fresh as springtime, spoke up and said, "I am Janell."

"Pleased to meet you, ma'am," Larry responded as he tipped his new Stetson toward her. He stood in the aisle, rocking with the moving train, talking mostly to Janell.

Tom interrupted, "Why don't you two sit together." Janell blushed, and Larry straightened up so fast, his head hit the train-car ceiling.

"Well," Tom said, "you two might as well sit together; you're doing all the talking as it is."

Janell asked Rachel if their sitting together would be proper, to which Rachel nodded yes.

"This is all so exciting to me. My parents brought me West in a covered wagon, and all I have ever seen was dry land and cactus. I lived at Fort Supply for a while, and then I went to live with the Summerses, to help with their little girl, Donna. Then, they adopted me. I am on my way to St. Louis to attend finishing school," Janell explained. The two young people exchanged stories for hours, even while the family ate the evening meal in the dining car.

Johnny Gail was full of questions, and everyone joined in with answers. A single answer lead to another one of Johnny's questions, every one ending in, "Why?"

Rachel mentioned that they had a ten-hour layover in Kansas City. She had seen a show bill advertising a show at the Royal Theater starring Eddie Foy. Tom mentioned that the show would start about an hour after they arrive.

Once in Kansas City, Larry helped Tom unload the trunks and luggage and put them in a locked storage. "Mr. Summers, are you sure these are all your trunks?" Larry inquired.

"You've never traveled with two women before, have you, son?" Tom laughed. "When does your train leave for St. Louis?"

"I am on your train," Larry said with a grin.

"That's convenient." Tom laughed. "If you like, why not go to the theater with us?" Tom asked.

"Only if it's my treat," Larry responded.

Tom answered, "Why not? But I'll buy dinner before we get back on the train."

The show was one of the best in Kansas City. Larry sat next to Janell. Later, Rachel told Tom that the young couple were holding hands.

"Let's let the baggage man load our trunks," Tom said.

"I can hardly move after such a meal," Larry chimed in. "The steak was great, but I've never seen lobster before. How about you, Janell, did you like the lobster?"

"Yes, Larry, but I wasn't very hungry. All the excitement, I'm sure."

For a few moments, the little ones chased each other around, happy to be outside again.

"All aboard!" shouted the conductor, and in a few minutes, their journey resumed.

They travelled all night. Tom was out like a light, and Rachel tended to the children. Another full day on the train gave Janell and Larry time to become better acquainted. Larry asked Janell if she would write to him once she got to school, and he gave her his parents' address.

"You may write to me in care of the St. Louis Finishing School for Girls."

They arrived at the station in St. Louis—what a bustling city it was! As Larry's train was about to leave for Poplar Bluff, he shook Tom's hand and said good-bye to the little ones.

He started to ask Janell if he could hug her good-bye. Instead, he grabbed her and kissed her and said, "I want to see you again." With that, he was gone.

A hack was waiting to take the family to the school. Professor Reneau met them in the library and welcomed them. He introduced them to Miss Deborah Keil, an English teacher with whom Janell would be staying.

After a short visit, Tom assured the professor that he would settle up with the school the next day.

Miss Keil joined them and they travelled to where she lived, which was near the campus. Tom unloaded Janell's luggage and asked her if she thought she would be happy there.

"Yes, I believe I will," she said, "but I will miss all of you so much!"

"We will miss you too," Tom said. "We will see you tomorrow after you get settled." Tom kissed her on the cheek.

Finding a hotel was easy; St. Louis was a growing city. Finding a room was a little more difficult.

"This room is a little cramped, but it is better than the stage stop!" Tom proclaimed. Tom and Rachel fell into each other's arms, laughing and crying too. "We have seen the best and worst in people," Rachel thought.

Johnny's "I'm hungry!" broke the silence of the moment. The shock back to reality brought everyone's attention on Donna, who was throwing things out the open window.

"Oh, Donna, don't do that!" Rachel scolded. Tom ran down two flights of stairs to try to retrieve the items. Unable to find anything, he ran back upstairs to their room.

The next day, Tom paid for Janell's schooling and her room and board in advance. After a tearful parting, the Summerses, without Janell, made their way downtown.

CHAPTER 23

Excitement in the Air!

"**L**ook at all the shops! Oh, look! There's a Chinese restaurant! Can we go?" Rachel asked.

"We'll see," Tom responded. "Let's go on down to the waterfront. There's the mighty Mississippi!" Tom told his family. In the distance, Tom spied a huge hardware store with a large sign spelling out, "Sommers Hardware." He asked the cabby to stop and let everyone out of the hack.

"Rachel, would you please take the children and go back to that nice restaurant and order something for yourselves and for me too. I'll be back and join you shortly."

Tom's steps were quick, his heart pounding. "I wonder, could this be my brother's hardware store? I pray it is!" He could hardly breathe as he opened the large wooden door. Tom was greeted by the image of his father.

"Are you the owner?" Tom inquired.

"Yes, I am," the one-armed man answered. He extended his good left hand to shake Tom's. "Who might you be?"

Tom ignored the question and replied, "This is the largest hardware store I have ever seen."

"Why, thank you, sir. We also sell to other hardware stores up and down the river."

"My father-in-law has a store in Leon, Iowa," Tom said.

The proprietor said, "By golly, I sell to him all the time. How is Mr. Lentz?"

"His son, Walter, is taking the store over. Lentz can't work anymore. We'll visit them on our way back home.

"Where is home?" the puzzled man questioned.

"I have a ranch in the Cherokee Outlet, Oklahoma Territory," Tom explained.

"You did not tell me your name," Mr. Sommers inquired.

Just then, a ship captain, and what looked like his entire crew busted in and loudly proclaimed, "Where's the boss? We need new rigging, and in a hurry, mate!"

"Excuse me, sir," Mr. Sommers said and went to wait on the impatient crew.

"I'll be back tomorrow," Tom said as he left with a lump in his throat. Outside in the warm summer afternoon, a young man wearing a white apron was setting up a display of the latest hand tools. Tom stopped and inquired of him, "What is Mr. Sommers's first name?"

"Why, that is my father. His name is John," the young man responded.

"Thanks," Tom said, holding back the tears. He hurried back to his family, who was waiting for him at the restaurant.

"What took you so long, Daddy?" Johnny Gail asked.

"I met a man who knows your grandfather," Tom replied.

"Oh! That is so exciting!" Rachel answered. "You better eat your supper before it gets any colder," she continued.

Back at the hotel, after the children were asleep, Tom told his wife, "I have found John!"

"What?" Rachel demanded.

"Yes, I am sure he is my brother, John, although he changed his name," Tom replied.

"I am so happy for you. Did he recognize you?" Rachel responded with a hug.

"I don't think so. We'll go back tomorrow, and I will tell him who I am," Tom stated.

After a sleepless night and a quick breakfast, Tom asked Johnny to go with him. "If you think Grandpa's store is big, you just look at this one!" Tom told his son as they entered.

"Good morning, sir! You are back, and who is this lad?"

"This is my son," Tom answered. "Have you lived in St. Louis all your life?"

"No," John answered. "I was born and raised east of Memphis, Tennessee, until the war."

"Brownsville?" Tom asked.

"How did you know that?" the curious man questioned.

Tom answered, "I am your brother, Tom!"

John Sommers was so shocked that he almost fainted. He sat down hard on a nearby crate and was brought to tears.

"My God!" he said. "I was told by the army that you were killed in the Battle of Stones River!"

"No, I escaped," Tom quickly replied.

"I thought you were dead all these years," John said as he stood back up, embracing his newly found brother. "When you came in yesterday, I thought it was odd that you wouldn't tell me your name. Now I know. Praise God, you are alive!" John continued.

Johnny Gail had never seen his father cry before. "Why are you crying, Papa?"

"Oh, we are crying for joy," responded John. "Come, I want you to meet my son. Look! Look, son," John said as they approached the young man who was arranging a new shipment of shovels.

Tom wanted to take in everything that involved his brother. He could wait no longer to meet his nephew. "And what is your name?"

"Thomas Jefferson Sommers," the young man replied. Tom was stunned. He remembered his mother quoting Thomas Jefferson, "God, who gave us life, gave us liberty." John broke the silence. "This man, this is your uncle. This is who you were named after, and this is his son."

Tom spoke up and said, "I am glad to meet you, Thomas. Yes, this is my son Johnny Gail. He was named after your father and the windy, stormy night on which he was born. I can't wait for you to meet my wife and daughter!"

"Thomas, I want you to go home and tell your mother that we will have four guests for dinner and to ready the guest rooms. Tell her I have found my long lost brother," Mr. Sommers ordered.

"Tom, please. We want you and your family to dine with us this evening and to reside with us during your stay. Here is our card," John said as he handed it to Tom. "We will expect you at 7:00 p.m. sharp." The two men shook hands and hugged again.

Tom and Johnny Gail returned to downtown St. Louis and headed toward the river to their hotel. Rachel had left word at the desk that she and Donna were shopping next door at Miss Madeline's Boutique.

"Boy, this looks like a fancy place," Tom said to his young companion as they entered the tall, etched, glass doors. "Fashions from Paris" was on the wall written in gold, and crystal chandeliers graced the carpeted dress shop.

"Oui, Monsieur, may we be of service?" asked a woman who looked a little overpainted and a lot overdressed. Her perfume floated around her like a song.

Stunned and speechless, Tom managed, "We are looking for Mrs. Summers and her daughter."

The uptown woman responded, "Of course, monsieur, please be seated. They will join you momentarily."

Awkwardly, Tom sat down on a satin-covered bench. Johnny looked out the window. "Don't touch anything!" Tom warned.

Rachel appeared in a lovely dress of pale-ivory silk embellished with Austrian beads. Donna joined her mother in a frock of soft-pink taffeta with a matching purse. Looking at his two beauties, Tom was filled with pride and, before Rachel could speak, said, "We'll take them both!"

"Oh, Tom, we can't afford these dresses! We were just trying them on for fun," Rachel whispered to Tom.

"They will be perfect for tonight. We are going to stay with my brother and his family. You stay here and pick out another dress. Johnny and I are going to the school and fetch Janell so she may join us for dinner. Be looking for a fine dress for her and some shoes also," Tom told his wife.

When the two returned, Janell tried on several fashions, modeling each one. "I like this red one."

"That dress is too bold for you, mademoiselle. Perhaps this blue one would be more practical," the attendant offered. After a few minutes, Janell had been strapped, laced, and buckled into a beautiful taffeta dress with bone and crystal buttons. "Mademoiselle Summers, this dress is exquisite on you. May I pin this lovely brooch straight from Paris on you for a touch of color?"

"No, thank you. I have a very beautiful brooch of my own," Janell responded.

"You ladies are beautiful!" Tom said as he turned to each one. "This is costing me fifty steers," he said to the owner of the shop as he paid for the dresses, "but it is worth it."

"Is there any relationship between you and John Sommers, owner of the hardware store?" she asked.

"Yes, I am his brother," Tom proudly answered.

"That is nice. Mr. Sommers's wife and daughter shop here all the time. You do know they are the richest people in town. Sarah Sommers inherited her father's import business and the fortune that went with it. Well, enjoy your purchases, and please visit us again soon."

"Boy, she's better than a newspaper!" Tom sighed as soon as they were safely out of the storeowner's earshot. The newcomers to the city were starting to fit right in. They chattered all the way to the hotel, filling Janell in on the good news. The ladies took turns showering after sending Tom and Johnny out to the parlor, where Tom read the latest newspaper. They could hear the girls laughing and going on about each other's new dresses and shoes and purses.

"You girls better hurry up! We don't want to be late," Tom cautioned.

They gathered up their belongings, and the hotel bellhop took their luggage to the awaiting hack. As the hack pulled up to 712 Washington Street, Tom explained to the children, "You want to be on your best manners now. Say 'Yes, ma'am,' and 'No, ma'am,' and 'Yes, sir' and 'No, sir,' all right?"

Tom looked up and, without thinking, said, "I didn't know they made houses this big!"

A coachman met them and assisted each one as they stepped out of the hack. Large white columns flanked the main entrance of the house. As Tom reached for the brass doorknocker; he could hear music coming from inside the house. "This is going to be an experience," Tom said to himself. A very distinguished-looking man answered the door. Tom said, "We are looking for the John Sommers residence."

"Sir, this is the Sommers home. They are expecting you," the butler told him. "Please follow me into the parlor."

John appeared and said, "May I introduce you to my wife, Sarah, and my daughter, Gabrielle. Darling, this is my brother, Tom, and his family.

"You are late," Mrs. Sommers snapped, shaking hands with Rachel and Tom. "Oh, there are five of you. I must tell the maid to set another place. John, you told me four. Now there are five guests," the haughty woman said, blaming her husband for the error. Staring at John, she turned abruptly and left the room.

Tom, feeling very embarrassed, apologized for his mistake. In the excitement of finding John, he forgot to mention his daughter Janell, who was settling into her first day at finishing school.

"Don't worry. We have plenty of room for everyone and plenty of food to eat," John assured.

Just then, the young man whom Tom had met earlier at the hardware store walked in and introduced himself. "Good evening. You must be the lovely Mrs. Summers."

"Yes," Rachel replied. She was standing close enough to notice the smell of whiskey on the young man's breath.

"My name is Thomas Sommers. May I assume these are your two beautiful daughters?"

"Yes, Donna and Janell," Rachel replied.

"One day, I hope to become a lawyer to better handle the family's finances. My grandfather, whom I am sure you have heard of, Senator Stephen Douglas managed quite well, and I want to follow in his footsteps. You know, he courted Mary Lincoln before she married the president."

"Dinner is served." The butler's announcement was a welcome interruption from Thomas's verbal pomp and circumstance.

The table was set with regal dinnerware, white linens, and more silverware and goblets than a china shop. Tom remembered days on the trail when he ate grass to survive. The first course was scalloped oysters, a favorite of President Lincoln's, and chilled cucumber soup. The main entrée was saddle of lamb "a la duchesse," with paper cuffs around the roast. Next came the gooseberry salad, garniture "a la jardinière" with hollandaise sauce. Finally came mincemeat pie for dessert. Silence reigned as the guests were stunned by the unfamiliar look and taste of each dish. Donna broke the silence by asking, "Why do the bones have socks on its feet?" referring to the paper cuffs on the ribs on the rack of lamb.

"Hush, and eat your dinner," Rachel chided.

Mrs. Sommers looked down her long nose and asked Tom, "John tells me you fought in the war. It's been years and years since then. My father knew President Grant before he became president. Where did you go after the war? John thought you were dead. With what regiment did you fight? We all thought you were dead."

Being the young boy he was, not understanding proper behavior, and being plain spoken, Johnny Gail said, "This meat sure is tough," right out loud. He looked around and saw everyone staring at him, especially his father.

"I guess maybe I got a dull knife," he said sheepishly.

When dinner was finally over, the men excused themselves to the parlor, where Roman punch, which was a blend of sherbet, rum, and champagne, was served, along with Cuban cigars of the finest quality for the men to smoke.

The women gathered on the veranda, where the summer breeze brushed over them ever so slightly. They could hear the men talking and laughing. "What a beautiful home you have," Rachel said to her hostess.

"My father built this for our family at the turn of the century. He was the driving force as St. Louis began to grow. What does your father do?" Sarah asked.

Rachel began to tell about her family living in Leon, Iowa, and owning and operating the oldest hardware store. But before Rachel could finish, Mrs. Sommers asked Janell about her schooling.

Janell looked at Rachel, and Rachel told Sarah that Janell was boarding with Miss Keil and preparing to begin school.

"Your dress is a bit drab for this part of the country, Janell. One must put their best foot forward. If only one could afford to shop at Madeline's."

Rachel was feeling a little warm and cleared her throat. "That is where we bought her dress, actually."

Sarah adjusted herself in her chair, sitting a little taller than Rachel and Janell, and replied, "Oh yes, I thought I saw that one on the sale rack. Perhaps a scarf would enhance it somewhat."

The lemonade was getting warm and the atmosphere cooler by the minute. The women excused themselves and made their way upstairs to their rooms, where the linens had been turned back with scented pillows awaiting each one.

Tom asked Thomas if he would show little Johnny to his room. "Yes, sir!"

"Good night, son. I'll be up soon," Tom promised.

Then Tom asked the most pressing question. "Why did you change the spelling of your name?"

John drew slowly on his cigar and waited to exhale. Finally, he said in a low voice, "Our father was so mean to us that I was ashamed to be known by his name. So when I learned he was dead—"

"Yes," interrupted Tom, "I saw their graves when I was leaving to go out West."

"So after I found that they had been killed, I headed north and changed my name," John continued. "I even had a young woman approach me, saying that she was my half-sister and that Molly McGee, a whore from Brownsville, was her mother. I sent her on her way, denying it but knowing it was probably true."

"Enough," said Tom. "I have forgiven him and tried to forget his evil ways. We were blessed with an angel of a mother."

Thomas returned and began to pour another round of punch.

"No, thank you. I know now why they call it 'punch'. I must call it a night. Thank you for having us in your home. See you in the morning," Tom said with an already splitting headache.

John had made plans to show his brother and family the sights of St. Louis the following day. They all piled into a surrey with three rows of seats. Two beautiful black Morgan horses and Ross, the driver, sped the happy troop first to the museum then to John's beautiful church.

"What about your store?" Tom asked John.

"Thomas will take care of it. Sometimes I think he does better there without me."

As they drew closer to the riverfront, John, beaming, said, "I want to show you my pride and joy. See there among all of the action? There, in the maze of steam paddlewheel boats, see that blue and white one—the *Sarah Gabrielle*?"

"Yes," replied Tom.

"That one is mine. I deliver supplies from my store up and down the Mississippi, also up the Missouri River to Kansas City, all the way to St. Joe; that's where the wagons pick up your father-in-law's supplies and takes them on to Leon, Iowa."

"This is all so exciting," Rachel responded. Johnny and Donna loved all of the activity too.

"I want to ride the boat. Please, can I ride?"

"We'll see, Johnny," his father replied.

"We will stop for lunch soon. Then, we'll go down on the docks so you can get a real good look, Johnny," his uncle told him.

John turned to Rachel and Janell and apologized that Mrs. Sommers will be unable to join them for lunch as she had a previous engagement.

As the young people watched the ships loading and unloading, John stepped back and motioned to Tom. In a low voice, he began this story. "I was mustered out of the army in 1864 as a corporal after I lost my arm. They were going to let me die. Guess I would have bled to death except for an angel of a nurse named Jenny. She sat by my side all night to keep my shoulder up to help stop the bleeding."

Tom stood there, tears welling up, but said nothing.

"When I was well enough to travel, she packed a few provisions for me, and I set out to find our parents. I came upon an Indian boy and his dog. I shared the food I had with them. We could not speak the same language, but we helped each other. The boy killed squirrels, and we roasted them over a quick fire. At the fork in the road, about five miles from our place, we parted ways. I headed for our home and found only ruins and the grave. That was difficult for me to accept. Then, I walked on over to the Allens' place to see Uncle Henry and Aunt Ethel, but there were new owners, and they did not know where the Allens had gone. I looked for over two weeks, but to no avail."

"Good afternoon, Mr. Sommers" was heard from every direction. Some of the crewmen tipped their caps to Mrs. Summers and especially to Janell.

"Men have come from all over the country to work here. The pay is low, but the work is steady. Here, Johnny, come. We can board the *Liberty*. It belongs to a friend of mine. See this wheel? This is how the captain or a crewmate steers this vessel. Each one must be careful not to run into another boat," John said to Johnny Gail.

Donna was busy feeding cookies to the seagulls and did not see the pile of rope in front of her. She fell head over heels into the wet mess. "Now, you're going to smell like a fish!" Rachel scolded.

"I'm sorry, but I promised to have Janell back to Miss Keil's quarters after lunch," Tom reminded his brother.

"Yes, we should go before Miss Janell gets kidnapped!" John laughed.

They delivered Janell to the door of her tutor. She said goodbye to her family again, thanking each one. "I will send Thomas over with the rest of your belongings tomorrow," promised John. "We are so glad to meet you."

About dusk, there was a knock on Miss Keil's door. She came to the door and asked the young man what he wanted.

"I am Miss Janell's cousin, Thomas Sommers," he said. "I have brought her luggage."

"Please come in. Set the suitcases there and please join us in the parlor."

Janell was pleased to see Thomas again. .

"How are you this evening, cousin Janell?" Thomas asked.

Janell blushed and said, "I must confess that I am not your cousin. My last name is Miller. Mr. and Mrs. Summers have the same as adopted me." Miss Keil excused herself and brought back cookies and buttermilk.

Thomas stood to his feet as Miss Keil entered the room. "I would like to ask your permission to escort Miss Miller about town."

Miss Keil stated, "You may come to call, but only on Sundays, as Miss Miller is dedicated to her studies. She must pass strenuous tests before she may be admitted to our school."

"May I escort both of you lovely ladies Sunday morning to church?" Thomas requested.

"Janell, do you care to go?" Miss Keil asked.

"Yes, ma'am, which church is it?"

"You may call on Miss Miller. My fiancé, Michael, will escort me. Please be here at 10:00 a.m."

"Yes, ma'am. Our family attends the Methodist church downtown. Will that meet with your approval?"

"Yes, sir. We will see you Sunday."

The two Summers families sat in reserved pews in a fine-structured building with lovely appointments, candles, pulpits, and a huge Bible on the altar. As the robed Reverend entered, escorted by three altar boys carrying candles to light the altar candles, the Reverend nodded to greet John and his family. Thomas and Janell joined the family behind them. The pipe organs dominated the first part of the service. Johnny Gail and Donna were all eyes as they had never seen anything like this church. The fifty-plus choir members filed in, and the service began.

Afterward, Janell introduced Deborah and her fiancé to John and his family. "Please join us for dinner on the grounds," Mr. Sommers said to both of them.

This was an annual summer event. Everyone who was anybody was present to see and be seen. "This is good for Janell to meet the highest class of this community," Rachel reminded Tom.

"I don't know; it seems stiff to me," he answered.

The boys and girls enjoyed themselves as they chased one another. Butterflies flitted from flower to flower. Ladies in large-brimmed hats gathered around white linen-covered tables to arrange the food. Folks had begun to place blankets on the beautiful green grass and to relax in the shade of the mighty oaks. More baskets of food began to appear.

It was a most lovely day. Janell and Thomas got better acquainted as John proudly introduced Tom and his family to all of his friends. "When are we going to see Grandpa Lentz?" Johnny Gail asked his father.

"In a few days, son; we will get back on that big black train and travel to Kansas City and then on to grandpa and grandma's," Tom assured his young son.

CHAPTER 24

Going Home, 1881

"Mother, Father, we're home!" Rachel called from the front porch.

"Oh, honey! It has been so long! Let me look at you. Come! Your father is waiting for you," Mrs. Lentz said as she picked up sleepy Donna and hugged Johnny Gail. "Come here, my darling daughter! And those children! You have done well, Tom. I salute you. You are blessed to have such a handsome family," Mr. Lentz exhorted.

The days were filled with many stories and lots of food. "Now I know where Rachel learned to bake!" Tom said to Mrs. Lentz.

"How are you feeling, Father?" inquired Rachel.

"I feel better now. Just being with all of you is a tonic. My legs are weak. I cannot walk, so I do what I can from this chair on wheels. Your brother, Walter, is head man at the store now," the elder Lentz explained.

One morning, Mr. Lentz told Rachel, "I want to take you to the cemetery where our family is laid to rest."

After a carriage ride south of Leon, the family gathered in front of Eherhart Lentz's tombstone in the Lentz cemetery. The inscription read, "Drummer boy for Napoleon." Eherhart was German, Mr. Lentz said proudly. He was my grandfather. "We are proud of our heritage, and I want you to be proud too." Rachel was heartbroken to leave. She missed her parents deeply. "We want you to come visit when you can," Tom said as he was loading the trunks into the carriage. Rachel had assured her parents that she was happy and that living on the plains was where she wanted to be.

"The trip to Dodge City was a long and dirty one. Soot from the engine found its way into everything they owned. The wind never stopped blowing. Rachel was staring out the window, lost in her thoughts, and was not very talkative.

"Is everything all right?" Tom asked.

"It is just so difficult to see my parents grow old. In twenty years, I will be old too!"

Tom replied, "You will always be young and beautiful to me."

Rachel snuggled up in Tom's arms as the train made its way through the night. The children were fast asleep nearby. Rachel stirred; a chilly sensation came over her. She felt weak but said nothing.

When they arrived in Dodge City, Rachel was pale and visibly ill. "I'm taking you to the hospital," Tom told her.

For days, she lay dangerously ill. "Malaria shows no mercy. It must run its course," the doctor told Tom. Captain Morgan and Sally Ann came and took the children to Fort Supply. Robert rode up from the ranch to spell Tom from the hours of staying with Rachel and the worry. After twenty-one days, Rachel's fever broke, and the doctor said she was "on the mend."

Tom and Rachel had become inseparable. He could not imagine life without her. He did not wire her parents, as it would have been very difficult on them, and Tom did not think they were well enough to make such a long trip.

After a brief stay at the Fort, their lives got back to normal. Janie White, the doctor's wife, went home with them to make sure Rachel rested and gained back all of her strength. Will knew to gather bark from the willow trees and scrape it into a powder. Mrs. White made tea from it to relieve the fever or headaches for Rachel.

Tom reminded everyone that it would soon be time for the fall roundup and the branding of the new calves.

CHAPTER 25

Colorado, Here We Come!

I n the year of 1885, the state of Kansas ruled that Texas cattle were quarantined from entering the state because of Spanish fever, also known as Texas fever. Longhorn cattle were immune from this deadly disease that was caused by the bite of a tick. Unfortunately, the English, or domestic, cattle were not immune. Kansas officials were taking no chances; all cattle coming into the state were stopped and inspected. The boundary of the quarantine line had moved westward across the state for years. It started at the railhead of Baxter Springs, Kansas, in the eastern part of the state and moved toward Wichita and on to Medicine Lodge, Hays, and finally, the entire state. Tom could no longer sell his cattle in Kansas.

A few years ago, he sold small amounts of cattle to the army at Fort Supply to feed the Indian tribes, but there was not enough income from that to keep his ranch solid. Tom talked this situation over with Captain Morgan at the Fort.

"I need another market for my cattle," Tom told him. The captain telegraphed the other forts and found that Fort Garland, in southern Colorado, needed a large number of cattle to feed the Ute Indians in the area. Also, there was a need in the nearby coal company to feed the miners.

243

Tom contacted the army at Fort Garland and the coal company near Walsenburgh, Colorado. After much haggling about the price by way of telegraph, Tom was mailed a contract from both. Delivery date for the cattle was to be on or before July 24.

Captain Morgan, who had been in that part of Colorado, stated that to get the cattle to the Walsenburgh coal mine would not be too difficult, but to go to Fort Garland would be another story.

"Son," he told Tom, "there's a range of mountains called the Sangre de Cristo that you must climb to get to Fort Garland." As the aging captain spoke, his voice changed and his eyes began to tear up. "The name means 'Blood of Christ.' The sunsets there are a red glow off the mountains that top out at over ten thousand feet high. Fierce winds and steep cliffs make traveling very difficult, but there is no more beautiful a place on this earth!"

Tom was relieved to find out that there was a narrow-gauge railroad that went west from Walsenburgh through Fort Garland and on to the gold fields.

"I will ship my cattle this year on the railroad," Tom declared. He telegraphed the railroad for the information and found out the hard truth. There were very few narrow-gauge cattle cars and no loading pens at Walsenburgh. The cattle would have to be driven all the way to Fort Garland. The distance was only fifty miles as the crow flies from Walsenburgh to the Fort, but it sounded like it would be rough going on the cattle and on the cowboys.

"Looks like we are going to find out if we are real cowboys or not," Tom said to his hands with a determined grin.

In early May, the Summerses began making plans to move the herd of Texas Longhorn to Colorado. "I think Johnny is old enough to go with us on the drive. He's ten years old and can ride as well as any man," Tom told Rachel. "I know," she responded. "He's almost a man. I would rather take him with me to see his grandparents, but I know you need him."

The men began gathering the cattle that they wanted to take on the drive to Colorado. Rachel and Donna packed for their trip east.

"Give my best to your parents," Tom said as he kissed them both good-bye. "I will come back from Colorado to Dodge City and telegraph you when I arrive."

Tom took the horse and buggy to the livery stable and arranged to leave them there for the two or three months that he would be gone. "Things sure are a-changin'," Tom told the new hands at the livery stable.

"Our business is sure hurtin'," the young man replied. "We haven't had a cattle drive in over six months."

Saddling up Ranger number two, Tom started back to his ranch. He rode from Dodge City straight through and arrived two days later. Robert Thornton, his foreman, greeted him. "Welcome home, Boss! Look who I hired."

Sitting beside Robert was a large man on a small mule. "This is our new cook. Wait 'til you taste his biscuits! That's what sold me. Tom, this is Jess Buchanan, from Arkansas."

"Glad to have you on board," Tom replied.

Robert continued. "Joe and Andy are getting the chuck wagon ready, and Jake and Will have finished gathering the cattle. We are ready to go!"

Johnny ran up to his father and asked, "How are we goin' to get to Colorado?"

"Well, son, I have an army map. We will go out West, following the Beaver River through 'No-Man's Land.'"

"Why is it called 'No-Man's Land'? Do they not let a man go there?"

"No, this area was a mistake when it was surveyed," Tom answered. "This land is north of the Texas Panhandle and south of Kansas. It is about forty miles wide, north to south, and one hundred twenty miles long. No state or territory would lay claim to it. The folks that live there are pretty much outlaws."

The army told Tom to wait until June to start the cattle drive, and they would supply a platoon of soldiers to travel part of the way with him through "No-Man's Land." Captain Morgan needed to transfer this troop to Fort Sumpter. In this troop were the Buffalo

Soldiers—a group of all-black soldiers, except their commanding officers, such as Lieutenant Elsworth, were white.

The army would travel with Tom's herd westward until he reached the Cimarron cutoff of the Santa Fe Trail then depart to the southwest and on to Fort Sumpter. From there to Fort Garland, they would be on their own.

The drive would follow the Beaver River until it petered out and then go along the Cimarron in New Mexico Territory then north into Colorado to the Purgatory River and northwest to the Cucharas River at Walsenburgh.

"This way, we will have water all the way," Tom told his crew.

The big day arrived. Provisions were on board, and even extra coats and long underwear were safely stored for the cold weather. Even though it was still July, vicious storms could happen in the big mountains where the tall trees grow.

"Head 'em up, move 'em out!" Each cowboy took his position to best move this herd of steers westward. The weather was unusually hot. Buzzards circled overhead looking for prey. The sound of the rock-hard earth meeting the hooves of a thousand bovines made an almost deafening roar.

"If only the wind would blow, it would cool us off a bit," Jake said to himself as he rode drag. He could hardly see or breathe because of the dust, even though he had pulled his kerchief well up over his nose and mouth. He took his canteen and poured water over his head to cool himself.

Seven days out, Robert, who was scouting ahead, came riding hard back to the herd with a band of outlaws chasing and shooting. Lieutenant Elsworth gave the command for the bugler to sound the charge. The well-trained Buffalo Soldiers rode directly into the swarm of bandits, shooting with great marksmanship, killing one, and wounding several others.

Some horses were shot out from under their riders. These men had no idea that the herd had an army troop with them. They quickly scattered in all directions, picking up the wounded as they rode by on horseback.

The moment that the charge was sounded, a much-dreaded stampede followed. Tom shouted to circle the herd to the left. After circling the frightened cattle for two hours, they finally came to a stop.

"Johnny, I am proud of you, son. You did well!" Tom said.

During the ruckus, Andy's horse went down with a broken leg from stepping into a prairie dog hole. He quickly shot his horse and laid down behind it as the cattle thundered around and over the dead mount. He could feel the earth shake as he lay there hugging the ground. When the last steer had found its way around him, Andy got up in a daze.

Jake rode up and said, "Here, take my hand." He lifted the shaken man to his horse.

That night as they made camp, the men compared stories. Robert looked at Andy and said, "Looks like you made love to a cactus."

"Feels like it too," he agreed.

"Jess, where were you when all the trouble started?" Will asked as he had been in the lead and could not recall where each man was.

"I've got a bullet hole in my hat!" Jess answered. "Me and the chuck wagon were bringing up the rear. We stayed back, letting you boys have all the fun."

The night was hot and muggy. Lightning could be seen in the distance. The land was as flat as a beaver's tail and as unforgiving as a scorned woman. From time to time, thunder echoed softly across the dry land, and they all prayed for a shower to cool things off.

Lieutenant Elsworth told Tom, "I will have a few troopers do night watch with your men."

"Thank you," Tom replied. "We will have to watch that storm. I wouldn't mind a little shower, but we don't need a storm coming this way to scare the herd again. I'll have Joe talk to the troopers and explain what is expected of them and how to handle the cattle at night."

As the men began riding slowly around the herd and singing to them, coyotes howled as if to join in. The men were thankful for the remuda of horses that they took with them so they could change mounts from time to time.

The word must have gotten around to the other gangs of outlaws that the army was along for this cattle drive; they had no more trouble with rustlers. Without the protection of the skilled soldiers, Tom was certain that the cattle drive would not have made it this far.

When the cavalry left at the Santa Fe Trail, Tom thanked them and wished them well. According to the map, it looked like they would have plenty of water on the trip, but when they left the Cimarron; the Purgatory River was bone-dry.

"Looks like the Cucharas River is another two days away," Tom remarked after studying the old army map. "There will be a full moon tonight. We will continue to drive the herd through the night as we need to get the cattle to water. We can rest when we get old!" Tom said with a dry laugh, feeling very old already.

As they approached the Cucharas River, the smell of freshwater stirred the weary cattle, and they began to pick up speed.

"Hold 'em back!" Robert shouted, but the herd was determined to get to the water. Man and beast reveled in the cool running water. The air was crisp and clean. Off to the west now, they could see the mountains.

"I've never seen a mountain before," Jake confessed to his buddy Andy. "Maybe we'll find gold!" he said. "And I hear the bears are twenty feet tall!"

"Yeah, and the women love you all night, if you can find one!" Andy was quick to respond.

"Boys!" Robert shouted. "Be sure to drink upstream from the herd where the water is clean." Joe answered, "Do not make much difference. I am going to drink it all anyway."

The next day, a lone rider approached. "Good day, gentlemen," the stranger greeted them. "Where you boys from?"

Robert answered, "We are from the Summers ranch in the Cherokee Outlet. Who might you be?" Robert inquired.

"I am Señor Cortez, and this is my land. You are welcome to rest here, but it's going to cost you," the rancher stated.

"How much?" Robert asked.

"Twenty dollars per day," the rancher replied.

"Our boss, Tom Summers, has ridden on into Walsenburgh on business, but I'm sure that will be fine and he will settle up with you. Where is your ranch house?"

"We are about six miles north, near the river. We are the Double T," the Mexican answered.

"Are we allowed to shoot game?" Robert asked. "We've seen some deer and antelope."

"Si, we have abundant game. Just be sure and bury the carcasses, or you will have bear in your camp!" Señor Cortez replied.

"It is beautiful country out here and different from what we're used to. We've never seen mountains like those two huge peaks to the west," Robert said.

"Those are the Spanish Peaks, but the natives call them 'Huajatollas,' the breasts of the world. They are over twelve thousand feet high, very beautiful and very magnificent!"

Tom and two cowboys from the mining company rode up and dismounted. Robert introduced Tom to the rancher.

"You are welcome to rest your cattle here on my land, señor, but I must ask you for reimbursement."

"We have been here two nights. What do I own you?" Tom asked.

"Forty U.S. dollars or gold pieces," was his reply.

Tom paid the fee and said, "Thank you. We may see you again next year."

Turning to Tom, Robert asked, "Is the mining company ready for the cattle?"

"Yes," Tom said, "these cowboys will help us drive and cut out the four hundred head they need. They have pasture on the east side of town to keep them."

Tom related to Robert that he was paid in gold, except for about two thousand dollars in greenbacks. "We're getting twenty dollars a head, and we've earned every penny," Tom said, remembering the stampede.

The cowboys from the mine helped drive the remaining six hundred head west of town to separate them and to let them rest before the journey over the mountains. Tom checked with the west-bound railroad, and as he had been told, there was no railroad corral and no narrow-gauge cattle cars to be had.

The only way to get the steers to Fort Garland was to trail them up and over what looked like an insurmountable challenge. The map showed they were only fifty miles away, but how tall those mountains looked to the flatlander cowboys!

"I don't know about your boys, but I am hungry!" Tom said as he turned Ranger II toward town. The miner cowhands lead them to the Miner's Café.

Just loud enough for Jess to hear him, Jake said, "Finally, we'll have some good food!" Jess tripped him as they entered the café.

"Check your guns at the door," the owner requested.

"Okay, but I hope you have plenty of good food," said Robert as he found a table and sat down. "Somethin' sure smells good!" He looked up and into the eyes of what he believed to be the most beautiful young woman he had ever seen. He was speechless.

Jake elbowed him and said, "Order up, man. What do you want to eat?" All Robert could do was smile.

Plates of home-cooked food were served all around, as well as some things the boys had never seen before: burritos, tamales, and red and green chili. Homemade beer was served in large pitchers. Tom asked Jake and Andy to relieve Will and Joe, who were watching the cattle, while they ate along with the miner cowboys.

"Joe, Will, and I will be out in the morning to relieve you," Tom promised and wondered what he was going to do about Jess, who more and more smelled of whiskey.

Tom began to ask around for a good guide to take them over the mountains. Robert asked Tom, before they left the café, "Would you find out if that young lady over there is married?"

Tom winked and said, "Find out for yourself."

Robert then asked Jake to find out the same thing, "And get her name!" Robert said.

"Okay," Jake said as he meandered over to the black-haired maiden serving sopapillas at the next table. "Are you married, and what is your name?" Jake asked boldly.

"My name is Rita, and I am not married. Why do you ask?"

Jake blushed. "My friend Robert wanted to know." When he turned around to look for Robert, he was gone. "Thank you, ma'am," he said and practically ran out the door.

The men found lodging in a small hotel. Next morning, Tom continued his search for a guide. Will, Johnny, and Jess went back out to watch the herd. Tom headed for the local saloon. It was early, but there were already a few customers.

A wiry-looking mountain man spoke up, "Heard you are lookin' for a guide."

Tom replied skeptically, "Now, how would you know that?"

"I just know. It will cost you fifty dollars in gold for me to take you over the Huajatollas, and I will be in charge. You and your men can choose to listen to me or die, not from my hand, but from the hand of God."

The man seemed to know what he was talking about, but to be sure, Tom asked him how many times he had been over the mountains.

"I was born there. It is my home. Do you want to go or not?" the dark-skinned man asked.

"Yes. You have a deal," Tom answered. "Only this one rule: no drinking until we are done with the job. What's your name?"

"Ray," he answered.

"What's your last name?" Tom asked.

"Knowing my last name will not get you over the mountains any faster," Ray grunted in reply. "Now, listen up. The first two days on the trail will be no problem. Trail the cattle west," he pointed to a low place between Baldy and Rough Mountains. "You'll wait for me there," he said with his hand out. "I'll take the gold now."

"I'm trusting you, and you sure as hell better be there!" Tom warned as he handed Ray a fifty-dollar gold piece.

Tom headed for the café. He went inside and sat down, barely recognizing the man seated with Jake and Andy eating breakfast.

"Robert? I didn't know you with a fresh shave and haircut! Those clothes look new too."

"I found out that Rita is not married, and I sure would like some time to get acquainted with her," Robert said.

Tom sent the two cowboys back to the herd and said, "We are leaving with the herd at first light. Tell Jess to stay sober. Have Joe bring the chuck wagon to town and pick up the supplies I'm buying today for the rest of the drive. Now, Robert, you are going to have two days off to do your courtin'. You know where to meet us in the valley, west of here. Be there on time to make the trip to Fort Garland."

"Thank you, boss!" Robert smiled.

About noon, Will came into the herd at a trot, finding Tom in the lead. "What's wrong?" Tom asked.

Will responded, "Nothing's wrong. We will be at the base of the mountains, in a couple of days with good travelin' all the way."

Tom replied, "Glad to hear that!"

Will continued. "Let's gather up the men, as I have somethin' to say."

Tom was a little surprised by Will, but he did not question. He simply held up his hand to stop the herd and motioned to the cowboys. The crew rode to Jess's wagon.

"Now that we're all here, I wanted to tell you that just over this hill is a church with a priest," Will told the men. "The priest is working in his garden—looks like he's all alone."

Tom said, "This I have got to see. Let the herd rest here awhile." Pointing to Jake and Andy, he said, "You two be the lookout 'til we get back."

As Tom and the men rode up near the outbuildings, they spotted a middle-aged man wearing a long black robe carrying water from a nearby stream to water his garden. Tom asked, "What are you doing way out here in the middle of nowhere? Are you alone?"

The small Mexican man replied, "The people who travel this trail are my church, and I am but God's hand to minister to their needs."

As Tom and Will talked with the priest, they learned his name was Father Francis and that he had lived there for five years. The father blessed Tom and Will and told them that he would bless their cattle and the rest of the drovers.

Will left and came back with the herd. He had tied a small steer to the chuck wagon. "Good idea," Tom said to Will. "Butcher it out and give it to Father Francis."

Joe approached the priest. "I believe in God the Father, and in His Son, Jesus Christ, but I have never been baptized." Father Francis responded, "I can help you there."

The men followed behind the Father and Joe to the stream, where Father Francis bent down and scooped up a handful of water, blessed it, then placed his hand and the water on Joe's bald head, saying, "I baptize you in the name of the Father, Son, and the Holy Ghost, amen." He blessed the other men and beasts as well.

"Thank you, Father; we will be on our way. Thank you and God bless you. We trust these supplies will be of use to you," Tom said as the men brought in sacks of flour, salt, and sugar next to the butchered beef. "There's enough salt here to cure the meat to help you get through the winter."

The men mounted up, said good-bye, and rode away from the church, the priest, and the shadow of the Cross.

Tom; son, Johnny; and the ranch hands started with the cattle the next morning. It was a cold morning; huge clouds were building up over the mountains. They had to ride hard to hold the herd back from running. After an hour or two, the steers went into a slow gait. Midafternoon, a light, cold rain shower began. To the cowboy's amazement, it began to snow; thunder rolled in the distance.

"Keep the herd together and start singin'!" Tom commanded. "Robert hasn't showed up yet. Jake, you take charge."

They managed to make it to a good place to camp for the night. "We'll take turns sleeping. I want all but two to be on watch. We're in new territory, so be careful," Jake told the men.

The snow continued through the night. The mountains loomed ahead, looking larger all the time. By now, everyone was covered with snow.

The second day broke early with cold winds, making everyone glad they had brought their long handles. Tom sent Will out ahead of the herd to blaze the trail.

"Jake, I want you to be on point with the cattle; start out slow. There are lots of auroras to watch out for."

The cowboys came to the base of the mountains and found a stream about three feet wide, snaking its way along.

"This is where we make camp!" Tom announced.

Johnny didn't waste a minute. He stripped off and headed for a large hole in the stream. He jumped in, gave a howl, and jumped out just as fast as he had jumped in. "I can't believe how cold that water is, and it's the middle of July!" Johnny said, shivering.

"Get your clothes on, and get ready for supper," Tom told him. Andy had shot two rabbits earlier, and Jess was making rabbit stew and biscuits.

The men spent two days resting and enjoying the spectacular views. "I wonder how Rachel and Donna are. They would love this country," Tom thought to himself.

On day three, here came Robert, all smiles. The gang teased him, chanting, "Robert's got a girlfriend!" Tom rode up and joked, "Well, are you married yet?"

The fire felt good—they all sat as close to it as they could. "Jess, we have to give it to you, that was great stew," Robert said.

The sun was setting behind the mountains to the west; the sky was bloodred. "I have never seen anything like it. The sky is ablaze," Tom said.

"Well, boys, I think I have been hoodwinked. That Ray fellow got my gold, and he's nowhere to be found. In the morning, two of us will start looking for a way over the top. Be close with the rations, because we don't know how long we will be in the mountains," Tom admitted.

Just then—hoof beats. The sound was bouncing off the mountains, and they all looked around to see where the sound was coming from. It was Ray, mounted on a fine-looking mule. "What are you lookin' at? I told you I would be here," the mountain man spoke.

"You and the cattle needed the two day's rest."

"How did you know we've been here for two days?" Robert asked.

"I could see you from my gold mine, way up there," he said as he swung his arm around above his coonskin cap.

But they could not tell which direction he meant. And he meant for them not to know.

Church on Taos Trail—Tom and cowhands stop with the herd at the old church on the Taos Trail on their way to FT. Garland, Colorado. Photo by Linda Riddle

CHAPTER 26

Over the Top

They were all excited as they saddled up the next morning. They were glad that they had good, strong horses and that they were shod in Walsenburgh.

"Ahead are the toughest five miles you will ever experience. Say your prayers. Let's go!" Ray said. Then, seeing Johnny, he said, "Wait a minute! Does this boy know how to ride and control his horse? If not, send him back now. This ain't no place for babies!"

"This is my son, John. He can ride herd with the best of 'em. Let's go!" Tom commanded.

For the first hour, it was a steady climb. The horses and cattle moved together. Ray pulled up his mule and took charge. "Now is the time for the chuck wagon to stop. Jess, you pull up the brakes, hobble the mules, and wait here. We will come back with ropes and pull you over the top. Be on guard for bears and don't let your guard down."

Again, Ray took the lead. "This may only take one day if everything goes well. Hang on to your saddle horns, that's what they are for! You there, watch where you are going. One slip and you and the horse are gone. We can't stop and get you."

The drovers pushed the unwilling cattle up the mountain, careful to keep them behind Ray. Sometimes they were almost single file as the rocks began to slide around them.

"Take it slow back there," Ray cautioned.

A large tree had fallen over the place where Ray had intended for the group to cross. He quickly lassoed a branch and dragged it out of the way. "Come on, what are you waitin' for?" he sang down into the valley.

Andy was busy looking back to check on the herd. He turned around with his mouth wide open and was surprised that a tree branch was in the way and got his mouth full of aspen. It bloodied his face, knocked several teeth loose, and knocked him to the rocks. He managed to catch hold of the stirrup and pull himself up. Jake, who was behind him by now, gave him a hand up. Andy's mare stopped the minute there was trouble, which enabled the man to reclaim his saddle.

"Are you hurt?" Jake asked.

"Only my pride, only my pride," Andy muttered.

The men pushed the longhorns with a constant slap of the lariat, a poke on the rump, or a whistle.

Robert noticed that he was having trouble breathing. His lungs hurt, and before he could say anything, he began to throw up.

Tom rode up alongside him. "Man, you're sick. What's wrong?"

Robert answered, "I don't know. I can't breathe. I heard the guys talking about high mountain sickness, maybe." Before he could finish speaking, he lost it again.

"Do you think you can make it down the mountain?" Tom asked. "You need to turn around and get back to the chuck wagon then go on into town. We will meet you in Walsenburgh in a week or two. Here are some greenbacks to hold you over," Tom said as he said good-bye to his best cowhand.

Tom made his way over to Jake and shouted, "Robert is sick! I sent him back, and you are the foreman now."

Jake called to Joe, "I want you to take up the drag. Watch for mountain lions 'cause I've seen tracks."

Riding over to Johnny, Tom asked his son, "How are you doin'?"

"I've gotta pee" was the answer.

"Not now, just hold it," his father replied.

"We're almost to the top, men," Ray announced. "We will rest about noon when the sun is straight overhead."

Wildflowers were blooming up and down the mountainsides—yellow, orange, blue, and white. The white of the aspen bark lay against the dark green of the pine and spruce, making a most spectacular landscape. Hawks soared overhead, looking for prey. Bright mountain bluebirds flitted and flew in the trees. As the men looked out over the valleys, they spied white mountain streams against the purple mountain landscapes.

"This is paradise, a place where God dwells," Tom said to himself, taking it all in. Suddenly, one of the hands hollered, a steer bawled, and rocks tumbling down the side of the mountain was all Tom could hear. A mountain lion crouching above on a jagged dike sprang into action and caught a trailing animal. Joe was unable to prevent it. The cat and steer made quite a sight as they fell down the mountain on a shale rockslide.

Ray motioned to keep moving. "Don't shoot. They'll stampede! Keep moving!" The cattle seemed agitated and thrashed and bawled all the more.

"We are almost to the top!" Ray called. "Hold them together!"

Each step was harder than the last. The herd even wanted to turn back. They were all short of breath, tired, and thirsty.

Johnny's horse stumbled and faltered. "Hang back, Johnny, I want to check your horse," Tom called to his son. Quickly, Tom lifted each one of Soldier Boy's feet and found one hoof with no shoe.

"Climb down, boy. Get my tools out of my saddlebag."

The herd reached the top. "What a view!" Andy said. He promised himself that he would come back to this place one day to hunt elk.

"Now, slow these boys down," Ray ordered as they started their descent. Beyond them was a huge valley, the San Luis Valley. "I call that Elk Valley," Ray said, "That's where we will rest and regroup."

Before them stretched the Trenchera River, winding along, making its way southwest.

"Time's up! Ten minutes is long enough. Get some jerky out of your bags, because we are going back to fetch Jess and the chuck wagon. Joe, you and Johnny stay here with the herd." Ray was all business as he prepared to go back up the mountain.

"Bears and thunderstorms," Ray said, "That's what'll give you trouble up here. Hope for the best; prepare for the worst." Ray took off, followed by Jake, Will, Andy, and Tom.

"See that eagle! He can soar way above the mountains and can see forever. He has no enemies 'cept the crow, and that is only when he gets down and walks on the ground. When his mother pushes him out of the nest, every time he falters, she flies under him and carries him back to the nest. She does this until he can fly on his own. When he gets older, he goes through a molting period. He pulls his own feathers out and would die except for the other eagles that help him and bring him fresh meat. If he were to eat dead meat, it would cause disease and kill him. It is a good sign when you see an eagle soar!" Will explained. Will did not talk much, but when he did, you listened.

The five men made better time without the steers and remuda.

"I bet it gets cold up here in the winter," Jake said to Andy.

Andy said, "I want to come back here and go hunting."

Ray heard them talking and interrupted, saying, "You'd better come prepared. These mountains will either make a man out of you or kill you. Few women come this way. The only woman I had up here froze to death two years ago."

When the men came within sight of the chuck wagon, they could tell something was wrong. The mules were cut and bleeding; one was down. Jess was nowhere to be found. There were two whiskey bottles under the wagon and a trail of blood down to the gully, where Ray found Jess with a slashed throat and gashes across his chest. Bear tracks! The men followed the trail of blood cautiously.

About fifty yards down the hill, Will whistled and called out, "Here he is!" A huge black bear lay flat out by the stream.

"Is he dead?" cried one of the men.

"We've got to make sure," Ray said, pulling out his revolver. He fired two shots into the head of the bear. "Stay sharp, boys. The smell of blood will bring more predators, so be careful," Ray reminded the cowboys.

They rode back to Jess's body. Nearby lay his Colt .45, empty. Apparently, he had emptied his pistol on the bear, trying to save the mules and then himself.

"Get the shovels out of the chuck wagon and bury this man," Tom said to Jake. After a few moments of silence and prayers spoken, the men returned to the job at hand.

"We must get this wagon over the mountain before nightfall," Ray said. The bears can smell this blood for miles around."

They unhooked the dead mule and put his harness in the wagon, then they tied ropes to the wagon so the remaining mules could drag the wagon to the top and all the way into cow camp.

When Johnny and Joe heard that a bear had killed Jess, a somber reality filled the camp. They knew that Ray was right about the bears and that these mountains were nothing like the prairie they came from.

"He will be missed. What a terrible way to die," Jake said.

Ray rode off into the mountains, and Tom figured that would be the last they would see of him. But in a little while, a shot was heard and there came ole Ray, pulling a dead elk behind his mule. Jake and Andy butchered it out real quick. Tom took over duties of cook and fixed a fine meal of elk steak.

"Why did you skin the elk over the ridge?" Johnny asked Ray.

"The bears will clean up the entrails tonight, and I sure don't want them in camp. I want four men to watch at all times through the night and keep the fire burning bright. You might wake up dead if you ain't sleepin' with one eye open."

More elk steaks were on the menu for breakfast before dawn. Ray looked at Tom as he was cooking and said, "I don't never brag on no one, 'cause it more than likely goes to their head and gets 'em killed, but for flatlanders, you and your hands managed yourselves and the cattle well." Then, turning to Johnny, he said, "Son, you did your dad proud. As far as I'm concerned, you are a man now. I picked up these Apache arrowheads near the old Spanish Fort over by Sheep and Rough Mountains, and I want you to have them as a remembrance of your first trip to these mountains."

"Thank you, Mr. Ray," Johnny replied. As Ray handed the handmade flintstone arrowheads to him, the young "man" asked, "What did you say was the name of those mountains?"

Ray looked across the broad valley then back at Mount Baldy and Rough Mountain and answered, "These Mountains are the Sangre de Cristos, which is Spanish for, 'the Blood of Christ.' This here is a spiritual place. It's one of those places that make a man think about his life—think about those things that are important, like respect for the land, killing only what you need to survive, the love of a good woman, and faith in God. Only He could give us such a place."

As Ray spoke, a red glow crept over the mountains as the blinding sunrise flooded the sky. "See what I mean?" Ray continued. "The bloodred color in the sky on the mountain ridge? I call them "The High Lonesome."

"Thank you again for the arrowheads," Johnny said to his new friend. "I sure would like to find some gold before we leave. Would you show me how?"

"Grab that skillet, don't burn yourself, and follow me."

The two unlikely companions headed for the winding stream through the thick brush.

Ray explained, "Young man, always look for a bend in the river or stream, like right here. Choose the side where the flow of the water is slow. You will notice black sand; if there is gold, that is where you'll find it. Now, squat down, hold the skillet with one hand, near the water. Get a handful of sand with the other hand, and put it into the skillet. Dip a small amount of water into the skillet as it flows by and gently swirl it around, getting rid of the sand on the top. Any gold will settle to the bottom. If you don't see any gold, just try again."

In the meantime, Tom was breaking camp and the boys were gathering the steers. "Looks like a clear morning although there are clouds piling up to the south," Tom said.

Johnny saw something that he had never seen before: two lumps of dull gold-colored rock. "Look, Mr. Ray. Look! Is this gold?"

Ray bent down and exclaimed, "Yessir! You have struck pure gold!"

Just then, Johnny heard his father calling, "Johnny! It's time to go." Johnny put the rocks in his pocket, thanked his partner, and joined his father.

Tom rode over to where Ray was standing. "Thank you, sir. You have been a good guide for us. Some of the best money I have ever spent. God bless you."

Ray mounted his mule. Over his shoulder he hollered, "Friendship is like the wind; there is no end. Thank you and Godspeed."

The cowpokes started out slow, enjoying the awesome view. The Trinchera River was clear and free running from snow in the higher elevations. Iron Mountain was to the right as they traveled. Passing the mountains on the left, they could see the Cuchara Range, as it was called on the old army map Tom carried with him.

"I think we should call that valley where we had breakfast Elk Valley in honor of the fine elk steaks," Andy said as he rode along.

In the evening, they made camp. Andy and Johnny rigged some poles and went fishing. Proudly, they brought back all they could carry of the finest brook trout. "Guess we earned our keep for a while," Andy remarked.

"Yes, sir! Now all you have to do is clean 'em, and I'll cook 'em." Tom laughed.

Johnny did not tell anyone about his treasure. After supper, he asked his father if he could borrow the skillet to pan for gold.

"I guess you can, but, Andy, you go with him and watch for bears," his father replied.

The boys didn't have any luck, at least no good luck. They came back to camp and took their turn at watching the steers.

Jake came into camp the next morning after riding herd most of the night. "There are fresh bear tracks all over, even down there where you guys were looking for gold."

"Okay," Tom instructed, "no more panning for gold, Johnny. It's too dangerous."

"The ranch you will inherit someday is worth more than gold; it's a good living," Tom remarked.

FT. Garland, Colo.—Long horns were brought to FT. Garland, Colorado to feed the Ute Indians by Tom and his cowhands. Kit Carson was well known in this parts.

Photo is taken by Linda Riddle.

Johnny replied, "I may want to be a soldier when I grow up, Pa. I can already ride and shoot when you need me to."

The land changed from rocky and buck underbrush and evergreen trees to hard ground, scrub brush, and sage. After traveling two more days, Jake, the new foreman, spotted a troop of soldiers in the distance.

"They are probably from Fort Garland," Tom said.

"Did you know that Kit Carson served there at one time?" Jake asked Johnny.

"Yes. I read about him. He was a famous soldier," Johnny said.

"We have come to escort you to the Fort," Captain Levings said with a quiet Southern drawl. "Looks like you have more than the six hundred steers we requested. What do you plan to do with the rest?"

"We are hoping to sell them to a nearby rancher. Do you know of someone who might buy them?" Tom asked the captain.

"Your best bet is to see a Spanish rancher, Señor Garza. His ranch is about five miles south, along the river that brought you here."

The cowboys and even the cattle seemed to know their journey was about to end. There was a chill in the air even though it was only the end of July. Mount Blanca loomed to the west.

"I can't believe I'm seeing snow in the middle of summer," Will remarked. The steers picked up speed and were easily put into the corrals at Fort Garland.

"We will count out six hundred steers in the morning, and then, you and I, son, are going to find Señor Garza."

The men bunked in an extra cabin. Johnny was all eyes and ears, being in the company of so many soldiers.

A large Gatling gun was setting on top of a man-made pile of dirt in the middle of the Fort. "Boy, would I love to shoot that!" Johnny exclaimed.

"Hold your horses, son. Only in extreme measures is that gun used," a soldier replied.

"Like an Indian attack?" Johnny questioned.

"Yes," Tom said, "now, let's go to bed."

In the morning, the captain appeared and said to Tom, "Here is your US Army voucher for the herd you sold us. Those Texas Longhorns are a tough breed to come clean from Oklahoma Territory and still have meat on their bones."

"Thank you, sir," Tom said as he shook Captain Levings's hand. "May my hands remain here while my son and I go to the Garza ranch to see if he wants the rest of my herd?"

"Yes, sir. No trouble at all," the captain replied. "Pace your-selves; it is hot out there on the desert. Stay close to the river and it will be cooler. You know, if you follow it far enough, it will take you to the Rio Grande," he continued.

Father and son saddled up and, like two well-seasoned cow-boys, headed for what they hoped was more cash at the end of a long and dangerous trail. Tom was astride Ranger II, and Johnny was the proud owner of a beautiful sorrel with white mane and tail that his father broke for him three years ago. Johnny named him Shooter and taught him to kneel so Donna could get up on him easier.

The sun broke out suddenly from behind the large, billowy clouds and was surprisingly hot. When Johnny reached for his canteen, he found it empty! It had been punctured, and now he was without water.

Tom said, "We'll have to buy you a new one. Looks like a bear may have tangled with that one."

The unforgiving heat beat down on the Summers men radiating up from the barren ground. "Pull your kerchief up over your nose to keep from burning your face," Tom told his son as he did the same.

In the heat, a few miles' ride seemed to take twice as long. "Let's pull up and rest under these cottonwoods and cool off."

They unsaddled the horses and let them cool down before lead-ing them to the water in the river nearby. Tom and Johnny scooped up some river water in their hats and poured the refreshment over their heads. For a few moments, they sat at the river's edge, silently taking in the cool.

"I miss Momma and even Donna," Johnny confided.

"Yes, I do too. We'll get home a lot faster than it took us to get here. Let's saddle up and get on our way," Tom said.

They brushed down their horses, threw the blankets on their back, and cinched up. As Johnny reached for the saddle to pull himself up on to Shooter, he felt a sharp pain in his left palm. He screamed and dropped to the ground. A big scorpion limped away.

"Here, bite this stick to keep from crying. This is what the Indians do," his father assured.

Tom grabbed a package of raw tobacco out of his saddlebag that he had planned to give to Señor Garza. He broke off a piece with his teeth and chewed it to soften and make it moist. Using it as a poultice, he put the wad of tobacco on his son's hand and said, "Hold this tight. It will pull out some of the poison."

Tom gave Johnny a hand back up on his horse, and they continued their journey. "We should be there soon, and we can have you looked at."

On the horizon, they could see what looked like water. "Is that a lake?" Johnny asked.

"No, it is a mirage. The heat waves make it look like water in the distance," Tom explained. Johnny's hand was bleeding, and he was beginning to look pale. "Here, I'll help you get a drink of water from my canteen." Tom was worried about Johnny and the extent of his scorpion-inflicted injury.

The searing heat bared down and was sapping Johnny's remaining strength. Riding through the cracked, dry buffalo wallows, they finally approached a beautiful hacienda with many barns and outbuildings surrounded by an adobe fence.

By now, Johnny was on the verge of falling off Shooter. Tom had put his foot in Johnny's stirrup so he could ride next to him and Johnny could lean against his father. A tall, dark-skinned man saw Tom and Johnny approaching and rushed to them.

"Señor, is the boy all right? He looks faint. We will help you."

The stranger reached for his knife, which he carried in a sheath on his belt. He deftly pierced the skin of Johnny's hand and pressed against his palm. "There, there is the stinger."

He quickly pulled it out with a small pair of needle-nosed pliers. "I will take you to the house and clean the wound. Come, señor. Bring the horses."

The dark man carried Johnny into the courtyard and into a large gathering room. "Whiskey does a good job for a man. It depends on how you use it," he said as he poured some over Johnny's wound.

"Now we will have a small drink," the man said. "Young man, you will be fine, but when it is cold, in winter, you will feel the sting once more," he continued.

Tom shook the man's hand and said, "Thank you. You have helped us greatly. Would you tell us where Señor Garza lives, as we would like to speak with him."

"Si, I am Señor Garza. How may I serve you?"

Tom answered, "My name is Tom Summers from Oklahoma Territory. My ranch is near Fort Supply. We brought Texas Longhorns to the coal miners in Walsenburgh and to the soldiers at Fort Garland. I have two hundred head left that I would like to sell."

"Come, we will retreat to the veranda."

Señor Garza clapped his hands and two young servants appeared. "Take our new friends where they can wash the dust from their faces, and bring me our best wine."

Johnny fell asleep. The two men told their stories as the wine flowed. A young man, who looked just like Señor Garza without the white hair and mustache, appeared. "Ah, mijo, venga! This is my son, Juan. He will own this ranch one day."

Johnny woke up and stumbled into the room looking like he'd been hung by his feet—clothes a mess, hair wild, and scratching his head. "This is my son, John. He is not at his best right now, but I'm proud of him. He's my right arm on our ranch and on this drive."

"Take the young Mr. Summers and show him our new colt," Garza beckoned to the boys. The two young heirs to their respective thrones raced each other to one of the buildings in the compound.

"I have named him Smoky because of his color," Juan told John, as they approached the colt.

"Señor Garza, do you have need of some of the finest cattle west of Dodge City? They are strong and hearty in the winters. They are immune to the Texas fever and most diseases," Tom exhorts.

"We will talk business after my siesta. We will talk of days gone by. Where did you grow up, amigo?" the elder man asked Tom.

"I am from Tennessee," Tom answered.

"Did you fight in the war of brother against brother?" Garza asked.

"Yes. It was a dark time for our country," Tom replied. "It was a time I would like to forget," he continued.

"I understand," the soft-spoken gentleman exclaimed as they looked out over large gardens and fields of oats and hay, which were irrigated from the river. They talked of dreams and disappointments. Tom revealed things to Garza he had told no man.

A short while later, a beautiful black-haired woman appeared. She paused before speaking to her husband. Tom stood to excuse himself.

"No, señor, you and your son would favor us with your company for dinner." Before their eyes was a banquet of the most colorful display of food he had ever seen. The men called the boys in. As they ate and talked, the meal became more than food for the body; it developed into a celebration of friendship. Señor Garza raised his glass and said, "Salud, a mis nuevos amigos! Peace to our new friends! The guesthouse awaits you to spend the night. We will talk business in the morning."

That night, as father and son readied for bed, Johnny told his dad, "I have found a new friend!"

"I have too," Tom answered.

Early next morning, the two ranchers and their sons saddled up and traveled back to Fort Garland. The air was fresh with the smell of sage. The red-tailed hawks prowled the air overhead, watching the ground for unsuspecting small prey.

"Beat you to the river," Juan called out to Johnny. The race was on!

"I am happy that our two sons have found each other," Garza said. "Life is hard out here on the range. Juan's two brothers died of the whooping cough two years ago. My wife and I still grieve."

Arriving at the Fort about noon, they immediately went to see the herd. "Your cattle are much larger than my Corriente," Garza said.

"That makes them worth even more than the price I'm asking!" Tom replied with a chuckle.

Tom motioned, and Jake, Will, and Andy moved the herd around for Señor Garza's inspection.

"I count two hundred sixteen," called Tom.

"Si, Mr. Summers, that is my count as well," responded Garza.

For Tom, the fun had begun—haggling for the price per head. Finally, Tom agreed to eighteen dollars per head for the heifers instead of the twenty dollars per head the army paid him.

"As far as I can tell, there are only thirty-five steers in your herd, Senor. The rest are good, healthy heifers; some bred back."

"Please follow me," Tom asked Garza. "I want you to see my herd of fine horses. My mules and chuck wagon are for sale also."

"How will you get home?" the Colorado rancher asked.

"We will take the Denver, Rio Grande to Walsenburgh, and on to Pueblo, then the Santa Fe on to Dodge," Tom replied.

That night, after Señor Garza and his son left for home, Tom asked his men what their plans were since this drive was almost over. Joe said, "I want to go back to the ranch in the Outlet with you."

Will, Jake, and Andy announced that they wanted to try their hand in the gold fields in Colorado.

"Fine," Tom said. "Tomorrow, you three pick out the horses you want. Jake, I want you to take Range II, and when you're through lookin' for gold, bring him back to the ranch. Also, you guys take what grub you want out of the chuck wagon as I am selling it, and the mules too."

The next day, the horse and cattle drive to the Garza ranch began. When they arrived, a feast was being prepared.

Tom asked, "What's all this?"

"My new friends have come to see me," Señor Garza responded with a hug and slap on the shoulder for Tom.

While they ate, the rancher told Tom that he didn't have need for the horses because there was a herd of wild mustangs on the mesa to the south in New Mexico territory. "But I might buy them if the price is right."

"Three of my hands will take one each; the rest are yours for twenty apiece."

"I will pay fifteen," the rancher said.

"That's not much for such fine horses," Tom said.

Señor Garza paused and then asked, "Mr. Summers, are you a gambling man?"

"Not really, what do you have in mind?" Tom responded.

"We will cut for the high card. If I win, I will pay fifteen per head. If you win, I will pay the twenty that you ask," Garza said.

They agreed to the terms and shook hands on it. The cards were shuffled, and each man drew. Garza drew a king and Tom, a three.

"Just my luck," Tom said good-naturedly. "Now, how about a hand-built chuck wagon and three tough mules?"

"Won't you need them next year when you have a cattle drive?" the señor replied.

Tom answered, "I will build another. I don't want to take it back over the mountains."

Garza replied, "I don't blame you, my friend. How much?"

Tom answered, "Wagon, mules, and harnesses—two fifty, firm."

"But you only have three mules. I will give you two forty," Garza countered.

"Deal," Tom said.

Later, Tom told Johnny about the "art" of negotiating. "I would have taken two hundred. You must learn to bargain; it's part of being a rancher and a cowboy. Buying and selling is like war.

The boys saddled up their chosen horses. Jake was on Ranger II, Will was riding a pinto, and Andy was on a coal-black mare. They packed up what food they could carry in their saddlebags. Jake reached his hand out to shake Tom's. "You know, I will be back to bring your horse to you—after I strike it rich, of course."

Andy said, "I have been with you almost twenty years; working for you is all I know, but I would like to try my luck at gold mining."

Tom told them, "You are like brothers to me. Go try your hand in the gold fields, but know that you always have a place wherever I am."

Tom tossed each man a twenty-dollar gold piece. They shook hands and then mounted up and rode west into the San Juan Mountains.

Tom watched three men he'd built his ranch and his life with ride away. He was happy for them to take a different trail, but he felt an emptiness he hadn't felt since the war. Tears welled in his eyes.

Johnny came to him and said, "Dad, come on. Let's go home"

The next day, Señor Garza had one of his men hitch up a wagon that was to take Tom, Johnny, and Joe back to Fort Garland. Before they left, Garza invited Tom and his family to come visit any time. "Mi casa es su casa."

Tom replied, "We feel the same."

Juan and Johnny cut their arms and rubbed their arms and their blood together. "You are my blood brother now," Johnny said.

Tom had always been a man of reflection. The trip to Fort Garland gave him time to rethink the drive. "We did what we had to do," Tom said, "We found some friends, but we lost Jess, and we were gone from home too long." Tom put his arm around his son's shoulder. "I'm not much for doin' this again. How about you?"

"No, sir," Johnny replied, "Well, maybe." The two laughed.

The mountains that loomed ahead north of Fort Garland were overpowering. Mount Blanca was at that time, believed to be the highest mountain in Colorado at more than fourteen thousand feet. Snow covered the highest points and remained in the valleys. Story went that it was the coldest part of the nation in the winter.

The three of them stayed in Fort Garland town for two days waiting for the next eastbound train to Walsenburgh. Their hotel room was small, but they spent most of the time walking around and talking to the locals. Everyone had gold fever.

The trains heading west were full of hopefuls chasing a dream. The sunsets were spectacular, showing the reds and golds in the whirls of clouds.

Their trip east over the mountains was treacherous. One of the passengers who was walking between cars fell from the train, down into a canyon. The train came to a grinding halt, and the brakeman and others tied ropes together and lowered themselves down to rescue the man. They hauled him back up even though he was dead, apparently from a broken neck. They opened the baggage-car door and threw the dead man in, right beside Tom's saddles and belongings.

Slowly, the engine began to pick up steam and, inch by inch, moved the immovable. A mighty blast of energy propelled the "Iron Horse" up the mountain. Now, they were literally on top of the world. The view was awesome.

They saw large herds of elk grazing on the lush mountainsides. At one time, there was a large bull on the tracks, trying to outrun the train, it seemed. Out of a window, they saw a large bear climbing a tree, and eagles soaring above in the sky.

The train stopped in La Veta, a small, friendly town. It was nestled at the base of the Spanish Peaks, where pioneers had settled, seeking a better life.

Arriving in Walsenburgh, Tom, John, and Joe looked up Robert. They found him working in the livery stable, fixing harnesses and caring for horses.

"I'm working here until I can talk Rita into marrying me," he told Tom.

"I wish you would join me here, Joe. There's plenty of work. Tonight, I want you to meet my Rita. If she will have me, we will buy a ranch and build a life together," Robert said. "Sorry I had to leave. It took me a week to get well. I wish I could have been on the drive. Well, that's not true. Being here, I have had time to get to know Rita and her family, the Bonses."

Rita's father, Nickanore, was born in Aguilar at the base of the Spanish Peaks on the east side. He was a coal miner. Mexican settlers founded the town of La Veta and erected a fort there to protect themselves from Indians. The evening was spent sharing their adventures. "We lost Jess," Tom told Robert. "He died protecting the mules and our rations from a bear."

The next day, Joe went to the train station with Tom, and Johnny and helped with their saddles and luggage.

"Thank you, Joe," Tom said, "Come back to the ranch as soon as you get Mr. Lovesick married off!" Tom shook his hand and handed him a twenty-dollar gold piece.

"What's that for, boss?"

"It's your bonus. We got those darned steers over the mountains and lived to tell about it. We couldn't have done it without you," Tom said, very much relieved.

Colorado Mountains—Rough terrain in the Sangre de Cristos Mountain Range, West of Walsenburg, Colo. After delivering cattle to the coal miners in Walsenburg, Tom and company drove more cattle thru these mountains to FT. Garland Colo., to feed the Ute Indians.

La Veta Pass, Colorado—Ruts from Wagon trains are still visible near La Veta Pass, Colorado, Tom and company bring cattle down this mountain into the valley and on to FT. Garland Colorado, about 25 miles south-west. The Riddles live 5 miles west of here, during the summer.

CHAPTER 27

Leaving the High Lonesome

"All aboard!" The whistle blew and the steam built to a mighty blast; the iron-willed monster began to move.

"Father, where are all those women going, and why are they dressed like that?" Johnny asked, "They're going to cook in the sun, no more clothes than they are wearing!"

Tom explained, "Those are 'ladies of the evening,' and they are probably waiting for the train going west."

Looking at one of the ladies dressed in red, Johnny thought to himself, "She said I was cute."

Pointing her out to Tom, Johnny said, "Pa, she seems nice."

"Try to stay clear of such women and find a proper girl to keep company with when you are older," Tom instructed his inquisitive son.

Their tickets were for the northbound train headed to Denver, although they would change trains at Pueblo and head for Dodge City. Tom pointed sights out to Johnny as they went, trying to keep his son's mind off the improper ladies.

"Do you think that Robert will get Rita to marry him?" Johnny asked. "He's old."

"Yes, I don't think he will have a difficult time talking Rita into marrying him," Tom replied.

"Where will they live? Will we ever see Robert again?"

"Do you remember when Robert went to the Texas Panhandle last spring?" Tom asked.

"Yes."

"There was a family out there that wanted to sell their ranch. Maybe Robert will buy it," Tom said.

With the sway of the passenger cars and the rhythm of the rail, by evening, everyone was very relaxed, and some were asleep. "Robbers! Robbers!" the conductor suddenly shouted. The train had slowed to climb a steep grade, there robbers would lie in wait and try their luck at jumping the train. Tom reached for his Colt .45 and prepared to defend the train.

Johnny said, "I wish I had my gun that's in the saddlebag!"

A beautiful young woman sitting across from the Summerses reached for her small .38 caliber Colt revolver, which was in a holster strapped to her upper thigh. Johnny's mouth fell open, and his chin almost hit the floor as he watched the woman slide her hand up her dress to the gun. He had never seen such long, beautiful legs. The woman handed Johnny the gun and sweetly said, "You may use this if it is all right with your father."

Johnny turned four shades of red. Tom thumped him on his head to bring him back to reality and said, "Aim for the horse and not the rider, son!"

One of the four robbers was riding full out and up close to the train, preparing to jump on the steps of the passenger car. Tom jumped to his feet, and as the would-be thief grabbed for the railing, Tom hit his hand with the butt of his gun. The robber lost his balance, fell off his horse, and rolled down the slope.

The conductor fired his gun twice, killing the gang leader.

Johnny stood up and shouted, "I killed his horse!"

The last of the marauders pulled up sharply and rode away.

"Where did you learn to shoot like that?" the long-legged woman asked John. Tom interrupted, laughing. "His mother can hit the head of a striking rattlesnake at ten paces!"

"What is your name?" Johnny asked. "Do you like to shoot, too?"

"My name is Maggie O'Reilly, and no, I do not like to shoot! I just carry my small gun for protection. If I had a good-looking, strong man like you by my side, I would not have the need for a gun," she said, smiling, "Are you going to Denver?"

"No, we are getting off at Pueblo and continuing on to Dodge City, on the eastbound train."

"Oh, I used to work in Dodge; I still have friends there," she said and continued to flirt with Tom. Tom opted not to ask what her occupation in Dodge was.

Tom helped Maggie down the steps of the train after they pulled into Pueblo.

"Good-bye, and good luck," Tom said, giving her a hug around the shoulders.

"All the good ones are married," she replied.

"John, let's get our saddles and belongings out of the baggage car. Then, I'm going to telegraph your mother and tell her that we will be in Dodge in two days. Please wait for me in the waiting room," Tom told his son.

Iowa

It had been a hot summer in Iowa. Rachel and Donna settled into the fast pace of city living in Leon. One of the first things on the agenda was to go to Kansas City on a shopping spree. Ella, Rachel's mother, made plans for the three of them to leave on the train.

"First, we must visit the beauty salon. We must all have our hair trimmed and nails polished," Mrs. Lentz reported. Reservations were made at the Royal, Kansas City's best hotel.

Days were spent shopping and visiting over tea, sharing details of frontier life. Mrs. Lentz was quick to point out the many wonderful things Rachel and Donna were missing because they lived so far away.

"Your father is not well. You must spend some time with him when we return. Hopefully, Johnny can come next time to get to know his grandfather."

The ladies returned to Leon with lots of new frocks and hats.

The Methodist church had been added onto, and a new preacher had been called. Rachel enjoyed spending time with her father. Many evenings were spent on the front porch—she in the porch swing and he in his wheelchair.

"I'm proud of you, Rachel. You have followed your heart and have a family that loves you," her father told her the night before he died.

When Rachel received the telegram from Tom, she sent one back, asking him to come to Leon because of her father's death.

"We are now going to Iowa where your mother and sister are. Your grandfather passed away, so I bought tickets to Dodge City and to Kansas City and Leon, Iowa," Tom told his son.

While they were waiting, they noticed an old man cleaning up the waiting room. He even picked up old cigarettes and tried to smoke them. Pretending to pick up used cigars and put them in the trash, he put them in his pocket. The man approached Tom and asked for change. The man's face was unrecognizable, but Tom knew the man's voice. He was older than his years, unkempt, and reeked of sweat and liquor.

"You are Jim Nickolson, are you not?" Tom exhorted.

"Yes," the confused man answered, "but who are you?"

"I am Tom Summers, you thieving son of a bitch!"

The old banker ran out of the building as fast as he could, with Tom shouting after him, "I'll bet the marshal in Dodge would like to get his hands on you!"

"Who was that?" asked Johnny.

"That was the banker that tried to cheat your mother and me out of our life's savings when you were just a baby."

"He looked like a bad man. Where'd he go?" Johnny asked, looking out the window as the man disappeared.

As they traveled across the flat Kansas prairie land, they began to see fields of growing grains.

Johnny asked, "What kind of grass is that, Father?"

"That's not grass. It's wheat. The wheat is ground and we use the flour to make bread. The farmers are taking over the land, whether we like it or not. Our way of life is changing right before our eyes! See that barbed wire fence? I am just not sure I am in favor of that."

That night, they stayed in the Beebe Iowa House in Dodge City. "This is the place that your mother, you, and I stayed almost ten years ago when someone shot up the room while we were gone. Sure hope it doesn't happen again," Tom said.

Johnny lay with his eyes wide open all night, listening to every creak and noise in the building, scared to death of another shoot-out.

Next morning, they checked at the livery stable and paid more rent for their buggy and Babe. "We are going on to Iowa," Tom told the keeper. "Look for us back in a week or two."

They boarded the eastbound train for Kansas City then on to Leon.

"What was Grandfather Lentz like?" Johnny asked.

"He was a proud, hard-working man who wanted to go west but stayed in Iowa and sold goods to people who were headed that way. When you meet your Uncle Walter, you will see your grandfather in him."

The funeral was large. Mr. William Lentz was well known and well respected. The Lentz family had a rich German heritage dating back to the 1500s. Most of the men in the family were craftsmen, gifted with talents of woodcarving and furniture making. William's youngest brother, Burl from Saginaw, Michigan, attended, insisting on making his brother's wooden casket.

The family stayed several weeks, helping to comfort Mrs. Lentz and to help her take care of business.

"Mother, it is time for us to go," Rachel said. "We must get back to the ranch. Why don't you come with us?"

Ella replied, "No, my place is here. I want to be near William," she said, crying.

"We will write often and plan to come back next summer," Rachel told her. "I love you."

Uncle Walter took the Summers family to the train depot and saw them safely on their way.

When they reached Dodge City, Tom settled his family at the Dodge House and headed for the livery stable. Tom told Rocky, the new owner, "I need two good horses to build my herd back up and a good trotter to pull the buggy. I want to trade Babe. She is old but would make someone a good delivery horse. She's the best there is."

After Tom did his horse trading, he drove Timber, the new horse and his buggy, to the station and picked up his saddles and luggage. He headed to the Mercantile to buy a new saddle.

"How is business?" Tom asked his old friend.

"No good!" was the reply. "No cattle coming to town and no riders to buy my goods," the old man said. I would sell this place if I could."

Tom interrupted. "I hate to see you do that. My wife and I have bought a lot of mighty fine things here."

The owner asked, "Is the sewing machine still working?"

"Yes, it is. I keep it oiled and it's doing good," Tom answered. Tom bought two saddles because the price was right—trading in his old ones.

Tom hurried back to the Dodge House. "Come, I want to show you our new horses and saddles. We will go eat lunch, and then I would like to drive out to Fort Dodge and see if any of my old friends from Fort Supply are stationed there."

Rachel said, "Would it be all right with you if Donna and I stay here in town and you and Johnny go to Fort Dodge?"

"That's fine, sweetheart," Tom said.

The two travelers rode the five miles east to Fort Dodge, only to find the Fort closed three months ago. They arrived back in Dodge late that evening and told their disappointing news.

The next morning, Johnny told his father that he wanted to find a jeweler to make necklaces for his mother and sister from the gold nuggets he found in the stream in Colorado.

"I didn't know you found gold," Tom said.

"I wanted to surprise you," Johnny answered.

"Well, looky there! You sure did!" Tom replied.

The girls went shopping, and the men found a jewelry store. "I can have these ready this afternoon, sir," the jeweler said.

"Fine, we'll be back," Johnny promised.

"Guess I better pay you your wages, son," Tom announced.

"Yes, sir!" Johnny agreed and, with a wink, said, "Don't forget my bonus!"

"It is so good to be back with my family," Tom told Rachel as they enjoyed their dinner at the Long Branch Restaurant, as it was now called.

The state of Kansas voted against whiskey and such, so there was no need for a saloon with the cowboys not coming to town.

"Maybe being dry will cut down on the crime," Rachel said to her husband as she laid her hand on his. "I'm happy that the two of you made it back safe and sound."

"Say good-bye to Dodge for a while; we're headin' home!" Tom said as he gathered up his family. Rachel and Donna rode in the buggy with the new trotter, Timber pulling. Tom and Johnny saddled up the two new mares.

"Donna, you get to name these two horses," Tom told his daughter, who was now eight years old.

"I want to name this one with the blaze on her face Dolly and the gray one Polly, after my cousins in Iowa," Donna proudly announced.

As they pulled into the stage stop, Edwin came out to meet them.

"Good evening, friends. I have bad news. Señor Hank was killed by Indians a month ago. My cousin, Benton is here to help me. Keep your guns on the ready; these are hard times, and many bandits come to steal and to harm us."

The second night was spent at Fort Supply, but Captain Morgan and Sally Ann were not there. Indians fatally wounded Captain Morgan, and Mrs. Morgan returned to Boston to be with her family.

The new captain, Leon Kidd, went into his quarters and came out with Captain Morgan's pocket watch and handed it to Tom. "Mrs. Morgan wanted you to have these," he said as he handed Sally Ann's collection of dolls to Rachel and the children.

"We are deeply touched and will treasure these gifts," Rachel told the captain with tears streaming down her face. "Both Captain Morgan and Mrs. Morgan will be greatly missed."

Rachel was overcome with emotion. The grief of losing her father, and now her dear friends, was too much. "Things are changing too fast! We are losing our family and our friends!"

They arrived home and started cleaning and unpacking, getting ready for the winter, one without their much-beloved cowhands.

About a month later, in early September, Johnny spotted three riders on the horizon. The dust was so thick, he could hardly make out if they were friend or foe.

He rang the alarm bell that he and Tom had nailed to the barn just for such a purpose.

When Robert, Joe, and Rita riding sidesaddle arrived, the family gathered to meet them.

"Get off those horses and come in!" Tom bellowed.

"Robert!" Rachel exclaimed. "It's wonderful to see you! Who is this beautiful young lady with you?"

Robert hugged Rachel and said, "It is so good to see you. I'd like you to meet my new wife, Rita Thornton. Sweetheart, these are my good friends, the Summerses. This is Tom, Rachel, Donna, and Johnny."

"Oh, Robert, how wonderful!" Rachel said. "We must have a celebration!" Rachel cried. "Come in, I know you must be tired from your trip. Please stay with us here in the main house tonight. Tomorrow, if you like, we can fix up the bunkhouse so you will have your privacy."

Looking at Tom, Rachel asked, "Why didn't you tell me about Robert and Rita getting married?"

"Well, woman! I didn't know if it would happen or not!" Tom replied.

The next morning, Rita was up early making homemade flour tortillas and burritos for everyone.

With a mouthful, Johnny said, "I hope Robert's wife stays with us for a long time!"

Robert joined in, "I do plan to keep her, yes sir! May I ask a favor? May we take your buggy out to the Texas Panhandle and see if that ranch I looked at last spring is still for sale?"

"Of course, when do you want to leave?" Tom asked.

"Today, if possible," Robert replied.

"Okay. Let's get Timber harnessed up and get you some traveling provisions."

The newlywed's hearts were filled with hope as they headed west.

The only cowboys on the ranch now were Tom, Joe, and Johnny. They rode out and began to check on the cows that were left on the ranch as they sold all the calves.

"Look at those hides. I've never seen such heavy hair on cattle before," Joe commented.

"You are right. What does that mean?" asked Johnny.

"We are in for a cold winter!" Joe stated. "Let's round up those cows and then I think we should start gathering and chopping wood."

They were glad that they lived near Wolf Creek, where lots of cottonwood trees grew. When they returned from checking the cows, they began chopping and cutting firewood. They also gathered deadwood and piled it all in the wagon.

Rachel and Donna arrived with sandwiches and lemonade and, after a little picnic, helped gather wood for the winter. Soon, they discovered pecans that had fallen from the trees.

"Let's get baskets and find all the pecan nuts," Rachel said. They worked until dusk and made plans to work again the next day.

"Why do we need so much wood?" Donna asked her father.

"If we don't use it this winter, we will have it for the next year," Tom commented.

They hauled wagon after wagon of wood to the house and even put some in the bunkhouse, stacking it as high as possible.

"We need to gather all we possibly can," Tom instructed.

Late November rolled around, and Will and Jake returned to the ranch.

"Where is Andy?" Tom asked.

Jake said, "Will and I could not find gold if we'd tripped over it, but Andy was different. He found gold in every stream we came to. By the time we were near Durango, he found the mother lode. He had buried some gold and had given us the map for safekeeping. One night, someone crawled into his tent and killed him with a knife. We didn't know about it until the next morning. Someday, we want to go back and try to find Andy's gold. We gave him a proper burial and then headed back here. On the trail, we knew we were being followed. When we got to La Veta, we heard this guy bragging about doing a job for a banker in Dodge City. He said he'd lucked out in the gold fields. He said, "I didn't have to dig one shovel of dirt! I struck it rich. My pal Andy found it for me!" Jake continued. "We told the sheriff in Huerfano County about it. Last we heard, he was somehow connected to the banker. His name was Sam, and he hasn't been found yet. We circled for a couple of days and then lost him."

Jake went on to explain that he and Will had to work odd jobs in La Veta to get enough money to get back. The wages they earned working for Tom were spent on gambling and fast living. He explained that the Carvers, some nice folks in La Veta, took them in. Mr. Carver started out looking for gold and ended up finding coal. Nora Carver, Jake said, was the best cook. "I wish I had some of her peach cobbler."

Mr. Carver told the story of how, for years, he and his father had walked around a huge rock near their well. One of the children needed an operation or she was going to die. For days, the whole family prayed for healing or for the money for the operation. One Sunday morning, Mr. Carver looked at that rock and had the feeling he should take it to the assayer. He loaded it up and found out that it was full of gold, that way Mr. Carver was able to pay for the surgeon that saved the young girl's life.

"We followed the railroad tracks over the mountains before we got to La Veta because we had no money to ride the train. We came back the way we trailed the cattle out there," Will said.

Jake confessed, "Will wanted to catch the train on the grade, but I wasn't going for that."

CHAPTER 28

Blizzard of 1886

Just before Christmas, Robert and Rita returned, full of big dreams and plans. "We bought the ranch," Robert said first thing. "It is a beautiful piece of land, with a small sod house and lots of corrals that need mending."

"How far away is it?" Johnny asked.

"It's about sixty miles southwest or two days' hard ride."

"Can you stay for Christmas?" Rachel pleaded, "We'd love to have you!"

"That would be wonderful!" Rita replied.

Supper was prepared and everyone sat together at the big table, all talking at the same time.

"We will surely miss you," Jake said.

Robert said, "Tom, I'm curious; what are you going to do with so much firewood? Looks like you cut down every tree on the ranch!"

Tom laughed and said, "Joe says we are going to need the wood for the long, cold winter that's coming."

"It had better get with it! So far, we haven't even had a freeze!" Robert replied.

"We even made an extra trip for supplies," Rachel added, "because we trust Joe. I talked Tom into buying a wagon full of oats for the horses."

The girls had fun preparing for Christmas, making bread and pies. The men cooked a calf over a pit. A large cedar tree that Tom cut down especially for Rachel stood in the corner; hard candy decorations hung from each bough. It was such a joyous time of singing Christmas carols, reading the scriptures, and teasing the newlyweds. A blazing fire in the fireplace invited the warmth of the season and the peace of the holiday.

In a few days, the Thorntons prepared for the three-day journey to their new home. They took their two pinto ponies and the mule, Big Joe. Rachel gave them two quilts filled with feathers and extra food for the trip. They headed out New Year's Day, 1886. It was warm that morning, and the sky was crystal blue.

"We will see you soon," Robert promised.

To the north, Robert could see dark clouds gathering. By midafternoon, a blue northern had ripped across the plains. A cold rain blew in first then hail. By sundown, the temperatures were below freezing, and a fierce north wind with blinding snow made travel almost impossible. The travelers found a grove of sumac and dismounted, and Robert piled their possessions to form a windbreak. He hobbled the animals to keep them close. The mule, Big Joe, stood against the wind, protecting the two horses that stood together. Man and beast clung on for dear life. Rita and Robert wrapped themselves in feather-down quilts, and covered their faces with woolen scarves. They huddled close and prayed for their lives.

The brutal blizzard made its way to the Summers ranch. Donna stared out the window, watching the snow. "Will Robert and Rita be all right, Daddy? Will they make it to their ranch?"

Tom replied, "I don't know, darlin'. I wish they had waited. We could all have braved the storm together. Let's ask the Lord's protection on them.

All night the wind howled like a banshee. Sleet pelted the windows, and by morning, the snowdrifts were three feet high and getting deeper. You could not see the sun; a winter halo filled the sky with an eerie light. Joe came to the house and told Tom that he would saddle up and go look for the couple.

"No," Tom said, "We have no idea where they are. I don't want to lose you too. All we can do is pray."

There was no stopping the blinding snow; it came at them like an angry woman, pushing the drifts higher and higher. The temperatures continued to plummet. The windowpanes became completely iced over on the inside, making lacy patterns on the windows. The house moved and moaned with the wind. Dodge, the mutt they found at the Fort, howled with the wind. Donna remained close to her mother as Rachel walked through the house, chinking the small holes around the windows and doors.

Outside, Will struggled against the wind to make it from the bunkhouse to the wagon. The wind tore at his coat and snatched his hat. A part of the tarp that covered the oats had been set free and was pulling the entire covering away. Once he reached the wagon, Will pushed handfuls of oats from a sack into his bucket and then held it close to his body to protect the precious food. He carried his cargo to the corral, walking backwards against Mother Nature, the wind whipping his long hair across his freezing face.

Three mares, a gelding, a stud, and their buggy horse, Timber, made their herd. To bring them safely through the blizzard was critical.

Will emptied the bucket of oats into the trough that was protected by a shed then broke the ice in the creek so the horses could drink.

When Will returned to the bunkhouse, he was half-frozen, and his teeth were chattering. Tom met him at the door. "Get in here and warm up!" Tom said they were going to break down two bunk beds and carry them into the main house.

"Jake, you and Will get the beds. Johnny, you grab all the blankets you can carry, and let's get to the house while we can," Tom shouted above the noise of the storm. Once inside, Tom instructed the men to set the bunk beds and the children's beds in the great room. "I want everyone to sleep here until this son of a bitch is over. Mother, bring all of the quilts and pillows and shut the door. Draw water, and fill every container you have. Will, bring in all the wood that you can and stack it high in that corner."

"Why, Boss, sounds like you were in the army," Joe teased.

"Hell, I was!" Tom replied. "Joe, I want you to be in charge of keeping this fire going. If it goes out, we all die," Tom continued, angry that Joe mentioned the army.

The stress was showing on Tom. "Rachel, Donna, bring all the canned food in here. I don't want them to freeze and break. We are going to need every last one."

Turning to Jake, Tom said, "Nail that side door shut so it won't blow open again."

It was a long night and a fretful one. Joe kept watch over the fire and kept it burning. Rachel stirred early to start breakfast. "I'm afraid I'm going to have to ration coffee and food to make sure we weather this storm," she told Joe.

"I'm sorry I spoke to you like that last night," Joe said to Tom. "That's okay, I'm just worried," Tom replied, "And we're all worried about Robert and Rita."

Rachel said, "They must be lost, or worse. No one could survive this storm!"

The blizzard raged. Will braved the storm to feed the horses again. He could not see in front of him and lost his bearings. He was gone way too long. Finally, he stumbled onto the porch and fell through the door, covered with snow. "I got lost on the way back between the bunkhouse and here. Thank God, I made it!"

Rachel made chili and beans for supper. Everyone tried to talk about anything other than Robert and Rita. Most everyone went to bed and tried to sleep, but it was difficult. About midnight, there were sounds like footsteps and a thud on the porch. Everyone jumped up to see what the commotion was. The door flew open, and there, with snow swirling around them like angels, lay Robert and Rita, their clothes and faces covered with ice. Jake, Joe, and Will dragged the two lifeless bodies into the house.

"Quickly, take off their clothes and wrap them in these blankets!" Rachel commanded. "Donna, get some water boiling for soup."

"Robert, wake up!" Tom gently shook his friend. "Robert, it's me, wake up!"

Rita began to stir.

"Rita, you are safe; you made it," Tom said as he knelt close by his friends.

"Where's Robert? I can't find Robert," Rita repeated over and over.

Dodge licked Robert's face, wanting his friend to wake up.

"Get some wet rags, Donna," Rachel instructed.

"Should I dip them in the hot water on the stove, Momma?" Donna asked.

"No, just plain cold water. Even regular water is going to feel warm to them," Rachel said, caressing Rita's face.

"Where's Robert?" Rita pleaded.

"He is right here, Rita. Right next to you," Rachel responded.

Rita tried to move. "Oh, I cannot move. Rachel? Rachel, I am so glad to see you," Rita said and then passed out.

Morning came slowly. Everyone was afraid that Robert and Rita would not last the night. Rachel offered water to Rita several times. Finally, she coughed and was able to drink.

"Where is Robert?" the young bride asked again.

"Right here by your side," Rachel replied.

"My baby! Where is my baby?" Rita cried out in her delirium.

"Rita, you don't have a child," Rachel reassured her friend.

"My baby, is he safe?" Rita cried. Rachel shook her head and wiped Rita's forehead.

Just then, Robert stirred. "I'm burning up," he groaned and writhed in pain. "Help me, please. Where's my wife?"

Tom answered, choking up with tears, "She is right here, Robert. You both are safe!"

Robert sat up, naked except for the sheets and blankets that covered him, and asked, "Where's Andy?"

"Andy is not here," Tom explained, "but you and Rita are safe. How in the world did you find your way back?"

Robert began to cry, "We were freezing to death. I had to kill the mule and skin it. Then we hovered inside the hide. The snow was piling up all around us. Rita had just told me that before we die, she wanted me to know she was with child. I prayed for God to spare us, to give our child a chance to be born and to serve the Lord."

With that, he slumped, and for a moment, they feared he had died. Then he began to moan and reach for his toes, which were turning black. Some of his fingers were painful and swollen.

"Where is Andy?" Robert asked.

Jake knelt down by Robert. "He is dead. I helped bury him."

"No, he is not dead. Just when there was no hope left, Rita and I looked up through the storm and saw Andy's face. Andy said, 'Come, follow me,' and we did. He led us the short distance to this house." Through the tears, Robert said, "We would not have made it without Andy."

It took about three days for Robert and Rita to regain their strength. Rachel and Donna waited on them and took care of them. They slept on the floor on pallets that were made for them, and they were given their clothing.

"Here is more broth," Donna said as she carried the soup to the couple. "What are you going to name your baby?" she asked.

Robert and Rita looked at each other and said, "Andy. Andy Thomas Thornton."

It was crowded in the ranch house with its nine residents plus Dodge and the cat. For entertainment, songs were sung and stories told. The men took turns bringing wood into the kitchen.

"I am glad you talked us into cutting all this wood now, Joe," Tom remarked.

After about five days, the storm let up, and they could see the sun. The white of the snow almost blinded their eyes. Tom asked Jake to retrieve all of the rope he could find in the bunkhouse and bring it to him. In places, snow was as deep as Jake was tall, but he made it back with his arms full of rope, nonetheless.

"Now, let's tie these ropes together and stretch them from here to the bunkhouse so no one gets lost again in case the storm acts up again," Tom instructed Will.

They found Robert's horses dead about fifty yards from the house. Jake and Will took the saddles and bridles off the horses and put them in the bunkhouse. The men fed their herd of horses and broke the ice again. The wind picked up; dark clouds reached toward the frightened men. The blizzard hit again with a vengeance.

The next day, Robert told Tom, "You are going to have to cut my rotting toes and fingers off."

Tom had not thought about the war for a long time, but Robert's request brought missing limbs and the smell of dying flesh to his mind and his nostrils.

Tom stared at Robert, knowing what Robert was saying and what he needed to do.

"Will, fetch the whiskey," Tom said somberly.

By using the ropes to guide him, Will made his way to the bunkhouse, wishing he were anywhere but here. He grabbed the whiskey, threw the horses some oats, and picked up a branding iron. "We'll need this to sear the flesh when its cut," Will said to himself.

Once inside, Will gave Robert the bottle and he began to drink. Tom looked at Will and said, "You know more about this than I do. I'll help you."

Not being a drinking man, Robert passed out in a short time. Will looked at Tom and said, "Put this branding iron in the fire."

Rachel spoke up, "Let me clean it up first," and went to work. Afterward, she placed it in the center of the fire in the fireplace.

Will told her, "This will keep him from bleeding to death when I'm through cutting."

"Now, Tom, you and Jake hold him down. Joe, bring me plenty of clean wet rags. Rachel, we're going to need bandages. Donna, I want you to close your eyes and pray for all of us. Johnny, bring me the sharpest kitchen knife you have after you've held it in the fire to sterilize it."

Will attacked the toes first; two toes on the right foot and one on the left had to go. "I'm only going to take this one finger now. If I have to come back, we can take another one later."

Will placed a stick between Robert's teeth and started. The stench of burned flesh was so terrible, Johnny opened the door to clear out the odor. Rachel bandaged Robert's seared stubs of toes and finger.

The blizzard raged again. Robert suffered bouts of fever, and Rita cared for him through the night. The smells of sweat, food, and healing skin set off Rita's morning sickness. She couldn't eat or drink for days at a time.

"How long will my sickness last?" Rita asked her friend.

"Not long," Rachel responded. "Now, you lie down and rest. We'll have a baby this summer, and it will all be worth it!"

"I don't believe the cattle can survive through this storm. I've never seen anything like this," Tom said aloud.

"Those Texas Longhorns are pretty tough, but I'll bet they ain't never been in something this severe," Jake replied.

"We are running low on provisions. Do you think there is any way we could bring down an animal to feed us?" Rachel confided.

Just then, Johnny shouted, "There's a calf outside!"

"Get the rifle, Son. We're going hunting," Tom said. They stepped outside with Johnny holding the .50-caliber rifle.

"There he is, leaning against the yard fence," Johnny said.

"Pull down on him, Johnny. Shoot him in the head!" Tom instructed his son.

It didn't take long to dress the calf; it was so thin, there wasn't much meat on its bones, but it would fill their bellies.

"Let's save some of this for Dodge and Princess," Johnny said to Tom.

"Yes, that's a good idea. Here, take this heart to your mother to cook for supper." Tom finished butchering the young animal and took the meat and bones to the bedroom that they had closed off from the rest of the house. When Tom came back to the porch, he caught a glimpse of a coyote carrying the hide between his teeth, running into the white blur of falling snow.

There was no reprieve from the constant blowing and falling snow. One of the windows cracked and fell out of its frame. Jake was quick to nail up an old blanket across the hole and then proceeded to take a chair apart and nail the wooden pieces across the window.

"We're not going to let this storm get the best of us," Jake said.

"Tom, the calf will help us a great deal. We have beans and pecans left, but we're going to be out of food in a few days," Rachel said with worry in her eyes.

Tom came up with an idea. He told Rachel, "I'm going to go gather up some oats and bring them into the kitchen. We will use the rolling pin and break up the seeds and boil them so we can eat them."

The oats kept them full. It was a good thing too, because the storm raged for a month.

After the Storm

"Mother, are we going to live?" Donna asked.

"Yes, Sweetheart, the Lord has provided."

The world outside was quiet at last. The snow looked like it had always been there, like a sculpture. Branches hung low with the heavy snow, and birds flitted here and there, searching for food. Jake grabbed a shovel and cleared the porch and steps, working his way toward the bunkhouse. He noted that part of the bunkhouse roof had caved in, but he was more concerned about the horses and cattle. Dodge followed cheerfully, barking and jumping into the snow banks.

In a week, the snow had melted some so that the men could get around on horseback. The horses fared rather well because they had some shelter and oats. Tom owned up to the men that if Rachel had not made him buy that wagonload of oats, "our lives would be quite different."

The men cleaned each horse's hooves, brushed them down, and saddled up. The five men rode out to check on the stock, riding the high drifts, doubtful that any survived.

"Boys, the first steer that we find—we butcher. We need something to eat," Tom told the men. They rode back early the first day, not knowing if the storm was actually over. Rachel, Donna, and Rita anxiously awaited their loved ones' return.

"Here they come!" shouted Donna.

As the men approached, Tom hollered, "We brought rabbit for supper!" Donna ran to her father, and he handed her three rabbits they shot. They rode out early every morning in hopes of finding the stray cattle. In the next two weeks, they found only two hundred of the one thousand that they once owned. Dead cattle were everywhere; one big bull was found standing but frozen to death.

Mud became the next enemy; footsteps bogged down in the black stuff and covered everyone's boots. The horses struggled, plugging along as best they could. Buzzards circled in the sky, signaling another carcass. Life and death were all around them. Spring flowers began popping up through the remaining covering of snow, and insects were a constant problem. Mosquitoes swarmed the faces of the men, and horseflies made life miserable for everyone.

A spring rain was a mixed blessing. It cleared the air but added to the mud. The snow was now almost gone. Robert and Tom rode alone in the pelting rain. They came to the canyon where the renegade Indians had taken the stolen horses. On the rim stood four horses: a paint and three chestnuts, all in good shape for having braved the weather.

"I wonder who they belong to," Robert said.

"I don't know, but let's gather them up," Tom said. As they approached, they saw the US brand on their rumps—army horses!

The four horses came to Tom. "They look hungry," Robert said. They roped the two larger ones and began to lead them back to the ranch. The two smaller ones followed.

"At least we will have a change of mounts until the army comes to get them." Tom told Robert. "I am sure happy that you are here to help me, Robert. You and Rita had a close call," Tom continued.

"Thank you again for taking care of us. I can't wait for our son to be born," Robert said.

"How do you know it's going to be a boy?" Tom asked.

"It has to be, so we can name him Andy," Robert boasted.

Later, Tom checked with Fort Supply, and they were not missing any horses. The captain at the Fort said to keep them. "We will telegraph around, and if you don't hear from us, forget it, and keep them."

While at the Fort, Tom and Robert heard horror stories about the storm of '86. He related later to his men the saga of the stage that arrived three days after the storm began. The horses pulled up to the stage stop. The passengers, who had covered up in a buffalo hide piled out when the stage stopped. The driver normally helped with the luggage, but this time he remained seated in the driving boot. Someone called to him. When he did not answer, a closer look revealed that although he was sitting up straight with the reins still in his hands, he was frozen. Some ranchers lost everything: their horses first, then their own lives. There were stories of horses slaughtered to feed their owners. It seemed like there were a few less dogs around too.

The two returned to the ranch, after picking up much needed supplies. The next evening, they were sitting out on the porch watching the fireflies light up the spring sky.

Robert told Tom, "I had enough money to pay for the ranch, and I did; but now I'm broke. I need to work for you, if you need me, so I can make enough money to get started."

Tom told his friend, "Rachel and I have saved some money. I am sure Rachel will agree with me that you and Rita can have what you need."

"But that is your hard-earned savings!" Robert resisted.

Tom assured, "The money is yours too. Without your help, I would not have lasted out here anytime at all. We are brothers, Robert, and Rita is our sister. Next week, all of us, including the women, will load up and go to your place and see what needs to be done," Tom told Robert.

"Why are you doing this?"

"Because I want to!" was Tom's reply.

Jake reported to Tom that they had counted three hundred and ten cows and fifty calves, many of which had drifted south, but most were healthy.

Jake reported, "I think several cows will calve later."

The women cooked for several days, preparing for the trip to the Thornton ranch.

"Glad we got an early start," Tom said to Rachel as they began their journey. I'm anxious to see their place.

The ladies chatted on the way, "We are so thankful for yours and Robert's safety and we can't wait for your baby to join us," Rachel told Rita.

"Can we start making baby clothes, Mother? I can sew pretty well now," Donna said.

"Yes, and we want to be with you when the time comes," Rachel said.

A few miles out, Robert spotted the site where he had to kill his mule and where he and Rita fought to stay alive.

"My dowry!" Rita squealed. "I didn't think we would ever find it! Now we can buy cattle and fix up our new home."

Nestled in a sumac bush lay the leather pouch that her father had made for her, and in it was the money he had saved to provide his daughter with a generous dowry.

"Father told me at my wedding that I had found a good man," Rita told her friends as they gathered up the pouch and pack saddle. In the distance, Johnny saw a brightly colored cloth; it was a serape caught in a sage bush.

The Thornton's ranch lay in the shadows of a series of bluffs. The small soddy was in good repair, but the large barn and shed were in need of help. The weight of the snow, no doubt, had destroyed the roof of each building and caved in part of the structures. The fences lay flat on the desert ground.

"Let's use the lumber from the shed to fix the barn," Robert suggested. "I can build a new shed later."

"Sounds like the thing to do," Tom replied.

The men chipped in, and inside two days, the barn was in good order. "We have a good well with sweet water too," Robert said.

On the third day, lo and behold, cows and calves began showing up. Jake and Will saddled up and went about counting the longhorn herd.

"Robert, your herd has shown up! We counted three hundred fifty cows and seventy calves," Jake boasted.

"That means I lost two hundred and eighty in the blizzard," Robert said, shaking his head in disbelief. "But we may find more later."

"Robert, Rachel and I need to head home. You could use some help. Which of the cowboys do you want?"

Robert replied, "These men are yours, Boss."

"No, sir," Tom retorted. "They are ours. No more cattle than I have, we can go together and split up the cowboys."

"Okay, then, I will take Johnny!" Robert laughed.

With a chuckle and wink, Tom replied, "You don't have to take him; I'll give him to you!"

Robert said, "No, Johnny's yours. Can I keep Joe? If he agrees, of course."

Handshakes and hugs all around, Tom headed for the buggy. Rachel reminded Rita that they would take her to Fort Supply when the time came for the baby to arrive. With a race to the next tree, Johnny, Jake, and Will were well ahead of Tom, Rachel, and Donna, as they headed home.

"Donna, would you like to ride Ranger II?" Tom asked his daughter.

"Oh, can I?" she replied.

Tom seated himself in the buggy, slapped the reins, and leaned over and kissed Rachel on the cheek. Looking at her intently, he said with a smile, "Well, hello there, pretty lady. This is the first time we've been alone for a long time."

In a month, Tom and Robert gathered one hundred head and drove them to Fort Supply to sell to the army. Being on the reservation, the Cheyenne Indians were now completely dependent on the government.

Summer brought the birth of little Andy. A new generation of cowboys had begun with this child of the plains. Everyone was busy working on their outbuildings and looking for cattle. Several fall days were spent gathering pecans and reminiscing about the blizzard.

"I hope it never snows like that again," Donna said. "I was scared."

For Christmas, the Thorntons, the Summerses, and the ranch hands gathered and had a grand time.

"It's special to have a baby with us at Christmastime," Rachel said with tears in her eyes, secretly wanting another baby. Tom squeezed her hand and gave her a small box wrapped in blue paper.

"Open it! We want to see!" Rita exclaimed.

"Oh, Tom, you are so thoughtful!" Inside the velvet-lined box was a beautiful cameo brooch.

"Merry Christmas, Sweetheart. Without you, we would not have made it through the blizzard," Tom said as he hugged Rachel

"Thank you, Tom. I love it!" Rachel replied.

In the spring of 1887, word came to Tom that there were about one hundred of his cattle marked with his Circle T brand running near the Red River, about one hundred fifty miles south.

"Those ornery critters drifted all that way during the storm," Tom thought to himself aloud.

The gathering of cowboys brought the cows and calves back. They crossed the Comanche reservation. At this time, Quanah Parker, a half-breed Indian, was their chief. The men holed up the herd at the Canadian River. Tom rode on into the reservation. By now, it was summer, and a hot summer day at that. Little brown Indian children played outside. Two dogs met Tom as he neared Chief Parker's home. As Tom looked around the reservation, he could not help but wonder to himself, "I thought a war was fought to free men. These men do not look free." Once, when Tom attended a meeting at the Cherokee Strip Cattleman's Association, he heard rumors that anyone living in the Cherokee Outlet would be pushed off in a few years. He wanted to talk to Chief Parker about the problem.

Greeted at the door by a tall young Indian, Tom was led into a larger room.

"Wait," the brave said to Tom.

A few minutes later, Chief Quanah Parker, now a grown man of influence and authority with the tribe, entered. The two men recognized each other.

"I remember you. You are the one who saved our people by giving us cattle when we were hungry," the grateful man said.

"It is good to see you again," Tom replied.

"I have a request. When I am forced off the Cherokee land where my ranch is, will you lease this land to me, the Comanche Indian land?"

Parker responded, "Many moons ago, you stretched out your hand to me. Now, I will do the same to you. When the time comes, we talk. You are my friend."

He offered Tom an invitation to join his family for the noon meal. Tom knew Parker would be offended if he did not accept. The squaws began bringing bowls of corn, beans, and Indian fry bread.

After the meal and good conversation, Tom said, "Thank you, Chief, for our time together. I must go now. My men are waiting for me down by the river."

In 1888, Robert and Rita brought another son into the world. They named him Hosa Jose. Tom and Robert were building their herds and working together. In the fall, they delivered one hundred steers to Fort Sill in the Southwest Indian Territory for the Comanche Indians. While there, Tom and Robert met a contractor who was building army houses at Fort Sill.

"Michael Johansen, it's sure good to see you!" Tom said and slapped his old friend on his back. "How in the world are you? Did you ever marry that pretty redhead you met in Texas?"

"Yessir, Tom. Why weren't you at the wedding?"

Tom replied, "I didn't know where you were, much less that you were tying the knot!"

The three men had supper together at Fort Sill.

"Mike, if I get Quanah Parker's permission, will you and your crew build me another house just like the one you built for me in the Outlet?" Tom asked.

"What do you need with another house? Did the one I built for you fall down?" the contractor joshed his friend.

"No! That is a good, solid house. We made it through the blizzard in fine shape. Where were you during the storm?"

"We were working over by Elk City and about froze to death," Mr. Johansen replied. "A rancher and his family took us in. They were good to us, but it was rough," he continued.

"The reason I want you to build another house for me is that there is talk of the government going to open up the land I'm on for settlers, and we will have to leave," said Tom.

"I will be glad to build you another home," Mike answered. "One thing, though, be sure your wife will make me homemade bread and jelly like she did the last time I was there!"

"It's a deal," Tom said, and the two men shook on it.

CHAPTER 29

The Land Runs

The Summers family enjoyed a break in their routine and made a shopping trip to Dodge City. Indian summer—the sun was bright but not too hot. Although it was fall, the land was still warm, and so were the days.

While the women shopped, Tom and Johnny whiled away the time, watching people. Tom picked up a newspaper and was not surprised by what he read, "Land Run in Old Oklahoma. On April 3 of 1889, there will be a run made into the center of Oklahoma Territory for all who want to settle a piece of land."

"I knew it!" Tom told his son, "We will be next. It isn't right. Our government has taken the land from the Indians. Now, they are having a land run for people to settle and grow crops and build fences in 'Old Oklahoma.' The next run will be on our land, the Cherokee Outlet." Wiping his brow, Tom continued, "There are already those who are crossing the Kansas border and sneaking into Oklahoma Territory and staking an early claim. They call themselves 'Sooners' because they were settling the land sooner than they legally should. Their leader is a man named Payne, and they want to be farmers. I think the farmers need to stay where they are and let us ranchers raise our cattle."

Johnny asked, "Couldn't farmers and ranchers work together? This is such a big country."

Tom replied, "I wish we could, but farmers build fences with barbed wire, and we ranchers hate any kind of fence."

"Who owns the land now?" Johnny asked.

"The United States government. The army got tired of rounding up Payne and each group of settlers who went into the Old Oklahoma territory. Every time the army would run them off, Payne would gather up more men and they would take out again," Tom explained. "Finally, the government came up with the idea of everyone who wanted land to line up on the boundary line, and when the pistol shot is fired, everyone scrambles for what they think will be the best farmland."

"Sounds like a mess to me," young Johnny said.

"It will be. Lives will be lost and claims stolen, as man is naturally greedy," Tom mumbled.

Just then, Rachel and Donna came back, laughing and planning on what they would do next. Tom asked Rachel to look at the newspaper headliners and said, "This land run will happen next spring, and then, we are next. We do not have title to the place where we live. We need to think about moving."

Everyone was quiet as the news began to sink in. "I don't want to move," Donna said.

"You'll be all right," Johnny told his sister. "It's a big world out there."

"Goodness, we've been at our place for twenty years. The Cherokees have been good to us, letting us lease the land because we took care of it and respected the Indians," Rachel said.

Tom interjected, "If we don't move, the government will run us off and we will lose everything. If we plan smart, we will be fine. Let's start for home, and then I will make a trip to see Chief Quanah Parker and try to make a deal where we can lease his land south of our ranch."

"But where will we go?" Donna cried.

"We will build about one hundred and fifty miles south of here, near Fort Sill in Oklahoma Territory."

"Father," Donna persisted, "why do we always live by a fort?"

"One reason, daughter, is we are safer living close to a fort; the second reason is we are safer living close to a fort," Tom joked, trying to lift his daughter's worry. "But first, I have to get permission from Quanah Parker, Chief of the Comanche."

"Quanah Parker must be a pretty important man," Johnny added.

"Chief Parker first fought the army out in the Texas Panhandle. When he found out that he could not whip them, he took up the white man's way of life. He now has a grand house on the reservation. He knows men who were three- or four-star generals. So to show his importance, he painted five large stars on the roof of his house. He also has five wives; I guess to show his importance too!" Tom joked.

After arriving home, four days later, Tom told his family that he would be leaving the next morning before daybreak. "John, you're in charge. I want you to look after the place and take care of your mother and sister."

"I will, father. You can depend on me," he replied.

The trip to Quanah Parker's would take four or five days in good weather. Tom packed hardtack, beef jerky, and apples to eat along the way. He sacked oats and carrots for treats for the big paint horse he was taking. Tom thought to himself, "I hope the chief is pleased with his gift; this is a fine horse and beautifully handmade saddle. He will especially like the silver stars on the saddle and bridle."

The first night out on the Western Trail, the moon was full: truly a harvest moon. It looked so close, you could reach out and touch it. Alone on the trail, Tom thought of his mother, who would tuck him into bed at night and say a short prayer with him, afraid the elder Mr. Summers would hear and start raising cane about her God-fearing ways. He would say, "What you need to fear is me."

Talking to himself aloud, Tom said, "I do not know how she put up with him for so long. At least she's at peace."

Sitting near the campfire, Tom stared at the flames, watching the sparks fly. He could feel the vibration of hooves coming closer. Three men on horseback approached, with masks covering their shadowed faces. One of them, the big one, had his gun drawn. Tom could see the glint of the barrel in the light of the fire.

Tom didn't move. The trio dismounted and walked over to where Tom was sitting. "We ain't killers. We just want your money," the leader demanded.

The second man spoke, "We are sorry to rob you, but we are hungry."

When the second man spoke, Tom recognized his voice.

Without so much as a flinch, Tom asked the man, "Didn't you ride for the San Antonio rancher, Charlie Reams?"

"Yes," the man said meekly, "I know you, but I cannot remember your name."

"Tom Summers."

The reluctant robber said to his partners in crime, "Put your guns up. We cannot harm this man."

Tom told them to drop their bandanas and set a spell. "I will share what food I have with you." With that, the hungry men began to eat.

"How is my friend, Charlie?" Tom asked, "Is he well?"

"No," the leader spoke. "He is dead—shot down in Dodge City."

"What happened?" Tom asked.

"Mr. Reams had learned that a man named Sam Perry, who had killed his brother and brother's wife, was let go by the judge for lack of evidence. Charlie went crazy! He rode to Dodge and called this Sam character out. Charlie was a good rancher and a good horseman but not so good with a gun. Sam shot him dead. Me and the boys went to Dodge and ambushed Sam and filled him with lead. We left that town in a hurry. The law has not found us yet. We took up a life of crime just to survive."

Tom answered, "Sam was a wicked man. You were right to kill him. Justice was done. I have a little money you can have if you are broke."

"Thank you," the leader said as Tom gave him a twenty-dollar gold piece.

"I think we will head for Mexico. We appreciate your help," they said as they rode away.

Tom failed to mention to the three that he had over one thousand dollars that he had hidden in a special place in his saddle. This was his stash to lease land from the Comanches.

When Tom rode up to Chief Parker's house, leading the beautiful paint, he was greeted by the Chief himself.

"Mr. Summers, I have been expecting you. Come and join me in my home." His house was grand, and by looking at it and the furnishings, you knew that he was in charge.

Tom stayed the night. The next morning, he was greeted to a banquet. "I make white man money now by leasing land. There is no land to buy because the government controls everything. They are even forcing our children to speak English," the Chief spoke, suddenly looking much older than his years. "The government sent most of our little ones off to boarding school to learn white man's ways."

The new lease for the Summerses was for five years and was straight west of Fort Sill with the Red River on the south. "I must return to my family quickly and begin making plans. We will want to build a home soon. Will the contractors and carpenters be safe to travel through your land?" Tom asked.

"I will see that they are," Quanah Parker promised.

After giving the Chief the gifts he brought, Blue Bonnet, the paint, and the handmade saddle, Tom rode back to the ranch. They decided that they needed to move as soon as possible and not wait until a bunch of crazy farmers come riding over the hill to stake their one hundred sixty acre allotment.

"This was good grassland, known for raising cattle and horses, but most years, the summers were dry. We don't have the forest, like in Iowa and Tennessee, or rich black soil. This is a harsh and unforgiving land, but desperate people do desperate things. When they find out there is free land for the taking, they will show up," Tom said.

A few days after telling his hands about their plans, Johnny and Tom rode to Fort Sill to look up Mike Johansen.

"The time has come," Tom told his friend. "I want you to build another home for us just like the first one, only Rachel wants a bigger pantry."

The men agreed on a price. Mr. Johansen said that the government contract would run out soon and that he and his men wouldn't have any more work until another government contract was let.

In a few days, Tom and Johnny were back at Quanah Parker's. Tom told him about his plans to build a home on the land.

"Of course, it will not be as grand a home as yours, but one you will be proud of. My wife is a fine cook. I hope you and your family will come and visit us," Tom said.

They loaded up in one of Parker's wagons. The chief was not getting around very well and could no longer ride his horse. He took Tom out to the place he had leased.

"It is the most beautiful piece of land, second only to mine," Parker said. "This is where you will want to build so that the sun greets you in the morning and the wind cools you in the evening."

Tom thought to himself, "We will be about twenty miles from the Chief's house and about thirty miles from Fort Sill, Oklahoma Territory. Tom rode back to Fort Sill to tell Johansen that the chief agreed to let Tom build his home on the land. Then, they all rode back out to the home site.

When father and son arrived back home, the snow was beginning to fall. What had been a wonderful summer and early fall turned into an early winter. On everyone's mind was the worry of another harsh winter.

"We better cut wood for winter," Tom said at supper.

"The men have been busy since you left, putting wood in the shed and stacking it behind the house," Rachel told her husband, "and Donna and I have been canning and drying food for the winter ahead."

Tom was full of information about the house, the chief, and the newly leased land. "It will take about six months to build our house," Tom said, "Of course, a lot depends upon the weather."

"Did you tell your carpenter that I want a larger pantry and more closets?" Rachel asked.

"You will have the biggest pantry on the plains!" Tom replied. He started to tell her he forgot about more closets, when they heard the men laughing on the porch.

Outside, the cowhands and Johnny were talking and laughing. Johnny was leading the conversation. All Tom heard was Johnny talking quietly and then "five wives."

"Johnny! Get in here!" Tom ordered. "We'll have none of that talk."

"Yes, sir," Johnny answered.

Donna was clearing the dinner table. Tom went back to visiting with his wife. "You know the army is going to run everyone off in about a year and burn all the prairie grass. Then the government will survey the land into one hundred and sixty acre plots that each settler could claim. I told Captain Kidd the last time I saw him that you cannot do that, but the captain replied, 'I have done a lot of things in my career that I did not think was right, but I have my orders. I have been in on some Indian fights that were wrong, but that was the way it was. The Custer massacre in Montana was terrible, but now Custer is apparently a hero. He and all of his men were killed. Custer was repaid for the evil he did at the Battle of Washita. In my opinion, he's not a hero!'"

Tom told Rachel the captain said when the time came, he would be moving them off—friend or not.

Rachel, the children, and Tom made a trip down to the new place because she had some ideas as to where changes needed to be made. By the time Robert, Joe, and the cowboys rounded up over twelve hundred head of cows, bulls, and calves, and made the big drive to their new place down south, their new home was nearly roughed in for the winter.

"As soon as we get settled in, I want to buy a piano for Donna to learn to play, and place it right there," she said, pointing to a space in the parlor.

They rode over to Fort Sill with a letter of introduction from Captain Kidd of Fort Supply. Colonel Arron Goss was glad to meet them. "We are happy you will be living near, and if you don't make any trouble, we will get along fine," he said.

Half-smiling, Tom answered, "We'll be fine until the govern-ment runs us off again."

The colonel replied, "Yes, I'm sure it will happen, for you know it will all be settled someday."

In the spring of 1891, when the house was finished, Tom and Will started loading a big wagon that Tom had rebuilt. Some of the cowboys were at the new ranch watching the cattle. Will and Joe stayed on to help with the move. Joe started out driving the wagon with his horse tied on behind. Will drove the buggy with Rachel and Donna on board.

"I'll be along. I have something to do," Tom said.

Rachel answered, "What's that?"

Tom's levity turned more serious, "Ain't no damn farmer gonna get this house!"

Will cracked his whip and they took off. Then Tom remem-bered something and rode after them. "Whoa!" he hollered, "Bring the buggy back to the house," he cried.

"Why?" asked Rachel. "Did we forget something?"

"Yes," Tom said, "the money box!"

They had a good laugh over that. Once it was loaded and tied down, the buggy and the precious cargo started up again. Later, Will told Tom that he did not know that the money box was hidden in the fireplace.

"Now, if I told you everything I know, then you would be as smart as me," Tom replied.

Tom took a five-gallon can of coal oil and walked into the old, empty house. He spread it throughout, saying good-bye to the home that had been so good to them. The south wind was blowing as he walked to the south edge of the porch. He struck a match and threw it into the wet coal oil. In an instant, the flames roared and began consuming everything in sight. Every corner melted and gave in to the heat.

Next, Tom walked over to the log cabin bunkhouse that they had worked so hard to build for their very survival thirty years ago. Tom could still see the beautiful cowhides they used on the roof and then changed to wood. With a knot in his throat, he poured more oil in the cabin and struck a match. In a flaming instant, part of Tom was gone. He watched as both buildings caved into themselves, taking their last breaths. He watched to see if the grass would catch fire too.

"Hmph," he said, "why should I care if the range catches on fire? The army is going to burn it all soon, anyway."

Although the fire had reduced the concrete to sand, the chimneys were still standing. Tom threw a rope over each one and pulled them over by hand. Then, he rolled up his rope, climbed on Ranger II, and headed south to the new land—no lookin' back.

One year later, the army came in and ran all the cattlemen off the land. A few raised a fuss and even went to court over it, but to no avail. The army was so strong that the problems did not last long.

At noon on September 16, 1893, the Run of the Cherokee Outlet began. People from all over the United States lined up on the Kansas border on the north and the boundary of Old Oklahoma on the south. At high noon, the army fired off canons and pistols, and the race was on.

There was a tremendous excitement in the air as wagons and buggies full of people and those on foot and those riding their fastest horses came to make their claim. Some folks had horses staked out ahead to jump on later to gain themselves an advantage. The trains that ran that day were told to run the same speed as the horses, about fifteen miles an hour.

The people that made the "Run" that day were those that did not have anything except a dream. People starting their lives over were the ones on the lines that hot September day. If you had a good farm in Kansas or a store in Missouri, you would not be there, but the dreamers were. Being the fall of the year was not a good time to begin a new life on the prairie because there was no time to plant or grow a crop or anything; but this was the way the government did things.

There were coal miners from Missouri and Arkansas who did not have anything and owed their next paycheck and their lives to the company store. Many of them slipped away in the night, traveling a long way on foot to be on the line for a chance at a better life in the

Cherokee Outlet, or "Strip," as some called it. The day ended with dreams fulfilled and others' dashed; the new landowners worked and schemed to survive. Many made dugouts in the earth to survive the tough prairie winter. They plowed and planted whatever they could find or worked for others to provide for their families. People pulled together for a better life or pulled apart, destroying what little they had.

CHAPTER 30

Life on Comanche Land

The Comanche Indians were still a big part of the Oklahoma Territory. They were people of the land. In earlier years, the young braves would slip into Texas to hunt the buffalo. The army would always round up the braves and return them to the reservation. By now, 1893, the buffalo were all but gone and the Indians contained; but the army was still hard on them—harder than they needed to be.

Although times were tough on the Indians, the army pampered the chiefs like Quanah Parker. One morning, a carrier from Fort Sill brought a message to Chief Parker, requesting that he attend the exposition in Fort Worth, Texas, the following week. City folks were anxious to see a real, live Indian, especially a chief, dressed in his tribal regalia.

Quanah Parker and the Comanche medicine man, a good friend of Parker's, went to the exposition. They were put up in the finest hotel in the city. When the two men got ready to go to bed in their strange surrounds, the medicine man, thinking that the gas flame on the wall was a candle, blew it out. By morning, he was dead.

Quanah, who was sleeping near an open window, survived but was quite sick. Geronimo, a chief of the Apache in Arizona and New Mexico Territories, had fought the army for more than thirty years. The army could not capture him. A lieutenant, John Reed, who was

311

accepted by the Apaches, met with Geronimo. After much talking and smoking the pipe, the army man got Geronimo to meet with General Cook, who convinced the great chief to surrender.

Geronimo was told that all the Apache would be moved by train to Florida and would live in a large and free reservation. Instead, his people were shipped like cattle in boxcars to a hot and swampy land.

Their new lives were like a prison, with little food and no freedom. In the early 1900s, they were herded up and shipped back to a new reservation near Fort Sill, Oklahoma Territory. This is where Tom met the heartbroken Geronimo.

The Cherokee Indians, with whom Tom had lived and fathered a child, were more than a tribe; they were a nation. Forcibly marched from the southeastern United States in the early 1800s, they were part of a journey called the Trail of Tears, where one in four Indians died on the trip. One thousand one hundred four died before they reached their new home in the Eastern Indian Territory.

The Cherokee were the only Indian people to develop their own written language. They also published their own newspaper, being the first to use both Cherokee and English. They drafted their own constitution and set up a public school system for their people. Numbering less than two thousand people, they built between fifteen and twenty schools by the mid 1800s, and two of these were schools of higher learning.

Life for the Cherokee was not as civilized as they wanted. Outlaws, whites and Indians alike, moved into the Cherokee nation to find a place of escape from the law. Caves in the area made perfect hideouts. Being a peaceful tribe, there was little law enforcement. Soon, the Indians had their own police force. Later, US deputy marshals were sent on patrol from their eastern boundaries at Fort Smith, Arkansas, but finding and capturing outlaws in the rough terrain and thick forest was almost impossible.

The Cherokee were also given a strip of desolate land called "the Outlet" or "Strip." This land was their hunting ground. It spread almost to the Rocky Mountains. Being a people of commerce, they decided to lease it out to ranchers. These ranchers could raise cattle and live on the land. Tom Summers leased his first ranch from these people. In 1894, Johnny, now eighteen, was taking more and more charge of the ranch operations. He was also quite the man about town at Fort Sill and Lawton. The cowboys had finished building the corral at the new ranch. It was there that they broke the wild mustangs that Tom had purchased from his old friend, Señor Garza. Garza brought a hundred head to sell to the army at Fort Sill, but the army only wanted ninety-six, so they culled four animals out of the herd. Tom bought them for next to nothing.

A new cowboy from New Mexico, Jeremy McCurry, was hired to break the mustang outlaws. Every morning, Jeremy and one of the wild horses could be seen working in the new corral. He had a way with horses—his own style. He brought a bucket of water from the trough and a handful of hay to the side of the corral and gently and quickly lowered his "saddle," made of two filled sacks of grain sewed together, onto the horse's back. He stood above on the high corral fence. Away the wild pony took off, hell-bent for election, bucking with the sacks flapping on either side until he was too tired to move.

Jeremy was able to break three horses this way, and he told Tom he thought the three would make good stock ponies. The fourth, Roany, was different. Roany was larger than most mustangs. He had a reddish coat, with an extra thick white mane and tail. He acted like a caged lion, pacing, snorting, and showing himself to be a force to be reckoned with. Jeremy told Tom, "I feel this horse is too wild to tame. Some horses are never meant to be broken. You will find one like this once in a while. If it was me, I'd turn him loose before he kills someone."

Upon hearing this, Joe walked up and boasted, "There no horse I cannot break!"

Jeremy continued, "That bastard is an outlaw stud. If I had not been near the fence when he bucked me off, he would have stomped me to death!"

Although Joe was fifty-plus years, he still wanted to try. Tom and John saddled up their mounts and both roped Roany around his neck. One man pulled one way, the other man the other direction, which controlled the horse somewhat. Roany was frightened, angry, and confused and kicked out. Will hurried in and, just like the Indians, grabbed Roany's ear, biting it and paralyzing the stud. Joe threw a saddle on the crazed animal while Will was wearing him down. Jake took the two ropes off the horse's neck. Joe put one foot into the stirrup, gingerly shifting his weight up onto the heaving mustang. On his command, Will let go of his bite on Roany's ear and jumped back.

Joe hung onto the halter rope with his left hand and gripped the saddle horn for dear life with his right. Roany jumped straight up and then whirled around, first to the right, then to the left.

"I've never seen anything like it!" Jeremy said to Tom.

Watching the situation intently, Tom said, "Enough! Let's get him!"

Just then, Joe started to lose his grip on the saddle horn. Johnny rode up as close as he could get to Joe and the stud and hollered for Joe to grab his arm and get away from the wild animal. Roany, determined to claim the corral, reared up, came down, and kicked midair. Joe was thrown from the saddle over the head of the monster and hit the ground hard. Like a demon horse, Roany leaped and stomped on Joe over and over, crushing him beneath his hooves. Tom quickly rode in and roped Roany and dragged him off Joe.

Tom hollered, "Will, open the gate!" He pulled the stud out of the corral. Roany ripped the rope out of Tom's hand and ran for freedom in a cloud of dust.

The men were gathered around Joe, who was bloodied and broken on the ground. Tom raced back to the center of the corral where Joe was lying and dismounted without breaking stride and rushed to his side. He was there just long enough to hear Joe say, "I am with my God."

The cowboys could not believe what had just happened. The silence was deafening, and their hearts were heavy as they gently picked up what was left of Joe, carrying him to the ranch house. Every bone in his body was broken. They washed him and dressed him in Tom's best suit. The next day, they took the dead man to a large hill on the ranch, dug a grave, and made a wooden cross.

"Wrap him in this Indian blanket," Tom ordered. "He always liked it."

Then, Joe was lowered into the grave. Tom began talking about his love and respect for his black friend.

"He has been with me, working side by side for over thirty years." Tom turned to the cowboys and said with tears in his eyes, "He was the first man I hired. He was my friend."

All the boys had something to say about Joe. The service lasted for two hours. Finally, they buried their friend, the man with no last name.

The following day, the crew took their rifles and rode out on the range. Thick black clouds came up fast, and they were greeted by lightning and thunder, like the sky was warning them to turn around and leave the outlaw mustang alone. The men strained against the wind-driven rain. About three hours later, Johnny found Roany in a draw, soaking wet. The rope around his neck was tangled in brush and a cottonwood tree. The more the stallion tried to free himself, the more embroiled he became.

Johnny fired three shots in the noonday air and waited for the other cowboys to show up. Here they came from all directions. Jake and Tom were anxious to find out what happened. "Why didn't you shoot him?" Tom asked his son.

Johnny responded, "We need to execute this outlaw!" They all agreed and dismounted with their rifles drawn.

CHAPTER 31

Romance in the Air

The Summers family settled into a routine in their new home in The Big Pasture of the Comanche Reservation. Letters arrived frequently from Janell. She was now department head of English. John Sommers, Tom's long lost brother, had paid Janell a visit, informing her of the drinking problem of his son, Thomas, and advised her not to keep company with him.

She wrote, "I am very busy with my teaching and administrative duties, so I have little time to be courted." The next letter told of her meeting a young man named Ralph Ridell. She said he was so big and strong that he could set a windmill head all by himself. That kind of job usually took two men to do it, so he was in high demand by people building windmills all over Missouri, Kansas, and beyond.

"I wish you could meet him. I have told him about you all," Janell wrote.

"I wish Janell would come visit us," Donna told her mother while they were busy making plum jelly. "She may have some pointers on what I should say to Justin Salder," Donna continued.

Ignoring her daughter, Rachel replied, "It would be wonderful to have her here with us. Would you finish putting the lids on the jelly jars, please? I need to rest a spell."

Unbeknownst to anyone, Rachel had been experiencing chest pains and shortness of breath. When the hot summer air was humid, her conditions worsened.

"It is just the heat. I'll be fine in a while," she said as she made a palette on the floor in front of a south window. Donna fetched a cold wet towel and hung it in the window, hoping for a breeze.

"This will help cool you, Mother. You just rest for now."

Tom, Johnny, Will, and Jake made plans to build a barn to store hay for the cattle. One night at supper, Tom told the family that he wanted to build grain bins on the ranch to hold oats.

"You know, it was oats and the good Lord that pulled us through that blizzard," he said as he took another piece of Rachel's lemon pie. Rachel could make a piecrust so flaky that it melted in his mouth. The lemon custard was so sweet and tangy that it just called for more.

"There are farmers in this area who are raising oats for the army and putting up grass hay. They're getting paid pretty darned good army scrip too!" Tom said.

Johnny, not very interested in building barns or grain bins, said, "I'm going to ride for Fort Sill tomorrow and see my friend Juan Garza. I haven't seen him since he joined the army."

Tom said, "Okay, you may go. Tell Juan hello for us, and tell him not to be a stranger." Tom knew that Señor Garza's heart was broken because Juan, his only son, left his ranch to become a soldier.

"I want to go too," Donna chimed in.

"No! I am not taking my little sister. This is a man's trip!" Johnny said with authority as he headed for the barn.

Donna had met a young lieutenant the last time the family was at Fort Sill, and she could not get him out of her mind. "Mother, do you think he likes me?" she asked Rachel, who had fallen asleep at the supper table.

"What? What did you say?"

"Do you think the lieutenant likes me?" Donna asked again.

Her mother answered, "I would say he does, the way he tipped his hat and smiled. Donna, would you do the dishes? I'm going to sit on the porch for a bit," Rachel said as she stood up. Her feet seem strangely heavy to her as she headed for the porch swing.

"I'll join you in a few minutes," Tom called.

Donna, who had grown into a beautiful sixteen-year-old young woman, said as she got up, more to herself than to anyone around her, "I didn't know what to say to the lieutenant that day. He probably thinks I'm stupid, but I'm not!"

The weeks went by as summer turned into fall. Donna was happy most of the time, singing and full of energy, although there were times of melancholy and moodiness. She loved to take rides on her horse, Chief, galloping all the way. Some mornings, she would saddle up and ride to the nearest neighbors, the Hughes. There was Mr. and Mrs. Hughes, Grandma Myrtle, three daughters, and a young son, who was crippled.

The family moved out west about fifteen years earlier in a covered wagon. One evening while Mrs. Hughes was cooking supper over an open campfire, holding her young son, the flames caught her dress, and she dropped Charlie in the fire. They were both badly burned. The fall injured his spine and he could not walk. Mrs. Hughes was never the same, physically or mentally. The three girls took over the care of their brother, their mother, and the home. The youngest, Elaine, was especially loving and caring. She and Donna became fast friends.

"Elaine, I'm just dying to know if Lieutenant Slader even knows I am alive. He has those big blue beautiful eyes that smile when he talks. He is a West Point graduate from New York City, you know."

Elaine stared at her friend.

"He talks funny, but I love it," Donna said with a sigh.

"What do you mean he talks funny?" Elaine asked the lovesick girl.

"You know, an accent, an Eastern accent," Donna implored. "I love the way he says, 'Yes, ma'am.'"

"Mary and I are taking Charlie to the doctor in Fort Sill next Monday. See if you can go with us," Elaine told her excited friend.

Monday came, and the three young women and Charlie headed for Fort Sill. The day dawned bright with a cloudless sky. The trip would take a few hours for the thirty miles. They would see the doctor, do some shopping, stay all night, and return the next day.

The doctor was optimistic about Charlie's condition. "I'm going to make an appointment for you in St. Louis. The finest doctors are there, and I think with some surgery, you will be able to walk again," he told Charlie. The doctor continued. "They can even do skin grafting these days to help with the scars from the fire."

Everyone was excited as they left the doctor's office. "This will help Mother so much, as she blames herself for all of this," Charlie said.

"Would you ladies and you, sir, do me the honor of having lunch with me?" The voice was familiar; the blue eyes and smile, too.

Donna almost melted but managed to say, "Have we met before?"

"Yes, ma'am. Your father, Mr. Summers, and I are good friends. I met you last spring. You and your family were just moving into your new home. How is your family?"

"My family is well, thank you," Donna answered. "May I introduce my good friends, Mary, Elaine, and Charlie Hughes. They are our neighbors."

"Pleased to meet you. My name is Lieutenant Slader. What is your pleasure? Brisket here," he said as he waved his glove toward the Yellow Rose Café, "or fried chicken with all the trimmings across the street at the Diner?"

"Charlie, you decide," Donna said.

"The town is quiet right now, but wait until Saturday night. The army boys come to town and mix it up pretty good," the lieutenant told his new friends. "Reminds me a little of New York City," he mused.

"Do you long to go back to New York City?" Donna asked.

"No, ma'am," the handsome lad replied, "When my obligation is done with the military, I want to find a ranch out West and raise cattle. Your father and I have talked about going into business together someday."

"The chicken was excellent, also the fried okra, just like I fix," Mary said, smiling at Lieutenant Slader. "Thank you for lunch. It would be quite neighborly if you would visit us sometime, and I will make you my prize-winning corned beef and cabbage," Mary boasted.

"Are you sure you don't want some plum pudding? They make the best!" the lieutenant said, blushing a little, but trying everything he can to prolong their parting.

Charlie saved the day. "I don't know about you girls, but I'm having dessert!"

"I would like more lemonade," Mary requested, smiling and trying not to giggle.

"Miss Donna, do I have your permission to call on you?" the lieutenant asked.

"I will ask my father," she replied.

Lieutenant Slader stood in front of Donna nervously, both of them staring at each other and both of them at a loss for words.

"Thank you, Justin. We have enjoyed your company and the lunch. I will have my father send word to you," Donna said as she smiled and held out her hand to the lieutenant. He gently took her hand and kissed it.

The girls spent time shopping, trying on dresses and sampling several fragrances from Paris. A whiskered man in a wheelchair asked if Charlie could join him in a game of checkers. The game was set up outside the mercantile on an empty whiskey barrel that had been cut in half.

"Please, sis! I'd rather play a game than go shopping!" Charlie begged.

"All right, we won't be long," Mary answered.

Charlie laid his crutches down and sat down on the porch in the shade from the hot afternoon, and the two men began to see who could outwit the other.

"I only brought a dollar with me," Donna told Elaine, "but I'm going to spend it all on this bottle of 'Toilettes de Perfume of Roses' in case Justin comes to call."

The girls also found some blue gingham fabric. Donna knew she and her mother could make a pretty new dress and said, "Mr. Ailey, would you please put this gingham and some thread on my father's tab?"

"Of course, Miss Summers! Beautiful fall day, isn't it?" Mr. Ailey said. "How is your mother?"

Donna looked a little disturbed about the question. "She has been a little tired lately, but I think she's trying to do too much as usual," Donna replied to Mr. Ailey and his wife, who was wrapping the cloth.

"Please give our regards to your parents," they said.

From a distance, Charlie could see the lieutenant approaching. The tall young man greeted Charlie and the older man with "Who's winning?"

"I am," the older gentleman said, "but just barely!"

Just then, the girls appeared in the doorway.

"Fancy meeting you again," Elaine said to the man in uniform.

"Ladies, my captain has given me permission to escort you back to your ranch tomorrow, whenever you decide to leave."

"Why, that would be wonderful! I mean, thank you, that would be most helpful," Mary replied. Donna blushed and adjusted her bonnet.

Elaine spoke up and said, "We plan to leave at 8:00 a.m. from the Fort Sill Inn, at the edge of town."

"I will be there," he promised.

Justin left and the girls could not stop giggling. Charlie teased them a little. "I hope we don't get attacked by wild Indians. You wouldn't even notice!"

The trip from Fort Sill to the ranch was a dream to Donna. All she could think about was, "Lieutenant Justin Slader," "Lieutenant Slader," "Mrs. Justin Slader," "Mrs. Donna Slader."

The sky seemed so much bluer than when they left the ranch. The wispy white clouds seemed to be dancing with each other as Lieutenant Slader led the buggy westward. Donna tried to not let him see her watching him astride his black stallion. Every so often, Justin would pull back and ride alongside the buggy. Charlie was involved in reading a book that his new friend Chance, who had beaten him two out of three at checkers, had given him.

Elaine and Donna were perched in the backseat. Charlie and Mary were in the front, with Mary holding the reins to a team of matching dappled gray geldings. They were about halfway home when Donna remembered that her father had asked her to order more nails for the barn.

"Oh no! What will I do?" Donna exclaimed.

"What will you do about what?" Justin asked.

"I forgot to place an order at the lumberyard for nails for father's new barn. He will never understand how I could forget such an important thing!"

"Don't you fret one minute, Miss Donna. I will place the order with Mr. Holderby when I return. What size, number six?" he asked.

"Yes, how did you know?" she asked.

"Well, that's the size you need when you build a barn!" They all laughed.

They stopped for lunch by a lonely willow tree growing by a small stream.

"We'll rest the horses and stretch a spell," the lieutenant said as he helped each one out of the buggy.

"Donna, you're not eating a thing. Where is your appetite?" Mary asked.

Elaine nudged her sister. "Never mind, that just leaves more for us."

The four enjoyed shelter from the unrelenting noonday heat. Storm clouds gathered in the west, but Justin assured them they were just dry weather clouds. The earth beneath them was parched from lack of rain, and the buffalo grass was now brown and crispy.

"We'd better get a-moving before some renegade Indians find us," Justin proclaimed. Helping lift Charlie into the buggy, Justin asked, "What's that you're reading?"

Charlie answered, "'How Do I Love Thee' by Elizabeth Barrett Browning. If I am able to walk again, I want someone to love me like this someday."

"I am sure you will walk someday soon," the lieutenant reassured. "You can even dance at my wedding!"

Everyone laughed, but Donna blushed. "Come, let's load up! If we hurry, we'll be at the ranch before you know it," Justin said, taking charge.

When they arrived at the ranch, everyone was tired and dusty. Justin joined the men as they went over plans to build the barn. The ladies brought out cold fried chicken, slaw, and fresh cherry pies Rachel made while they were gone. Rachel asked Mary, Elaine, and Charlie to stay overnight before they headed for home.

Next morning, Donna pulled Elaine to the side and excitedly said, "Lieutenant Slader has asked me to the Fall Dance at Fort Sill! Father said I could go. Will you help me make a dress? It has to be the most beautiful dress ever! I want it to be special. Blue, like the color of his eyes." Donna was so excited, she was about to burst. "Did I tell you he touched my hand before he left? I'm never washing it!"

"Yes, I will help you, but first we must order material from the Sears catalogue. I think blue taffeta would be perfect. And you must have new boots. I saw some in the catalogue with lace at the top. Oh, and a corset! One must draw in their waist to be in fashion. Your petticoats must be white with lace—rows and rows of lace!" Elaine exclaimed, almost as excited as Donna over the invitation.

"Oh no! My hands are so rough, what will I do about these awful hands?" Donna cried.

Elaine said, "Don't worry, I know what to do. You cut milk-weed, strip the liquid from the stems, and rub the milk over your arms and hands. That will soften your skin like a baby's bottom."

"Oh, Elaine, what would I ever do without you?" Donna squealed, hugging her friend.

A big dance was something to get excited about. Everyone at the ranch seemed to be making plans and looking forward to the event, working faster and harder to prepare for it and winter.

The year was 1896. Tom had seen many changes in his lifetime. He had felt the lash of his father's whip, the pain of war, the empti-ness of lost love, and starting from scratch with little smarts and a lot of good fortune. He would tell his son, Johnny, "I do not believe in luck. I believe in hard work."

Now Johnny was talking of joining the army. Janell had a life of her own, and Donna had found her a fellow.

CHAPTER 32

The Loss of Rachel and the Gain of a Son-In-Law

"Brand every one of those young-ins," Tom shouted. "We will be back in a day or two." Rachel had not been well. Tom and Rachel were headed to Fort Sill. The visit to the doctor did not go well.

"Your wife has a weak heart, and the beat is irregular. There is nothing I can do," he said. "I want her to rest and get some help around the house."

Turning to Rachel, he said, "Take these pills if you feel anxious. They will help you rest," Doctor Holvick said to Rachel as he looked away. Whispering to Tom, he said, "Bring her back, Tom, if she gets worse."

Rachel sat close to Tom as they rode back to The Big Pasture in the buggy. "I love these Indian summer days, Tom, and I love you," she said. "Everything is going to be okay."

Elaine came over and stayed a couple of days as they cut and measured and stitched and sewed "the dress" for the dance. The girls giggled and sang as they sewed. Rachel helped by sewing pearls down the front. "You will be the belle of the ball," Rachel told her daughter.

"Here," she said, "I found this in my travel bag. It is the evening bag my mother gave me. It's from Paris. It will match the pearls on your dress."

When the Summers family arrived at the dance, Lieutenant Slader met them outside, by the door. As Justin helped Donna out of the buggy, he said, "You look lovely." The music was playing and many couples were already dancing when Tom and his family entered the ballroom. "May I have this dance?" Justin ask. He and Donna joined the party. Tom sat wistfully watching his little girl. She reminded him of Rachel when they were first married. She was just as beautiful.

Rachel took Tom by the hand and said, "Will you dance with me?"

"Yes, yes, of course, but are you up to it?"

"I've been taking care of myself," she admonished. "Now, be quiet and dance. I am the one who taught you, remember?"

Tom led his wife out on to the dance floor to the strains of "The Viennese Waltz." He took her in his arms; she felt like a feather.

"You look so beautiful tonight, sweetheart," he said with a smile. As the song neared the end, they realized that everyone else on the floor had stopped dancing and had formed a circle around them, just watching two people happily married, still in love, and moving as one. When the last note was played, applause greeted them. They smiled and made a slight bow as Tom led Rachel off the dance floor. Something was different this time. She did not feel like a feather; she felt heavy on his arm. Their friends were clapping, and she was smiling and waving to the crowd. When she reached her chair, however, she was pale and limp.

"Tom, would you take me to our room?"

Tom helped her to her feet. "Don't say anything to anyone, please. I don't want to cause a stir," she pleaded.

They were spending the night in the officers' quarters that were nearby. Even though Rachel was still the petite woman Tom had married, she felt like a ton of bricks as he opened the side door. He barely got the door open and he could feel her go down. He picked her up in his arms and carried her into the officer's quarters. All of the houses at the Fort had a flight of stairs in front. As he carried her up each step, he realized that he was not the young man he was once.

Tom laid her on the couch and tucked a pillow under her head. She was quiet.

"Don't leave me," he pleaded.

"It won't be forever," Rachel said sleepily. She closed her eyes and passed on.

For Tom, the silence was deafening, yet one could still hear the party going on, the band playing, and people laughing in the hall below. Rachel had not disturbed the dance, and that was what she wanted. Tom ran back to the hall and found Dr. Kreger by the punch bowl. He grabbed him by the arm and practically dragged him up the stairs to their room, where Rachel lay.

Tom's eyes were wet and wild with desperation. "Rachel's sick! She is very sick! Can't you do something?"

The doctor took a long look at her, took her pulse, felt her head and her heart.

Shaking his head, he said, "Tom, I'm sorry, she's gone." There was a scarf on the chair next to her. He grabbed it and covered her face.

"Tom, I'm so sorry. Is there anything I can do?" he asked.

"No, you can't do anything! She's gone. My Rachel is gone. Just leave me alone with her."

Tom sat on the floor next to his beloved and talked to her about their lives and their past. He prayed long into the night. Later, Dr. Kreger came back with some soldiers and a stretcher and asked if they could take her. Through his tears, Tom said, "Yes, but be careful with her."

The next morning, he walked over to where the children were staying and had them come with him to the parlor.

"What's wrong, Father? Where is mother?" Donna asked.

He took Donna's hand in his and said, "Your mother died in my arms last night." John was speechless and just stared out the window. Donna was hysterical, so Tom held her while they both cried.

Two days later, on November 10, 1896, Rachel was buried at the military cemetery. They knew the cemetery was only for soldiers and their family members, but Colonel Jackson made an exception. He said, "You know, this is the frontier, and she was part of us. We want to keep her here."

Tom thanked him, knowing in his heart that he still considered himself a military man.

Several of their friends came back to the ranch with them. They talked into the night.

"Where is she?" Tom asked. He knew where she was, but God, he missed her. She was everything to him; more than a wife and companion, she was his closest friend.

Six months later, in May, Lieutenant Slader asked for Donna's hand in marriage. Tom thanked the lieutenant. Tom told him he was lost without Rachel, but he would talk it over with Johnny and Donna. Then, expressionless, he asked, "Do you have to marry her?"

Justin replied, "No, sir. I do not have to marry her, but I sure do want to."

When Tom called his children together and told them that he wanted to talk about Donna marrying her soldier man, Donna said, "Yes, Father, please say yes! I love him like Momma loved you—with all of her heart."

Johnny stared out the window and said, "Of course, I want the best for my sister. He has a good education from West Point and seems like a good man." Then he laughed and said, "I hate to admit it, but I arm wrestled him the other day, and he beat me. That proves he can take care of himself!"

Reaching out to his daughter and hugging her, he said, "Then, it's a done deal. I will welcome him to be my son-in-law. We're going to have a wedding!"

Johnny, Donna, and Tom had been at Fort Sill for several days, and it was now time for Tom to get back to the ranch.

"Donna, if you want to stay here a little longer to get things done for the wedding, John and I will leave. Maybe the lieutenant can bring you home."

"That would be wonderful, Father. I will miss you, but we will get a lot of planning done. Mrs. Briggs said I could stay with them anytime I needed to."

Since the time the Summers came to The Big Pasture, Mrs. Briggs had been Rachel's dearest friend. She was almost like a mother to Donna.

The buggy ride to the ranch gave father and son an opportunity to talk.

"Mother was my rock, and I never told her," Johnny said. "Now I never can tell her." Tears filled his eyes.

"She knew, son," replied Tom. "She knew you loved her very much."

They arrived in the late afternoon. Will came out and took care of the horses. Johnny and Tom walked into the house. It was lonely and cold. The life and heart and soul of the home was gone, and emptiness was everywhere. Tom put his arms around Johnny and they both cried.

"Dad, when Donna leaves, it's really going to be hard on you," Johnny told his father.

"I know," replied Tom, "you and I will manage things together. It's your ranch now."

The wedding plans were a blur to Tom. Elaine helped Donna make her dress. A large reception was going to be held at the Fort right after the wedding. Family members who could not make it in time for Rachel's funeral came for Donna's big day. Walter and his family arrived from Iowa. John Sommers, Tom's brother, came alone; his wife was in Europe. "Just as well," Tom thought.

Janell arrived with her beautiful daughter, Jean. Justin's parents arrived from New York. The Sladers met Janell at the train station in Kansas City and got acquainted on the train ride.

Mrs. Slader asked Janell why her husband was not with her on the trip. Janell replied that three months after they were married, he was killed.

"How?" the surprised Mrs. Slader inquired. "By Indians?"

"No," Janell explained, "my beloved Ralph had just finished a major job. He had set a large windmill in place for a rancher in Kansas. He climbed down, and instead of going into the house for a drink of water, he took a drink from the stock tank. The typhoid fever took him. I never had the chance to tell him I was carrying our daughter. Then, I lost my wonderful mother, Rachel," she explained.

Across the miles, lives, friends, and families were talked about. In conversation, the Sladers said they were going to a wedding—the same wedding. Janell said, "You will love Donna. She is a lot like Rachel."

As the handsome gray-headed father of the bride walked his lovely daughter down the aisle, his thoughts returned to the summer day in Iowa when he married Rachel. "Doesn't seem that long ago," he thought to himself. "Where did the years go?"

He looked at Donna on his arm; she looked so much like her mother, and she was wearing the necklace Tom had given Rachel.

"I do," and it was over. Elaine's mother came up to Tom, seeing tears in his eyes, and said, "I'll bet you hate to see your little girl getting married!"

"No," he said, "it's not that. It's because her mother is not here to see her."

Mrs. Hughes responded, "Oh, Tom, you know better. She's here. She's here in spirit and she's here in deed."

Then Tom turned to Donna and Justin and said, "Here is a gift to the bride and groom: a new horse and buggy from your mother and me."

Headlines from the local newspaper in 1898 stated that Spain should not have control of the country of Cuba. For most of the folks out west, this was of no concern. "It just doesn't make any difference," Tom told the barber that morning.

Before long, the battleship *Maine* was sunk, and there was talk of war against the Spaniards. War was declared, and Teddy Roosevelt was going to get a cavalry together and fight the Spanish in Cuba.

"I met Mr. Roosevelt a few years ago, when Quanah Parker invited him on a wolf hunt," Tom told his son, Johnny. "He seemed like a fair and honest man," Tom continued.

Johnny was caught up in the war and wanted to join Roosevelt's "Rough Riders," as they were called.

CHAPTER 33

Tom Goes to New Mexico Territory

It seemed like fate that Donna and Justin had bought a ranch near Cimarron, New Mexico Territory. The year was 1906. Johnny Gail had gone to the army but did not return. Now there was talk of The Big Pasture Ranchland being turned over to the settlement of the government. Tom wrote to Donna about this turn of events, and she answered that he should come and live with them and bring Ranger II, the stud horse.

Tom had been alone for eleven years. He was sixty years old now, and he felt like he was getting to be an old man.

"No," Tom said to his longtime friend and cowboy, "I'm going to the New Mexico Territory alone. You need to go on. Find you a good woman and take what you want from this life. Do you have some other place to go?" he asked.

"Yes. There is a widow woman that has a hardware store in the town next to Fort Sill. If she'll have me, I believe I will marry her," Jake said.

Tom sold everything he had to a livestock buyer in Lawton, Oklahoma Territory, a town not far from Fort Sill. "Put the wagons, buggy, saddles, and harness up for sale too," Tom told Mr. Roth.

"Why you selling out?" Roth asked. "The settling of Big Pasture is just a rumor."

Tom told him, "It will be more than a rumor shortly." Sure enough, the government moved into The Big Pasture in 1906.

Tom wrote a letter to Johnny and took it to the Fort for him to read if he ever returned. "It has been eight years, but there's still a chance he's alive," Tom told the Captain. "I'm going to New Mexico Territory to help my daughter and son-in-law on their ranch."

Tom decided not to burn the house and barn. He would give it back to the Comanche Indians on the reservation. It was on their land anyway. He allowed that he had burned all that he was going to burn. He talked to his banker and told him to wire his money to his new bank when he wrote to him with the address. Then, he wrote to his brother, John, and told him to come visit and bring Janell.

Tom took three thousand dollars out of the bank with him. The new "gold" was not like gold used to be: it was paper. It didn't weigh as much.

He saddled up Ranger II, his stud, the colt from his first ranch horse almost twenty years earlier. He rode Ranger to Fort Sill and visited Rachel's grave, knowing she really was not there. Then, he started out through the Texas Panhandle to Cimarron, New Mexico Territory.

"Come on, let's go," he said to Ranger, "No lookin' back."

No Lookin' Back/ Is this Tom Summers or Ted Riddle?

ABOUT THE AUTHORS

Photo by Three Sisters Old Time Photo—Branson, Mo.
Authors Linda and Ted Riddle

Ted Riddle was born near Red Rock, Oklahoma and graduated from Oklahoma State University. He owned and operated his ranch of longhorn cattle and wheat in Northern Oklahoma, where he raised two daughters and built a log home. He is past president of The Oklahoma Chapter of the American Agriculture Movement, an organization to save the family farm. When he quit ranching, he pursued his electrical degree by supervising the building of electrical sub-stations and wind farms throughout the mid-west. Ted retired in 2009.

Linda (Love) Riddle was born in Delta, Colorado, moving at a young age to Spenard, Alaska near Anchorage, continuing her education in Kansas and Oklahoma. She raised three sons and co-owned and operated the Daylight Donut Shop in Tonkawa and Blackwell, Oklahoma for many years.

Linda studied art at Northern Oklahoma College in Tonkawa with Gene Dougherty, Larry Stephenson and Audrey Schmitz. She also studied with Barbara Bartels of Taos, New Mexico and La Veta, Colorado, earning several awards. She was published for her art and poetry in The Harvest Magazine at NOC and wrote a weekly column for The Tonkawa News.

Linda married Ted Riddle and was his project coordinator for several years. They now divide their time between southern Colorado and Branson, Missouri.

CPSIA information can be obtained
at www.ICGtesting.com
Printed in the USA
FFHW020945241019
55716100-61580FF